DEVIL SAHIB

DEVIL SAHIB

Marjorie Shoebridge

W H ALLEN · LONDON
1988

Printed and bound in Great Britain by
Anchor Brendon Ltd, Tiptree, Essex
for the Publishers, W. H. Allen & Co. Plc
44 Hill Street, London W1X 8LB

ISBN 0 491 03428 8

For Paul and Sheila

Chapter One

Zara Deane stared at her father with disbelief. 'You cannot really mean it, surely?'

The tall man standing by the hearth, his outstretched arm resting on the mantelpiece, turned his smile on her. It was a charming smile and one which had disarmed many a creditor. His still dark hair was only a little flecked with grey and his slim figure in its well-cut coat and breeches, brocade waistcoat and immaculate linen, gave him an air of rich elegance.

'But why, Father?' Zara asked, although she knew the answer.

'It is marriage or a debtor's prison, my child.' His tone held amusement. 'Would you have me in the Fleet or Newgate? Mrs Makin is by far the most comfortable alternative.'

'She is twice widowed, Father, and if gossip be true, is not – not –' she floundered.

'Not quite a lady?' he prompted. 'True, my dear, but she has pretensions to Society, and since I have the entrée, the – er – arrangement will satisfy us both.' He paused, looking down on Zara. 'Did I forget to mention that she is extremely rich?'

Zara tried to hold back her smile but failed. 'Oh, Father, you are incorrigible! I gather that her previous husbands left her in that happy state or you would not be proposing this course of action.'

'Indeed not, yet the lady is not without charm in her own right.' He shrugged. 'Since King Edward's succession, a fortune earned from trade has not the stigma it once had. I believe I can bear it.'

'When is the wedding to be?'

'Very soon. One cannot let slip such an opportunity.' He moved from the hearth and came towards her, taking her hands. His expression was no longer one of amusement.

'Your mother was a lady, and I loved her dearly. She understood the flaw in my character and took me, none the less. She has been gone these five years and I am a man of straw, tossed by every wind and whim of my nature. I shall never change and Mrs Makin quite accepts that I shall be an expensive acquisition, just as your grandfather did.' His mouth curved with remembered humour. 'Thank God for lawyers, or you would be joining me in the Fleet. Forgive me for taking Mrs Makin but needs must when the devil drives.'

Zara rose and kissed her father's cheek. 'Am I not a Deane, too? Take your Mrs Makin, Papa, with my blessing. As for myself,' she shrugged, 'should I take the first gentleman who asks me, do you think?'

'Not unless he is rich, my darling, for though you don't gamble, your own tastes are expensive.'

They laughed together, easy in their relationship, but Zara felt a pang of regret that soon she must share her father with another. They knew each other so well, sharing the Deane restlessness, the urge to take chances, the dreams of adventure.

Zara was twenty-four years old, tall and dark-haired, her slim carriage as elegant as her father's. The afternoon dress she wore as she climbed into the carriage after leaving her father was simple, but deceptively so. A coffee-coloured gown trimmed with Brussels lace and the high neck enhanced Zara's own slim white one, her dark curls dressed were high beneath a tiny hat trimmed with cream roses. A short squirrel cape lay over her shoulders.

She sighed as the coachman wheeled the carriage towards the corner of the road where one of her contemporaries lived. Most of them, she reflected, were now sunk into domesticity, talking of nothing but husbands and babies, in the world or imminent. Their tones were rather more guarded in her company as if, being unwed, she must be protected from the secrets of procreation.

She turned her thoughts to Mrs Makin. A handsome dark-haired woman, shrewd-eyed and obviously infatuated with Charles Deane, a handsome dandy and rake, for there was no denying that her father had all the charms of both.

6

Now that father, and Mrs Makin, had forced her hand, Zara considered, without enthusiasm, the gentlemen of her own society. She would have to choose one or engage in what she sensed would be polite warfare with Mrs Makin when she became the second Mrs Deane.

She was greeted in the drawing room by her old school-friend, Eleanor Farnes, now a wife and proud mother of two. She steeled herself to listen indulgently to a recital of the children's progress while sipping tea and nibbling sweet cakes. But today was different. She found herself being introduced to a man of above medium height, brown-haired and uniformed. She smiled and held out her hand. It was taken in a warm clasp white blue eyes under dark brows regarded her gravely.

'Captain Ralph Browne, Zara,' said Eleanor proudly. 'I haven't seen him since we were children and now he is captain in the army of India. Isn't it exciting?'

'Miss Deane, I am honoured to make your acquaintance. Cousin Eleanor has been telling me of you.' The smile he gave her was a little shy and she saw the tiny white lines round his eyes crinkle in his tanned skin. A man who looked often into the sun, she guessed.

Zara felt a quickening of interest. 'Are you on leave, Captain?'

'Yes, ma'am. Just two weeks left before I sail. Since I happened to be in London, I took the opportunity of visiting cousin Eleanor and I am very happy that I did. She has received me most graciously and I cannot thank her enough.' Though his words were directed at Eleanor, his eyes did not leave Zara's face.

'Take off your hat and gloves, dear Zara,' said Eleanor. 'And tell us all the scandal and gossip. It is an age since I attended a party let alone a ball, for I have not yet trained the nurserymaid to entertain little William while Nanny is busy with baby Patience.'

Zara laughed. 'Really, Eleanor, you cannot expect Captain Browne to be interested in female gossip.' She smiled at him. 'For myself, I would rather hear of India. Do you find it exciting, Captain?'

7

'Quite exciting, Miss Deane, although there has been little trouble lately. A few skirmishes with tribesmen, that is all,' he shrugged. 'Since the Mutiny in '57, long before my time I fear, it has been mainly garrison duty.'

'You speak as if you regret not being involved in a thing of such magnitude.'

'Well, I am a trained soldier with duty to King and Country.'

'Oh, I am sure you would rise to the challenge if trouble broke out again.'

'Indeed, and welcome the opportunity, should it arrive.'

'And how do you pass your time when you are not fighting tribesmen, Captain?' Zara accepted the cup of tea from Eleanor abstractedly and returned her gaze to Captain Browne's face.

'Polo matches, hunting and sometimes a tiger shoot. That is usually from a howdah perched on an elephant's back.' He went on to acknowledge modestly that he was a pretty decent shot and the proof lay spread-eagled on the floor of his bungalow in the Lahore cantonment.

'How truly exciting,' said Zara, and Eleanor asked what the ladies did, for they must surely need entertainment of a different kind.

'Parties, balls and picnics, I suppose?' she enquired rather wistfully. 'I have heard of such things.' She turned to Zara. 'Just imagine, my dear, all that sunshine, a house full of servants and not a thing to do but enjoy life!'

'There is no need for you to repine, Eleanor,' Zara smiled fondly at her friend. 'You too, have servants and when the nurserymaid is to your satisfaction, we shall see you back at the balls and assemblies.'

Eleanor brightened. 'Of course. And you must now come upstairs and see how much bigger the children have grown and how healthy they look since your last visit.'

'Which was only last week!' Zara reminded her. 'But yes, I would like to see them.' She caught Captain Browne's eye and he smiled, shaking his head as she raised an eyebrow.

'I have already been privileged to meet my new niece and nephew, if that is the correct relationship, though I doubt it for I am merely a cousin of their mother.'

'Ralph found them enchanting, did you not, Cousin?' Eleanor asked complacently.

'Most enchanting,' he said gravely. 'Were I ever in the delightful position of husband and father, I would be content with two such perfect creatures.'

Outside the nursery door, Eleanor laid a detaining hand on Zara's arm. Her fair curls bounced as she cocked her head. 'Do you not think my cousin is handsome and charming?'

'Well, yes, but I barely know him.'

'He has taken a strong liking to you, my dear. I can tell by the way he looks at you. One could hazard a guess that he is enamoured.'

'One could,' said Zara crisply. 'And certainly I would expect it of you for you have always been of a romantic disposition. Why is it, do you suppose, that all one's friends become matchmakers after their own marriages? Don't talk nonsense, Eleanor, but open that door so that I may view the children.'

'Well, I think he is interested,' said Eleanor with a toss of her curls. 'And from what I gather, he was great-aunt Matilda's favourite nephew and she left everything to him so that makes him rich, too, although I would not be so vulgar as to ask how much. I am sure she was a wealthy woman.'

Zara smiled to mask the sudden leap of her heart. 'Then he would have no difficulty in finding a wife, provided, of course, that she is prepared to live in India.'

Eleanor giggled. 'I am sure you would be, dear Zara, for you have always craved adventure, even as a child at school.'

Zara let her laughter bubble up inside her. 'Perhaps it is as well that he sails in two weeks' time or you would have the poor man bound in matrimony, like it or not.'

They viewed the children and Zara said all the complimentary things expected of her, then they returned to the drawing-room. Zara picked up her hat and gloves.

'Thank you so much for tea, Eleanor. I really must go now. Father and I are attending a concert.' She held out a hand to Captain Browne. 'It has been a pleasure to make your acquaintance. I hope you enjoy the rest of your leave.'

'Do escort Miss Deane to her carriage, Ralph,' Eleanor said, a mischievous smile on her lips.

'I fully intend to do that, Cousin,' Ralph said and he and Zara left the room.

As he handed her into the carriage he held her elbow for a moment longer. 'May I call upon you, Miss Deane?'

'If you wish, Captain. I shall be delighted to hear more of India.'

'In the morning, Miss Deane?'

At Zara's nod of assent, he shut the carriage door and stepped back, bronzed and slim in his scarlet tunic and close-fitting blue breeches. The autumn sun glinted on burnished buttons and well-polished leather, touching the brown hair with an auburn sheen.

On their return from the concert hall where they had listened to a performance of Mozart concertos, Zara's slightly abstracted air communicated itself to Charles Deane. They entered the drawing-room and he surprised her by calling for wine. He was a temperate man, strong drink not being among his vices, and they had dined after the concert, drinking only a little white wine, usually sufficient for them both.

'Sit down, my dear, and tell me what is on your mind. If it is serious, then this wine will calm you. If not –' he shrugged, smiling. 'Then you may at least enjoy it, for it is one of the few fine wines left in the cellar.'

As Bates, the old butler, placed the silver tray and crystal glasses on the wine table beside Mr Deane, he stroked the bottle lovingly, his old eyes reminiscent.

'You're right there, Mr Charles. I remember the day we received this consignment from Bordeaux. A well-stocked cellar we had then, for the mistress's father was most partial and liked to keep a good cellar.'

When he had retired from the room, Charles Deane grinned at his daughter. 'Yes, indeed, and he drank most of it himself, the old reprobate. Dear God, the lectures I endured on the profligacy of my ways, but that old villain thought nothing of buying a whole season's yield from his favourite vineyard. However, my love, it is not of the dear departed we speak but of yourself. Tell me, what is it that taxes your mind?'

'Why should it be anything, Father?'

'Well, you don't usually frown over Mozart, which was, to my mind, performed quite expertly. Neither do you look through old friends when we dine at the Savoy.'

Zara's eyes widened. 'Oh, no, don't say that. Did I really cut someone? How dreadful!'

'No, no, my love, I was only teasing.' Charles Deane laughed aloud. 'But you did frown. I cannot deny that you had me wondering. You are not being dunned by some upstart milliner, are you?'

'Nothing like that, Father, I assure you. I am keeping within my means, though, like you, I find it hard to resist the latest fashion from Paris and have resolved to avoid Bond Street for the next quarter.'

'Then what is it? Mrs Makin?'

'Not directly,' Zara said slowly. 'Though naturally, it will make a difference in our lives. Will you be at home in the morning?' she asked abruptly, her hazel eyes regarding him seriously.

'If you need me to be at home, my darling, then I shall certainly be at home. Can you tell me why?'

'Of course. I went to tea today with Eleanor Farnes. She has a cousin staying with her, a Captain Ralph Browne, on leave from India.' She paused, then fell silent.

'And?' her father prompted.

'He has asked if he may call on me tomorrow. I agreed.'

'Where is the problem? You don't need a chaperone for a morning visit.'

'I – I would rather like you to give me your opinion of him.'

'Ah, yes, I see. He has shown interest? And you, my love? Does he interest you?'

Zara took a reflective sip of wine. 'He is quite charming, quite handsome and according to Eleanor, quite rich. He is stationed in a town called Lahore.'

'H'm,' said Mr Deane slowly, his tone amused. 'He does seem to have the right qualifications.'

Zara rose and moved restlessly about the room, coming to stand before her father. He looked up. 'Would life in India appeal to you?'

11

'He made it sound exciting and yes, quite frankly it would.' She met her father's eyes. 'He has but two weeks left of his leave in England.'

'Yes, I understand now. Should you encourage or discourage his attentions since you know little about him, save his kinship to Eleanor?' He rose and put his arms about her and Zara leaned her cheek on his chest. 'Don't worry, my dear. I will meet your Captain Browne in the morning and take his measure. A father may ask a question or two, most casually of course, which might be a little indelicate for a young lady.' He held her away from him and smiled fondly. 'I am quite experienced in deviousness, you know. I can pick out the rum card in a whole pack.'

Zara laughed. 'Do that for me, darling, for I swear the thought of riding elephants and playing croquet with the Colonel's lady has quite taken hold of my imaginaion.'

When Ralph Browne stepped through the door held open for him by Bates, he was impressed by the splendour of the wide hall. Well-polished tables and cabinets stood about, each adorned by silver vases filled with crysanthemums. The staircase wall was hung with oil paintings all bearing the elegance of the differing costumes of their times. Hazel eyes watched him from each face and bore, in some degree, the likeness to the face he had seen yesterday.

On being relieved of his hat and gloves, he was led into a long, sunny drawing-room. Here again, there were flower-filled vases, a Persian rug stretched almost the width of the room, comfortable brocade-covered chairs and couches and more silver. The room spoke in muted tones of expensive elegance. He was not to know that elegance stopped short above stairs, for Zara had set out the hall and drawing-room with all that remained of value. It was an impressive show and Captain Ralph Browne was duly impressed. He had as fine an eye as Charles Deane when it came to recognising the genuine and his casual glance round the room convinced him that the Sèvres pieces, the silver bowls and gold carriage clock were exactly what they purported to be. He strolled over to the hearth and was examining a gilt-framed miniature when he heard a soft step behind.

He turned, expecting Miss Deane, but found himself looking into a pair of amused eyes. 'A Holbein original, Captain, and said to be an ancestor in the family line, but I daresay you guessed that, for the likeness to my daughter is quite remarkable. Wouldn't you say so?'

'Indeed, sir, and for that reason I was observing it closely. Please excuse my obvious interest for I was not doubting its authenticity.'

'Naturally not. By the way, I must introduce myself. I am Charles Deane and I take it that you are the visitor my daughter mentioned.'

'Yes, sir, Captain Ralph Browne, 16th Queen's Lancers, stationed in the Punjab.' He smiled. 'And you, sir, need no introduction really since Miss Deane has inherited the family resemblance most markedly.'

Charles Deane gave his lazy charming smile and waved an elegant hand. 'Be seated, Captain. My daughter will join us presently.' He moved to a chair himself and Ralph Browne observed the slim, expensively attired person of his host, noting the gold hunter watch and the diamond pin in the silk cravat.

'Will you take coffee or something a little stronger, Captain?' queried Charles Deane.

'Coffee, if you please, sir. I am not a great drinker and certainly refrain when I hope to converse with a lady. An aroma of drink is not likely to commend itself.'

Charles Deane nodded. 'Nor would it have done to me, Captain. I admire a temperate man, since I am one myself.'

Ralph Browne nodded gravely, thankful that he had made the right decision. To win the daughter, he must impress the father and above all, he was determined to win Zara Deane. It was a favourable beginning and one on which he hoped to build his future. Since escorting Zara to her carriage yesterday, he had thought of nothing else. The dark-haired beauty with her stunning smile and manner, the elegance of her gown smoothly clothing the slim perfect body had filled him with desire. She would put every other female in the shade,

13

including the Colonel's wife, in the garrison town of Lahore. A rich and beautiful wife on his arm would make him the envy of every other officer. But time was not on his side. He silently cursed his ill-luck in not contacting cousin Eleanor before. He came out of his thoughts to meet the hazel eyes of the man opposite. Those eyes were clear and guileless. Mr Deane had the appearance of indolent good nature, a father prepared to chat amiably to any guest in his house.

'Africa was it, Captain?' Mr Dean's brow wrinkled in thought. 'Ah, no, I believe my daughter mentioned India.' He shrugged and smiled charmingly. 'It is all so far away and one forgets these outposts of Empire. Punjab, you said. I distinctly remember. Where is that precisely, Captain?'

'North-west India, sir.'

'Ah!' said Charles as if he understood perfectly. 'North-west, eh? Always fighting someone or other there, aren't we? Good prospects for advancement, what?'

'We're not fighting at the moment, sir. The army is in strength in that region and I have every expectation of reaching higher rank.' He smiled, recognising that Charles Dean's geographical knowledge was of the vaguest, for his host wore the bemused expression of an aristocrat who saw little beyond the fringes of his own circle.

'I daresay it takes money to live in style out there –' Charles waved a hand as if he'd forgotten just where it was already.

'No problem there, sir, for I have considerable income,' Ralph assured him.

'Too bad that you are here for so short a time, Captain. I should have enjoyed a discussion on India. I am sure my daughter will be most entertained for she has an inquiring mind. Can't think where she gets it, but these modern finishing schools, you know –' He raised a quizzical brow in tolerant acceptance.

Both men turned, rising, as Zara came into the room, her morning dress of apricot silk, wide-skirted and tiny-waisted, billowing about her. The high, ruffled collar seemed to enhance the pure oval of her face and under the simply styled dark hair, her hazel eyes were warm.

'Forgive me for keeping you waiting, Captain.' She

14

extended a slim cool hand. 'I am sure my father made up for my brief absence and you missed me not at all!'

She brought with her into the room a glowing presence like perfumed sunshine and Ralph Browne could only bow and stare, touching the fingers briefly before they were withdrawn. He found his throat constricted, his breathing ragged, for she was even more beautiful than he remembered.

'I am the one to seek forgiveness, Miss Deane, for staring at you so. I am overwhelmed by the vision.' His smile was shy and self-deprecating. 'It is good of you to receive me so kindly, both you and Mr Deane.'

'Nonsense, Captain.' Zara laughed, enchanting him further. 'I should have been most disappointed had you not come, for I long to hear more of your adventurous life.' She looked at her father. 'Did Captain Browne tell you that they shoot tigers from the backs of elephants?'

'Good God!' said Charles Deane, his eyes widening. 'How precarious it sounds. How do you mount the creatures?'

Ralph Browne found confidence returning and explained that the mahout ordered the animal to kneel while the hunters climbed into the howdah. He set himself to the task of absorbing Miss Deane's complete interest in the life and activities of a garrison town in India. He had not felt quite easy under the bland gaze of Mr Deane, but his daughter's interest seemed genuine enough.

He drank coffee almost absent-mindedly as Zara plied him with questions and he sought to answer them fully.

He was startled when Mr Deane consulted his splendid hunter watch and reminded Zara that they were due to lunch with the Admiral and his lady.

'And you know, my dear, when the Admiral says eight bells or twelve bells, or whatever the naval jargon is relating to time, he means precisely that! Ah, well, young Rodney will smooth things over for your sake.'

'Oh, my goodness,' Zara said on a breathless laugh. 'I was so engrossed that I quite forgot the dear old Admiral. What is the penalty for tardiness in the Royal Navy, I wonder?'

Captain Browne rose quickly. 'The time has passed so swiftly and enjoyably, that I must beg forgiveness again.' His

15

smile was rueful: 'How dare a mere Army Captain allow an Admiral to be kept waiting? I will instantly take my leave with warmest thanks for your hospitality.'

Zara walked him into the hall where Bates waited with cap and gloves. Ralph bowed over Zara's hand. 'I have so enjoyed this call on you.'

'So have I, Captain.'

Ralph gazed into the bright hazel eyes. Was there a hint of regret in them? 'May I call again? I can think of no better way of spending my last week or so.'

'Why, Captain, what a sweet thing to say. I shall be at home on Friday if you care to call.'

'Indeed I do care, Miss Deane. Until Friday, then?'

Zara returned to the drawing-room and regarded her father questioningly. He gave a lazy smile.

'He's yours for the taking, my love. I never saw a man more dumbstruck when you flowed into the room like a perfumed butterfly. I agree with your assessment of him. He is ambitious and fully expects to rise in rank.' His eyes crinkled with amusement. 'You may find yourself a Colonel's lady if you take him, my love.'

'How splendid. By the way, who is this Admiral we're lunching with?'

Charles Deane laughed. 'Spur of the moment invention. I thought he had stayed long enough and the mention of young Rodney, whoever he is, might spur your Captain into movement.'

'And you called Grandfather an old villain!'

'Well, my love, you came in on cue so what does that make you?'

'A villainess, I suppose,' she said, laughing.

'Order the carriage, will you, darling?'

'The carriage, Father? Why? We have no luncheon appointment.'

Mr Deane shook his head. 'My dear Zara, you really must learn to carry deception to its proper conclusion. If your swain is as love-struck as he appears, he may hang about the pavements, hoping to catch sight of you driving away to take luncheon with the Admiral and the so eligible Rodney. What

16

would he think if we remained behind closed doors?'

'Devious man!' Zara said, repressing a chuckle. 'Where shall we go?'

'A drive into the country, then take tea and cream pastries by the river at Hampton Court.'

Captain Ralph Browne continued to frequent the drawing-room of the Deane house. He was welcomed in cool friendly fashion by Zara who contrived with great skill to look a little different each time. A new hairstyle, a switch of frothy lace collar from a pink velvet gown to a turquoise silk, gave her the appearance of being possessed of an extensive wardrobe. She had learned to buy expensively when Charles Deane was in funds, varying her trimmings and accessories when he was not, and achieve for herself a reputation for flair and originality. Her own allowance, guaranteed under her grandfather's will, was merely a few hundred pounds a year, a sum which Charles Deane could not touch.

To give him credit he had not tried, for he loved the daughter who was so much like himself. His skill as a gambler and member of many clubs suited his nature perfectly, for he was a gentleman without deep ambition to tax his mind with business.

Only the advent of a new breed of gambler, some said from the American South, had resulted in Charles Deane losing a great deal of money and, doubting his skill to win it back, convinced him that matrimony with Mrs Makin was a surer bet. She was prepared to meet his debts and allow him to continue, within prescribed bounds, in return for his name and a certain standing in Society.

The constant visits of Captain Browne, his charm and conversation, had imbued Zara with a vast longing to see for herself this exciting land of colour, exotic flowers and spicy fragrances, its bazaars and plains, majestic hills and jungle. She knew, if he asked, that she would marry him and adventure into that alien continent.

They walked in the park on those mild autumn days, watching the lazy flutter of falling leaves, gazing up at the enormous beeches, deep copper against the pale blue sky.

They strolled along paths, footsteps muted by a carpet of russet-hued, crackling, curling, dead leaves. When the air turned cool, Zara wore a fine wool gown, a fur-lined pelisse and muff of matching fur. Her cheeks glowed in the crisp air and Ralph's eyes glowed as he looked at her. He took her arm more frequently, warning her of this tree-root or dip in the path, and Zara was quite happy to allow herself to be so guided.

Young nannies wheeling perambulators and young girls, dreaming of flirtations, cast admiring glances at the erect red-jacketed military man with the bars of rank on his epaulettes, the blue breeches on the long legs encased to the knee in fine leather boots. Zara, too, was observed by acquaintances, who bowed and beamed on the handsome young couple, envious or wistful, hoping or remembering.

Zara glanced up at the angular, tanned face of the man pacing beside her. 'Take off that cap for a moment, Captain Browne,' she said.

He looked startled. 'What? Take off my cap? Why?'

'We are passing under a beech tree and I swear that your hair colour will match those dying leaves.' She smiled, cocking her head.

'My dear Miss Deane, it is not proper for a soldier to appear hatless in public. I could be arrested on the spot for being improperly dressed.' He glanced around.

Zara's smile became mischievous. 'Do you expect to find a military policeman lurking in the bushes? Do indulge me, just for a moment, won't you?'

'Well –' he began doubtfully, and was so lost in the contemplation of her face that he failed to notice a slender, almost leafless branch.

Zara burst into laughter as the twig accomplished her request and Ralph's cap tilted, hovered, then fell to the ground by the path.

He flushed, looked annoyed, then caught Zara's laughing eyes.

'How absolutely splendid,' she said. 'Just when I thought you would refuse and go terribly King's Regulations on me.'

Ralph smiled weakly, then jumped as a voice behind said in

a strong cockney accent: ''ere y'are, guv. Good as new.' And a small urchin rubbed a grubby woollen elbow over the glossy peak. 'Worth a tanner that, eh, guv!' and the shrewd young eyes assessed both Ralph and the smiling lady.

Ralph took the cap, restraining an impulse to cuff the impudent urchin. Instead he smiled tightly and turned back to Zara. 'Talk about blackmail,' he muttered and pulled out a white linen handkerchief to polish the cap brim. He glanced at Zara and saw that her smile was on the boy.

'Tanner, indeed! You'll get a dodger and like it.' She opened her reticule and tossed the boy a silver threepenny piece. 'Hop along, young 'un. You've had your money's-worth. Depart forthwith!' The words were spoken casually, as if to an equal, and Ralph stared.

But the urchin understood and grinned, knuckling his head and bobbing. 'Yes, Miss. Right away, Miss.' He turned and stumped away on knobbly little legs.

Zara looked at Ralph and saw the astonishment in his eyes. 'Good heavens, Captain, have you never been trailed by an urchin before?'

'Well, yes, we have swarms of beggars in India but –'

'He was not begging, Captain, just hoping for an opportunity to earn a copper. There are hundreds like him. No need to make a fuss.'

'No, no, of course not. I was just surprised at the way you spoke to him.'

Zara's eyes narrowed consideringly. 'You feel it was less than ladylike? Would you have me faint or threaten to send for a constable? He was doing no harm and he took my meaning perfectly. He won't be back. Now – where were we?'

Ralph smiled. 'Until fate – in that tree branch – interfered, you were persuading me to remove my cap.'

'Yes, indeed, and do you know, I believe your hair is a little too brown to call it beech-leaf colour.'

Ralph bowed. 'May I now return my cap to its rightful place?'

'Of course,' and she watched in amusement as he gave the cap a final examination before putting it back on his head. 'You are a very meticulous man, Captain.'

19

He took her arm, his good humour restored. 'And you, Miss Deane, are most ladylike. I cannot imagine you ever having the vapours in any situation.'

'The vapours? Good heavens, no. How insipid! The Deanes have more backbone than that.'

Three days before Ralph was due to leave London, Zara was delighted to find that both the Deane and the Farnes families had been invited to the same ball, to celebrate the engagement of a schoolfriend of both Eleanor Farnes and Zara. Since Ralph was a Farnes house guest, he was also invited.

'How splendid,' said Zara when he told her. 'You will find the greatest assembly of pretty girls under one roof that you could hope to meet in London in a twelvemonth.'

'I believe I have already met the prettiest,' said Ralph gallantly, 'without even attending this ball of Lady Saltby's. However, since there will be equally an assembly of gentlemen, my only fear is that I shall be left on the outskirts of those who surely must want to dance with you!' His blue eyes smiled into hers. 'You will allow me a dance or two, I hope? I waltz quite reasonably and am pretty good in the galop, I believe.'

His eyes were so bright and his smile so charming that Zara felt an excited flutter of the heart. Yes, she would take him, she vowed, provided he asked, of course, and a gentleman did not waste his time calling so frequently on a young lady without raising expectations.

On the night of the Saltbys' ball, Zara wore a splendid creation of cream satin and lace.

Her dark hair, brushed to a satin finish, was piled high, a few curling tendrils on her forehead. Diamond eardrops and matching neckcollar accentuated the slim neck and smooth shoulders visible in the décolletée neckline. Cream satin slippers, matching elbow-length gloves and an ivory-sticked fan, hand-painted with birds of paradise, completed her attire.

As Charles Deane slipped a silk cloak about her shoulders in the hall, he nodded approval.

'Quite magnificent, my pet. One might suppose you the

greatest heiress in London, not the daughter of a man hovering on the brink of being incarcerated in the Fleet.'

'One must keep up appearances, darling, even when the tumbrils roll. You have taught me that yourself.' She turned to face him. 'You are quite splendid yourself.' Her voice caught in her throat. 'I shall leave you happy with Mrs Makin?'

He smiled. 'You mean to take the gallant Captain?'

'I believe I must. It is the only way for both of us. He is the key to adventure and really most attractive.'

'And rich.'

'And rich,' Zara echoed and they smiled at each other in complete understanding.

The ballroom of the Saltby London house still held its Regency splendour. The fragrance of massed flowers in every niche vied with the perfumed ladies, and the colours of gown and flower dazzled the eye. The focal point was, of course, the radiant Miss Saltby and her smiling fiancé, flanked by their parents as they stood at the head of the stairs greeting the guests. Zara and Mr Deane offered their congratulations, kissed or bowed to the family and moved on, their places being taken by the next in line.

A concealed orchestra was playing in the gallery above, masked by enormous pots of fern and evergreen. Beyond the ballroom, smaller rooms were set aside for gentlemen who preferred card-playing, billiards or just conversation where they might smoke their cigars. A lounge stood at the disposal of ladies only, a comfortable chintzy room where they could gossip and drink tea, leaving their charges to the more energetic pursuit of dancing. Zara knew the house well. She also knew that her father would not remain long at her side, preferring the card tables, yet good breeding would not permit him to desert her until she was established in the company of friends. A few couples were already dancing when Mr Deane took Zara on to the floor.

They moved with grace and fluidity, their bodies so attuned and alike in structure, that their steps required no conscious thought but flowed together like strands of the same skein. Their progress brought the required result and

Charles Deane left Zara in the company of Eleanor Farnes, for once entrusting her precious babies to Nanny, and accompanying her husband and house guest.

Zara gave her hand to Ralph Browne, her brilliant smile to the rest of the company, then she was whirled away in the arms of the Captain, much to the chagrin of a posy of young females who had been eyeing the handsome scarlet-jacketed Captain with covert interest.

'How impulsive you are, Captain,' Zara protested, laughing. 'You barely allowed me to exchange a word with Eleanor. I hope she will not feel insulted for you really should have danced with her first.'

'She will forgive me,' he said confidently. 'She knows that I have been watching the door and how would I have felt if, when you arrived, I had been engaged on the floor with no chance to claim you before someone else whisked you off. I could not take that risk.' He glanced round the room. 'There is more than one gentleman's eye upon you, Miss Deane.'

His own blue eyes smiled down and Zara felt again the flutter of excitement. She had not been as close to him before. He really was attractive, she thought, his skin clear, teeth white and that air of military authority. He danced well, too, although without the supple grace of her father. Yes, indeed, she could well be very content as the wife of this man.

During the evening, she noted with amusement and a little pride, that when he did not dance with her, he danced with no one else save his cousin Eleanor. At every opportunity he claimed her, more times than was advisable unless a man had marriage on his mind. She wondered if he was fully aware of the rules of Society.

'Captain Browne,' she said gently. 'Your attentions, although flattering, are causing comment. It is not usual for a gentleman to attend so constantly upon one lady. You would not have the guests here think that I am fast or flighty, would you?'

He stared down at her. 'I am convinced they could not.'

'Or yourself be put into a position of dishonour?' She smiled at his frown. 'Etiquette is such a bore at times but one really must retain one's character. You should not dance with me again, Captain. More than twice with the same partner will have the matrons and chaperones believing that you are toying with my affections, as they term it, and that alone would compromise you most dreadfully, and I do believe this is the third time you have partnered me.'

His frown did not lift. He looked down on her intently. 'I have been long out of England, Miss Deane, and am not acquainted with such correct procedure but never would I put you in a position that might reflect upon your character or my own. I ask your pardon for being less than circumspect.' He paused. 'We have known each other a short time, I know, but would you consider it presumptuous of me to beg interview with your father?'

Zara looked into the grave face. 'Why, Captain Browne, there is not the slightest need for such an action, I assure you.' She smiled. 'I was merely teasing. I am not an under-age girl at her first ball. My character is quite without stain and has no need to be lifted into respectability by a gentleman of honour.'

He smiled then. 'You mistake me, Miss Deane. I was not linking the one with the other. My mind had been set before this ball. Your interest in India and the life we lead has encouraged me to hope that your interest might be expanded to include a cavalry officer who holds you in the highest esteem.' He paused again and Zara looked into the earnest face where a boyish smile suddenly showed. 'Should you feel obliged to decline, I will, as you put it to the urchin in the park, depart forthwith, a broken heart in place of a – a dodger, was it?'

Zara laughed. 'Please do call, if you're determined on it, Captain.'

'I am quite determined on it, Miss Deane.'

Zara sat close to her father in the carriage as they made their way homewards. Ralph had rejoined the Farnes party after kissing her hands in a warm gesture.

Charles Deane was pleasantly happy, exuding an aroma of good cigars and wine. He had won enough at the tables to satisfy more urgent creditors. He was aware of Zara's silence but did nothing to disturb it. Their spasmodic conversation related only to the ball and the newly engaged couple. She would tell him her thoughts when she was ready.

At the foot of the stairs, Zara kissed her father on the cheek. She half-turned away to mount them, then glanced at him.

'Captain Browne wishes to call on you tomorrow morning, Father.'

Charles raised his fine brows and a smile touched his lips. 'And what would you have me say to that, my love? Do you mean to take the gallant Captain?'

Zara nodded. 'Yes, I believe I must. A new life for both of us, Father. Mrs Makin, I think would not wish the encumbrance of a stepdaughter with tastes just as high as yours. It would not be fair to ask the lady to pay my bills too and since she will virtually control the purse strings –' She shrugged and laid her palm on her father's cheek. 'Besides, I would really like to go to India.'

Charles Deane reached for her hand and dropped a kiss in the palm. 'India, yes, I can well imagine you will make an impression there, but to achieve it you must take the man too. Apart from the obvious attribute of money, he is a pleasant, correct and reasonably good-looking man, an officer with prospects. Do you care for him, my darling?'

'I think I could be content, a dutiful, faithful wife. I cannot let this opportunity slip, Father, just as you cannot with Mrs Makin.' She laughed suddenly. 'If the alternative is the Fleet, then I'm for India! Good night, Father.' She picked up her skirts and turned for the stairs.

Chapter Two

Charles Deane was at his most charming when Captain Browne was shown into his study the next morning. He assumed an expression of amused tolerance as he indicated a chair with a wave of his elegant hand.

'I would prefer to stand, sir,' said Ralph Browne, holding

himself stiffly, eyeing his host with a nervousness he could not quite conceal. 'Has Miss Deane spoken to you, sir? I mean, to inform you of the nature of my visit?'

'But of course, Captain. I assume your intentions are honourable?'

'Yes, indeed, sir.'

'Then do sit down, my dear fellow. I do so dislike suitors who insist on pacing the floor.' He looked into Ralph's face and smiled kindly. 'Puts one in mind of watching a game of lawn tennis, all that bobbing about.'

Ralph obeyed, sinking deep into an armchair while Mr Deane took the advantageous position of standing with his back to the empty firegrate.

'I suppose it is a very common occurrence, sir. Anyone as beautiful as Miss Deane –' He hesitated, seeing the fine brows draw together.

'My dear fellow,' Charles said a little coolly. 'I do not keep a register of suitors, I assure you.' He strolled across the room and seated himself behind the leather-topped antique desk. He glanced sideways at the folded newspaper, then looked at Ralph, who had climbed to his feet, the hint of a flush on his cheekbones.

'I will come to the point, sir. I would like your permission to offer for your daughter's hand in marriage. I esteem her most highly and would do all in my power to make her happy.'

'You would take her off to India?'

'She has shown great interest in that country, sir, and I can promise her a life of great comfort in Lahore.'

'Since, as I believe, you have only a few days left of your leave, how do you propose going about it? Even if she agrees to your proposal, it could be months before she reaches India on a passenger liner.'

'Yes, sir, I quite expect that, but if Miss Deane will consider an official engagement.'

'Ah, yes, I take your point. An announcement in *The Times* will discourage other suitors.' He gazed musingly into the earnest face. 'Engagements can be broken, Captain, should either one of you have a change of heart.'

'Never, sir, on my part. To allay any doubts of my

character, I would have you contact my Colonel's wife who is in England at the moment. She takes ship back to India in January to rejoin Colonel Lacy. May I give you her address? She would be delighted, I'm sure, to chaperone Miss Deane on the voyage – should she accept my offer.'

'You're a determined young man, Captain.' Charles leaned back, smiling. 'A chaperone already picked. I'm surprised you have not already booked her a passage!'

'That would be rather presumptuous, sir, since she has not yet accepted me.'

'Very true, Captain, but she has spoken of you in most kindly terms.' He rose, holding out his hand. 'You have my blessing, Captain. I will take you to the drawing room now. Zara will be waiting.' As he opened the study door, he paused. 'You know, that's not a bad idea of yours to book a passage for Zara on the ship that carries your Colonel's lady. With a liner ticket in her hand – first class, of course, Zara will be honour bound to use it and she is a most honourable girl.' He patted Ralph's shoulder and laughed. 'A splendid idea. How could she resist taking advantage of it?'

As they moved into the hall, Ralph Browne reflected on the words and found something highly commendable in them. Although Mr Deane had given him credit, unintentionally or not, on the value of booking a passage for Zara, Ralph felt that a ring on her finger and a liner ticket in her possession might swing the balance in his favour, and he wished very much for that.

Zara was standing by the window as they entered the drawing-room. She turned her head and looked at him gravely, then her gaze passed to her father. Behind Captain Browne, Charles Deane gave a small nod and Zara turned a faint, almost distant smile on the Captain.

Now that the moment of decision was here, Zara wondered if she was being quite fair to the man who stood before her. Had he more time at his disposal, he might eventually have become aware that the Deanes, although well-born and accepted everywhere, were not quite what they appeared. Of course, she argued, they had never claimed riches, but the fact of putting every object of value within range of his eyes was in itself a deceit. But did it matter, since he was not a poor man himself, according to Eleanor who should know the business of her own family? By accepting him, she was herself freed from Mrs Makin's charity which would have been most irksome, since her own allowance was woefully inadequate for her tastes. Now she and her father would be clear of creditors and what could be more comfortable than that? Great passion was the stuff of novels and could hardly be thought of in the context of a convenient marriage. She shrugged mentally and stepped away from the window, holding out her hand.

'Good morning, Captain Browne. I am happy to see you.'

Ralph took her hand. 'And I you, Miss Deane. Most happy since your father has received my request with the greatest kindness. May I speak clearly of what is on my mind and in my heart?'

'Please do, Captain.' Zara withdrew her hand and sat down on the couch, spreading her skirts.

Charles Deane retreated to the doorway. 'I think this is an occasion where the presence of a third party is undesirable. I shall be in my study when you have finished your private converse. Come to me there if my advice is needed or any difficulties present themselves.' He smiled and closed the door behind him.

'Miss Deane – Zara – I believe you are in no doubt as to the reason for my presence. May I have the privilege and honour of asking you to become my wife? My most earnest endeavour will be for your happiness and comfort if you would but consider a home in Lahore with a man whose heart you stole at our first meeting.' He sat beside her on the couch and took possession of both her hands, looking at her intently.

'Captain Browne – Ralph – I accept your offer most readily and the privilege is mine since you will be, at the same time, sharing your other world with me in addition to being my dear husband.'

Captain Browne kissed her hands. 'You will allow me then to purchase a passage for you, together with a ring?'

'Of course.' She smiled.

'And announce our engagement in *The Times*'.

'If you insist. You seem most determined on this course.'

27

'Since there is no time to marry before I sail, and I would infinitely have preferred that, I must be content with binding you to me with all the means left available. Even so, I shall dwell in uncertainty of mind until I hear that you have embarked for India under the protection of Mrs Lacy.'

Zara was touched. she leaned forward and kissed his cheek lightly. 'I shall not fail you, Ralph.'

They joined Mr Deane in his study where a celebratory glass of champagne was drunk, then Ralph left to go to the offices of *The Times* newspaper. He promised to return by mid-afternoon, bringing with him a jeweller so that Zara might choose an engagement ring to her own liking from the great variety to be displayed to her.

'Well, my darling?' asked Charles Deane, pouring more champagne.

'Very well, I think, Father.' Zara sipped reflectively. 'Unless he thinks better of it when he is back with his regiment.'

'Nonsense, my dear. It is common practice for King's officers to look about for brides on their home leave and your Captain Browne will consider himself very well pleased that he has attached to himself a well-born girl of beauty and charm.'

Zara smiled. 'A little past my girlhood, Father, but not yet too decrepit to contemplate my future without youthful enthusiasm.'

'We shall both be comfortable, you with that rather serious young man and I with my indulgent Mrs Makin. She has a French chef, you know, and from what she says, an excellent cellar.' He raised his glass in a toast. 'To us, my darling. To comfort and contentment which is, after all, the true basis of our lives.'

Zara raised her own glass. Comfort and contentment were values to strive for, naturally, but could one not wish, just a little, for passion and high adventure? Adventure there must certainly be in India, new and exciting, but passion? She checked herself, but remembered the love that her parents had had for each other, the exchange of looks, the touch of hands, the almost visible bond of love in all its variety of

28

meaning. A rare thing, perhaps, that perfect union, a gift not bestowed on every mortal. To be 'respectably settled' was enough for most people. What made Zara Deane so special that she wanted more? She gave herself a silent admonition. Needs must when the devil drives, her father was fond of saying. She must hold to that adage.

'Comfort and contentment,' she murmured. 'Not to be found in Newgate.'

'Indeed not,' Charles Deane agreed. 'Let us drink to those poor wretches who could find no alternative.'

Eleanor Farnes was delighted when she read the announcement of their engagement in *The Times*.

'Ralph never said a word,' she complained to Zara. 'I would never have thought him so secretive, but then, he had to make sure of you first. I was never in doubt for a moment that he intended to have you from that first meeting.' She cocked her head to look into the face of her taller companion. 'And I suspect, dear Zara, that your own intentions were just as determined.'

Zara laughed. 'Really, Eleanor, you make me sound like one of those female spiders weaving a gossamer web to catch an unwary mate. Do you know, I do believe she eats him afterwards!'

Eleanor gave a faint scream of protest. 'Zara, please! Whatever will you say next? You always did read too many serious books at school. It is not necessary, you know, to be so well-informed about everything. Husbands go in fear of clever wives. It is not natural in a female and much to be deplored.'

'Nonsense! Father always encouraged me and how can one converse intelligently without knowing any topic to converse upon?'

'Well, I will not engage you in argument for I confess you will have the bettering of me. Let us talk instead of your trousseau. I assume you mean to buy it here and I know the very couturier for he made my own wedding gown.'

Zara allowed herself to sink under a welter of suggestions and ideas of what would be proper to carry to India in her luggage. Since Ralph had undertaken to present her to his Colonel's wife before he left, Zara rather thought that that lady's advice might be sounder since she knew the climate and conditions of Lahore.

Mrs Lacy proved to be a slender, elegant lady of middle age. She had a gentle abstracted way with her but professed herself charmed to be having Zara's company on board ship in January. Zara took to her immediately, this tall fair lady with the marks of many Indian summers on her face.

As they drove away, Ralph smiled at Zara. 'She is a most amiable soul but inclined to vagueness. I hope she will remember the sailing date herself.'

Zara, who, with her father, had over the years learned to read characters rather better than most, smiled, but suspected that Mrs Lacy's vagueness of manner disguised a sharp mind, unfashionable perhaps, but the thought intrigued Zara. She would be an interesting companion on the voyage. There would be others on the ship too, she learned. Wives returning to their husbands after depositing their progeny in good boarding schools, young female relations taken out on visits and of course returning officers from various regiments and stations.

On the night of Ralph's leave-taking, he took her in his arms and kissed her on the lips, holding her very close. Zara found it a pleasant experience. She knew she could be content with this tall, brown-haired man who treated her with serious deference.

The blue eyes met hers as he drew back. 'You will wear my ring throughout the whole voyage, will you not?'

Zara looked at him in surprise. 'Of course. Why should I not?'

His smile was disarming. 'It is a long voyage and my fellow officers will have the advantage that I lack. You will be sometimes in their company and it is not unknown for shipboard acquaintanceships to develop inadvertently. I pray you will not allow these fellows any familiarity.'

'Do you consider me so untrustworthy? Really, Ralph, I take that badly.' The hazel eyes were cool. 'Am I now to be thought of as flirtatious and light-minded?'

'Ah, forgive me!' His hands rested on her shoulders, holding her from turning away. 'I doubt your conduct not at all, but knowing my fellow officers, I must deplore their ease of manner with ladies of whatever station. I seek to warn you of what you might expect and to be forearmed against impropriety. My ring on your finger will be a discouragement to any man of honour but, alas, there are those who would ignore such niceties. Please believe that I trust you implicitly. I meant no slight on your own character. That is above reproach.'

He was looking at her so intently that her flush of anger faded. She had misunderstood. He was warning, not admonishing her as she had at first supposed.

'Forgive my sharpness,' she said smiling. 'You need have no fear since I am no young thing to be bowled over by flattery. And you forget, I have Mrs Lacy to guard me. Her position as the Colonel's wife must deter the most persistent, unless he is a brigadier or field marshal and holding that rank would not, I think, be of a flirtatious character.'

'Certainly not those that I have met,' Ralph said, his manner easy again. 'A rubber of bridge would be more to their taste.'

'Then I shall be quite safe and you have no need to fret. Shall we join Father for dinner? The gong has been sounded twice and Bates will be out of temper if we continue to ignore it.'

Chapter Three

The first awareness that she was not alone on deck came to Zara Deane on the warm sultry air. She was standing by the stern rail of the ship, staring mesmerised at the long phosphorescent wake that spun away into the starlit night. A faint drift of cheroot smoke reached her but she did not move, reluctant to identify its source and make her presence known. Some gentleman, unable to sleep, was taking the air, just as she was herself, she supposed. He must move away presently and at this moment, she was not eager for company. Wearing a deep blue wrapper over her pale cotton nightdress, she hoped for invisibility against the night sky.

The small cabin she shared with Miss Pringle had been suffocatingly hot, for Miss Pringle did not care for dangerously open windows, for they were on the boat-deck and any passing man might glance in. And quickly move on, thought Zara morosely, for Miss Pringle snored. It was said that some of the male passengers, properly accommodated forward, of course, took out their bedding and laid it on deck as they approached India. Naturally, this was not quite the thing for ladies, but Zara wished she could flout the conventions and do the same. She almost sighed aloud but remembered in time that the scent of cheroot was still in the air.

She leaned forward a little to watch the wake curve away and the lacy scarf she had draped over her head slipped. Raising a hand quickly to grasp the ends, she found them gone and her loosened dark hair flung itself about her shoulders. She turned, her gaze dropping to the deck at her feet. The breeze took her hair and flung it wildly about her face, obscuring her view. She pushed it out of her eyes and stared about. The stranger was momentarily forgotten and she started as a harsh, male voice cut through the night.

'What the devil –' The words were sharp and irritable, then a brown hand reached out and scooped up the handful of lace that had drifted to the deck.

Zara stared at the hand, her gaze progressing upwards to a tall, barely discernible figure against the bulkhead lantern. He stepped closer and she glimpsed a dark, bearded face. He held out the scarf.

'Yours, madam?' The accent was definitely English and she was relieved.

Zara nodded. 'Yes, thank you.' She reached for the scarf. 'I'm sorry if it startled you.'

'Almost dropped my cigar, which would have been a waste of a good one.' He turned to the rail then looked at her over his shoulder. 'Why are you on deck? What brings you out of the dovecote?'

Zara stared at him, seeing the sardonic curve of his mouth and the raised dark brows.

'The what?'

'The dovecot, where gather the respectable matrons returning to India and their loved ones. That area aboard ship is commonly referred to in such terms.' He regarded her speculatively for a moment. 'I take it that this is your first trip to that jewel in the crown of Empire?'

'Yes, it is.'

'With your husband?' he asked.

'I am not married.'

He laughed softly. 'Ah! So, it is the fishing fleet for you. I wish you good hunting, madam.'

'I haven't the faintest idea what you are talking about.' Zara said stiffly. 'I am joining my fiancé in India, if it's any business of yours. As to why I am on deck, well, I find our cabin extremely stuffy and my companion a trifle – er noisy.'

'You mean she snores?' There was no disguising the amusement in his words.

'I would rather not discuss my cabin companion.' She looked up into the dark face and spoke hesitantly.

'Are you in the habit of frequenting this part of the ship?' She had tied the scarf about her tumbled hair again.

He understood the implication of her remark. 'Certainly not in daylight and rarely at night, so you will be free to take the air whenever you choose should your companion continue – er – noisy.'

'I would expect the view to be much the same from the officers' accommodation,' Zara said.

'Indeed, but I am not in the officers' accommodation. I am a civilian, ma'am.'

'Oh, I see,' said Zara, although she saw nothing and the stranger did not enlighten her. A collector, administrator, a planter? She wondered at herself for being here at all, having a conversation in the middle of the night with a strange man. How shocked Miss Pringle would be.

She sighed without realising it. 'I must go back to my cabin. If Miss Pringle wakes – I mean – if my companion

33

wakes and wonders where I am –' She broke off as his soft laugh came again.

'So, you are sharing a cabin with the delightful and determined Delia.' It was not a question but a statement and Zara stared into the smiling face.

'Are you then acquainted? And why do you describe her in those words?'

'We have met in happier times. Quite a delightful girl but her determination shows too strongly.'

'I don't understand you.'

'Of course not, since this is your first trip and your fish has already been caught. To my knowledge, delightful Delia has made three trips and her line continues to come up empty.'

Zara shook her head. 'You talk in riddles, sir, and though I cannot quite understand you, I sense that whatever it is you are saying is most disrespectful. My companion – indeed all of my companions on this voyage have been most kind and considerate. I will not listen to any disparagement of them.'

'And quite right too,' he said, surprisingly. 'And with that attitude, you will fit very well into the life of a memsahib. I daresay you play bridge and croquet?'

'Why no –'

'But you surely embroider delightfully and produce pretty watercolour pictures?'

'Not exactly –'

'Pianoforte? The harp? You sing, of course?'

Zara frowned. 'What a lot of strange questions. Why are you asking? And does it matter if I do none of those things? What one is expected to do in England is surely of no consequence in India.'

The stranger shook his head sadly. 'On the contrary, ma'am. One might transpose an English drawing-room to India and find the only difference a punkah – that is a ceiling fan, with a native attached to the end of the rope.'

Zara was well aware that she should have ended this conversation long ago, but curiosity held her still. What a strange man he was. She was not afraid of him for he leaned against the rail and kept his distance. The night was less dark now and a faint rose colour on the horizon heralded the dawn.

She saw him a little more clearly. Fully dressed in well-cut tail coat, he was slim and long-legged, his neckcloth seeming undisturbed by the warm night. A dark, curly beard and fine moustache, his hair looked a little too long, certainly compared with the clipped hair and neat sidewhiskers of the army men. She could not see his eyes but had the impression that they were dark. He hadn't asked her name or given his own. Perhaps it was as well. If he belonged to some civil administration, she was unlikely to see him again. He made her feel a little uneasy, for there was an underlying mockery in his words, making her feel like a child in the presence of erudite elders and not quite understanding the conversation.

She glanced out to sea. A faint rim of gold edged the horizon. The man followed her gaze.

'The false dawn, but nevertheless, a signal for parting, ma'am. It would never do to start a fluttering in the dovecote. Reputation is a delicate flower. You must guard it well and hold silent on our meeting.' He bowed and swung away, soft-footed into the shadows cast by the ship's bridge.

Zara went slowly back to her cabin. The air had cooled a little and she slipped into her bunk, glancing over at the sleeping girl sprawled on the other bunk. Since they were both unmarried girls, it had been suggested they share a cabin. Delia was blond and slightly anaemic-looking, with hard blue eyes. She had an abundance of gowns and the weary hauteur of one who has travelled extensively and sees nothing new under the sun. The stranger on deck had known Delia. Was it true that Delia had sought and failed to find a husband in India? What had he called it? The fishing fleet, yes, that was it. There were so many eligible young officers in the British Army of India that only the arrival of a ship bearing English girls could solve the problem of bachelorhood.

She glanced over at Delia again. The light had strengthened and the lines of discontent on the girl's face were softened by sleep. She felt a stab of pity mixed with understanding and exasperation for the girl. If she dropped her air of superiority she might fare better in the husband stakes. Good heavens, she thought in amusement, I am beginning to believe that strange man with his joky talk of fishing fleets. And the dovecote? Well, indeed, it was a remarkably apt description, for the ladies fluttered and cooed over trivialities.

Zara thought of these things as she lay on her bunk. She recalled Ralph's last embrace, the kiss that had lingered on her lips and his plea that she take the first available passage to India. She felt a sense of excitement, for they were due to dock within three days and Ralph had promised to meet her. Her thoughts rested for a moment on the stranger. He had not talked of hunting and polo as Ralph had done, but of the life of a memsahib as if it was exactly the same as life in England. Surely her new life would hold more adventure. She mentally dismissed the stranger. As a civilian he would know nothing of army life.

She did not stroll on deck in the small hours during the next two nights, but on her last evening aboard she felt restless and quite unable to sleep. Miss Pringle had almost driven her to distraction with her packing. Such a quantity of bags and trunks brought from the hold, to be packed and repacked, deciding first on one outfit, then another for the following day, that Zara gritted her teeth in sheer exasperation. Darkness had fallen long before Delia seemed satisfied with her choice but even so, the array of unstrapped boxes choked the small cabin, ready for a change of plan as dawn broke.

The night was warm and Zara had tried to sleep, but the claustrophobia caused by the piles of baggage and the still closed window drove her out into the cooler air. Standing by the stern rail, her loose hair lifting from her warm face and neck, she surveyed the ship's wake. It was not the best position to catch her first glimpse of Calcutta but she could not go forward for that was where the men were quartered. Perhaps when the ship turned to effect entry, a view might be obtained.

'Port or starboard,' she murmured. 'Not straight in, surely.' She leaned her elbows on the rail, staring into the starlit night.

'She'll anchor in the roads, ma'am, and wait until ordered to a berth,' said a soft voice, and there was the fragrance of cheroot smoke on the air.

Without turning her head, Zara spoke as softly. 'Why,

thank you, sir. You have relieved my mind. I would like my first view of Calcutta to be clearly seen.' She glanced sideways at the dark figure leaning on the rail a few feet away. She could not distinguish his features, only the faint outline of his profile. It was difficult to judge what kind of face he had for the beard and moustache disguised all but the strong nose and well-shaped head. Ralph was clean shaven, his frank, open countenance revealed to the world. She could not recall having seen this man during the long voyage from England until three nights ago. Did civilians use another deck, she wondered? Surely not, she decided, for he seemed quite at home on this part of the ship.

She realised with a start that he was watching her. With the moon beyond his shoulder the pale light illuminated only her own face. All she could see of him was the glint of teeth as he smiled and the shine of his eyes.

'You have an expressive face, ma'am. You are wondering, yes, about me – or do I flatter myself?'

Zara considered a denial but shrugged instead. Why not be honest? 'To be truthful, yes. Most people on a voyage of this length make the acquaintance of almost everyone on board, yet I do not recall seeing you before the other night.' She saw his teeth glint into a smile.

'In response to your wonderment, I will say only that I did not board ship in England.' He turned away then and she sensed that he would permit no more questioning on her part.

For a long moment, they both stared silently into the night, then Zara spoke softly.

'What is it like, this country of which I know nothing? Oh yes, I hear of balls and such from the ladies, tiger shoots and the like from my fiancé, but what is it to you and those beyond the garrison towns?' She smiled in the darkness. 'An English drawing-room life transposed to India, as you implied? How do you, a civilian, look upon this vast continent?'

'Like a lover returning to a mistress – if that sentiment does not shock your ears.'

She knew he looked at her sideways but she kept her gaze forward.

37

'Punjab means the land of the five rivers with the foothills of the mountains to the north. The word Himalaya means abode of snow. Lahore, your destination, is set between two of the rivers, the Beas and the Ravi.'

'How do you know I go to Lahore?'

He gave a soft laugh. 'Because of the company you keep. Since you are much with Colonel Lacy's wife, it is quite a simple deduction. Shall I continue with my geography lesson?' he asked mildly.

'Please do, and forgive my interruption,' Zara said in a slightly muffled voice, and stared hard into the darkness, determined not to respond to the amusement in his voice.

'Indeed, madam, you are quite forgiven and when I tell you there is no finer view, save with the eye of an eagle, than that area between and beyond the rivers, I am sure you will agree when you have seen it for yourself. I hope you will be allowed the opportunity.'

Zara glanced at the dark face. 'Allowed? What should prevent me?'

'Your fiancé, perhaps, or moral pressure.'

'I don't understand you.'

'It is not necessary to be a high-born Indian girl to be kept within the confined circles which they call purdah. Memsahibs do not venture far afield save in groups. One might almost term it white purdah.'

'That sounds quite nonsensical,' Zara said sharply. 'You exaggerate, I think. I haven't travelled so far to see nothing of the country and its people.'

He straightened and gave her a little bow. She saw he was smiling. 'I wish you luck, ma'am.'

The cigar butt arced into the sea, then he turned and was gone.

The midday sun was so intense that few of the ladies had ventured out near the rail as the ship lay at anchor in the roads. Zara, a wide straw hat shading her eyes, stared over the brilliant water towards Calcutta. The whitewashed buildings of the harbour threw back the sun's glare and the scene shimmered as through a haze.

She brought Ralph to mind. The tall, brown-haired man, tanned and slim in his well-cut uniform. She glanced at the ring on her finger. In the two weeks of their acquaintance, she had gathered little about him, save that he had no family. Did it matter that she knew him so little? He had proposed marriage and here she was, committed to a course of action that would not have arisen, had not her father contemplated remarriage. He was perfectly entitled to marry again, she admitted honestly, but Mrs Makin was not the kind of stepmother Zara had expected. She shrugged away the comparison with her own mother. It was no longer of consequence for her new life was about to begin.

She turned from the rail and sought the comparative coolness of the lounge where the ladies were congregated.

The fierceness of the sun had eased a little by the time the ship slid into its berth. Carriages and wagons lined the pier as the bags and boxes were swung down. The rails were lined now with straw-bonneted ladies, watching anxiously as their possessions were unloaded. Army officers, shepherding new recruits, left first, to be marched away, then the holds were awash with native porters, humping enormous loads on their heads as they ran, sure-footed, down the gangway.

A tall man in a linen suit, a panama hat set at a jaunty angle, strolled casually down the gangplank. Zara, noting the swing of his step and the curve of his profile, leaned forward a little over the rail, vaguely aware that there was something recognisable about him. The stranger she had met twice on deck? She was almost convinced of it, for his hair sat on his jacket collar and the dark beard was curly. As he reached the foot of the gangplank, he turned and glanced up at the lined rail. His mouth seemed to twitch with amusement and he raised the panama politely before turning his back.

A breathless gasp swept through the ladies. Zara's hand, half raised to acknowledge the polite gesture, fell to her side and she looked into the shocked faces about her with puzzlement.

'How dare he return!'

'What outrageous cheek –'

'That man is lost to all decency! And on this ship, too.'

Zara stared into the chalk-white face of Delia Pringle. The blue eyes were hard as flint, the mouth tightly pursed.

'What is it? Who is that man?' Zara asked of no one in particular.

The ladies regarded her silently for a moment, then one took the lead. 'Of course, you are not to know, my dear, being a stranger to India, but that man is a scoundrel, a disgrace to the army – fully deserved to be cashiered.'

'What – what did he do?' asked Zara faintly.

The ladies exchanged uneasy glances. 'There was a scandal involving a native girl. She was found dead in his bungalow. We really should not talk of it now.'

Delia gave a short harsh laugh. 'Found dead is not in the least true. She was stabbed to death and he did it! Blood everywhere and he drunk on the floor beside her.'

'Delia, my dear –' protested one lady, but Miss Pringle turned on her savagely.

'He denied it, oh yes, of course he would, but they should have hanged him for murder.' She swung away abruptly and hurried down the companionway.

There was another uneasy silence until one lady broke it. 'Poor Delia. She was quite convinced that he would offer for her but then this happened.' She sighed. 'I don't pretend to know why he is here, but be warned, my dear, for he is a dangerous man. We knew him for a rake but that –' she shuddered slightly. 'And he a major too. Major Richard Deverill, though, of course, he no longer holds the rank which he disgraced.'

Chapter Four

It was eminently desirable, Zara thought, to keep a discreet silence where the stranger was concerned, and she did not make the mistake of gazing after him. It was shocking enough to have spoken to him twice, alone and in the darkness of the night, but now he had the reality of a name and an unsavoury record. Delia Pringle's outburst, together with the amusement he had shown in speaking of Delia's fishing line coming up empty, convinced her that he was a callous and hurtful man, capable of raising false hopes, then dashing them down. Had he amused himself at Delia's expense while keeping a native girl as mistress?

Zara pulled her thoughts together. It was shocking and ungentlemanly behaviour, but it was history now and really no concern of hers. She knew that her own feelings should be as shocked as the ladies', and yet she recalled the tone of voice he had used when speaking of the land of the five rivers and 'the abode of snow'. Almost an endearment in the timbre as if he loved the land and stood in awe of the Himalayas.

She saw Ralph then, and everything else fled from her mind. He was seated astride a large bay horse, his uniform immaculate, a solar topee on his head, shading his blue eyes. They were scanning the decks and from her position by the rail, she raised a hand, waving it wildly to attract his attention. He saw her and his taut body seemed to relax as if he had been expecting her to decide against the journey. He raised his riding crop in salute then urged the horse forward, its huge hindquarters scattering the porters and fruit sellers. A small brown child overbalanced and sprawled chuckling in the dust before his approach and the horse stepped delicately over the little body, without Ralph's direction. He seemed unaware of the scowl thrown at his back by the woman who scooped up the child.

Zara had drawn in her breath sharply, fearing for the infant's safety, but a hand touched her arm reassuringly.

'An impetuous fiancé you have there, my dear,' Lucille Lacy commented. Zara looked into the face of Colonel Lacy's wife. She was smiling indulgently. 'Safe enough, my dear. Those cavalry horses are trained to avoid such things. Except in the charge and then, my goodness, they go mad with hooves and teeth too.'

'Well, now that he has seen me I hope he will keep the creature stationary.'

Mrs Lacy's gaze was considering. 'Don't let your first words be of reproach, Miss Deane. Gentlemen are not keen

41

on that, and we do depend on them greatly out here. You will find the life very different and our tongues more guarded.'

Zara smiled. 'Thank you, Mrs Lacy. I believe that you are telling me that the rules of conduct are – perhaps – more strictly observed here than in England.'

'You understand me well, Miss Deane, for, after all, we have only ourselves to turn to.'

'Does your husband meet you, Mrs Lacy?'

'Alas, no. He is probably out on manoeuvres or is called to a staff meeting. We are thrown much into our own company and seek such diversions as we may arrange.'

The stranger's amused words floated treacherously through Zara's mind. 'Like bridge and croquet?' she hazarded.

'Exactly. Do you play the piano, Miss Deane? Such a delightful accomplishment, though I fail sadly in that respect myself.'

Zara's breath caught in her throat as she tried to quell the ripple of laughter. 'Oh, indeed, Mrs Lacy,' she managed on a gasp. 'I fail most miserably in that matter, too, and pray do not ask if I sing, for I don't, but my embroidery is considered quite reasonable although my watercolour paintings run shockingly into each other.' She was unable to hide her amusement as Mrs Lacy stared in astonishment, before her mouth curved into an answering smile.

'My dear Miss Deane, I am not interviewing you for a position as governess.' The pale lined face seemed to light up and she gave a most girlish giggle. 'Those diversions merely pass the time for matrons and hopeful young girls. You will be far too busy for such things, having engaged yourself to a charming young man.' Her faded blue eyes sparkled for a moment and she looked about her casually to gauge who was in earshot. 'You are pretty and original, my dear, but do not, I beg of you, be too original. Husbands do not care for their wives to be different, preferring merely a genteel extension of themselves. I think I need say no more for you are sharp enough to know what I mean.'

It seemed that half the carriages on the Lahore train had been hired to convey the party of English ladies north-westward,

42

and Zara was pleased to have Mrs Lacy insist on her company in the first carriage. The matrons and single girls, including Delia Pringle, were installed in following compartments and they in turn by the enormous amount of baggage which filled two further carriages. Zara watched, fascinated, as troopers led their mounts into the rear vans and she admired Ralph's efficiency, though he seemed, she thought, a little too grim in his treatment of a reluctant horse, or a slow-moving trooper.

Mrs Lacy sighed and leaned her head on the velvet cushion. 'So much more comfortable, now that the lines have been laid. Do you know, my dear, that when I first came to India as a girl, we travelled for weeks in most uncomfortable ox-carts, making only a few miles a day. If we outpaced the slower baggage carts and lost sight of them, it was possible we had lost our possessions altogether. And the dak bungalows where we spent each night were most unsavoury. The food was ill-cooked, the servants surly, and my dear, the mattresses most suspect.' She glanced up. 'Ah, here is your fiancé, my dear, come no doubt to determine if all is well.'

Ralph stood in the doorway. 'Indeed, ma'am,' he said with a quick smile at Zara. 'But also to ascertain your own comfort in strict accordance with the orders laid on me by my Commanding Officer. Should the slightest lack of attention displease you, I shall immediately be deprived of my commission and most probably court martialled into the bargain.'

Mrs Lacy laughed. 'Then I shall certainly hold my tongue should the need arise for I will have no officer brought low on my account. But everything has been splendidly arranged, Captain, and so I shall tell my husband.'

'Thank you, ma'am,' Ralph said. 'My duty and pleasure is to serve you.' He hesitated fractionally. 'Would you consider it improper of me to speak to Miss Deane on the platform? She will be in full view of your goodself, naturally.'

'Not in the least improper, Captain, for I am sure you are both dying to have a private conversation, after being apart for so long. Shall we say ten minutes?'

Ralph helped Zara on to the platform and they stood outside the door of the compartment. He took her hands and kissed them lightly.

'I am most gratified that you came, Zara. Every moment since my return, I have worried that, on reflection, you must surely change your mind. The two weeks of our acquaintanceship seemed hardly sufficient reason for you to entrust your future into my hands.'

'Your worries are at an end, my dear, for I stand before you.' She regarded him gravely. 'You look tired, rather as you looked the day I met you at Eleanor's, and yet you were then on leave.'

To her surprise, a slight flush appeared under his tan. 'And not surprising, for then I was bored with my own company and now I have this tedious task to perform. Had it not been that you were of the party, I should have delegated the escort to my lieutenant.'

'But, Ralph, you have been most efficient. Mrs Lacy was very complimentary.'

He smiled but there was something in his eyes she could not read for in truth, she knew very little of this man, her knowledge being surface only.

'To rise in rank, it is necessary to please both the Colonel and his lady.' His smile warmed. 'Forgive me, Zara. You are marrying an ambitious man. Does that displease you?'

'Why, no. I suppose every man has ambitions to rise in his chosen profession. It is no fault, quite the reverse, and I will do all I can to help you.'

He squeezed her fingers gently and leaned forward to kiss her cheek. 'We can be married in Lahore as soon as it can be arranged. I knew I had chosen right the moment I saw you. You have an adventurous spirit, or you would not be here. We shall deal well together, I am convinced.'

'You make it sound like a business venture, Ralph, and I do not wish to marry in such haste. You must allow me time to acclimatise myself to the country and become acquainted with the life of a soldier's wife. Since I cannot flee the country without great inconvenience, I would learn something of it first. Do not press me into the role of wife too soon. Let me enjoy my newfound freedom a while longer. Perhaps a month or two.' Though she made her tone light and teasing, she sensed that Ralph was not pleased. 'Is it too much to ask?'

'Of course not, my dearest. I just wanted us to be together as soon as possible. It was selfish of me to hope you cared as deeply –' He broke off and looked away, his expression remote. She noted subconsciously the paling of his blue eyes.

Zara laid a hand on his arm, touched by his brief show of emotion. 'Oh, Ralph, I'm sorry. I have no wish to hurt you, since you have done me the honour of proposing marriage. By all means go ahead with the arrangements, but allow me a few weeks to get my bearings.'

He turned to her, his face alive again, his pale blue eyes darkening to brilliant blue. His lean brown features were smooth, the sun of India tracing the lines about his eyes and mouth. Mrs Lacy's skin was similar. Would she too, find her fine skin become like soft leather? No wonder Delia had such an assortment of wide-brimmed hats and parasols among her luggage.

'I must return you to your chaperone, my love. It would never do to displease such an important lady in the hierarchy of Lahore.'

Zara caught the undertone of cynicism. He stood back and bowed correctly, including both ladies in the gesture of politeness.

When the last piece of luggage had been stowed and wicker hampers containing food and drink had been placed in each compartment by the servants of the railway hotel, the engine whistle shrieked imperiously and the train shuddered into movement.

Mrs Lacy smiled up from her comfortable window seat. 'Marriage to you, my dear, will have a most settling effect on Captain Browne. Young officers are apt to run a little wild without the guiding hand of a wife.'

'Really? In what way?' Zara was genuinely interested, but Mrs Lacy's expression became suddenly wary. 'Oh,' she said vaguely. 'Harmless pursuits in the main, gambling, wagers, that sort of thing and – er – perhaps unwise company.' She attempted to dismiss the subject but Zara said on a laughing note, 'By unwise, I suppose you mean "ladies of the night". Is that not the name for them?' She looked innocently into Mrs Lacy's shocked face. 'Come, ma'am, I am four-and-twenty

45

years old and have lived my life in London. I am not a simpleton.'

Mrs Lacy gave a stifled giggle. 'No, you are certainly not that and yes, to be truthful, our bachelors have discreet relationships.'

'Not always discreet enough, I imagine,' returned Zara, remembering the stranger on the ship.

'You refer, I believe, to poor Major Deverill. Quite incomprehensible. He was a difficult man but most charming. Such a waste of a brilliant career and no question of his guilt, of course.'

'Do you not wonder at his return to India?' asked Zara. 'The ladies were most taken aback when they saw him quit the ship.'

'I don't wonder at it at all, my dear, for he had a great love for this country. A man like that will make his way somehow.' Mrs Lacy closed her eyes and leaned back her head.

Zara accepted it as a signal for the closing of that topic of conversation. Yes, she thought, the stranger's words on the ship revealed his affection for this land. A clever and not too scrupulous man might make his living in some way outside the protection of the army. She began to think of Ralph. She was determined not to be rushed into matrimony however hard he pressed. She must inevitably marry him sooner or later, there was no turning back from that, but for the present she was happy to absorb herself in this new life.

The steam engine puffed and thundered north-west, billowing plumes of sooty smoke enveloping the train one moment, then being blown aside by the hot wind from the plains. It was impossible to open the window without receiving a coating of grime and the heat was oppressive. Zara glimpsed village women in loose-fitting cotton saris and envied their freedom of movement. She supposed the garrison ladies retained their corsets and stockings, just as they did in England, but how wonderful it must be to go bare-legged with only one cotton garment for cover. She fell asleep on the thought.

Contact with Ralph and the other ladies on the train could

only be accomplished when the train halted on its long journey. Station hotels provided meals and accommodation and the chance to stretch one's legs. Ralph was always at hand on these occasions, backed up by native officers of the regiment, to translate or harry the hotel servants into providing whatever the ladies wanted. The hotels were efficiently run, the staff friendly and helpful, and quite able to cater for every taste of the Europeans. A slight over-enthusiasm to make every dish have the flavour of curry, even the fried egg at breakfast, amused Zara, but she decided she quite liked the taste of it. Only the sacrosanct teapot escaped, for which she was grateful as a great deal of tea was drunk.

Darkness fell with surprising rapidity in India, she realised, for indeed there was hardly any twilight and the night arrived at precisely the same time throughout the year. Ralph managed to spend a few minutes with her at every halt but most of his energies were taken up by supervising the feeding of his men and horses.

'We disentrain at Lahore tomorrow,' he said, 'provided one of those confounded cows does not take it into her head to occupy the railway line.'

'A cow on the line?' asked Zara in surprise. 'Surely its owner will keep it out of such danger?'

'He will urge it, to be sure, but the driver will stop the train and blow off steam, they always do, until the beast gets tired of the noise and removes itself. Those animals are sacred to the Hindu and they will coax, not beat it away.'

'Ah, I see.' Zara shrugged. 'Since we are, after all, in their country, we must abide by their customs. It seems only right and proper.'

'When you have been here a little longer, my dear, you may find your patience becoming overstretched. It is always "tomorrow, Sahib, tomorrow". Time has no meaning here, except with the army.'

Zara looked into Ralph's grim face and decided against inquiring about further customs. She would learn soon enough. Since he had taken on this escort duty for her sake alone, she must show him her appreciation. She tucked her arm under his elbow and smiled up at him.

'I am convinced that no lady on this train has had the slightest cause for complaint. Your praises will be sung into every ear, including that of Colonel Lacy. You have performed this escort duty splendidly, even though it is not to your taste. For myself, I thank you most kindly. It was thoughtful of you to greet me in person, for everything is so strange and new to me.' She lowered her voice confidentially. 'Had you not come, I might have turned tail and hidden in my cabin until the ship turned about for England.'

She saw the flash of alarm in his eyes and regretted her light-hearted joke. 'No, no, I did not mean it, truly. You take me too seriously, Ralph.'

He frowned a little. 'You should not make remarks that have no foundation in fact. Flippancy is something to be avoided. People misunderstand.'

Zara felt her heart sink. He really was very serious. Perhaps this escort duty was too much on his mind.

'Father and I are in the habit –' she began but Ralph cut her off.

'Your father is not here, Zara. I have the responsibility of you now and I take that seriously.'

Zara could not stop herself from saying. 'It seems the responsibility lies too heavily upon you. I have no wish to be a burden and have never considered myself in that light, but since you point it out to me –'

Her cool tone had brought a flush to Ralph's cheeks. 'You are my fiancée since my ring is on your finger. Perhaps I do not take that as lightly as you, but it is a position I will not relinquish whatever you choose to call it.'

Zara withdrew her arm and clasped her hands together, feeling the hardness of the diamond on her left hand. How simple to take it off and drop it into Ralph's hand. What then? Home to England and to the house where Mrs Makin was already Mrs Deane? No, pride would not allow that. She was committed, having accepted Ralph's proposal, his ring and the expense of a passage to Calcutta.

She looked up at him, smiling. 'You cannot change me overnight, Ralph, from a flippant girl into a matron of sober respectability. It is not in my nature, though if it will please you, I shall endeavour to become staid and conventional.'

He smiled then. 'Not too staid, please, but conventional by all means. You will understand what I mean when we join the garrison. We all live by the strictest of rules. One cannot be different.'

When Zara joined Mrs Lacy in their compartment, she was silent, reflecting on the conversation. The memory of the stranger's words came irritatingly into her mind. Transpose an English drawing-room to India. You will find little difference. Surely he was joking, but his words tallied so well with what Ralph had intimated that she knew had meant every word.

'Damn the man!' she muttered, then realised that she had spoken the words out aloud, for Mrs Lacy's amused gaze was resting upon her. She flushed. 'I beg your pardon. That was most unladylike.'

'But relieved your feelings, no doubt, though I must admit it seems a little early to be damning your fiancé. What has the poor man done to deserve your censure? You did mean Captain Browne, I take it?'

Zara met the shrewd gaze and thought quickly. It would not do for the Colonel's wife to know that she had been twice alone in the middle of the night with a completely strange man. And that one a cashiered officer and, according to Delia, a murderer.

She avoided a direct reply by saying, 'I fear Captain Browne may yet rue the day he met me in London and proposed this course of action. He takes responsibility for me so seriously that when I ventured a joke on turning tail in Calcutta, he was not at all pleased.'

'You must not blame him, my dear. He has a high sense of duty, my husband says, and devotion to duty does not always include a sense of humour. I am sure he will be more amusing when he has discharged this task of escorting us to Lahore. Just think what trouble he would be in if he mislaid one single dove from the late dovecote!'

Her eyes twinkled and Zara laughed. 'You are right, of course. I suspect he would find it less irksome to ride into battle.'

As Mrs Lacy dozed, Zara considered the landscape passing swiftly by. The fertile valleys with their brilliant green rice fields were left behind as the train climbed. In the land of the five rivers which was the Punjab, she had learned that wheat was better suited to the soil than rice, and she glimpsed the golden fields glinting under the sun. Higher still, although they would not be travelling so far, was the 'abode of snow', the vast Himalayan mountains, the barrier of sheer cliffs that divided northern India from Afghanistan. Tomorrow they would reach Lahore and there her new life would really begin.

Chapter Five

The carriage drive from Lahore railway station was a delight to Zara. Small brown laughing children strove to compete with the horses, grimy hands outstretched.

'Begging, of course,' Mrs Lacy said, smiling. 'They will all swear to being orphans in the hope of a few coins being tossed to them. I cannot resist them myself but one shouldn't really encourage them.'

The children fell back as a native cavalryman came alongside and shouted at them. The reddish dust thrown up by the hooves of the escorting horsemen hung in the still air. Through the haze Zara glimpsed a nosegay of flower-patterned parasols in the following carriages. Mrs Lacy caught her eye and smiled wickedly.

'Being the Colonel's wife, my dear, has its advantages. My carriage takes precedence in the line, and we avoid the dusty wake of others. However, a parasol is still essential for the sake of your skin.'

Her smile became vague as Ralph galloped alongside. He looked hot and harassed, his face filmed by dust.

'Almost journey's end, ma'am,' he reported. 'I have sent two troopers ahead to clear the road. There appears to be some procession barring the way.' He touched his cap with the whip handle, gave Zara an abstracted smile and galloped on.

'A funeral,' commented Mrs Lacy as the line of carriages passed a long column of people.

Zara saw the uncovered face of a very old wrinkled man turned skywards as he lay on some kind of stretcher carried shoulder-high by dark-faced men. Garlands of flowers were around the dead man's neck and covered his body. Veiled women followed the cortège. The heavy perfume of flowers swept over the ladies in the carriage.

'Where are they headed?' Zara asked. 'I know nothing of their customs yet.'

'To the burning ghat beside the river, for I believe they are Hindu. Their bones then go into the Ganges after the burning, for the Ganges is their sacred river. That is their custom, but the method of disposing of the body varies according to their own religions.' She glanced ahead. Her face brightened. 'The garrison, at last. We have lived here so long, it is like a homecoming for me, far more than England was.'

Zara gazed at the whitewashed bungalows with interest. In a semicircle, with gardens of their own, they faced a great expanse of grass, short-cut and yellowing. Beyond the grass were barracks for the troopers, stables, and what looked like a parade ground.

Tall trees, the blue-flowered jacaranda, stood sentinel beside large-leaved plantains, all new to Zara. Steps led up the front of each bungalow and each step held a potted plant, its blooms startlingly vivid in shades of yellow and crimson. Bougainvillea bushes adorned the plain white walls, colours rioting through scarlet to purple.

The carriages broke line as each headed to its own destination. Mrs Lacy's carriage halted in front of what seemed to Zara a vast assembly of dark, white-robed figures. Zara looked at them with curiosity and Mrs Lacy smiled about amiably. A middle-aged man, stiff and dignified in his starched white tunic, turban and a red cummerbund led the greeting, palms together as he bowed.

'Welcome, Memsahib. The light of your presence has returned to us.'

'It is good to be back among friends. This is Krishna, our

51

khitmagar, our major-domo, my dear. Is all in readiness for our guest?'

'All is ready, Memsahib.' The man bowed to Zara, his dark face impassive. 'If the Missie Sahib will follow the girl.' He waved to a slight, round-faced youngster. 'She will attend you as ayah if it pleases you to have her.'

'Why, Krishna,' exclaimed Mrs Lacy. 'Is she not your granddaughter, Sushila?'

'Yes, Memsahib.'

'Such a little one when I left and how pretty she has grown.'

'She will serve the Missie Sahib well,' the major-domo said in a voice of authority. 'That is, until I have arranged her marriage.' He turned, waving a hand in dismissal to the assembly of cooks, gardeners and grooms who had gathered to show respect to the returning Colonel's lady.

Mrs Lacy said, 'When you have refreshed yourself, my dear, we shall take tea on the veranda.'

Zara followed the girl indoors, down a passage and into a long, cool room. In its centre stood a four-poster bed. From the supports hung white mosquito netting curtains, already drawn. The heavy shutters of the window were thrown back and a faint breeze came through the partly opened window. Sushila showed her the small dressing-room. It contained a marble-topped washstand laid out with soap and towels, while beside it stood an ornate hip-bath already filled with warm water.

Zara undressed and climbed into the hip-bath with a sigh of satisfaction. Mrs Lacy had spoken of the derzie, the man who could cut out and stitch dresses to any pattern or picture shown to him. This was not the place to wear velvet or heavy satins. Lightweight dresses of muslin and cotton were essential and perhaps a reduction in the number of petticoats usual in England. She supposed that corselets and stockings must be retained for their lack would be obvious, but how nice to go barefoot and draped only in blouse and flowing cotton sari like the ayah.

The water about her waist rippled to her suppressed laughter as she thought of the shock waves through the garrison if she dared dress like that. It would not do to scandalise the ladies and embarrass Ralph. Life here ran on very well-regulated and conventional lines. The standards of English Society must be maintained at all costs. She had learned that lesson from the moment of boarding the ship. It was up to her to play the role she had allotted to herself on accepting Captain Browne's offer of marriage. She stepped from the bath, towelled herself dry, and slipped into a fresh clean dress.

On the threshold of the drawing-room she paused and looked about. A long room, white-walled and high-ceilinged, its floor red-tiled. A large-bladed ceiling fan moved the air slowly above a collection of rattan chairs and low tables.

The room opened onto a veranda which ran the full width of the building. It was shaded by blinds of rush matting which could be rolled up and tied when the sun passed over the house. Bungalow, Zara corrected herself. Even buildings with stairs were called bungalows, an Indian word.

Mrs Lacy was already on the veranda, presiding over the tea tray. 'Ah, there you are, my dear. So nice to drink tea exactly to one's own taste and Krishna does it excellently. Sit down, my dear, and enjoy this cool little breeze while we may, before we are driven indoors by the mosquitoes and flying ants.'

Zara accepted the fine bone china cup and gazed over the compound. Every building seemed to be whitewashed into eye-searing brilliance as the sunlight caught them.

A trumpet shrilled in the distance. The glow of the sun lessened as it began its descent to the hazy horizon that seemed to reach up with dusky fingers to pull it down.

'Evening stables,' commented Mrs Lacy. 'Soon, the flag will be lowered and the troopers dismissed.' She paused as a trumpet sounded from farther away. 'A different call and coming from the north.' Her face brightened. 'Could it be that my erring and faithless husband has recalled to mind my existence?' She rose and moved to the veranda rail. 'Good heavens, I feel quite excited. How ridiculous!'

Zara joined her, smiling into the suddenly youthful face. 'Nonsense. I would guess that Colonel Lacy swore most fearfully when he learned that duty must take him from the garrison at the very moment of your arrival in Calcutta.'

Mrs Lacy's soft laugh was almost girlish. 'What a thing to say, but I daresay you are right. He is a most excellent husband yet I will not tell him so for men think enough of themselves without flattery.' She laughed again. 'My dear Zara, I cannot think why I talk in this fashion to you. It is most unlike me to share my thoughts, save with my husband. Why do I do it?' She looked inquiringly at Zara. 'Not even with the Major's wife, who is a good friend, can I speak so easily.'

Zara smiled. 'I have long suspected that your upbringing was not of the conventional. I believe that we have that in common.'

Mrs Lacy tried to look prim and failed. Her lips curved in remembrance. 'I should not say it, but Papa was everyone's idea of a non-worldly cleric. We girls, after Mama's death, were brought up by a dear old aunt, quite as vague as Papa, for she was his sister. Being the youngest of four girls I had no real mentor. Then I met dear James who was not the least put off by my unconventional manner. Indeed, he declared it would be an asset in an army wife.'

'But now you are the Colonel's lady,' teased Zara, 'and must act accordingly. What a burden you bear, like Caesar's wife.'

Mrs Lacy laughed delightedly. 'How very right you are. You understand perfectly. One can only escape into one's own mind when things become tedious.'

Zara recalled Ralph's comment on Mrs Lacy's vagueness. She guessed that few people ever penetrated beyond that public mask, perhaps only she and Colonel James Lacy. Zara felt a surge of affection for this lady. She turned her gaze to the horseman galloping across the maidan, that great expanse of grass. Even without looking at Mrs Lacy, she knew this slender, grey-haired man riding so easily in the saddle, his mouth smiling, must be Colonel Lacy. She moved away from the rail and through the drawing-room into her own bed-room. She sat down on the bed. Would she, herself, ever hang over a veranda rail, stars in her eyes, to greet a returning loved one? Could Ralph inspire such love in his wife? Perhaps. Only time could tell that story.

Zara dressed simply for dinner since most of her clothes required pressing. There had been a small laundry room on the ship, but it had been so crowded with helpless females who had never laundered a garment in their lives and were disposed to harry the two junior seamen allocated to them, that Zara took care of her own clothes. Unlike Delia, her cabin companion who had changed her outfits at least six times a day and was finally left with a mountain of rumpled dresses, Zara had discarded a number of petticoats and shifts, wearing only the minimum for the sake of decency.

She wore a high-necked, green cotton dress whose creases had shaken out reasonably well and her hair was piled smoothly on the top of her head, leaving her neck and face free of curls that might adhere to her skin in the heat.

The sun had quite gone by now and the noisy cicada insects were making their nocturnal presence known. From the distant horse-lines, fires twinkled and the aroma of curry and spices came to her. This was the scent of India, mixed with the heavy perfumes of flowers and humanity, horses and leather. She lifted her face, breathing it in. It seemed alien and exotic, a far cry from the beeswax and delicate flower scents of her English drawing-room. She smiled to herself. How exciting it was all going to be. So much to see and learn before allowing herself to be forced into the mould of an army wife.

The lamps had been lit and the table set with silver and crystal. White-robed servants moved about under the eyes of Krishna whom Zara glimpsed as she moved towards the veranda.

A man turned at her step, a hint of surprise in his eyes, then he was smiling and holding out a strong brown hand.

Mrs Lacy's chuckle drifted towards her. 'Did I not tell you, James, that Miss Deane was very much out of the ordinary?'

'As always you were right, my love. How do you do, Miss Deane? Captain Browne did not describe his fiancée adequately. I thought to meet a shy, young thing with a longing to rush back to her Mama. I usually do, you know, but here I see a self-possessed and most elegant young lady.'

'How do you do, Colonel?' Zara smiled, taking as immediately to this man as she had done to his wife. 'Your present opinion is, no doubt, arrived at with the help of your lady. I might yet prove a disappointment to both you and my fiancé but I will not rush home to my family, you may be sure. There is so much here to learn and to see. I thank you for greeting me kindly.'

The shrewd eyes in the thin, clever face held approval, Zara thought. 'That I firmly believe, Miss Deane, even on so short an acquaintance. One loves or hates this country. There seems no other way. I hope you will come to appreciate its diversity.'

'It will not be for the want of trying, Colonel.'

He seemed to hesitate fractionally before saying, 'Do not be in a great hurry to quit my roof, Miss Deane, however much Captain Browne wishes it.'

Zara raised her brows in surprise but the Colonel smiled. 'It is natural that he will be impatient and I have nothing to say against your fiancé, but marriage is a commitment to this country and you must be very sure. Apart from that, my reasons are purely selfish.' The lines about his eyes crinkled as he smiled again. 'I have never seen my wife in such good spirits, almost the girl I married, and I feel sure that you are the main contributing factor.'

'You flatter me, Colonel, but I confess we have much in common.'

They both turned at the sound of a horseman crossing the maidan.

'I invited Captain Browne to dine,' Colonel Lacy said. 'Freed from the duty I placed on him, he is now eager to enjoy your company again.' He moved to the veranda steps as a syce (groom) ran up to take the reins tossed to him.

Ralph came up the steps at a run. He saluted the Colonel, then removed his cap and bowed to both the ladies.

'It is good of you to invite me to dinner, ma'am, on your first evening at home.'

'Not at all,' Mrs Lacy murmured. 'I knew you would be eager to see Miss Deane, without half the garrison families calling on you for help and advice.' She smiled serenely.

56

'Captain Browne performed his duties most excellently, I may tell you, sir.' She glanced at her husband. 'Though I fear it was not a task with great appeal.'

The Colonel smiled and took her arm, leading her along the veranda. 'But well enough done since all our doves are safely back in their nesting boxes.'

Zara looked after them, smiling. 'They are so kind, Ralph, I begin to feel quite at home here.' She looked up at him and found his eyes on her.

'Don't feel too much at home, for I have another waiting for you.'

'Let me get my breath, Ralph,' she protested. 'I have seen nothing yet, save from a carriage or train window.'

'Marriage will not prevent you seeing anything you wish.' He was smiling, but she sensed that he intended persuading her into an early marriage.

She could not understand the feeling of resistance welling up in her. She would not be rushed, as Colonel Lacy had advised, though Ralph was looking extremely handsome, well shaven and free of the dust of the journey. Even sweat-soaked and harassed-looking, she had seen the single girls eye him speculatively. And why not, since he was polite and charming to them all. He was attractive, certainly, but she needed to know him better, discover the deeper qualities under the exterior of a well-bred man.

She was saved from a reply by the sound of the dinner bell. Over the meal, the conversation was well conducted by the Lacys, a little talk of the regiment, an account of the activities on the ship and at the garrison and then it was time for Ralph to take his leave.

He and Zara stood on the veranda steps as they waited for the syce to bring round his horse. The night was dark but bright with stars and lights from across the maidan where the troopers had their quarters.

Ralph kissed her as the sound of a horse being walked came nearer. Zara felt her heart quicken as he held her close. She leaned against him, her senses submissive with tiredness and the two glasses of wine she had drunk.

'Don't keep me waiting too long, Zara,' Ralph said in her

ear. 'I want us to be together under one roof. My bungalow only lacks you, my darling.'

A memory stirred. 'You said you had a tiger.'

'What?' He drew back to look into her face.

'The one you shot.'

'Ah yes, I have that, but he's lonely company for a man.'

Zara laughed and slid her arms around his neck. 'Don't seek to play on my sympathies, Ralph Browne. I will never believe that a young, handsome bachelor could ever be lonely. Bachelors, old or young, have always been an asset at any hostess's table.'

Ralph smiled and glanced over his shoulder towards the syce and the horse. He detached her arms gently.

'I do not deny that I have been guest enough at other people's tables but I would seek the opportunity of returning their hospitality as soon as possible. It is not the thing for single men to entertain ladies in their bungalows. One needs a wife in order to observe the proprieties. However, you must be tired, my dear, so I bid you goodnight.'

He drew back and turned to the steps. The syce handed up the reins as he mounted. Zara stood by the veranda rail and watched until Ralph was out of sight beyond the maidan. It was going to be all right, she thought. Ralph would prove an excellent husband in his quiet way. A conscientious soldier, he had proved that on the journey, and the Colonel had hinted nothing reprehensible in his character. She smiled into the darkness and made her way to her bedroom.

Chapter Six

Some three weeks after Zara's arrival in India, the Rajah of Batala held a durbar. Since all English officers and their families were invited, there was much discussion in the drawing-rooms of the garrison relating to what should be worn.

'The Rajah holds audience, my dear,' explained Mrs Lacy.

'Traditionally, it is for the local people to lay their problems before their ruler. He delivers judgement, rather like a magistrate. But, of course, since he has invited us to his court, there will be a great deal more to it than that.'

On the appointed day, a cavalcade of carriages left the army station. Each carriage held a complement of splendidly attired women, gloved and hatted. It had been thought polite to attach a length of veiling to each hat, for bare-faced women were considered bold. Even the poorest peasant woman veiled her face in the male presence.

Heading the column was Colonel Lacy and his senior officers, mounted on superbly groomed horses, the regimental banner and British flag whipping in the breeze, and surrounded by a phalanx of junior officers. The two lines of sowars, the native mounted soldiers, kept strict station along the length of the cavalcade. The sun shot sparks from bridles and lances, turbaned heads gazing haughtily forward.

Zara was impressed and said so. Mrs Lacy smiled.

'I believe that is the idea. Our strength must be seen and respected by those who would have us leave. We are not short of enemies as recent history has shown.'

Zara looked about her, seeing the small villages huddled together. The river Beas lay beyond, giving the land its fertility. The paddy fields she had seen from the train windows lay more southerly with the gatherers standing ankle-deep in water. Those fields had been emerald green oases in the brown landscape. Wild bougainvillaea hid the peeling paint of timber or stone-walled buildings in the villages, giving the dull surroundings an air of festivity. Women with baskets or pots on their heads paused to stare impassively at the passing carriages. Children stood silent, large-eyed, deterred from approach by the dark-featured cavalry escort.

When they turned towards Batala, the road became rutted, the hard-packed earth throwing up spurts of dust beneath the horse's hooves.

'It is always the same in the dry season,' sighed Mrs Lacy. 'Where the bullock carts have ploughed through over moist earth the ground dries hard as iron into ruts. We really should build a road for the Rajah but one cannot interfere. Luckily, the road is quite short.'

The palace, when they reached it, was not quite the turreted, gold-domed edifice of Zara's imagining. Certainly large, with an immense courtyard, but a gathering of lower buildings round a main structure, rather like a hen surrounded by chicks. A single dome looked over flat tops of varying heights, balconies and archways festooning the view. Despite its careworn appearance, the palace stared with weary grandeur over the countryside.

A closer approach revealed the carved stone doorways, the intricate work of some long dead craftsman. Marble steps led up from a portico under which the carriage halted.

Once inside, Zara revised her opinion. The great hall was laid in mosaic, depicting scenes from mythology, she supposed. They passed between lines of robed and dark-faced men, old, young, some ragged, some flamboyantly dressed. They stared silently over the shoulders of the palace servants as the Europeans passed. The air was stifling, the heat and smell of bodies pungent.

'Petitioners,' whispered Mrs Lacy. 'They bring everything to the Rajah from disputes over a yard of land they believe a neighbour has included in his own property, to the exorbitant interest a usurer has demanded.'

Zara glanced back. 'So many of them.'

'That is because the Rajah holds fewer durbars than he used to do. He is an old man, and his people are not yet sure that his son, the Yuvaraj, will have the same understanding. Consequently, they wait until it is the Rajah himself who holds durbar.'

They were in a long, stone-walled corridor, the scent of crowded humanity being replaced by waves of heavily perfumed air. Numerous curtained archways led off into shadowed rooms; the quarters, Zara supposed, of the palace occupants. More than one archway revealed a flight of shallow, marble steps leading to those balconied rooms she had seen from the outside.

A wide archway faced them. The booted feet of Colonel Lacy and his officers drummed on the stone floor, accompanied by the rustle of long skirts and subdued murmurs. Guarding the archway were tall men, lean-faced and bearded. Dark eyes watched without expression from under turbans. Each man wore round his waist a broad sash housing the curved blade of the tulwar, the weapon of the northern tribesmen.

As Colonel Lacy halted before them, he removed his plumed ceremonial helmet, holding it under his arm. His officers followed suit. The guards stood aside and without a word being spoken, the garrison party moved into the audience chamber.

A section to one side held seats and to these the Colonel led his party. To their right and opposite the archway was a dais and in its centre, a high-backed throne. A gold-tasselled canopy stirred above it, curtains of gold cloth almost concealing the throne chair. High windows, stoutly grilled, let in the sunshine which glittered on the embroidered cushions beside the throne. Low, carved tables, ivory inlaid and set with precious stones, were positioned at intervals between the ladies. Each held a dish of highly coloured sweetmeats.

Zara found herself between Mrs Lacy and Delia Pringle. Delia was gazing at the sweetmeats with an expression of distaste.

'I wonder when those were set out,' she murmured.

'Does it matter?' asked Zara. 'I'm sure it was a kind thought.'

Delia shrugged and gave her a pitying look. 'They have probably been here for hours with the flies crawling all over them for they are so highly sweetened. I would not wish to be struck down with dysentery.'

Zara eyed the sweets doubtfully. Purple, green and bright blue, most unusual colourings. She glanced at Mrs Lacy who had heard Delia's remark. 'A little pretence of enjoyment, my dear, then slip them into your reticule. The servants' children adore them but for us, Miss Pringle is probably right.'

Zara jumped as a discordant trumpet note sounded. Cymbals clashed and a blast of music wailed from some hidden instrument.

'I should have warned you, dear, of the signal for the Rajah's entry,' Mrs Lacy smiled and looked towards the throne.

The curtains were flung back and a man who must have approached from behind the dais was seated on the throne. Quite old, thought Zara, with his sparse grey-streaked beard. But even from where she sat, she could see the dark eyes held an alertness at variance with the lined and sunken face of age. She had expected the exotic attire of some Arabian Sultan but the Rajah was almost a replica of the warrior guards on the entrance arch. Plain robe and turban, the only embellishment on the jewelled sheath and hilt of the tulwar strapped about his waist.

She was aware then of other figures lowering themselves on to the cushions at his feet. A man, possibly in his late twenties, sat nearest. His robes held colour and Zara noted the rings on his fingers. Slightly below and on the other side of the Rajah sat a woman, a fine gauze veil beneath brilliant black, long-lashed eyes. The veil was too sheer to disguise her features and Zara looked with interest at the most beautiful woman she had ever seen.

Zara looked a query at Mrs Lacy who replied from behind the lace fan she was moving gently.

'The young man is the Yuvaraj, the heir. The woman is the Rani, wife of the Rajah.' She smiled at Zara's surprise. 'Stepmother of the Yuvaraj, my dear, for the Rajah took her as his second – or was it his third wife – I can never remember.' She smiled vaguely as Delia turned her head. 'A very beautiful woman. But Indian girls are usually quite beautiful in their youth and the climate does not affect them as with us. So sad that we lose our complexions after a few years. You are lucky, my dear, to be dark-haired. It is we fair-skinned who suffer most.'

Zara saw Delia's lips tighten, a faint flush mantling her cheeks. She remembered that Delia had come to this continent three times already, according to that man on the ship. She looked down at her hands quickly, understanding Delia's preoccupation with creams and lotions on the ship, the parasol and wide-brimmed hat she was never without. So fair-skinned a girl must necessarily guard her precious pink and white complexion especially, the thought came unbidden, one who desired a husband so fervently. She would not be here otherwise. She glanced at the Colonel's wife who was staring into space.

To bridge the silence, Zara said, 'Do the Rajah's people present their petitions first?'

Mrs Lacy looked at her. 'Oh no, my dear. The reception takes place now with whatever entertainment the Rajah has provided. It is only after we leave that the people are allowed in. I suppose they prefer it that way and not under the eyes of the Europeans.'

'I suppose so, but that means they will have to wait in that crowded hall.'

'They are quite used to that for they are a most patient people. They even sleep on railway platforms while waiting for a train they know will arrive sometime. Today, tomorrow, it makes no difference. Nothing is done in a hurry. Time has little meaning for the people of this land.'

Delia turned her pale, aristocratic face towards Zara. 'You will soon learn that from the servants. When you ask for something to be done, it will always be: "Soon, Missie Sahib, maybe tomorrow, Missie Sahib".'

Her tone was so scathing that Zara wondered why Delia came to India at all, then remembered the man on the ship. Three times Delia had come, all in the hope, he had implied, of catching herself a husband. She must not think of him, that man who had been cashiered in such disgraceful circumstances. And poor Delia might have married him. One could understand her bitterness, but that was no fault of the country. There would be other chances for Delia. Of course she might have been wildly in love with that dreadful Major Deverill, but Zara rather doubted it. Her bitter disparagement at the ship's rail was more likely the fury of a woman who had been played false by a handsome and eligible King's officer. His own words on knowing that Delia was on the ship were more of amusement than of love lost.

Zara smiled ruefully to herself. She was in no position to cast any stone. Hadn't she accepted Ralph for reasons that suited her and not because she was wildly in love with him? She glanced over to where he sat, his smooth, brown hair reflecting the sunlight as he bent his head courteously to some word being expressed by Major Fraser. The Major was a red-faced, stout man of good humour, rather like his plump, good-natured wife in appearance. A pleasant couple, thought Zara, who had met with kindness from them both.

Ralph glanced over his shoulder to where she sat. He smiled and she returned his smile, feeling a surge of affection for him. How much sounder a base for marriage was affection than wild love that must surely burn itself out in time? She felt Delia's eyes on her but did not look at the girl, fearing to see either dislike or contempt in her gaze.

A group of men had seated themselves, cross-legged, beside the dais. Sitars, tambourines, and many flute-like instruments lay in their laps. A man squatted before an assortment of drums. The Rajah raised a hand and they began to play, a strangely weird but not unpleasant sound, Zara decided. Not at all like the music she had been used to for it held an earthy yet haunting quality. The Rajah was nodding, the young Yuvaraj was listening impassively, but Zara's attention was caught by the Rani. Her brilliant eyes were fixed on the players, her expression as rapt as if she had been in another world, a paradise of the senses. Her body seemed to keep rhythm with the music although she never moved, save for the long-fingered hands moving on her lap like a dance in themselves. Had the Rani been permitted she might have answered with her body the lure of the music.

The Rani's hands quietened as a different strain of music was taken up. From behind a vividly worked screen of silk, a troups of dancers emerged, greeting the Rajah and his court before whirling into intricate movement of neck and arms, a bending and swaying of lissom bodies. Wrists and ankles were encircled with golden chains from which tiny bells hung, sweet tinkling sounds that complemented the music.

'Professional dancers from Gujrat,' whispered Mrs Lacy from behind her fan. 'Every movement of the hand tells a story. They are expressing joy and satisfaction for the season's bounty.'

Zara nodded, her eyes still held by the scarlet and gold costumes, the smiling girls with flowers in their hair, painted faces and eyes outlined with kohl for added lustre. The music stopped suddenly and the girls sank into the folds of their billowing skirts, heads bent towards the Rajah.

As they filed away, Zara turned to Delia. 'That was wonderful. Do you not agree?'

Delia shrugged. 'I have seen them before. They are the Rajah's favourite dancers.'

'But so graceful, and what beautiful costumes and jewellery.'

'It is their trade to look spectacular,' Delia said. 'And I grant that it is quite startling to the newcomer.'

'Well then, as a newcomer, I found it enchanting,' Zara went on with an attempt at friendliness. 'And the Rani, who must have seen hundreds of performances, was almost for joining them, I swear.'

Delia's lips curled but her smile held more cynicism than humour. 'I don't doubt that for a moment. It is rumoured that she herself was a dancer of note before she caught the old man's eye.' She looked away from Zara and studied the row of officers rising to their feet.

Zara observed the speculative glance which seemed to rest on Captain Ralph Browne for longer than on the other young officers. Zara wondered about that look. Delia and Ralph must have known each other before Ralph's home leave. Had he been on Delia's list of possible husbands? If so, it had obviously come to nothing and Delia had set her cap for a man of higher rank. What a devastating mistake that had been. Yet Zara had to admire the courage of this girl who had returned once again to the place where the scandal and her own involvement with the Major was drawing-room talk, abated perhaps but still common knowledge.

The ladies were rising and moving towards the cane chairs and tables spread about the hall where the dancers had been. Fruit drinks and silver plates of spicy food lay on each table beside gem-encrusted goblets. The royal court had come forward, mingling with the officers. Colonel Lacy was talking to the Rajah.

Mrs Lacy laid a hand on Zara's arm. 'The Yuvaraj is coming this way. He delights in acquainting himself with our lady newcomers.'

Was there a cautionary note in her voice, Zara wondered, and looked towards the Prince of Batala with interest. He was of the warrior breed like his father, his aquiline features hard and hawkish. About thirty years old, she judged, strong-boned and lean, moving with the soft-footed litheness of a hunting leopard.

He halted before them, inclining his head slightly.

'We are honoured by your return, Mrs Lacy, and doubly honoured that you present us with yet another flower of your native country. Such beauty will add lustre to the Punjab.'

He looked directly at Zara as Mrs Lacy murmured her name and the smile on his lips was half-mocking in its politeness. The dark amber-touched eyes met hers with an intensity that was almost imprisoning and although his gaze did not waver, she felt that her whole appearance was under inspection. From the veiling that darkened her hazel eyes, down her body in the tight-waisted gown, to the slender length of leg in soft sandals, she felt the caress of his eyes as if he had touched her with sensitive fingers.

Something warned her that this was a trick, a game to be played to test female susceptibility to flattery.

She smiled. 'Your Highness is too kind. I doubt my presence will make the slightest difference to the beauty that already surrounds us.'

'You find our country beautiful, Miss Deane?'

'Beautiful and fascinating, your Highness. I am grateful for the opportunity of seeing it for myself.'

'Then we must thank the estimable Captain Browne for luring you to our country. I hope you will find it worthwhile.' He turned his head as Delia Pringle came near. His eyes took on a malicious gleam. 'Ah, Miss Pringle. It is good to see that you have returned to us yet again. Old friends are always welcome.

'Thank you, your Highness,' Delia said in a flat voice.

The Yuvaraj smiled. 'You will take refreshments, ladies?'

He turned and beckoned a servant carrying a laden tray of fruit drinks.

'Thank you, Highness. A kind thought,' said Mrs Lacy, smiling warmly.

The Prince bowed. 'Excuse me. I have not yet observed the civilities with the delightful lady of Major Fraser.' His bland smile encompassed all three ladies. He indicated the goblets in their hands. 'The juice of the passion fruit. So delectable when tasted in its young ripeness before maturity sours it. Is that not also true of life?' He turned away, the half-smile of mockery very plain on his face again.

Delia glanced down into her goblet. 'I shall not risk it,' she said, setting down the goblet and making her own departure.

Mrs Lacy sighed. 'A difficult girl. She really should not let her feelings show so obviously. People can sense these things only too well.'

Zara asked curiously. 'How does the Prince view his beautiful stepmother? There cannot be much in age between them.'

'I suppose not but as women are of little account here, I doubt he thinks of her at all. She is his father's woman.'

Zara looked towards the Rani who stood, eyes downcast, a few paces behind her husband. She was taking no part in the conversation between the Rajah and the senior British officers yet her very immobility indicated attention and understanding. The long-lashed, kohl-ringed eyes moved under their heavy lids, convincing Zara that little escaped her encompassing glance. Men bowed and ladies smiled as they moved past her but she engaged no one in conversation. With such a husband, one supposed she might by tradition have been kept in purdah, her femininity guarded from all male eyes except those of her husband. In contrast to the stark attire of the Rajah, the Rani's scarlet caftan over silken trousers was liberally worked with gold thread. Jewels glittered about her neck and arms and in the soft gold-studded sandals.

Captain Ralph Browne detached himself from the group of officers and came towards Zara. He bowed formally to the wife of his Commanding Officer then asked Zara if she was settling into the routine of garrison life. His manner was as polite as the occasion and Zara answered in the same vein, smiling at the correctness expected of a junior officer.

To Zara's surprise, she found the Yuvaraj heading their way again. She had supposed his attention was mere politeness, going the rounds of the ladies, a duty he performed in lieu of his father.

This time the hooded eyes rested on Ralph and she could not doubt the malicious amusement in them.

'Ah, Captain Browne,' he said smoothly and Ralph turned his head with a quick movement. 'I have already met your fiancée, Miss Deane, but have not, until this moment, had the time to offer my congratulations.'

Ralph's bow was stiff. 'Thank you, your Highness.'

'Do not thank me, Captain, but rather the fates that set Miss Deane in your path. Guard her well, for I read envy in other men's eyes.' He laughed softly. 'Set your seal firmly upon this treasure, Captain, or you may yet lose it.'

Ralph stiffened, a slight flush touching his cheekbones. The Yuvaraj watched with interest.

Zara interposed with a light laugh. 'You divert yourself at our expense, Highness, and though your words are flattering, I am not a goat or sheep that must have its owner's brand upon it. And yet –' she gave the Prince a look of amusement to equal his own – 'I could wish that my own countrymen were as silver-tongued as the Prince of Batala.'

'Well said, my dear,' Mrs Lacy came to her aid. 'It is not the way of our menfolk to sink us in flattery, yet I confess to liking your words, Highness, though that you utter them to every female I have not the slightest doubt.'

The Prince's eyes rested upon her with what seemed genuine fondness. 'In the face of two such unflatterable ladies, I shall retire defeated.' He bowed. 'Farewell, ladies. Captain.'

Ralph smiled with his mouth but his eyes remained cool. The Yuvaraj left them and Ralph followed his departing figure with a strange look in his eyes.

'I can't say that I like the fellow,' he declared. 'Too familiar by half.'

'Because he flattered me?' challenged Zara. 'Come, Ralph, you cannot take his words seriously. He was merely acting the pleasant host since his father appears to be above talking to ladies.'

'That is exactly true,' Mrs Lacy said. 'I have never yet exchanged a word with the Rajah. I find the Yuvaraj charming too, and don't forget, Captain Browne, that he will be the Rajah himself in due course. We shall need his friendship then.'

'You are quite right, ma'am,' Ralph relaxed and smiled. 'Perhaps it was just his flattery that caught me on the raw.' He looked at Zara. 'I am not a patient man by nature. I should feel easier if we had a date settled for our marriage.' He turned on his heel to Mrs Lacy. 'May I earnestly appeal for your aid, ma'am?'

There was a slight tearing sound as his spur caught in the hem of Zara's gown. They all looked down to see a length of lace flounce trailing on the floor.

'Oh my God, I'm sorry.' Ralph said, horrified. 'These damned spurs – I beg your pardon.'

'It is nothing,' Zara said. 'I need a stitch or a pin in it, that's all.' She raised her skirt from the ground and looked about. 'There must be a private room I can go to.'

Mrs Lacy beckoned a servant who nodded in understanding.

'Follow him, my dear. Do you wish me to come with you?'

'No, no, it will not take a moment. I have some pins in my reticule.'

She smiled at the servant as he led her out of the audience chamber and down a curving corridor, across a small hallway into another passage with doors leading off. What a warren of a palace, Zara thought. How on earth did the servants ever find the one they were seeking? The air was full of the scents she had come to know, wood smoke, musk, and the sharp tang of spices. The servant halted, sweeping back a door curtain to bow her into a small room. The curtain dropped and she heard his sandalled feet moving away.

She glanced about her. Cushions, a small iron stove, a charpoy. Someone evidently slept here on that low bed.

Opening her reticule she searched for pins, then lifted her skirt to secure the hanging piece of lace. She took a few paces across the floor to be sure the temporary repair was secure and she was ready to leave.

Her hand rose to the curtained archway and held still. She had noted vaguely on her entry that the panelled walls were painted, but had not taken in the subject matter. Now she stared, her eyes growing wide. Like a theatre play where every scene progresses to a climax, so the paintings ran. Each panel depicted an act of love. At first a young girl dressed richly enough for a bride. Enormous black-ringed eyes gazed submissively into the hawk-like features of a warrior, armed and booted. The panels formed a frieze round the room and Zara's eyes followed them with stunned fascination and complete absorption. The round, impossibly round-breasted girl, voluptuously hipped, lay in most unlikely positions, her doe-eyed unsmiling face accepting the attentions of the rampant male with incredible composure.

Zara blinked dizzily. The paintings were crude but held a vivid earthy quality that brought them to life. Really, she should not have looked at them but turned her back in shocked distate as Delia would have done. She bit her lip, aware that her clasped hands were damp with a sudden warmth. How strange. She wanted to laugh. Not hysterically like some swoning maiden of the last century but laugh because love was really as depicted in these paintings and not the dainty hintings of young matrons over the Crown Derby teacups. Bridal lace and wedding bells were not the end but the beginning of that secret life, the knowledge of which correct Mamas kept from their young daughters.

With her hand on the curtain, Zara glanced back at the predatory face of the lover, the fierce supremely arrogant look of a man who took what he wanted. Life with Charles Deane had not cocooned her in ignorance and her mind was well-informed, but not quite as well-informed as this. She took a deep breath to restore her composure.

A soft flutter of footsteps in the corridor brought her face to the curtain. The servant returning for her? The steps halted some distance away. A hiss of silk, then a soft murmuring voice. Not the servant; a husky female voice, she decided, and stepped into the corridor herself. It was deserted. She looked about her. Which way, now? She had been too concerned with keeping her skirt from trailing on the ground to count the turns and twists of the corridors.

The palace was quiet, no sound of voices from the audience chamber. The thick stone walls were sufficient barrier. She moved to the right, remembering the small square hallway. Past that she had only to continue to reach her destination. Reaching the hall, she stopped. More than one corridor led from it. She frowned, trying to recall any distinguishing feature. How long could one wander in the palace without meeting a living soul? Not long, she supposed, by the vast number of servants the Rajah employed.

A low murmur reached her and she noted an open door. It was simple. She would ask. Standing on the threshold, she looked into the room. It was shadowed, the only light coming in from a high, grilled window. Two figures stood there, clasped tightly in each other's arms. The figure of a woman, dressed richly in scarlet and gold, had her arms about the neck of a tall, black-bearded man. The slender arms blazed with jewelled bracelets and from where she stood, Zara caught the heavy scent of musk. She was murmuring still, the tone of her voice pleading though Zara only sensed this for the words were not in English.

She began to retreat as silently as she could, her skin damp with embarrassment at the thought of interrupting such a private scene. She knew she had not made a sound but the man's eyes rose, black, angry eyes that stared across the intervening space. He did not call or put away the woman, just stared at Zara with a disturbing intentness.

Zara turned and fled down the nearest corridor, her heart thumping painfully. The fierce-looking man with the woman in his arms was not the Rajah, but the woman he held in a lover's embrace was, without doubt, the Rani.

Chapter Seven

Zara stood for a long moment outside the door to the audience chamber regaining her breath. She smoothed out her skirts, ran a hand over her hair and tried to compose herself. Gradually her heart stopped its pounding and she moved slowly between the carved pillars, her gaze holding steadfastly towards Mrs Lacy, now in conversation with Major Fraser's wife.

They glanced at her as she approached. Mrs Fraser smiled. 'You should have come to me, dear. I have all manner of things about my person, including needle and thread. My husband teases me that I carry supplies for a month of camping in the Moffusil, but he will not hesitate to ask if I have such a thing as a headache powder or a pipe-cleaner on me. Not to mention a cure for indigestion!'

Her eyes in the plain, homely face twinkled good-humouredly. 'Oh, I know it is not elegant to carry a reticule as heavy as a suitcase, but I make no pretence to that, being merely of good yeoman stock from Somerset.'

Zara laughed, liking the woman's plain speech. 'Elegance never cured a headache nor indigestion. You are a wise lady, Mrs Fraser.'

'Not wise, dear, just commonsensical. One has to be with four children and a climate like this.' She heaved a vast sigh from the ample depths of her bosom. 'Thank goodness they all thrived and are safely in England with my sister, poor soul, who never dropped a foal in her life.' She stopped, reddening. 'Oh, my goodness, and you an unmarried lady at that. What will I say next?'

'Dear Mrs Fraser, I am not entirely ignorant of the terminology of the country. My father had racing friends who were always talking of sires and dams when they discussed mares in foal.' She paused, then said with a half-mocking smile. 'I do believe there are similarities applying in the human race.'

72

Mrs Fraser's muffled gasp was overlaid by the light, amused laugh of Mrs Lacy. 'Zara, dear, you must not be so forthright or you will shock your elders. They maintain the fiction that young females are pure and simple, their minds on lofty things, like what they shall wear for the Governor's ball and will their dance cards be full, and which handsome officer pays the nicest compliments. Important things like that, you understand.'

Zara bit her lip. 'I understand,' she said demurely.

As she drifted away the two older women exchanged looks. 'No mother,' murmured Mrs Lacy.

'That accounts,' replied Mrs Fraser. 'Girls too much in the company of fathers tend to have broader views.' She followed the direction of Mrs Lacy's gaze.

'A most proper young man, Captain Browne.'

'Most,' said Mrs Lacy slowly.

Zara's steps had taken her towards the group of which Ralph was part. As she glimpsed Delia amongst them, her pale face animated instead of bored, she decided against joining them. As she turned away, the Yuvaraj moved to her side.

'Ah, Miss Deane, I find you for once alone, which is my good fortune,' he said with a slow smile. 'No doubt I shall be scowled away from your side by the gallant Captain in a moment but for now I should like your opinion, and praise, of course, for this most beautiful trophy of my hunting skill.' He indicated a shallow alcove in the wall to one side of the Rajah's throne. 'See, it hangs beside the one my father killed when he was young. Is mine not finer by far?'

Zara looked at the two tiger skins pegged to the walls. There was little actual difference in size but age and moths had taken their toll of the older one.

'A truly splended skin, for which your Majesty's modesty of speech did not prepare me,' Zara murmured, slanting an amused sideways glance at him. 'Worthy indeed of a Prince.'

She caught an appreciative glint in his eyes as she went on smoothly, 'Of course, if your esteemed father should ask me the same question I should, of necessity, reverse my opinion, for he looks quite fierce enough to have me thrown instantly into your deepest dungeon.' She thought of that warren of shadowed and dark corridors leading heaven knows where, and her shiver was not exactly play-acting.

The Prince's handsome mouth smiled. 'I will protect you. Rely on me, Miss Deane. Should such a fate befall you, I will, personally, and at great risk, storm that dungeon and escape with you into the night. No doubt I should receive much honour and rich reward from the King-Emperor.'

Zara laughed. 'I should insist upon it most strongly, but I beg you will not put it to the test!'

They were smiling at each other when Captain Browne joined them. 'You appear to be enjoying some joke. May one share in it?' He was frowning.

The Yuvaraj's face smoothed into bland politeness but Zara sensed the mutual dislike of these two men.

'I have been admiring this splendid tiger his Highness was kind enough to show me. A tiger shoot sounds most exciting. Is it customary to use elephants?'

'Safer than on foot, although that is done too. The beaters are sent out to drive the tiger towards the elephants and on to the rifles in the howdah.'

'I would love to take part,' Zara said. 'And I should be equally proud of my tiger skin. Of course I cannot shoot but I might learn how to do so.'

Both men looked at her, the Yuvaraj with sardonic humour and Ralph in astonishment.

'You?' he said. 'My dear Miss Deane, it is quite out of the question. Ladies do not participate in such dangerous pursuits. You are joking, are you not, though I fail to see the humour of it.' He glanced sharply at the Yuvaraj. 'I hope your Highness has not put this notion into my fiancée's head for I should consider it ill-meant.'

'Of course he has not,' Zara cut in. 'If the notion is ridiculous, it is certainly of my own making.' She was annoyed with Ralph who seemed quite unaware of it, but she sensed that the Prince was aware and amused by it. She stared directly into the dark eyes. 'I thank you for your kindness and hope we shall meet again, your Highness.'

The Yuvaraj inclined his head but said nothing. Ralph

bowed, then took Zara's arm. 'The ladies are preparing to leave.' He led her a few paces then said, low-voiced. 'It is not to your credit to be seen in such close converse with a man who is virtually a stranger to you.'

Zara stopped and removed her arm from Ralph's hold. 'The Yuvaraj is not just any man, he is the host. Since the Rajah is not disposed to mingle with mere women, the Prince is doing his best to make up for that deficiency. I fail to understand your objections.'

Ralph made an impatient movement with his hand. 'I don't object to that but to his particular attention to you. It has been commented upon.'

'Indeed?' The hazel eyes that looked into Ralph's face were bright with indignation. 'By whom, may I ask?'

'It was Miss Pringle who drew my attention to the fact. It was a kindness, she said, to point out that you both were almost out of sight in that alcove.'

Zara drew in a steadying breath. 'I take it that Miss Pringle would consider it a grave danger to her reputation to be for a moment out of sight of the whole garrison and in such company. What an exceedingly proper young lady she is.'

Ralph studied her face for a moment, then said somewhat patiently, as one would to a child, 'We are a small community and you will find that everything is noted and spoken of. We must all abide by the standards and observe the rules, however ridiculous you find them.'

'Well, I understand that, but you were rather hard on the Prince. I thought him charming but obviously you did not agree. Did you need to frown on him so ferociously?'

'I should frown on any man who claimed your attention. Do you deny me that right?'

Zara was slightly mollified but not wholly convinced that that had been his reason for removing her so abruptly from the Prince's side.

During the drive home Zara was silent, going over in her mind the events of that day. She liked the Prince but Ralph seemed not to approve of his efforts at friendship. To be jealous of the Prince was ridiculous since they were engaged to marry. Protecting her reputation then, which thoughtful Delia had pointed out was in danger of being tarnished? Perhaps it was his own reputation that was threatened. He had once said that he was an ambitious man. Could an officer rise in rank if his wife had sinned, however slightly and unknowingly? He had agreed without demur that Delia Pringle was exceedingly proper.

She stared moodily over the countryside. It was unworthy of her to think of Ralph in this way. She turned her thoughts back to the palace and the hard, dark face of the man with the Rani in his arms. It had been an unblinking stare as if he were memorising her. She hoped they would never meet for it had been a cruel face. What would the Rajah do if he discovered his wife's infidelity? The sun's glinting rays struck sparks from the hem of her gown. The pins, of course, and with that thought, the room in which she had repaired the torn lace flashed through her mind. Dear God, those paintings! It came to her suddenly that every male face had the dark slanting eyes and sensual mouth of the Yuvaraj! She thrust the images away with resolution and turned her head to find Mrs Lacy regarding her.

'Did you enjoy the experience, my dear?'

'What?' asked Zara, startled.

'The durbar, what else? You have spoken no word since we left the palace.'

'I'm sorry. Yes, indeed, it was splendid.' She hesitated. 'Were you serious when you talked of the things a girl should keep her mind on, you know, ball gowns and dance cards?'

Mrs Lacy laughed. 'Not entirely, my dear, though it does seem the main topic. What else had you in mind?'

'Joining a tiger shoot?' Zara ventured hopefully.

'Out of the question, my dear, though rich, eccentric ladies have been known to do it. We amuse ourselves with croquet and archery. Most ladies consider those activities strenuous enough.' She regarded Zara thoughtfully. 'You may ride, of course, but only with an attendant groom, if you should desire it.'

Zara's face brightened. 'Oh, I would indeed. I was beginning to think that everything exciting was restricted to men.'

'Yes, my dear,' Mrs Lacy said placidly. 'If you are referring to the dangerous sports I believe Captain Browne would tell you the same thing.'

'He already has,' Zara said moodily. 'And read me a lecture on impropriety.'

'Good heavens!' Mrs Lacy was startled. 'Whatever brought that on?'

'The Yuvaraj was showing me the pelt of a tiger he shot. It hangs in a sort of alcove to one side of the Rajah's throne. Ralph seemed to think it improper of me to be alone with the Prince and almost out of sight in an alcove.'

Mrs Lacy smiled. 'Just like a man to make a fuss about nothing. Perhaps he wanted to speak to you particularly and was annoyed not to find you alone. It would certainly have been more improper to upset the Prince by refusing to look at his tiger skin.'

Zara nodded and decided against telling Mrs Lacy that Ralph had not come looking for her until directed by Delia. Despite his assertion that he would frown on any man who claimed her attention, she wished he had not found it necessary to mention Delia.

The carriage turned in the last stretch of road, past the old banyan tree with its hanging, rope-like branches, ever seeking to reroot themselves in the earth. Through the small mango grove, dense-leaved and weighed down by ripening fruit, on to the metalled road leading to the cantonment. The road swept around the grassy maidan and the Lacy carriage drew up before the long, white building.

Zara raised her gaze to the distant mountain range. The sun was low and the snowy summits were touched with gold. The Himalayas, the abode of snow, the mighty barrier between Northern India and the wild land of Afghanistan. A wild land and wilder Tribesmen, Colonel Lacy had told her, a bleak, comfortless place where men were a law unto themselves and extended no friendly hand to those who were not of their race and religion.

Early the next morning, Zara put on her riding habit and joined the Colonel on the veranda, taking a cup of tea from the

77

khitmagar as she waited for the syce to bring round a horse. The Colonel rose, dropping his breakfast napkin on the table. He smiled into Zara's animated face.

'I wish I could go with you but my office is knee-deep in most important pieces of paper, every one more urgent than the next, or so I am led to believe by my staff. Half of them are nonsense, of course, but one hesitates to point that out to the General.'

Zara smiled into the lean, brown face under slightly greying hair. 'Well, if you will be a Colonel, you must take the consequences.'

'Indeed, but had I known it would turn me into a pen pusher.' He shrugged and gave her his quizzical smile before going lightly down the veranda steps.

The ride was most invigorating for Zara. It was the best part of the day, the early morning when the air was cool and sweet, the dew still on the grass. In all too short a time the sun would send down its brazen stream on the earth, taking up the moisture and baking the ground anew. She glanced over her shoulder at the groom, mounted on a strong-looking horse. She stroked the neck of her mount, silky and warm. Soon it would begin to sweat and they must return to the bungalow.

She raised her gaze to the Himalayas, shading her eyes under the brim of the white pith helmet. Mist covered all but the foothills, hiding the peaks and crags. The roof of the world, they called it. Did people really live up there, or just exist in hardship and cold? Over there, eastwards beyond Kashmir was Tibet, the land of Buddhism whose monasteries were built on rock and served by ochre-robed, almond-eyed priests. Beyond Afghanistan, there was Russia and China. What a vast Asian continent. Man was as the ant upon it.

'Missie Sahib. It is time.'

She turned to smile at the groom. 'You are right. I was contemplating my insignificance and what a terrifying thought that is.'

The groom stared, uncomprehending. 'Lacy Memsahib expecting very soon.'

They cantered back to the cantonment, skirting the bazaar where merchants had already set up their stalls, past straggling lines of peasant women, brimming baskets of vegetables for market on their heads. Despite the weight, or perhaps because of it, she mused, their carriage was erect and sinuously flowing, a variation of the book on the head as practised in finishing schools.

The familiar scent of woodsmoke, curry and spices, horses and saddle polish hung over the army lines. It was still early but a small canvas-topped carriage was drawing up outside the Lacy bungalow. As she came nearer, Zara recognised Delia Pringle and Mrs Fraser. Her heart sank as she remembered the invitation issued by Mrs Lacy. It was too soon after the durbar yesterday for her to feel anything but annoyance at Delia's slyness.

She drew rein and called a greeting to Mrs Fraser who responded cheerfully.

'Good morning, Miss Pringle.' Her greeting to Delia was cooler.

Delia's pale eyes took in the healty flush on Zara's face, the cloud of ruffled dark hair as the rider removed the pith helmet. Zara flung aside her riding skirt to free her booted leg from its side-saddle posture, enabling her then to slide to the ground. Delia's eyes narrowed on the glimpse of long slim legs.

'Did you have a nice ride?' queried Mrs Fraser.

'Wonderful,' Zara answered. 'Do you ride, Mrs Fraser?'

'What? At my age and with the weight on me? My dear, it is an activity I leave to the young and slim like you, though I must confess that few of our new young ladies take advantage.'

'And you, Miss Pringle?' Zara asked in tones of sweetness. 'Surely you will not give me the same answer as Mrs Fraser?'

Delia's parasol opened with a sharp click. From under its shade, the pale eyes met Zara's warm hazel ones.

'I don't care for horses and my skin is far too fine to risk its ruination under a hot sun, and I really prefer not to look like a gypsy.'

She turned and mounted the veranda steps, her wide skirts billowing. Mrs Fraser pursed her lips then smiled as she saw the amusement on Zara's face.

79

'As long as you don't get over-heated and get sunstroke, my dear, I cannot think of a healthier exercise.'

'And if I get sunstroke, I shall immediately apply to your reticule.'

Mrs Fraser's bosom heaved in a chuckle and she too mounted the veranda steps.

Zara handed the reins of the horse to a waiting syce and followed, going straight to her room to wash and change.

The early morning rides became a habit with Zara. They gave her a wonderful sense of freedom, away from the somewhat cloying atmosphere of gossip over teacups, the small talk in drawing-rooms, so beloved of matrons. The young females seemed not averse to the delights of the croquet lawns, the rounds of calls to take coffee and the small parties held frequently in the mess hall. These were occasions when the young unmarried officers found themselves in great demand as partners, dancing to the music of a regimental band. Zara, too, enjoyed the dancing though it was a far cry from any London ball she had attended.

Ralph stayed by her side throughout and only he solicited dances. Since they were official engaged, she could hardly blame him for frowning on any other approaches, but she began to feel that her freedom was drawing to a close. Ralph became more pressing on the matter of their marriage and she realised she could not delay much longer. She had been in India for a month.

Alone one night in her bedroom she asked herself why she delayed. She had come to Lahore to marry Captain Ralph Browne. There was no alternative. Why should she even think of it? In England her father had married Mrs Makin, she knew that from his letter. He found himself surprisingly content, he had said, for the new Mrs Deane was generous, kept a good table and welcomed his friends. His fondest hope was that his dear Zara was finding life exciting and that serious young man, Captain Browne, was making her happy.

Zara stared out of her window into the velvet darkness, half-hearing the noise of the cicada and the bull-frogs from the river bank. Happy? What did happy really mean?

Contentment, such as her father had and presumably the matrons on this station, or something vibrant and joyful, filling life with delight?

She could not, and should not try to fault Ralph. He was most correct, a promising young officer who knew to a degree how things should be done, how one did not stand in conversation with a syce and discuss horses and how one did not swing up a brown baby who had tumbled in the dust. Yes, Ralph was very correct and serious and, she paused, and quite – quite without that sense of humour she had shared with her father. She sank on to her bed slowly, thinking about it. Was it this that had made her uneasy at the thought of tying herself for life to Ralph Browne?

Colonel Lacy could make her laugh, but he was the Colonel of the regiment, not an ambitious young officer whose behaviour must be noted when promotion was considered. She thought of the half-dozen lieutenants at last night's party. Their behaviour was as impeccable as Ralph's, yet their conversation with the young ladies seemed to provoke great amusement. She remembered watching one group as she stood by Ralph's side, wondering what they found so humorous. Then Ralph had touched her arm, indicating the arrival of a Colonel from another regiment and giving her a brief account of his career, in tones of admiration.

Zara lay back on her bed, staring into a future that seemed like a long, confining, well-regulated tunnel of bleak sameness. She knew that she loved the country already but she also knew she did not love Ralph. But she was here and he had paid for her passage, would expect her to honour the promise she had made when he put the ring on her finger. There was no escape. She had to go through with it. She buried her face into the pillow and finally sleep came.

Chapter Eight

Zara's early morning forays over the countryside suffered an unexpected and unwelcome blow. She had carefully avoided any reference to them when in Ralph's company but in so small a circle, nothing could remain unnoticed for long.

'I'm told you exercise that young, part-Arab mare of the Colonel's each morning,' he commented one evening as they strolled in the cool air of the Lacys' garden, past the long-leaved plantain trees and the papaya fruit bushes.

'I do,' said Zara lightly, resisting the impulse to ask if he had learned of it from Delia. 'She is a sweet-natured and lively young thing. I have grown fond of her.'

'Nervous, I should call her,' Ralph said in a considering voice. 'I am not sure that I approve of her suitability.'

'You don't have to, since I am the one who rides her and I find her superbly suitable. Or is it my handling of her you doubt?'

'No, but I suggest a steadier horse, one better fitted for a gentle canter.'

Zara felt an upsurge of anger and was glad of the shadowed night which hid her expression. She fought hard to speak in a reasonable tone.

'I have no wish for a fat, steady horse who will do no more than amble at his own pace. Farah is as glad of an early morning gallop as I am.' She knew the moment she had used the word 'gallop' that she had said the wrong thing but she went on blithely. 'The air is wonderfully refreshing at that time, the light still pearly grey and the dew on the leaves, long before the sun takes the freshness from the day.'

Even in the darkness, with only light from the veranda lamps streaking the garden, she knew Ralph was frowning. Dear God, not another lecture.

'I shall speak to Colonel Lacy,' he said. 'It seems to me that both horse and groom are unsuitable.'

The lighting of another lamp on the veranda illuminated their faces. Ralph's tight-lipped and Zara's outraged.

'Really, Ralph.' Zara said in a shaking voice. 'You take too much upon yourself. I am quite capable of controlling the horse in a gallop and since the groom keeps pace with me, I cannot see why you should think it necessary to speak to Colonel Lacy.'

'I think you have been used to your own way for so many years, my dear, that it has made you a trifle headstrong. I don't blame your father, he is a man of charm, but without the guiding hand of a mother, your spirits run a little too high. You must curb them, my dear, and take example from wiser heads.'

'Like Miss Pringle's, I suppose? I am sure she was your informant since she has seen me return from my ride.' She felt childishly spiteful as she flung the words at him, but really, it was too much to have her behaviour criticised and reported by the sharp-eyed, pale-faced girl with the permanent look of distaste.

'Very well,' said Ralph. 'If you would rather I did not speak to the Colonel, I will not, but you may dispense with the groom in future for I will ride with you. I have no duties at such an early hour.'

Zara's heart sank. 'There is no need to put yourself to the trouble, I am quite –'

'It is no trouble, my dear, in fact I should enjoy it and be keeping an eye on you at the same time. I would hate to see you take a tumble and make me wait even longer for our marriage to take place. You must admit that I have been very patient in allowing you such freedom – but there, we shall leave the subject for the moment. We shall be more private on our morning rides. Let us go indoors now. I think we have been too long alone outdoors.'

Zara accepted his arm and moved towards the veranda steps with a feeling of complete frustration. She had been allowed her freedom, he had said, implying that it was high time she responded to his generosity and rewarded his patience. The word freedom had a hollow ring to it since Ralph barely let her out of his sight anyway.

It was quite coincidental that on the first of their rides the following morning they met the Yuvaraj. The Prince of Batala was out hawking, as was evident from the hooded bird on the leather-gauntleted hand. He glanced their way but made no salutation, though Zara thought she caught the flicker of a sardonic smile.

'Good morning, Highness,' Zara called, refusing to be daunted by Ralph's frown.

The two heavily bearded and armed men, the Prince's escort, closed in, one on each side of their charge. Their dark intent eyes were fixed on Ralph. Zara looked at the long, curved tulwars in their sashes, the blades honed to a sharpness that might decapitate a man with one stroke. Behind their backs, the holding straps running diagonally across their chests, were the long rifles of the hillmen, the chased silver-stocked jezails.

She turned to Ralph. 'The Prince's men are quite fearsome-looking, I'm sure you will agree. It behoves one, in my opinion, to smile, lest they take it upon themselves to slit our throats.'

Ralph seemed to become aware of the hard stares and he allowed his expression to relax.

'Good morning, Highness,' he said without a smile. 'Have you had good sport?'

The Prince gave him a cool glance and there was something malicious lurking in the way his eyes flashed from one to the other of them.

'Alas, no, and now my opportunity is gone.'

'Gone? In what way?' Ralph's sharpened tone was probing.

The Prince waved a hand languidly. 'Frightened off by the thunder of a horse's hooves. You ride a heavy-footed beast, Captain Browne. Oh, do not mistake me, I doubt not your ability, but the horse is a cavalry horse, after all, and you are a cavalry man.' He switched his gaze to Zara. 'For myself, I admire grace and elegance in both horse and rider.' He raised a dark brow at Ralph. 'And I see both in Miss Deane. Do you not agree with me?'

'Yes,' said Ralph briefly and stiffly. 'I am sorry to interrupt your sport. Good-day to you, Highness.'

84

The Prince shrugged. 'It is of no consequence. There is always tomorrow and yet tomorrow.' He inclined his head gravely. 'Good-day to you both.'

As they rode away, Ralph turned in his saddle to frown over the dry plain with its rocks and waterless stream beds. Later, when the rains came, the empty nullas would become foaming torrents, encouraging the thin soil to a brief flowering of whatever lay dormant. The fertile wheatfields lay farther to the west, closer to the river which guaranteed their fertility.

His frown remained as he looked at Zara. 'What do you suppose the fellow meant about lost opportunity?'

'It seems quite logical,' Zara said carefully, 'that small desert creatures are easily frightened. The noise of our approach must surely have driven them into cover, just as his Highness said. I see no other interpretation of his remark.' She gave a little laugh and urged Farah into an easy gallop. 'You sound most suspicious. What on earth has the poor man done to make you doubt him? He is merely out hawking, not planning some treacherous action.'

Ralph caught up with her. 'I would not put that past him. He has no love for us.'

'Really, Ralph. This conversation is becoming quite ridiculous.'

'Is it indeed.' He looked closely at her. 'You showed no particular surprise on meeting the Prince. I take it your paths have crossed before?'

She stared at him. 'Since he is on his own land, why should one be surprised to see him?'

Ralph's expression darkened. 'You evade my question.'

'I saw the Prince last at the durbar,' Zara returned coldly. 'And I resent the implication in your question.'

'That is because you know so little of the man, only his flattery. You see a handsome, charming man, every girl's idea of an Eastern Prince, but beneath the charm he is a libertine and it amuses him to play with people, as a cat with a mouse.'

'How can you know this?' asked Zara, wide-eyed.

'There was a scandal, hushed up of course, which I prefer not to discuss, involving the Yuvaraj and an innocent female of our community. She was packed off home in disgrace. It is my duty to protect you from any such danger until we are married.' He paused, communing darkly with himself. 'Even then I shall not approve of any private converse between you.'

'Surely as a wife, the danger of seduction will be over?' Zara spoke sweetly, annoyed by his assumption that she would bow to every husbandly dictate. 'After all, you spoke only of an innocent female.'

Ralph's eyes narrowed. 'An indecorous remark, if I may say so.'

'You may say what you will, Captain Browne, but you will permit me the same liberty. I have lived twenty-four years in London and am not likely to cast myself at the feet of a handsome and charming Indian Prince. You insult my intelligence by treating me as a girl of simple mind who must be watched and frowned upon.' She pulled Farah to a halt and scowled into Ralph's astonished face. 'I strongly suspect, Captain Browne, that after all, we are not suited to each other.'

The colour rose in Ralph's face. 'Nonsense,' he said sharply. 'We are engaged to marry and marry we shall. I will make the arrangements myself since you will give me no definite date. By delaying this matter, you lay me open to the jibes of my fellow officers who threaten daily to cut me out. I have not spoken of this before but you may guess with what difficulty I have defended your right to choose.'

'Yes,' Zara said slowly. 'You are not a man to turn things off with a laugh.'

'And do you find fault with that?'

Ralph's voice was hard, almost accusing, and Zara knew that here were the makings of a serious quarrel if she let temper overtake her. Even in their time alone, he was always the correct young officer. She had thought his behaviour constrained by the presence of superior officers, or dignity upheld before his juniors. But surely a healthy young man, finding himself alone with the girl he was to marry, might fling correctness aside, and act the lover? Her father had alluded to his seriousness and Mrs Lacy to his perfection of manner. Was there nothing of the impetuous passion in him or did he just desire the married state to set seal on respectability? Was a married man deemed a steadier prospect when promotion was considered?

'Well?' Ralph asked, and Zara started, coming out of her preoccupation. She spread her hands in a gesture of helplessness.

'It is only human to joke at another's expense. The fault is in taking it too seriously.'

'We cannot alter our natures,' he said stiffly.

Zara felt the spasm of anger. 'Yet you would try to alter mine!'

'For your own protection. That is my duty.'

'And what, may I ask, is your pleasure?'

He frowned. 'I don't understand you.'

'I wonder if you ever will! We have been alone for more than an hour and all you have done is lecture me. Betrothed couples do not always spend their time so.'

'What are you suggesting?' Ralph looked hard at her.

'We could dismount by that stream yonder and spend a few moments of idle flirtation in the manner of lovers. You have neither kissed me nor reached for my hand. I tell you, Captain Browne, this lack of loving attention is very lowering to my self-esteem.' Her smile was teasing but missed its mark as Ralph glanced about him.

'I should not be unwilling to admire the stream with you but as you see, the hour has advanced sufficiently to bring out the workers.'

'And Captain Browne would not care to be seen kissing a lady in public!'

'Quite so. Such activity is best conducted in private and not under the eyes of the native population. Be sensible, my dear. This is neither the time nor the place. We must hurry now or I shall be late for duty and you for breakfast with Mrs Lacy.'

'Quite so,' Zara said crisply. 'That would never do.' She urged Farah into a trot.

'There is no need to adopt that tone, Zara.' Ralph drew level. 'If you were my wife, there would be no need for flirtatious dalliance by streams. My bungalow is quite ready to receive you and this situation cannot go on indefinitely. I have a houseful of idle servants awaiting your arrival. Since I take meals in the mess, they are an unnecessary drain on my resources, don't you see? Mess and bar bills are not inconsiderable, either. Forgive me for drawing this to your attention but I have to point it out.'

'Yes, I do see and I am sorry. I confess I didn't give a thought to the expense you have incurred on my behalf.'

'And how should you, my dear. Your station in life has never brought you into contact with such mundane matters. Your father shielded you, as was his duty.'

As they neared the Lacy bungalow, Ralph leaned towards her and pressed her hand. 'I am sorry if you feel it ill-mannered of me to speak of money but I am impatient to step into your father's shoes and become your true protector.' He smiled. 'Can you blame a man for becoming a little edgy and moody at the waiting?'

Zara shook her head, answering his smile. 'It is I who am at fault. I have been thoughtless in regard to money.'

'As to that, it is quite as it should be and there is not the slightest need to trouble your mind in the future. I shall be only too happy to administer your own funds when your father releases them on our marriage.'

As if a soft woollen cap had been pulled over her ears, Zara's stunned mind hung suspended, hearing nothing but a dull beat that must have been her own heart thumping.

Ralph was still speaking when her mind functioned again. A second or two, that was all it could have been and her mouth, she realised, still held that idiot smile.

' – if you will consent, of course,' he was saying, and his face held a question.

A moment of panic, then she remembered. Her funds, yes, that was it. She nodded. 'Yes, of course –' There was no time to say any more for Mrs Lacy was waving from the veranda.

Ralph touched the brim of his solar topee with the handle of his whip, gave a warm smile, then turned his horse towards the maidan.

Zara mounted the veranda steps to be met by a flow of words from Mrs Lacy. It was not until later that she had the time to ponder the implication of Ralph's final words.

Was it possible that Ralph was not the rich man Eleanor

Farnes had led her to believe? A rich man did not talk of bills and a draining of resources. At least, none of those she had come into contact with. Supposing his inheritance from Aunt Matilda was very much smaller than Eleanor had assumed? One could, no doubt, live on an army officer's pay, supplemented by a reasonable private income, if one's tastes were not too extravagant, that is. And a man of careful nature would keep an eye on expense and not wish to outrun himself by unnecessary bills, such as he had explained.

But what of the remark about her own funds being released? What funds? An invention of her father's, without doubt. Her quarterly allowance was so small as to be ludicrous. 'Funds' was much too grand a name for those few hundred pounds a year. Of course, both she and her father had given the impression of wealth, as was their habit. Charles Deane's way of paying his tailor's bill was by ordering another suit and hoping to cover the cost of both at the gaming tables.

Ralph Browne was under the impression that he would be gaining a rich wife, an impression fostered by Charles Deane, with herself equally to blame. Well, it was poetic justice on them both if Ralph was no more than moderately wealthy. Quite funny, really, but not in the least laughable. The feeling that she was right began to grow more strongly. It could account for Ralph's frowning protectiveness and his appeals that she set a marriage date. He feared to lose her, that much was certain, but which loss was the more important, herself or the imaginary funds? Did he love her? Enough to forgive her deception when he knew the truth? Now there was a question with great doubt attached to it. Correct, very proper and mildly affectionate, she could never envisage Ralph as a passionate lover. Even if he was fabulously rich and forgave her generously, could she go through with the marriage anyway?

The more she thought of being Ralph's wife, the more the thought dismayed her. She did not love him, did not want him with body or mind. Despite her casual upbringing, she knew that if she really loved a man, it would not matter a jot if he were rich or poor. She who had determined to marry for money now faced the consequences of her folly. He evoked no wild feeling of love in her, just a dull resentment.

Surely a girl was entitled to be swept off her feet, even though it might be for a short time only and not be a good basis for marriage. She remembered the toast she and her father had drunk to comfort and contentment. But Charles Deane had known that special time of love with her mother. Mrs Makin, though no doubt quite admirable, was second best. Could Zara Deane content herself with second best, never having known the first?

Chapter Nine

Although their rides the following mornings took them in different directions, Zara and Ralph met the Prince each day. Despite Ralph's muttered curse, there was no polite way of avoiding the confrontations for they had come suddenly upon the Prince's party as they rounded a grassy hillock. Coincidence? Zara doubted it. The Prince had the air of an expectant host and his smile of welcome held no surprise.

Was this to be the pattern for all future rides, Zara wondered. A simple matter, indeed, for him to receive intelligence on their direction. All information led to the Prince of Batala, if such was his whim, and his whim appeared to be the discomfiture of Captain Browne. The glinting mockery in those slanting dark eyes convinced her that she was right. Why did he put her in mind of a sleek hunting animal testing the weakness of his prey? And why had he chosen Ralph for that role? It amused him to see Ralph bristle, that was certain.

It struck her that during her previous rides with only the groom for company, she had never once seen the Prince. Why only now when Ralph was with her? She acknowledged that he might have avoided meeting her for reasons of courtesy and regard for her reputation, but could not now resist the impulse to bait Ralph.

This morning the Yuvaraj was not alone with his two armed escorts. Beside and slightly to his rear was a short but very fat Indian, mounted on a bony, depressed-looking horse. Two pairs of dark eyes watched their approach steadily.

The Prince, in close-fitting white jodhpurs, an embroidered waistcoat over white silk shirt, inclined his head, the jewel in his turban sparkling in the morning sun. The half-smile was on his lips as he watched Ralph.

The fat man gave an expansive grin. 'Ah, Captain Browne, it is delightful indeed to meet an old friend. I have looked for your company before this time but alas, I have been disappointed. You must come and drink a little tea with me soon, I insist upon it. Is it not time and beyond, my friend?'

Zara took an instant dislike to the fat, oily-faced man who sat in sweating discomfort on his horse. Surely such a coarse-looking man was no friend to Ralph? She glanced at the Captain and saw that his face was pale beneath the tan, his lips tight-set, but he made no comment.

The fat man turned his smile on Zara. 'I give you greeting, Missie Sahib. It is good for the Captain Sahib that you arrive for there has been much expectation in waiting for so happy a day. I trust all will be resolved to satisfaction.'

Zara stared from under raised brows at the questioner. 'Since I am not in the least acquainted with you,' she returned coldly, 'I fail to see what my business has to do with you.'

The man's smile faltered and he glanced at the Prince who made a dismissive gesture and spoke in a voice of dangerous calm.

'The honoured lady is right. Your tongue is impudent, your words offensive. I gave you no leave to address the Missie Sahib. Go, Hassan, before your tongue betrays you into unpardonable indiscretion.'

A sheen of sweat glistened on the man's forehead and his eyes did not quite meet the Prince's. There was fear on the face that lowered in submission.

'Yes, Lord. I go in silence and shame under your displeasure.' He pulled on the reins and the bony horse turned and shambled away, its rider swaying heavily, like a man unused to horseback travel.

Ralph looked after him for a moment, then turned to face the Prince, some of his colour returning. He still said nothing and Zara had the uneasy feeling that the scene had been arranged by the Prince of Batala. He had let the man talk, then cut him off abruptly with a thinly veiled threat that brought naked fright to the man's eyes. And yet she could think of no reason for the Prince's action, if her instinct was right. The two men were facing one another, Ralph's expression grim and the Prince's impassive.

A dark brow rose quizzically. 'An old friend, Captain, yet you honoured him with no word of greeting. Was that wise?' The Yuvaraj's voice was low and silky, yet amused.

'He lies if he claims me as an old friend,' Ralph's voice was also low but forceful. 'His kind would claim friendship with the devil if there was any profit to be made out of it!'

'Ah yes, his kind,' the Prince murmured. 'You are acquainted with his kind, naturally.'

Ralph shrugged. 'Isn't everyone in Lahore? His kind are as thick as the leaves on a mohwa tree.'

The Prince smiled suddenly. 'Indeed, and are quite as useful in times of shortage.' His glistening smile turned on Zara. 'The mohwa is called the food tree, for one may eat the fruit and flowers and its seeds are ground for cooking oil. An apt comparison, Captain, though I doubt Hassan would agree.'

Ralph shrugged again. 'It is of no concern to me.'

'Nor to me, Captain. I find the man quite tedious with his requests for durbar, but how can I refuse to advise when I am their lord Prince and it is the tradition? Many of my people prefer audience with me rather than the Rajah, especially in delicate matters, you understand, for my father's judgements are strictly in accordance with Holy Writ. Most admirable, of course, but inclined to harshness. With me they open their minds to reveal many secrets.' He shrugged as if bored with the conversation and gazed into the distance at the speck that was the man, Hassan. 'Such a foolish, greedy fellow, yet he has grounds –' He left the sentence unfinished and glanced at Zara.

Was there a hint of satisfaction in those dark, amber-touched eyes, as if some amusing scheme had pleased him by its result? She could not begin to guess what had been in his mind, yet Ralph had lost colour on seeing the man, Hassan. Why should that be?

The ride back to the garrison was conducted in silence, Ralph's expression so forbidding that Zara dared not ask him the meaning of it all, if meaning there was. Her mind was relieved as they approached the bungalow, for Ralph smiled.

'Forgive my preoccupation, Zara, but I have been pondering on the Prince's lack of conduct in subjecting you to the attentions of a man like Hassan. For myself, I can stand his dislike and air of superiority over men who are not his blood, but I thought he held all English ladies in high regard. The discourtesy put me quite out of temper, I confess it.'

'Who is Hassan?'

'A city merchant of quite unsavoury reputation.'

'Yet he implied a friendship with you.'

'His class always do, even if the matter is merely an army transaction. It is sometimes necessary to deal with all kinds of merchants to keep the garrison supplied.'

Zara felt the tension drain from her. There had been nothing sinister in the meeting with Hassan, after all. Ralph's paleness had come from suppressed anger, his silence an unspoken criticism. One could not rebuke a Prince, especially before one of his subjects. Ralph's correct soul must have been shocked to its very foundations by the merchant's impudence of address to his fiancée. The Prince had seemed unaware, perhaps deliberately so, of Ralph's stiff outrage.

Zara leaned towards him as the horses rode shoulder to shoulder.

'Dear Ralph,' she said warmly. 'You are far too protective towards me. There is no need, I assure you. I am quite level-headed and not given to swoons and hysterics. I told you that in London.'

'But this is not London.'

'I know. This is wonderful, exciting India, but I remain the same Zara Deane.' She glanced back over her shoulder at the towering mountain peaks. 'The abode of snow. Have you ever been into the mountains, Ralph?'

He shook his head. 'No. They are unsafe.'

'The mountains?'

'No, the tribesmen who live up there. A most inhospitable breed. They delight in watching their enemies die slowly, I'm told, though I've never been in action against them. In fact,' he smiled, his face very handsome in the morning light, 'I have seen no action at all! What a confession from a soldier!'

Zara laughed. 'Well, you are hardly to blame for that.' Her glance fell on the cavalry sword, its scabbard swinging at Ralph's hip. 'You have not then been obliged to defend yourself with that?'

'In practice only.' He patted the hilt. 'But I hope I shall use it in honour should the occasion demand.'

They parted as usual at the veranda steps. Mrs Lacy gave him her slightly vague smile.

'Come to dinner tonight, Captain. I believe there will be just the four of us. I have mislaid my engagement book but Zara will remember if we have engaged ourselves anywhere. She is so correct about these things.' Her smile embraced them both as she reached for the teapot.

Ralph looked pleased both at the invitation and perhaps, Zara thought, at Mrs Lacy's reference to her correctness. Had she said that on purpose? Zara sank into a seat and fixed Mrs Lacy with a hard stare.

'Have you really mislaid your engagement diary?'

A pair of mischievous blue eyes gazed back. 'No, dear, but I thought it would please him to know that I see nothing out of the ordinary in your conduct.'

'My conduct?' Zara's stare widened. 'Would you care to be a little more explicit?'

'Of course, dear. It is that silly girl, Delia Pringle's fault. She is so envious of you that every time the ladies gather her tongue will not stay quiet in her head.'

'What have I done to be the cause of gossip, if that is what you are implying?'

Mrs Lacy hesitated, her expression a little troubled. 'Such nonsense, of course, for why should you not take an early morning ride if you wish it?'

'What on earth is there to criticise in that? Ralph has taken to joining me, whereas I took a groom before.'

'Exactly, my dear. Delia has the impertinence to wonder out aloud why Captain Browne should think it necessary to accompany you himself in place of the groom.'

'I see,' Zara said in a hard voice. 'And what conclusion did she arrive at?'

'That you were meeting someone in secret and knew Captain Browne would not approve. Delia said it most laughingly as if it were mere fantasy but people remember these remarks and pass them on. I spoke quite sharply to Delia at the time and she apologised and said she meant nothing.'

'And who should I be meeting? Did she choose a lover for me? Major Fraser perhaps, or Lieutenant Thompson? There is quite a wide choice.'

'The Yuvaraj.'

Mrs Lacy's words fell into a sudden pool of silence. Zara stared, unable to speak for a moment. Mrs Lacy, a little pale herself, stared back.

'Dear God, the Yuvaraj!' Zara said after a stunned moment. 'Why him?'

'I wondered that myself and I have been giving the matter some thought, Zara. I have come to some very unpleasant conclusions.' She leaned forward. 'I have not spoken of this before because it seemed irrelevant, but Delia was for ever seeking Captain Browne's company before he went on leave.'

'But I understood her expectations were in the direction of the officer who was cashiered, Major Deverill.'

'That is true, but Richard Deverill did not see it that way. After his disgrace he left the country and Delia looked about her for someone else. She is a very shallow creature and Richard did not break her heart yet she played on it to gain sympathy.'

'From Ralph?'

'Well, yes, dear, but he went on leave and came back engaged to you. Delia decided a home visit was called for and left soon afterwards. She didn't stay in England long.'

'And now she is back. What is she trying to achieve?'

'What indeed? I can only think, and this is mere supposition, mind you, that she has not entirely given up hope of Captain Browne. There was a scandal last year involving the Yuvaraj and a young English girl.' Mrs Lacy stared unseeingly over the veranda. 'It is too preposterous, I am imagining too much. Delia is not as clever as that.'

Zara frowned. 'You are thinking that if Ralph believes there is something between the Yuvaraj and myself, he will cry off and I shall be sent home in disgrace, leaving the field free for Delia to regain Ralph?'

'Oh, my dear, I was thinking exactly that!' Mrs Lacy looked horrified. 'She is not clever but very sly.'

'I know. She is aware of dislike between Ralph and the Yuvaraj and played on it very well at the durbar by pointing out to Ralph that my reputation might suffer if I lingered in that alcove where the Prince's tiger skin hangs. He also warned me that the Yuvaraj's attentions were being remarked upon. I am sure the only one to remark was Delia!'

'Oh dear,' said Mrs Lacy, helplessly. 'And Captain Browne is so correct in his manners. You must marry him quickly before Delia has time to make any more trouble.'

Zara blinked and looked down quickly into her teacup to avoid the gaze of her hostess. Her heart thumped, throwing up an instinctive barrier against that suggestion, but her mind accepted that the advice was sound. She should marry Ralph, had expected to marry Ralph, had been prepared to compromise for comfort and contentment, but now her wits seemed to scatter in confusion as if she were a mouse in a cage, seeking a way out. It had all been in the future, time to spare, time to enjoy this new experience before committing herself. But time never stood still. Like the days of one's life, like the ending of a season, time caught up and ran its course. And time had run out for Zara Deane.

She laid down the cup and saucer with infinite care and looked at Mrs Lacy.

'Marry in haste to thwart Delia?'

'It would not be in haste exactly, would it?' The blue eyes were uncomfortably shrewd.

'No. I have, as you suspect, been putting off the moment.

There has been so much to see and learn,' she finished weakly.

'Which will not disappear after marriage,' Mrs Lacy returned drily.

'No, it is just – just that I feel overwhelmed by the thought, like a flower must feel when it is pressed into a scrapbook and is thereafter rigid and completely conformable.' She smiled but her lip quivered. 'I have never been so – so watched over. It is quite unnerving. So ridiculous, isn't it?'

But Mrs Lacy did not smile, nor dismiss her words as nonsense. She sighed. 'I know what you mean and Captain Browne is so correct, a model soldier, my husband says, who overlooks not the slightest thing.'

'He is ambitious.'

'That accounts for it, of course. He will become a major in no time.'

'And even more correct,' Zara said gloomily.

The two women looked at one another and both began to laugh.

'Oh dear,' said Zara. 'I really am making a cake of myself. You know, I cannot help feeling that Delia would make him a far better wife than I.'

'And what should you do then, may I ask?'

Zara stared over the veranda at the distant snow-clad peaks of the Himalayas. 'Is there any call for lady explorers, I wonder?'

Mrs Lacy laughed and rose from the table. 'Come, my dear. We'll make a start on it by exploring the bazaar. There are many fine craftsmen who excel in silver and copper work. You will want fine rugs and hangings in your new home. Bachelors never give a thought to decoration.'

Since the weather had turned sultry and the bazaar would be crowded and dusty, Zara wore one of the simplest dresses the derzie had sewn for her. A pink-flowered, full-skirted cotton, with puffed sleeves and a scoop neckline. Her English clothes were packed away in a tin trunk, wrapped carefully in tissue paper and unbleached cloth. Light-weight sandals from the chutler man were more the thing as leather tended to acquire a film of mildew in the humid atmosphere.

Ram Das, the coachman, starched into straight-backed

magnificence, the regimental flash on his snow-white turban, flicked his whip with haughty disdain at the foot travellers, clearing a way for the carriage. His black-bearded, military-moustached face, the black eyes that looked down arrogantly, guaranteed the carriage easy passage. Ignoring the presence of bullock-carts, pony tongas and rushing rickshaws, he drew the carriage to a halt in the middle of the narrow alley, thereby blocking all movement. No one seemed to object but waited patiently, their faces incurious, as the ladies alighted.

'One hour, Ram Das, if you please,' Mrs Lacy said and Ram Das inclined his magnificent visage and said nothing. He climbed back on to the carriage seat from which he had descended with inexpressible dignity to open the carriage door. Relieved of his charges, he whipped up the horses and sent them racing down the alleyway, leaving the inferior traffic to follow in his dusty wake.

'Like Jehu, son of Nimshi,' murmured Mrs Lacy.

'Or Icarus, son of Zeus,' returned Zara.

'Yes, indeed.' Mrs Lacy smiled. 'Yet he has never harmed anyone. A kind man, really. He has six children and adores them all, even the girls for whom he must provide dowries when their time comes.'

The dust of Ram Das's brisk retreat had settled but the air was full of odours as they moved between high-piled stalls. Mangoes, orange-coloured and glossy-skinned, lay on wicker trays beside the round, fat tree-tomato, the stems of small, still green bananas vied for space beside papaya fruit and guavas. Chillies, peppers, tall conical piles of ground spices, cinnamon, ginger, yellow saffron floated their sharp scents in the nostrils.

Vying with the odour of massed humanity, dung, and the slow-burning braziers over which sweating shopkeepers cooked pilau and chapattis for the long-distance merchants, was the perfume of flowers. Looking incongruous beside the busy market stalls were shrines with small effigies of the gods, from the elephant-headed Ganesh to the goddess most feared, Kali the destroyer, whose disciples of earlier days were stranglers. Offerings of flowers, small brass bowls of rice, trinkets of silver adorned each shrine and Zara was fascinated by the reverence bestowed on the myriad gods and goddesses. High over the market stalls, a Muslim minaret looked down from secret eyes.

'Here is Silver Street,' announced Mrs Lacy. 'I will take you to my old friend, who calls himself the Silver Raj. You must not show interest in any of his wares or the price will be raised quite exorbitantly. You must haggle fiercely. It is a game we play and I believe he would be most disappointed, not to mention disdainful, if you meekly accepted the asking price.'

Zara looked about her at the glittering silver chains, necklets and bangles that hung on every inch of wall in the shadowy, cave-like preserve of the Silver Raj. Goblets, filigree-edged fruit baskets, teapots and engraved trays covered the low counters set within the interior, and between these she and Mrs Lacy were bowed in by a smooth-faced man of impressive size.

'Ah, Lacy Memsahib, I am honoured that you come to my poor establishment once again.'

After the introduction of Zara, he said, more as a statement than a question, 'You will take coffee while I spread my wares before your most discerning eyes?'

He clapped his hands as Zara and Mrs Lacy seated themselves on low stools. A small dark girl appeared from behind a curtain in some deep recess. She carried a round brass tray on which stood a tall-necked coffee pot and two tiny brass beakers. Her smile was a shy flicker of the lips as Mrs Lacy thanked her. The girl poured a thick dark liquid into the two beakers and disappeared behind the curtain. A spiral of steam rose from the liquid, giving off a pungent aroma. Mrs Lacy raised the beaker to her lips and took a tiny sip. Zara did the same. It was her first introduction to the thick, bitter-tasting coffee so beloved of northern men. She would have preferred tea with milk but smiled in appreciation as Mrs Lacy was doing though she could see that the older woman's smile was as fixed as her own. Mrs Lacy glanced at her with a slight shake of the head. The look seemed to warn that if she drained her cup too quickly, it would immediately be refilled.

The merchant laid a rug before them and knelt on its corner. On the rug he laid a selection of his silver trinkets, delicate filigree work like fine cobwebs. Fruit and flower designs worked into shapes and suspended on silver strands, so finely drawn they appeared fragile. Remembering Mrs Lacy's advice, Zara pointed to one particular necklet, grouped with matching bracelet and earrings.

'That one is quite pretty, but so are they all, if one is interested in filigree.'

The man sank back on his haunches and fixed Zara with a bright eye.

'What?' he said in exaggerated horror. 'Two ladies with eyes like the eagle who chooses his prey with just such a discerning eye? Dear Lacy Memsahib, you will be the ruination of me for the young Missie Sahib has pointed out my pride of collection. Now she will beat down my most reasonable price until I am forced to beg in the streets. How can I sell my pride? It is quite priceless.'

'In that case, we must go elsewhere for something that has a price,' Mrs Lacy said equably.

'But as a special favour to you, memsahibs, shall we say twenty rupees?'

'Shall we say eight?' returned Mrs Lacy. 'That is if Missie Sahib is interested.'

They both looked at Zara who had been examining the necklet. 'Why, the droplets all around this chain are shaped like mangoes and between each is a furled leaf. How exquisite.' She paused, schooling her expression from delight to uncertainty. 'Well, perhaps I will think about it.'

'Fifteen rupees is nothing to its true value, Missie Sahib. See, I will put it about your neck. Look into the mirror there by the entrance where the sun will catch it. Does it not enhance your beauty most wonderfully?'

Zara looked into the mirror, delighted by the effect of the delicate tracery of the necklace. Behind her the stalls of the market were reflected, people pausing and moving on, passing in and out of her view. She brought her gaze back to the necklace. Yes, she would take it, along with the matching bracelet and earrings. A face swam into her vision, a fat, sweating face, and she frowned. There was something familiar there. Ah, yes, it was the merchant, Hassan, who had been with the Prince, the one Ralph called an unsavoury character. She saw him bend and disappear into a small Judas gate cut into the high door.

The Silver Raj was holding out the earrings. She smiled, taking them from him, and began to adjust them on the lobes of her ears. Then she stood back, gazing at the effect. Quite delightful and impossible to refuse this purchase. As she began to turn the tiny screw of one earring, another figure stopped by the merchant, Hassan's, door. A tall, uniformed figure who paused, glancing quickly up and down the alley. He then bent and entered through the small gate. Zara was convinced that the tall, brown-haired man had been Ralph. Ralph and that man, Hassan? Army business, she supposed, just as Ralph had said, although why deal with a man one disliked? Many merchants would be eager to sell their goods to the garrison.

She removed the earrings and necklace, handing them back almost absently. The silver merchant noted her abstraction and hastened to renew her interest.

'For you, Missie Sahib, I will make a special price. Ten rupees. Is that not reasonable?'

Zara glanced at Mrs Lacy who nodded.

'Very well, I will take the set.'

As they left the silver merchant and were passing the low gate where the two men had disappeared, Zara glanced towards the inscription above the door. It was written in English and Hindi. The name Hassan was large but the script of the smaller writing was discoloured by damp and peeling paint.

'Hassan,' Zara said. 'What kind of a merchant is he?'

Mrs Lacy glanced up and her lips tightened. 'A merchant in misery, according to my husband.'

'What does that mean?' Zara asked in an astonished voice.

Mrs Lacy bit her lip, a soft flush staining her cheeks. She looked vaguely uncomfortable, as if she regretted her words. 'The man is a money-lender. There are many such about.'

She took Zara's arm and steered her firmly past the Judas gate.

Chapter Ten

That night, Zara wore her new jewellery. The delicate filigree necklet was light upon her skin above the wide neckline of her sea-green muslin dress. The sleeves were wide and three-quarter length, so the bracelet showed to advantage. With the earrings in place and her skin scented with toilet water, she made her way to the veranda.

Colonel Lacy's voice came clearly and she heard the murmur of Ralph's reply. Ever since she and Mrs Lacy had returned from the bazaar, she had been wondering about Ralph's reason for visiting the place of the money-lender. It had been more a cautious than a furtive approach. There were many eyes in the bazaar and a British officer in uniform could not be unobserved. Why the caution if the matter was army business? And surely it must be, for Ralph could not need the usual services of a money-lender, could he? Since he had spoken of expense in maintaining an idle staff, he was probably not quite as rich as he would have liked, but that was a long way from being in debt. She thought of the man, Hassan, and the Yuvaraj's part in that scene that morning. Two most unlikely allies in a game of – what?

As she stepped on to the veranda, Ralph and the Colonel rose. Ralph came towards her with outstretched hands, pulling her gently towards him and kissing her cheek. She glanced into his face, surprised. He was usually very formal in the presence of others, but now he squeezed her fingers and smiled. The blue eyes in the tanned face were very bright, his expression smooth and untroubled. He reminded her of the young officer she had first met in Eleanor Farnes's drawing-room. Mrs Lacy joined them, relaxed and elegant. Colonel Lacy touched her shoulder in a gesture of affection as he moved past her chair to the drinks tray.

'You always look charming in blue, my dear,' he said.

'I know, James, which is why I wear it,' she responded,

smiling. 'I always bow to your preferences like a good wife.'
She glanced at Zara. 'I am too old-fashioned to change my
ways, but I am firmly convinced that young women should
not bow so readily, allowing their husbands to become
despots.'

'Do you accuse me of being a despot, my dear?' Colonel
Lacy asked mildly. 'Why, you have twisted me around your
finger these twenty years. I have never needed to act the
despot since your judgement has always been sound.'

'There you are then,' announced Mrs Lacy triumphantly.

'And where would that be?' he asked in amusement. 'I fear
your logic has confounded me.'

'It proves my point that a female who can think will never
go far wrong, for we have our instincts to guide us and do not
need to be corrected and lectured.' She beamed at her
husband, then raised a deceptively limpid gaze to Ralph.
'Don't you agree, Captain Browne?'

Ralph looked a little taken aback. 'Well, ma'am,' he said
cautiously. 'To a certain extent that is true, but instinct alone
cannot be infallible all the time, surely? A guiding hand and
greater knowledge can prove the more reliable.'

Zara, watching closely, realised that Mrs Lacy, while
not saying outright that Ralph was being too severe on his
bride-to-be, was nevertheless hinting that it was so. Zara
smiled inwardly, knowing that Ralph's correctness could
not be dented by her words even if he understood the
implication.

Mrs Lacy leaned back in her chair. 'So, Captain Browne,
you think little of female intuition. Unlike my husband you
dismiss our judgement as feminine foolishness –'

'My dear,' cut in Colonel Lacy, eyeing his wife with mild
surprise. 'You are quite the Turk tonight. How can one argue
such a point when standing on opposite sides of the fence?'
He laughed lightly, squeezing her shoulder. 'It would never
do for men and women to understand each other perfectly for
there would then be nothing to discover. Now, stop teasing
the poor fellow. He will not know whether he is on his head or
his heels.'

Mrs Lacy relaxed and looked into Ralph's face. 'Forgive

me, Captain,' she said in a soft voice. 'Such a silly thing to get heated about. I think I am a little tired. Shall we go in to dinner?'

The round table of Kashmir walnut was set with lace table mats, a low brass bowl of early roses in the centre. Lamplight glowed on the crystal and silver and the slow-moving punkah over their heads stirred the air in a semblance of coolness. White-robed under-servants held out the chairs while the khitmagar, the dignified head bearer, held a chilled bottle of wine for the Colonel's inspection. The Colonel nodded approval and the meal proceeded through clear soup, a local white fish, sliced chicken in herbs and spiced sauce, and finished with cold sorbet. In each brass fingerbowl a tiny rosebud floated, adding its fragrance to the centre bowl of blooms.

The conversation had been idle and amusing with the Lacys at their most charming.

Ralph's brown hair caught the light, reminding Zara of the beech leaves in Regent's Park. He was just as handsome, deferring to the Lacys and meeting her own gaze with a measured half-smile and eyes that seemed to hold a quality of anticipation. Almost, she mused, as if he held something to himself, suppressing it until the right moment. Good heavens, she thought, I am indulging in that feminine foolishness Mrs Lacy calls our female instincts. And yet there was something different about Ralph. He was assured and relaxed, not the tight-lipped, watchful-eyed man of the morning rides who had expected the Prince round every curve of the hills, nor the possessive man at the social functions. Here, of course, she was under his eye and he had no need to glower at any male approach. Was it this that gave him his air of relaxed confidence?

'Coffee on the veranda?' suggested Mrs Lacy and they rose to move outside.

The veranda lamps were still burning and in the small circle of light an ice-bucket glinted on the bamboo drinks table. A frosted bottle stood in the depths of crushed ice.

'What's this?' asked Colonel Lacy in surprise. 'A bottle of champagne? Where did this come from?'

'Without your permission, sir,' said Ralph. 'I asked the khitmagar to arrange it, but with your permission and the graciousness of Mrs Lacy, I would like to make an announcement.'

Zara looked at Ralph's flushed face, then at the bottle nestling in the ice. A spasm of alarm tingled her nerves. Her instincts had been right, after all. Ralph had held something to himself. That curious half-smile had been one of satisfaction. For what? Something to do with his business in the bazaar? Of course not. A business agreement did not call for champagne.

Ralph looked directly at Zara. 'I went today to the garrison church to see our regimental padre.' He smiled. 'The arrangements for our wedding, my dear. It is to take place in exactly two weeks' time.'

'What?' exclaimed Zara. 'Why did you not tell me you were going?'

Ralph's eyes stayed fixed on her, the lamplight making dark pinpoints in the pale blue gaze. He smiled.

'But I did, my dear, and you gave me consent to arrange everything. Surely you remember? It was only yesterday, after our ride.'

Zara remembered vividly her moment of blankness before Ralph's voice came back to her. Something about consent. Dear God, had she really given him permission to arrange everything? She recalled her own vague murmuring and silly nodding head, but thought he was talking of her funds. Her funds? A bubble of hysteria began to mount within her but she forced it down and set her teeth, fixing a smile on to her face. The Lacys were congratulating Ralph and wishing them both great happiness.

Zara looked into their kind faces and felt an almost overwhelming impulse to burst into tears and scream in anguish that it was all a mistake. She didn't want this champagne in her hand, didn't want to be married and if she did, it wouldn't be to Captain Ralph Browne. Instead, she sipped her drink and smiled with stiff lips.

Mrs Lacy rose and set down her empty glass. 'Do forgive me. I am so very tired and any more champagne will go to my head.' Her eyes scanned Zara's face keenly. 'You are a little pale, my dear. Take a turn in the garden with Captain Browne before you go to bed. This day has been quite tiring. All that walking about in the bazaar.'

Colonel Lacy glanced at his wife. 'You went into the bazaar today? I am not surprised that you are tired. Such a hot, sultry day. Come, my dear, take my arm. Our guests will excuse us.'

Zara looked at Ralph. He was staring at her. No, not at her but at the filigree necklet. He was perfectly still, his expression taut. She noted the slight movement of the champagne in the glass that had been half-raised to his lips. Then the glass continued upwards and he swallowed the contents, leaving Zara to wonder if she had imagined the faint tremble of his fingers.

She set down her glass and rose, moving to the veranda steps. 'There may be a breeze in the garden. It will be a little cooler, anyway.' And in the darkness, she thought, I can take this stupid smile off my face.

Ralph followed her and seemed oddly silent for a man who was to marry in two weeks' time. Zara let the darkness, whispering leaves and the fragrances of climbing roses sweep through and relax her. She turned her face to Ralph and broke the silence.

'I see you noticed my necklet. Do you like it?'

'What?' Ralph seemed to come out of an abstraction. He gave her a smile. 'Very pretty. Yes, I noticed it and it suits you very well. Where did you get it?'

'In the bazaar.'

'Naturally, but who sold it to you? There are many silver merchants.'

'A man who called himself Silver Raj. Does it matter which one?' She watched his eyes, seeing a flicker of something in them that made her feel strangely uneasy.

He shrugged. 'Not in the least. They're all there to make a profit.'

'Mrs Lacy argued the price for me. I believe it was quite reasonable.'

'Did you buy anything else in that street?'

'No, although I saw many things of interest.'

The blue eyes sharpened. He raised his brows. 'Such as?'

Zara was surprised by his tone. 'Good heavens, how can I remember everything I saw?'

She wondered then if she should tell him that she had seen him go into the place of the money-lender.

He made the opening himself by saying casually, 'I passed through the bazaar myself today but I did not catch sight of you.'

'Oh, is that the way to the garrison church?'

He looked at her sharply as if scenting sarcasm. 'No, it isn't, but I had some business to attend to.'

'Yes,' said Zara. 'In Silver Street, wasn't it?'

Ralph stopped walking. 'You saw me?'

'Yes.'

'You saw where I went?'

Zara nodded.

'How did you manage that when I never saw you at all?'

'I was at the entrance of the Silver Raj's shop, trying on my necklet before a looking-glass.'

'I see. So you saw me go into Hassan's place.'

Zara nodded again.

'So now you want an explanation?'

'I am not asking you for one, but I did think it curious since you said yourself that he was an unsavoury character.'

He looked down and smiled ruefully. 'Forgive my somewhat probing questions. I had to know what you saw. Did Mrs Lacy see me too?'

'No, she was inside the shop.'

'Good.' Ralph stared at the tree shadows for a long moment. 'I am afraid,' he said at length, 'that I can't give you a complete explanation since it involves someone else. I told you the man was a merchant. He is a money-lender, too, as I am sure you have guessed. My business with him was on behalf of a fellow officer and strictly in confidence.' He gave a humourless laugh. 'A fellow can get into debt out here quite easily, living beyond his means and running through money like water. When once he gets into the hands of a fellow like Hassan, he never gets out, unless he resigns his commission and makes a bolt for it.'

He looked down at her and she saw the bitterness in his eyes. She shivered, remembering the fat, sweating man beside the Prince on the hillside. His eyes had been cruel.

'But what does your – your friend hope to gain by your visit to Hassan?'

He shrugged. 'Time. Time to make a recovery and pay off the debt.'

'How can he do that if he has no money?'

'Borrow elsewhere if he can, gamble for high stakes, make wagers, that sort of thing.'

'But he could still lose and be further in debt.'

'Exactly.' He put an arm about her shoulders and kissed her on the mouth. His body felt warm, his lips moist, the scent of the wine on his breath. He drew back and touched her cheek with his finger. 'What must you think of my lack of ardour on this of all nights. This damned haggling with the money-lender –' he raised and dropped his shoulders. 'There'll be the devil to pay if the Colonel finds out. What would you advise the poor devil to do? What would your famous female instincts suggest?'

'Marry a rich woman, perhaps?' Zara said lightly, thinking of her father's solution.

'Good God!' She heard his sharp intake of breath. He was looking at her intently. 'Why did you say that?'

'Why not?' she asked in surprise. 'It's not an unusual practice. Does it shock you to think of marrying for money? Would you find it quite unprincipled?'

He was silent for a moment. 'You would not think badly of a man who did that?'

'Would you think badly of a woman who did?' she parried.

He frowned. 'We are talking about a man.'

Zara considered, thinking again of her father. Mrs Makin had enough common sense to know that Charles Deane was not in love with her. He would show her kindness and courtesy, be a faithful husband and treat her with well-mannered affection. His one love, apart from his daughter, was the gaming table. Mrs Makin knew all this and accepted it as the price of marriage to Charles Deane. Zara admired her for it. But there lay the difference. Mrs Makin knew she was being married for money.

'Yes,' Zara said slowly. 'We are talking about a man, an officer and presumably a gentleman. Should he pretend love and hope to be forgiven later when the truth came out as it surely would? Or would he not care for forgiveness, once in control of her money? No, that would not do, for this mythical rich woman might resent it and create the very scandal he sought to avoid. A deceived woman,' she said, thinking now of Delia Pringle who had perhaps deceived only herself, 'can be quite vindictive.'

She paused, studying Ralph's face. She had let her time pass by, but now she must tell Ralph the truth, so that the arrangement for marriage could be cancelled before the news spread round the garrison. It would be too hurtful to let him suppose she could go through with it. As they were on the subject of debt and deceit, alone here in this quiet garden, she must be honest. It was exactly the right moment. She drew in a deep breath.

'Ralph, I must speak to you honestly before it is too late. Your announcement tonight surprised me and in front of the Lacys I could not protest.'

He laid a hand on her shoulder, his face close to hers. The blue eyes looked almost colourless in the lamplight. 'Why should you protest?'

'Because I feel there should be honesty between us –' Zara winced under the suddenly hard fingers. 'I think it is only honourable,' she said on a gasp. 'And you are hurting me.'

He released her. 'I'm sorry,' he said stiffly. 'What are you implying? That I have been dishonest with you?'

Zara stared at him, feeling genuine shock. 'I was not implying anything of the sort. I just wish to make clear my own position. To avoid later recriminations, if we marry, it must be understood on both sides. I wish to be perfectly honest.'

'Why do you say – if we marry?'

The hard look was still on Ralph's face and Zara found it difficult to go on, but she had to put an end to it as gently as she could.

'You have been very kind and patient but I cannot live up

109

to your expectations. You are so correct and I resent correction. You have called me headstrong and that is true. You cannot turn me into a perfect garrison wife. In fact, I have deceived you from the first by pretending to be something I am not.'

Ralph's response surprised her. She had been staring down at the grass but glanced up quickly into his smiling face. The hard look had gone. He raised one of her limp hands and kissed it.

'Dear Zara. Did you think I was deceived by your pretence?'

She stared, wide-eyed, unable to speak as he continued.

'A man can tell if he is loved and I know very well that I only rate fondness in your eyes. I shall not ask for wild passion. I am perfectly willing to accept you as you are. What is all the fuss about?'

'But, don't you mind that I have nothing to offer you? It was all pretence.'

'I proposed to Miss Zara Deane who did me the kindness of saying yes. She is here and that is all that matters.' He paused, gazing down into her strained face. 'I am keeping you from your rest. You have had a tiring day. Stop fretting about unimportant things and think of our wedding. Will you ride in the morning or stay quietly indoors?'

'I will ride.'

'Very well. I will see you as usual.'

He escorted her to the veranda steps and watched as she mounted them. She glanced over her shoulder. He raised a hand, then turned to stride to the stables for his horse.

Zara undressed slowly and slipped a light dressing gown over her nightdress. She sat on the bed, trying to sort out her thoughts. What had she achieved in the garden? Precisely nothing, since Ralph was intent on going ahead with the marriage. She didn't love him. He knew and accepted it. She tried to think back. Had she made it clear that she was poor? He would take her as she was, he had said. A girl who was merely fond of him? She could not believe he would be content with that. He was not a man of wild passion. That she could believe for he had shown her none. She shook her head

110

in puzzlement and frustration. The position was exactly as it had been before he produced the champagne. What was it they said? Hoist with one's own petard? She blew out the lamp and lay down on the bed staring into the darkness. Tomorrow she must make things crystal clear to Ralph.

She lay for what seemed a very long time, her mind refusing to relax. A band of tightness clamped round her brow turned into a headache. She must sleep but her throat was dry and her eyes burned. She sat up and pushed away the mosquito netting, swinging her legs to the cool stone floor. The shutters were open, letting in the hot night air and by the light of the stars she crossed to the marble washstand. The earthenware chatti pot held the drinking water in coolness and she filled and refilled a tumbler, grateful for the relief it brought. The damp facecloth cooled her hot cheeks.

She was about to move back to bed when some movement outside caught her eye. Looking through the unshuttered window she saw a figure squatting under a tree. The white turban and white robe stood out in the darkness. Of the wearer she saw little, except that he was very dark-skinned and heavily bearded. Was he one of the servants? Surely they were all in bed by now. This man was sitting relaxed, as if waiting. She leaned on the window sill to get a better view. A burglar? He was not in the least furtive and was making no pretence of hiding.

From her left a board creaked. There was someone on the veranda. The man didn't move but his head turned towards the sound. Someone descending from the veranda into the garden. The man rose then and waited, still half in the shadow of the tree. He stood very still, listening.

A whisper drifted through the night air: 'Shaitan?' A hint of amusement was in the whisper.

Zara frowned. Shaitan? Was that the name of the man under the tree? Who was calling to him? An accomplice? She saw the gleam of white teeth in the dark face as the man moved forward a pace, hand outstretched. It was gripped by another and two figures stood close together. The second man, a little shorter, wore a hooded robe of dark material, wide-skirted and held about the waist with a tasselled cord.

111

The bearded stranger – she could not see the face of the other – jerked his head interrogatingly at the dark bungalow. A brief touch of moonglow showed up the face, then he turned, drawing the second figure deeper into the shadows. In that moment of illumination, Zara sensed something familiar in that face. Had she met him before? Where could she have met this bushy-bearded man who was very tall by Indian standards? So tall he must surely be able to look over any head without difficulty.

She stifled a gasp, her skin prickling coldly with vivid remembrance. That hard unblinking stare over the Rani's head! That man, the Rani's lover, had been the one waiting under the trees. But waiting for whom? And why in the middle of the night?

Chapter Eleven

'Good morning, Colonel.' Zara smiled brightly although her head ached and her eyes felt tight from the sleepless night. 'I hope Mrs Lacy has recovered from our excursion?'

Colonel Lacy smiled and poured a cup of coffee for her. 'She is still sleeping.'

'I am sorry to have tired her. It was selfish of me to keep her so long in the bazaar when she had seen it all before.'

'Nonsense, my dear. The bazaar has always delighted her and she enjoyed showing it to you. That was a very pretty necklet you bought. The Indians are so clever with their artistry.'

'What is the common language here, Colonel? I would so like to be able to speak with them.'

He raised a brow in surprise. 'You are unusual. Most of our ladies never learn more than a few words. They consider it more proper for the people to speak English.' He laughed. 'Of course it is essential for we officers to speak the language, but there lies a problem. Urdu is perhaps the most common in these parts although each region has its own language and

112

dialect. There are literally dozens of different tongues, Tamil, Hindi, Gurkali, Kashmiri, Singhalese, Persian . . .'

'Stop,' said Zara, laughing. 'One would need many lifetimes to learn them all.' The Colonel was rising to his feet as Zara asked. 'What does shaitan mean?' His eyes met hers steadily but she noted the surprise in them.

'Shaitan?' he said smoothly. 'It means "devil". Where did you hear that?'

'I – I'm not sure,' she said, feeling a slight embarrassment as the thought struck her that the second man last night could have been the Colonel. He was tall, almost as tall as the bearded man, and if it had been him it was a secret meeting and none of her business. She wished she had not spoken but it was too late and he was waiting for her reply.

She wrinkled her brow. 'Was it Ram Das, who drove like one of the furies, scattering all before him? Would anyone have shouted abuse?'

'I'm sure they would and calling him a devil is mild to some of the remarks they hurl at each other.' He smiled, relaxed. 'I must go. Do you ride with the Captain this morning?'

She nodded and he went down the veranda steps to the waiting syce holding the reins of his horse. Zara sipped her coffee thoughtfully. If the word she had heard last night had been one of abuse, why had the bearded stranger grinned? He would understand the language. Perhaps it was occasionally used as a term of affection, just as an Englishman might call a close friend a sly dog, or a wily old bird.

A puff of dust approaching across the maidan recalled her to the present. Her heart sank as she recognised the rider. Today she must be truly firm and make it quite clear that her so-called funds were nonexistent.

Ralph rode up as the groom assisted her into Farah's saddle. He looked relaxed and cheerful and she felt ashamed by her pretence, but knew she must not falter in determination. Dear God, what if he forgave her and insisted on going ahead, declaring that Great-Aunt Matilda's legacy had been more than generous!

They cantered over the shorter grass where the flocks had

113

grazed and made for the lower foothills. Ralph glanced about him.

'I wonder where the Yuvaraj is riding today?' His tone was cynical though he smiled as if it didn't really matter. 'I dare say we shall come across him whichever direction we choose.'

He looked at Zara and she smiled. 'I believe you are right. He must have many informers among his people who keep him in touch with every movement in the garrison. Why do you suppose he pops up wherever we go? Is it just a game of idle amusement?'

'Perhaps, but apart from knowing it annoys me, and I swear he enjoys that immensely, I feel he has more than a passing interest in looking at you.'

'What? You can't be suggesting that he has designs on me! But that is too ridiculous!'

'You said he was charming and you were quite cross when I rescued you from him at the durbar.'

'Only because I didn't wish to be impolite and he was being very charming. I think you imagine his interest in me. There are so many beautiful Indian girls about, why should you suppose he holds me in any favour?'

'Why, indeed?'

Ralph's tone was dry and Zara frowned. 'Why are you talking in this vein?'

Ralph half-turned in his saddle to smile at her. 'It would not disturb me this morning if we did meet the Yuvaraj. It would give me pleasure to watch his face when I announce our wedding plans.'

'Why? He knows of our engagement.' She gave him a puzzled look.

Ralph laughed. 'But a married woman is different. He has never interested himself in wives, save to be respectful and impeccably well-mannered.'

'Good heavens, Ralph!' Zara said impatiently. 'You are thinking again of that poor girl who was sent home in disgrace. Is that why you hate the man? What was she to you that you hold him so guilty of wickedness? Were you fond of her?'

'No, but she was an innocent, trusting girl who fell under his spell and ruined her life.'

114

'Really, Ralph, you make it sound like a Victorian melo-drama! She is probably quite happily married now with two children and a fond memory of a handsome Indian Prince.'

'You take it very lightly,' he said, frowning.

'Well, it does take two people to achieve a seduction. Or are you saying it was an attack upon her by the Prince? It seems most unlikely and Prince or not, he would be in grave trouble.'

Ralph opened his mouth and closed it again, reaching hastily for Farah's reins. His eyes narrowed as he pulled round the horse.

'What is it?' asked Zara, clinging to the pommel. 'Why did you do that?'

'I saw the flash of a jewel down there in the valley. I've decided against letting the Yuvaraj have his amusement this morning. Come, we'll make for that ridge and ride along the crest towards the mountains.' He handed back Farah's reins. 'If you feel strongly about it, you may give him a distant wave.'

'I thought you said it would not disturb you to meet the Yuvaraj today?' Zara said curtly. 'Now you turn tail and almost unseat me into the bargain.'

'I'm sorry, but this is a route he will not expect us to take. You will be able to look more closely at those mountains you spoke about, "the abode of snow", wasn't it?'

Zara glanced up. The lush foothills of the Himalayas lay visible from the top of this crest. Higher up the ground was rocky, meeting the snowline. Above, hazed in early mist, rose the immense snow-clad peaks.

'How stately and magnificent,' she said, her crossness forgotten. 'Can people climb to the top?'

'I've never heard of anyone doing it but in Nepal there are sherpas or guides who will lead people up part of the way. I believe the air is too thin for survival at any great height.'

'Could we reach the snowline?'

'I expect so. But it is farther away than it looks. It would need a proper expedition.'

'Let's see how far we can go.' She spurred Farah forward and the half-Arab flung back her golden mane and surged on joyfully, her dainty legs stepping firmly and surely.

Ralph followed on the heavy cavalry horse. Zara rode on, exulting in the cool wind which blew, she imagined, right from the top of the snow peaks, roaring down the incline and into the foothills where it stilled and allowed the sun to stroke it with warm fingers.

Although Farah would not have outpaced the cavalry horse in a headlong charge, she was a swift little mount, her very fleetness of foot carrying them well ahead. It is said that a horse senses the mood of its rider and responds in kind. Zara's exhilaration infected Farah and she moved like Pegasus, the mythical horse, as if on wings.

Ralph called something but the wind blew away the words. Zara glanced back and saw the heavier horse labouring to keep its large feet in the track that had become more rocky. She drew Farah to a halt and looked at the mountains. It was true. They still seemed as far away as ever. Below the crest they had been riding on she saw a rough-grassed plain, a small valley set with trees. The sparkle of a stream caught her eye. She turned in her saddle and waved, indicating the place to Ralph. He raised a hand in acknowledgement. He was so far behind that Zara knew she and Farah would be at the stream long before the cavalry horse had negotiated the descent.

'Come, my beauty,' she said aloud and turned Farah's head. They could rest a while and water the horses before returning to the garrison.

Farah picked her way down the hillside and the scent of herbs, crushed by her hooves, rose. Blue speedwell, lavender and red clover, the air was full of the perfume, so familiar to her that she was surprised to find them here. But why not, it was a magic country? People grew roses, anemones, petunias, violets, and many more. With so much travelling and the exchange of plants, one scarcely knew which flowers were indigenous to which country these days.

She reached the stream and dismounted, loosening Farah's girth straps, and leading her to the clean running water. It looked crystal clear but she must ask Ralph if it was safe. They drank only boiled then chilled water in Lahore. Dysentery was something unpleasant, to be feared and avoided. While she waited, she lay under the shade of a willow tree, her pith helmet beside her. How beautiful it was. They had never ridden so far before or in such a direction. It would take them ages to get back. She turned on to her side and looked up as a bird sped from a willow branch to hover above the water, then darted down in an exotic flurry of colour. A kingfisher! She lay silent, enchanted by its beauty. The flash of blue-green wing as it hovered momentarily held a metallic iridescence. Short-bodied and short-tailed, it had an impressively long dagger-like bill. A brief turbulence, a scattering of rainbow droplets, then the kingfisher was back on its willow branch, a fish clamped firmly in the darting dagger. In a second the fish was swallowed whole, then the kingfisher sped upstream, barely inches above the stream's surface, to disappear into the rush-fringed bank.

Zara heard the heavy hoofbeats and blowing of the cavalry horse. She rolled over and sat up. Ralph looked down on her crossly.

'Didn't you hear me call?' he asked curtly. 'Mount up. We shall be late back.'

Zara smiled up lazily. 'It's so beautiful here. What does it matter if we're late? The Colonel knows we're together. No one will worry unless we don't get back at all.'

'I have my duties to attend to.'

'Well, I'm sure the army won't fall into disarray because Captain Browne is half an hour late at his desk.'

'Half an hour? It will take us at least an hour to reach the garrison. We should have turned back long ago. I believe you deliberately ignored my call. That was wilful, and dangerous, too.'

Zara rose, brushing the grass from her skirt. She looked at the sweating cavalry horse. 'Well, you might at least dismount and let that poor horse drink from the stream. Can't we drink too? It looks perfectly clean.'

'It probably is but we've no time.' He looked about him then up to the mountains. 'This is not a good place to linger. Please mount up.'

'It looks peaceful. What do you mean?'

'Take a look across the valley. It has been grazed, probably by nomads, and they're not all friendly towards us.'

'You mean hill people, the ones you told me about? Aren't we too low down the mountains for them to bother us? If it's only goat-herders –' She broke off, narrowing her eyes on a spot among the crags.

'What is it?' Ralph's voice came sharply.

'Nothing, I think, but I caught a bright glint of something up there on the hillside.'

Ralph looked where she pointed and his voice took on an urgency.

'For God's sake, mount up, Zara! We're sitting targets for any trigger-happy tribesman.'

He wheeled his horse as Zara ran for Farah, half-dozing in the shade. Ralph was already moving and had made no attempt to help her mount. She scrambled into the saddle and brought Farah round.

'Come on,' he shouted and his nervousness infected her. Was there a grinning tribesman lying hidden in the rocks, his finger tightening on the trigger of the silver-chased stock of his jezail? Was the barrel moving, covering their flight, waiting for the right angle before firing? Farah blew indignantly through her wide nostrils, as if this sudden change from dreaming inaction to headlong gallop was a slight on her high-born dignity. She reacted by choosing the softer ground, the grassy slopes, veering round sharp-edged rocks, unlike the heavier horse that took a direct route over stone and earth alike.

Ralph looked over his shoulder. 'Keep up,' he shouted and Zara saw that his face was pale under the sheen of sweat.

At that moment, a shot rent the air and a plume of dust leapt into the air five yards away.

Farah jinked sharply and Zara clutched the saddle to prevent herself being thrown off. She remembered with a chill of fear that she had not tightened the girth straps again before she mounted. Now the saddle was loosely held and any more sudden veerings by Farah could unseat her. She gripped the knee pommel with hand and stiffened leg. A useless gesture really for if the saddle went she would go with it.

Another shot, but from a different direction! The bullet ploughed a furrow ten feet ahead of Ralph. She thought ridiculously of the tiger hunt as told by the Yuvaraj. The beaters drove the quarry on to the guns in the howdahs. The first shot here had achieved the same purpose, driving them into the ambush set up by the second rifleman.

On the rock beside which they must pass, a figure rose, a tall, baggy-trousered man in long tunic and coloured shirt. The glinting barrel of a jezail was cradled by his bearded chin. White teeth flashed as the round muzzle pointed directly at Ralph. Zara saw no more for Farah stumbled and the loosened saddle pivoted. She clutched the golden mane but it ran through her fingers like silk. Farah swerved in terror as the saddle thumped into her side and Zara's fingers were jerked from their hold on the reins.

'Ralph!' she screamed and the earth came up to meet her. She fell in the way she had been taught, protecting her head and curling into as much of a ball as time allowed. The ground met her shoulder with a thump and the breath was knocked from her lungs. Thank God, she thought vaguely, that grass was softer than rock. She might have a stiff shoulder but there were no bones broken, and she had not landed on her head.

She rolled, coming to her knees. Farah! Where was the creature? Then she saw her beloved horse, long tail swishing irritably as the saddle still bounced against her side. But Farah was not waiting for any adjustment. Beautiful Farah, her golden coat now patched with sweat, was far away from Zara and heading at speed towards the garrison.

Ralph? She saw him turn in a wide circle away from the menacing gun. She sighed with relief. He was coming back for her. That cavalry horse could carry two. He was almost up to her when a bullet split the ground between them. Ralph veered and looked up to the rock. There were now two men, both grinning and following his moves with the barrels of two rifles.

Zara had no idea of the capability of the jezail, whether it was a single or multiple loading rifle, but whichever was true, the men were quick to reload. She sensed in some bewildering way that the shots had not been aimed to kill. They could have hit their targets much earlier for the hillmen were reputed to be excellent marksmen. Was this just a game to frighten the feringhee, the foreigners? Neither she nor Ralph had been hurt.

Another bullet whistled through the air, barely inches in front of the muzzle of Ralph's horse. Zara flinched as dust flew into her eyes. When she could open them again, the big horse was almost on its haunches as Ralph pulled back on the reins. The horse protested, blowing noisily through distended nostrils, and the whites of his eyes showed. Dust flew from under the stamping hooves and Ralph was having difficulty in controlling the beast.

Zara rose to her feet. 'Ralph!' she called. 'Help me. Your horse can carry –'

Her words were drowned by the crack of another shot. The horse shied away from the wind of its passage. Zara began to run. She saw Ralph hesitate, his face very white. The hillmen glanced at Zara indifferently. One set his foot on a rock and began to reload his jezail. The second man laid aside his rifle and drew from his sash a wickedly gleaming tulwar. He began a quick descent to level ground.

Zara felt her theory crumble and terror took her. They like their victims to die slowly, Ralph had said. The knife is slower and creates exquisite agony, much more enjoyable than a quick bullet in the heart.

'Ralph!' she screamed, her senses shredding. 'Your sword –'

Ralph made no move. He looked dazed, his eyes caught by the glittering tulwar blade that flashed hypnotically as the man scythed the air with the casual ease of a warrior accustomed to its use. Ralph's eyes flickered to the man reloading his jezail. There appeared to be some difficulty. The second man reached the ground.

The pass between the rocks was clear, for a precious few moments unguarded. Ralph looked at Zara briefly. She almost screamed again as she read his eyes. She knew with dreadful clarity what he was about to do. He was frightened, terrified, and the moment was here and now, the moment to break and run.

120

He whirled the big horse and dug in his spurs. The horse reacted to the drag on its bit and bounded forward, strong haunches bunching with effort. Past the man with the tulwar, now still and staring, they charged for freedom.

'Ralph!' Zara screamed again, her voice cracking with shock. She still could not believe he had deserted her quite so cold-bloodedly. He had been frightened, but so had she. His sword was still in its scabbard. He had not even attempted to defend her! Hooves thundered and Ralph, bent almost double over the sweating horse, did not look back.

Zara stood very still, staring after the receding figure, and the tears ran hotly down her cheeks. Ralph had saved himself at her expense, leaving her to the mercy of these savage tribesmen. Dear God, how could he have done it? She covered her face and wept, sinking down on to the grass.

Chapter Twelve

The spasm of crying lessened and the tears of shock dried on Zara's face. She dropped her hands and stared fully into the empty distance. Then she felt the stirrings of anger. Ralph was a coward! The gallant Captain Browne, who had pledged his sword in honour if the occasion demanded, had turned his back on honour. Two men only and he had not even made a fight of it, but fled the field in a palsy of terror.

What would he tell them back at the garrison? How could he explain her absence when he was seen to be without a scratch? A desperate battle against overwhelming odds would hardly do since he was unbloodied and still had the shine on his sword. At least it delayed the need of confessing her poverty, she thought wryly.

She came to herself with a start. Dear God, it didn't solve her own problem. She glanced fearfully towards the two men. What did they intend to do with her?

Her eyes widened as she looked at them. The jezails were laid aside, the tulwars back in their sashes. They sat relaxed on the rocks, talking softly and sucking beedis, short brown cigarettes. It was almost as if she didn't exist! She climbed to her feet, wincing a little from her bruised shoulder. The conversation ceased and the dark eyes regarded her silently. Both rose then, flipping away their cigarettes. One turned his head and gave a shrill whooping whistle. The other, surprisingly, smiled.

'Good,' he said and brushed his cheeks with his fingers as if wiping away tears. 'Go now.'

Zara frowned, perplexed. The dark eyes were friendly. Had they been waiting until she had stopped crying? Shooting at them one moment then politely averting their eyes from the sight of her grief?

In answer to the whistle, two shaggy ponies cantered into the clearing. There were no saddles and the hair on their backs and flanks was dusty and uncared for, but they were bright-eyed and healthy. They were caught by their rope bridles. One man swung himself up and the other gestured to Zara to mount. She hesitated.

'Where are you taking me?'

The man nodded. 'Good. Go now.'

'Where?'

He nodded again. 'Good. Go now.'

Zara realised that he had no other English words, none that he was admitting to, anyway, and shrugged, reaching for the bridle. Without a saddle she would have to ride astride. Thank heavens it was only a pony, stolid and unmoving, not a tall, nervous horse. She used her childhood method of mounting, twining her arms about the pony's neck and sliding herself, stomach first on to its back, right leg crossing over, then coming erect with the reins in her hand. The two men grinned and surprised her by clapping like children. The second man swung up behind her and took the rope bridle from her fingers. He smelled strongly of sweat and tobacco and many more unidentifiable aromas. He did not clasp her waist but seemed at pains to hold himself away from her. Was he being polite, she wondered, or did her own scent repel him? Somehow, she had stopped being frightened, for they were treating her with respect. But where were they taking her and would something frightful be waiting when they arrived?

The way became rougher, the ponies skidding on loose pebbles but retaining their sure-footed stolidity. It grew hotter as the sun rose and Zara had to narrow her eyes against the brilliance of sun-touched rock. One of her captors had rescued her pith helmet, handing it to her politely, and she was grateful for its protection. Even so, her face and neck felt gritty with dust and perspiration. The cotton shirt she wore, once crisp and white from the ayah's flat-iron, was limp, streaked with dirt and grass stains.

Were the mountains coming nearer? Perhaps, but there was no cooling in the air. Her throat was dry and she could only taste salty dust on her lips. She turned her head.

'How long?' she asked the dark face behind.

He grinned, nodding. 'Good,' he said and began to hum to himself.

'I might as well talk to the mountain,' she muttered, favouring him with a glowering look. He stopped humming and beamed broadly as if her look had pleased him. He called something to the second man who glanced appraisingly at Zara then nodded, appearing also pleased.

Zara shrugged and turned her gaze forward again. What they had to be pleased about was beyond her. Did they imagine she would not be missed? Ralph must surely have reached the garrison by now. However he explained it, Colonel Lacy would muster a troop of cavalry and set out in pursuit. She was comforted by the thought that an English girl does not just disappear into the hills without a hand being raised to search her out. Someone would come and find her, alive or dead. Her mind halted there abruptly. She didn't want to die, but what were her prospects alive? What was it all about? Even if they released her now, she had no horse and all this twisting and turning up rocky tracks had confused her sense of direction. The mountains were still ahead, of course, but was Lahore directly south or to the east or west?

It must be about midday, Zara judged, for the sun was overhead. Her back ached, her thighs were sore from contact with the pony's rough coat. Without stirrups she could not ease her position. The sun-scorched rocks began to dance in her vision and she felt dizzy and sick, sick of this endless progress that seemed to be taking them nowhere. She bent forward over the pony's neck, her stomach cramping with fatigue and hunger. Since last night she had drunk only a cup of coffee with Colonel Lacy. A puff of dust, kicked up by the pony's forelegs, gusted into her face. She began to cough, particles rasping in her throat. The effort was painful and hurt her chest but she couldn't stop.

'Water,' she gasped, her eyes misty and streaming.

The second man alighted from his pony and stood looking at her, a concerned expression on his face.

She dragged in a deep breath. 'Pani, damn you! Bhisti wallah!' Her knowledge of Urdu was woefully inadequate but the man radiated relief and a flurry of words followed. Her own escort dismounted, the rope halters were thrown forward, and the two men half-ran, dragging the ponies between tall rocks.

Zara heard it then, the faintest sound of running water. A twist in the track, then she glimpsed the wonderful sight of a slender spurt of silver, issuing from a rock face. She half-fell from the pony's back, recovered her balance and began to move towards the tiny waterfall. Although her legs were unsure, neither man attempted to touch her but stood watching, broad smiles on their faces. She sensed that the smiles were not of derision but gratification that they had understood her need and provided for it.

She knelt near the rock, reaching out to catch the fall in her cupped hands. It was the sweetest, finest drink she had ever had. She cupped her hands again and again, throwing water over her face and head until her shirt was soaked and water ran out of her hair. Crystal clear and cold, straight out of the mountains, she surmised, and was reluctant to leave it, but the hillmen were making flapping gestures with their hands. She knew the movement of beckoning, not the European upward curve of the palm but a downward flap as if paddling water. She sighed, feeling much stronger, and returned to the pony.

'Good,' her travelling companion said, not as a question, but a statement.

'Very good,' she said and smiled at him.

He blinked and looked embarrassed. Why, she wondered? Because I am a foreigner, an unveiled woman and a smile is an encouragement? Perhaps, she thought hazily, only a bad Indian girl goes unveiled and smiles upon men.

The track wound on interminably, the shadows lengthening until the sun was low in the sky, turning the snow-capped peaks into pink icing sugar. Eventually the ponies paused on a plateau of rock. The air was cooler, the rocks bare of dust as if some invisible broom had swept away all dust and sand.

The two men dismounted. Was this the destination, wondered Zara, gazing round? It seemed like any other part of the hillside they had been climbing for so many hours. No sign of habitation, no people, not even a goat stirred the silence. The men grasped the rope halters and began to lead the ponies across the plateau to a small incline that boasted an area of tussocky grass. Beyond, the hills rose again. Zara gazed up at them despairingly. Surely they were not to proceed on foot? She doubted the ability of her legs for that. They were aching abominably already from the pony's rough flanks.

Once on the grass, the men indicated that she should dismount. She slid thankfully down. Her knees gave way and she sank on to the grass. watching the men remove the rope halters. One man skirted a rock and disappeared, returning a few minutes later with a battered metal bucket that slopped water. From a sack in his other hand he poured oats on to the ground in front of the ponies. Zara clasped her arms about her shoulders and waited. She hoped they would feed her too.

A hand flapped in her direction and she rose wearily. She followed the man who had brought the water and oats. Round the curve of the rock he stopped and pointed. Zara gazed over another small plateau of rock and saw that a wide cleft had been roofed over with bamboo sticks, twined through with branches of fir and ferns. The earth floor was covered by matting, the walls lined with a jumble of weapons and cooking pots. In front of the cave-like construction was a circular area of stones, containing dead ashes.

125

The man lifted a tall-necked earthernware pot. He stabbed his chest with a dark, grimy finger.

'Bhisti wallah,' he said and burst into uproarious laughter.

Water carrier, he is saying, thought Zara, and moved forward. The man handed her a tin mug and she filled it from the clay pot that held in the coolness of water. She sat with her back to the rock, legs outstretched before her, and watched the man build a nest of twigs and dried grass inside the ring of stones. He glanced up at the hazy sky then used a tinderbox to fire the grass. When the twigs were alight, he laid flat stones amongst them and brought a blackened cooking pot from the cave. Into this he poured water and set it upon the stones. From under half-closed lids, Zara saw him skin and chop into pieces a small animal, dropping chunks of meat into the pot. A few leaves, a handful of spices were tossed in, then he took a twig and applied it to the end of another small brown cigarette produced from beneath his shirt. He sank back on his haunches and Zara's eyes closed as sleep overcame her.

She woke to darkness, except for the glow of the fire. The sky seemed close, the stars brilliant as twinkling crystals of ice. She shivered, for there was a coolness in the air and she wore only a cotton shirt. She looked about quickly, warily. Where were her captors? The murmur of voices came to her and she saw them squatting, Indian fashion with only their feet on the ground. With every joint protesting, Zara climbed to her feet, stretching her shoulders and arms. The two men stopped talking and one rose.

Zara stared at him steadily as he came near. Her dark brows were drawn into a straight line and the hazel of her eyes caught pinpoints of gold from the flames. Her fingers curled into fists and she stood tensed, her face expressionless, only her eyes moving to follow the man's progress. She was not aware of the fierceness of her look but the hillman circled her cautiously as he would a tigress and made no attempt to come close. He pointed to the cave, speaking words she did not understand. A brief glance showed her a pile of goatskins and a couple of vividly coloured blankets. He rubbed his shoulders and mimed a shiver.

Zara nodded but stayed where she was. The man shrugged

126

and picked up three metal dishes. Only then did Zara become aware of the aroma of cooked meat. Fragrant steam spiralled upwards from the pot, barely moving in the still air. As he turned towards the fire, Zara moved to the cave mouth and pulled out one of the bright blankets. The man glanced over his shoulder and nodded, grinning, then began to ladle food into the three dishes.

Zara swung the blanket about her shoulders, feeling its immediate warmth. It was soft and woolly, like a hand-knitted mohair coverlet, and smelled only faintly of goat. She took the dish handed to her and waited to be given some eating implement but since the men were using their fingers she had to do the same. Flat cakes of bread lay on the hot stones and with one of these she managed to eat her meat and wipe up the liquid as they were doing. After so long without food, she ate hungrily and whatever it was, she decided, it was good.

One of the men rose and picked up his rifle, slinging it over his shoulder. He disappeared into the darkness. Keeping guard, she wondered, and stifled a yawn. The other man pointed to the cave and mimed sleep, then he too, picked up his jezail and moved away in a different direction. Zara sat for some time by the dying fire but neither man came back. She found her eyelids drooping and had to keep jerking herself awake. Finally she rose and went to the cave. She could not hope to stay without sleep throughout the entire night. If they meant her any harm, there was nothing she could do to prevent them. In a way, they had been kind, she reflected as she lay down on the soft skins, for they had not bound her, nor used any force to bring her here. Food and water and a warm blanket had been provided, but what was it they wanted? There had to be some reason for this abduction. Sleep claimed her before any answer presented itself.

Zara woke to the chill of dawn and lay still for a moment, wondering at the pearly greyness that filled her vision. She pulled the blanket closer about her shoulders and stared up at the fir-branch roof. Her sleep had been profound and undisturbed, the foliage bed comfortable, but now she needed the comfort of privacy as in her dressing room at the Lacy bungalow. She threw back the blanket and stood up. No one would make camp here unless they were within reach of water. She moved to the cave and entrance and gazed out. The tussocky grass looked stiff, slightly frosted, and she saw the hobbled ponies with goatskin rugs tied to their backs, as if the night had been cold. How high were they? This early chill was far sharper than any she had experienced in Lahore.

Lahore? What would they be doing now? Almost twenty-four hours had passed since she and Colonel Lacy had drunk coffee together. She stared about cautiously. There was no sign of the hillmen. A voice to one side made her jump and whirl about. A familiar dark face grinned, showing strong white teeth. He made that curious flapping gesture and turned away. Zara followed. He led her through a narrow cleft, the packed earth beneath her boots covered by goat droppings, and they emerged into a small clearing. A spindly stream of water trickled silently out of a sheer rock face to fill a shallow indent on the hillside. A few bushes surrounded the pool. The man pointed and nodded encouragingly, then backed away to disappear the way they had come.

Zara unbuttoned the long skirt that covered her riding breeches and draped it between two bushes beside the cleft. As long as this makeshift curtain was in place she could not be spied upon. After the completion of her toilet, she tied back her hair with its ribbon and tried to brush the stain of travel from her clothes with a dried fir branch. A small willow leant over the pool and she remembered someone telling her that a soft furry twig was the usual toothbrush of many Indians. The air was less chill as she retrieved her skirt and made her way back through the cleft. As she turned on to the grassy plateau she stopped, her eyes widening in surprise. Squatting by the fire and blowing the ashes into life was not one of the hillmen but a girl. She wore baggy trousers, a brightly coloured tunic and a small cap from which a veil hung. A plait of black hair fell over one shoulder as she fed the embers of the fire with twigs.

As Zara started forward, the girl glanced up and quickly drew the veiling across her nose and mouth. Her large dark eyes stayed only a moment on the English girl, then she bent to her task again. Zara moved to the cave mouth. A high-pitched giggle followed her and she turned sharply towards the girl by the fire, but her face was unsmiling. From a bend in the path came another girl, a smile still on her face, her arms cradling a wide wicker basket. She caught sight of Zara and her smile faded. Behind her walked one of the hillmen.

This girl was dressed similarly to the other but her veil was in place. Above the veil her dark eyes were merry, due, no doubt, to the spirited interchange with the hillman. Feeling like an unwanted guest at a party, Zara scowled and went into the cave. The sun came up, its rays reducing the frosted grass to a soft green. The goatskin blankets were taken from the ponies and their hobbles removed. A pot began to steam on the fire, the other hillman appeared, and they both sat with their backs to the warming rock, smoking their beedis, watching the two girls.

Zara sat with her hands about her knees, staring moodily at the four of them. their conversation was friendly, even bantering, the girls stifling giggles with hands flat over their mouths, the men grinning and nudging each other. What, in the name of heaven, did they need her for? If the whole episode had been a joke, a spur of the moment thing, one of them could have carried her to the outskirts of Lahore and left her there to make her own way on foot. Since Farah, and Ralph too, had deserted her, it seemed only sensible. Why bring her up the mountain? Were they bandits, enemies of the British? Was she to be ransomed? She rested her chin on her knees, frowning. If only she could communicate with them and know their intention instead of being forced to guess.

Her gaze rose to the girl coming towards her, a bowl in her hands. The girl with merry eyes smiled, holding out the bowl.

'Chota hazri, Missie Sahib.'

'Breakfast,' said Zara, answering the shy smile. 'Thank you.'

'Very good,' the girl said.

Zara nodded. 'Porridge for breakfast. It smells good.'

'Very good,' the girl repeated. 'Salt, yes? I learn from memsahib.'

Zara stared. 'You learn from memsahib? So you speak English?'

The girl shrugged. 'Some little, maybe. Not pleasing memsahib. I go.'

'What is your name?'

'Soonya.'

'Well, Soonya, can you tell me why I am here?'

The girl shook her head. 'I asking. Raschid say big secret thing.'

'Big secret thing?' Zara scowled in the direction of the two men. 'Big secret to me, too.'

Soonya said, 'You not come by wanting?' She seemed surprised.

Zara began to eat the oatmeal mixture. It was thick enough to cling to her fingers. It tasted like spiced porridge cooked in strong milk, probably goat's milk.

'No, not by wanting. My – my companion was British officer. They –' she nodded towards the hillmen. 'They fired their jezails at him and took me prisoner. It is very serious. The soldiers will come to punish them. I hope they understand that.'

Soonya looked grave. 'That is bad. We are peaceful, not like Afghan peoples. Not wanting soldiers of white Rajah to burn our villages.'

'Then you must tell Raschid to take me to Lahore.'

Soonya nodded. 'I will tell but Raschid is sometimes fool.' She shrugged and picked up the now empty bowl.

'Is Raschid your husband?' asked Zara.

Soonya smiled. 'He is my man, little good, little bad, sometimes big fool but woman need man for – for' her brow wrinkled as she sought for a word in English, 'for being safe – when bad men look at me.'

'You mean he is your protector against other men?'

'Protector.' Soonya tried the word slowly and seemed to like it. 'Protector. That is good word. Raschid, my protector.' She nodded vigorously. 'You have one protector, Missie Sahib?'

Zara thought of Ralph and her expression hardened. 'Before Raschid came I thought I had.' She clasped her knees again and rested her chin on them.

Soonya moved away on bare dusty feet, her thoughts made uneasy by that hard look. The Missie Sahib's eyes between narrowed lids were watching Raschid with an unblinking stare, like those of a mountain cat awaiting the right moment to spring. Soonya shivered, trying to dismiss the thought, and yet this Missie Sahib was not like the plump, soft-faced, shrill-voiced memsahib she had served for a short time in Lahore. This one was hard and had clever eyes. She had smiled and spoken to Soonya as an equal, not as a foolish servant who must be told everything twice. Working for English memsahibs was all very well for those docile Hindu women but she, Soonya, a Muslim hill girl, was not to be ordered about by lazy memsahibs and idle house servants.

She walked over to Raschid and stared down at him. She spoke in the hill dialect. 'This thing is not good. The Missie Sahib will kill you. Already the soldiers are searching.'

Raschid rose and took her arm roughly. 'You talk like a foolish child.'

'But I do not act like one,' Soonya said, regarding him steadily.

Raschid raised a hand to strike her but Soonya did not flinch and Raschid's hand fell to his side. Soonya had only put into words what he had begun to think himself. He and Mahomet had planned it so carefully. They had imagined the wondrousness which would result from their action. He and Soonya, Mahomet and Rahti, the girl now sanding out the oatmeal bowls. Life was good here in the hills. Always water streams from the mountains, plenty of wood and fruit from the trees, the goat-herds to provide food and warm clothing and, of course, a woman. She was the most essential part in a hillman's life. Who else would do the work and carry the burdens when they moved camp? A man's job was to ride and care for his pony, discuss weighty matters in the shade of the trees, and chastise the women who delayed in their duties by chattering like parakeets at the water hole.

Raschid frowned fiercely into his woman's face. 'It is not for you to know,' he said, asserting his superiority. 'This is man's business. If Mahomet and I choose to bring a gift, it is no concern of yours. Go about your business, woman.' He

131

presented his back to her deliberately, signifying the end of any further talk between them.

Soonya turned away and went to squat beside Rahti, absently wiping out the bowls with a handful of damp grass. A gift, Raschid had said. What gift? She had seen no freshly slaughtered animal in the camp, nor had any traders passed lately. If Raschid and Mahomet had robbed a rich merchant, they would be full of the news, recounting how they had surprised him, relieving him of all his silver rupees. No, this was some big, secret thing.

The brass pot she had been holding fell from her fingers and bounced on the rocks. It must be the Missie Sahib! They had gone down to the lower lands, armed with tulwars and jezails to find a gift of sufficient importance. For him! For that giant of a man with his quick tongue and piercing eyes, the leader they were expecting back at any moment. Allah protect us, she muttered, and drew her veil over her face.

With this thought her uneasiness increased. He had not sent them to do this thing. If he needed a woman, there were many in the villages, but he had never taken one, it was said. So why should Raschid and Mahomet risk the wrath of the soldiers by stealing one of their women? But nearer at hand was another wrath if their rash action displeased him. And if it did, what would become of the Missie Sahib?

Perhaps she would please him and their gift be well received. She tried to comfort herself with the thought, but glancing sideways towards the cave mouth, she met the brooding stare of those light, gold-tinted eyes. She averted her gaze quickly. Stupid, stupid Raschid and Mahomet! The Missie Sahib was not a simple woman who would think it an honour to be chosen as a gift for their leader. Soonya pulled her veil higher and rocked back and forth on her heels.

She started as her name was called. It was the Missie Sahib and her eyes were fierce. Soonya rose reluctantly. Standing before Zara, she kept her eyes firmly on the ground and waited.

Zara had followed keenly the interchange of words with Raschid and expected her to return to the cave mouth. Soonya had not done this but had squatted by the fire, her

132

expression puzzled. The clang of metal on stone as Soonya dropped the pot, the quick widening of her eyes, then the retreat behind her veil had sent a chill of fear through Zara. Soonya's mind had worked on the puzzle. She had reached a conclusion and was afraid.

Zara broke the silence. She spoke harshly. 'Well? Raschid told you, didn't he?'

Soonya shook her head, her eyes still downcast. 'No, but I see his mind clear. He thinks to bring great gift for Devil Sahib who has no woman of his own.' Her gaze rose miserably to Zara's. 'I think maybe, he bring great trouble instead.'

Chapter Thirteen

Zara stared into Soonya's face, hardly able to believe what she heard.

'Do you tell me that I have been brought here to give to some man as a gift? This is monstrous! I demand to be taken back to Lahore immediately.'

Soonya said hopefully, 'He is great leader, very strong, very fierce. Everyone afraid of Devil Sahib. Maybe he like you very much and bring honour to Raschid and Mahomet.'

'Devil Sahib!' Zara laughed harshly. 'What a ridiculous title.' She was on her feet now, trying to bury her fear in a show of temper.

'Is his name, Missie Sahib, true name not leader name.'

'Soonya, this is the most ridiculous thing I ever heard. People cannot give other people away.'

'Here,' Soonya swept her arm upwards towards the mountain peaks, 'All the time goat people and hill people sell daughters, maybe sometime give away to save feeding.'

'But I am not one of the goat or hill people,' snapped Zara. 'Our customs are different. Men in my country do not take their women in this fashion. It is against the law and brings them trouble. You must tell Raschid that he will be caught and put into prison.'

133

Soonya considered this solemnly. 'Is hard,' she said eventually. 'To catch in mountains. Raschid and Mahomet do stupid thing but Devil Sahib very clever for hiding.'

'If this – this Devil Sahib is so clever, he will know that his men have done a stupid thing and return me to my people.' Soonya said. 'I think he not liking your people, Missie Sahib. Maybe he not liking prison too, if he take you and get caught by soldiers.'

Zara sat down suddenly on the flat-topped rock at the cave's entrance. Her whole body felt limp, her legs too weak to hold her upright. Of course they wouldn't take her back for fear of the soldiers shooting on sight. Whoever was with her would, at the least, be accused of her abduction and if not shot would be taken into custody to face that charge. Since women were of so little account, who would risk it?

She tried to think clearly. What were the alternatives? Leave her here or force her to go with them? She looked across at the two hillmen, remembering Ralph's words, and a shiver passed through her. They might have looked like pleased children who had successfully divined her wants, but they were not children. They were tough, rangy hillmen capable of cruelty, indifferent to hardship, who looked on their women as little higher than beasts of burden.

'It is the will of Allah,' Soonya said.

Zara gazed up blankly into the large dark eyes, the finely chiselled features of the hill girl, and turned her head away, trying not to let her dejection show.

'Allah is not my god,' she muttered and moved further into the shadowed cave where she lay down on the fir-branch bed, her face to the stone cliff wall. She heard Soonya move away, then for a long time there was only the sound of murmuring voices, the cry of a wheeling bird and the whisper of breeze-rustled leaves.

She must have dozed, her mind sunk into the blankness of despair. She woke, her face still to the rock. It was dark, yet she knew she could not have slept through the entire day. There was no sound, no murmuring of women, no whisper of leaves. Her heart jerked painfully as her mind sought a reason for this utter stillness. Childhood horror stories, victims walled up alive, flashed through her mind. Her breath caught in her throat as she stared towards the cave opening. Chinks of sunlight filtered in, surrounding a solid object. Something black and menacing filled the space. A giant boulder heaved in to block the opening? Walled up, walled up, her mind screamed and blind panic brought movement. She was on her feet, the scream coming from the depths of her being.

Then the wall moved and sunlight blinded her, forcing her hands to cover her eyes. The darkness was gone and she peered, blinking to look upon the same scene as before. Two veiled, crouching girls were stirring the fire. Beyond were the ponies, heads stretched to the grass. Zara sank on to the bed again, her shocked mind trying to bring reality into focus. A dream, a ghastly nightmare? No, she knew she had not been asleep so deeply. Something had momentarily blocked the light then been removed. Not something, her wits told her, but someone. Someone had stared down at her, standing so still that her sleep-drugged mind had created its own fantasy.

Someone. It could only have been the man they were waiting for, the man they called Devil Sahib, the leader they had planned to gratify with a gift, the gift of herself.

The perspiration of panic was cold on her skin. She huddled into the farthest corner, her hands clasped tightly about her knees, and waited.

The cave, although it was not really a cave but a thatched shelter between a cleft in the rocks, did not have much depth. A tall man stretched to full length would leave little room. Was this the lair of Devil Sahib? The name and thought of him made her shudder. The word Sahib was a mark of respect and not confined to Europeans. A high-born or high-ranking Indian might just as easily have the respectful word attached to his own name. But surely this leader was a bandit, a lawless man. Why else would Soonya talk of evading pursuit and hiding in the hills? And she had slept on this man's bed!

The thought brought her to her feet, a fresh panic flooding through her. If he came again, she was trapped in this confined space. His body had filled the entrance, like the boulder of her imagining. She must get into the open, to the company of the girls, although even they would be no

135

protection if she was dragged back. She snatched up her pith helmet and jammed it on her tousled head. The girls glanced up as she approached, their eyes unsmiling above the veils.

She squatted down beside Soonya. 'Where are the men?' Her voice was low and husky as if there was some special need for quietness.

Soonya jerked her head toward the path along which Raschid had led Zara that morning, the place of the tiny waterfall and small pool.

'Why?'

Soonya gave her a sideways look and her reply seemed touched with cynicism. 'Devil Sahib very angry but not saying bad things in front of women. That bring shame on Raschid and Mahomet. They beat us then to bring back honour.' She shrugged, her words very matter-of-fact. 'Devil Sahib knows this. How can women work if hurt bad?'

'You let your men beat you?' Zara asked, horrified.

Soonya shrugged again. 'It is way of man.'

They sat in silence for several minutes, then the sound of crackling twigs under booted feet came to them. Soonya and Rahti sprang up and went into swift action. Mahomet and Raschid appeared. At the same time, Soonya and Rahti engaged themselves in brisk conversation, one chopping vegetables which she dropped into the pot set on the fire while the other girl fed it with pieces of wood. Zara did not understand their words but she was impressed by the ordinary, cheerful, everyday scene the girls were presenting. They did not glance at the men but continued to chatter and peer into the pot as if it had their entire interest, to the exclusion of any other thoughts.

Zara stared at the pot too, her head lowered. She sensed, rather than saw, the hesitation of the two men, then they passed the fire and moved to the edge of the clearing. The strong smell of beedi smoke drifted back as they sat back on the rocks.

One of the men turned his head and shouted something, Soonya listened, then looked at Zara.

'Raschid say I take you now to Devil Sahib. He wish talk.'

Zara peered up from under the brim of her helmet. 'Talk?

136

What about?' She knew it was useless to ask but it delayed the moment of confrontation.

Soonya shrugged. 'He tell Missie Sahib. Come.'

Zara rose, shaking the dust from her long skirt. She felt her hands trembling but she fought to hold an expression of resigned disapproval on her face. She thought to argue that a gentleman should wait upon a lady, not the other way about, but she knew that Soonya would not understand and anyway, Zara knew her position to be too precarious to risk disobedience. An enraged hillman might think it necessary to beat her into submission, so as not to lose face.

As she followed Soonya, she wondered if Devil Sahib might be open to reasoned argument. Very angry, the girl had said. Did that not suggest her abduction was not to his liking? Might he lend her a pony and point her towards Lahore? Her spirits began to rise a little. She could only prove an embarrassment, an unnecessary burden to his way of life. Surely she could convince him of that. If he was as clever as Soonya had said, the last thing he would want was the British soldiers scouring the hills for her.

Soonya stopped and pointed. She gave Zara a nervous glance and hurried back the way she had come. Zara looked, narrowing her eyes against the sun. She could only see the shape of a man for he stood in the rock shadows while she faced into direct sunlight. She had the impression of height, a long tunic, and wide trousers tucked into knee-high boots. He looked very large.

A hand pointed, indicating a rock, lower than the one on which he was standing. She knew he meant her to sit down on the lower level. It was a masculine ploy, one her own father had used when he required to intimidate a caller. It gave a man the advantage of appearing to look down his nose at the inferior person almost beneath eye level. She almost smiled but restrained herself. This was not a European gentleman but a hillman she must take care not to enrage. As she approached, she noted uneasily that his hand lay on the tulwar hilt. She sat on the rock. It was not in the shade and the sun still prevented her from seeing him clearly. That he was dark-skinned and heavily bearded was all she could make out.

137

The long moments stretched out and he did not speak. Zara grew tired of looking into the sun and lowered her head, staring instead into the water of the pool. The low, intent voice made her start. Her gaze flew upwards but still she could not see his face.

'Why do you ride so far from your people?'

'It – it is not forbidden,' Zara answered as calmly as she could.

'Dangerous,' the voice said. 'There are many dangers in the foothills.'

'I know.' She could not refrain from adding caustically. 'I met two of them.'

He made a sound that might have been a low laugh but Zara doubted it as he went on in a hard voice.

'Only a woman of little sense rides alone.'

'I was not alone –' she began but he interrupted.

'But far ahead, which is nearly the same. Why?'

'Because I wanted to fly and Farah had wings.'

'Farah? Ah yes, the little horse that threw you from her back.'

'She didn't throw me. I forgot to tighten her girth straps. The saddle slipped.'

'But she was unfaithful and ran home. Just like your companion.'

There was such scorn in his voice that Zara started to her feet, resentment flaring.

'Sit down,' he ordered.

Zara obeyed, knowing that his scorn was justified. Raschid and Mahomet would have given him a detailed account of Ralph's hesitation and eventual flight. She stared into the pool gloomily, thinking of Ralph's defection.

'A frightened horse,' he went on, 'can be forgiven, but a frightened man, never.'

'Your men had rifles and two against one –' her voice trailed away.

He gave an exclamation of disgust. 'They would not have killed him. I have forbidden such things. It was amusement for them to bring fear into the heart of a British soldier. Like children they make fun.'

'I suppose that makes it all right! They were just having fun! Yes, indeed, I quite understand. Now can I go home?'

'You have money to buy a horse?' His tone was amused.

'No. I have no money with me but when I get home I can –'

'You can shout to the soldiers and have me arrested? You think I am stupid like Raschid and Mahomet?' The amusement was gone from his voice. It became fierce. 'Do you know why they brought you here?'

Zara thought of what Soonya had said. Perhaps she would be wise to appear ignorant. 'I lost my horse and I was far from Lahore. I thought they meant well and would help me.'

'Oh, yes, they meant well, the fools! By Allah, they meant well and it leaves me no alternative but to accept the gesture.'

Zara felt a quiver run through her. Did he mean to take her as they had planned? A gift for Devil Sahib who had no woman of his own? A shadow fell across the pool and she looked up quickly. He had not moved but the sun had dipped behind the mountains. She saw him more clearly now but he was even more hidden for he had pulled the tail of his turban across his face. She saw only the dark eyes in the dark-skinned face. Eyes, very dark and piercing, eyes that had stared into hers before, the fierce unblinking stare above the Rani's head! She choked back a whimper of fear and dropped her face on to her knees, shutting out the sight of those cruel dark eyes.

She had no strength to move, even when a rattle of pebbles warned her that he had changed his position. He now stood over her and she could hear his breathing.

'You remember me, Missie Sahib. I see that you do. It is most unfortunate for now I must keep you.'

'They will come looking for me,' Zara said desperately. 'You will be found and punished.'

'Do not threaten me, woman,' he growled, 'or you will suffer for it. Hold your tongue and obey, like Soonya and Rahti. No one will come tonight. Tomorrow at dawn we move camp.' A mocking note came into his voice. 'Go back and sleep under the fir branches. You will not be disturbed. I am too weary to have any need of you – tonight.'

Zara stumbled down the track, her booted feet skidding clumsily over the loose stones. Her wits felt dulled by the

139

knowledge that this man, this Devil Sahib, was keeping her, as the two hillmen intended. He had been angry at their action, according to Soonya, but had no intention of jeopardising his own safety by returning her to Lahore because she had seen him in the palace with the Rani. But what did that encounter signify? The Rani might have a hundred lovers for all she cared. She could tell him that she had spoken of it to no one, which was true, but even if he believed her, he would keep her here to protect the Rani and make sure of her own silence.

Damn Ralph for tangling his spur in her lace flounce! She would never have seen the embrace if she had not needed to repair the damage. Would Devil Sahib have let her go if they had not faced each other over the Rani's head? Probably not, for he was still a brigand and had made it clear that he had no wish to come upon a search party of British soldiers.

She had reached the clearing and now must face the curious eyes of the two men and two girls. Her shoulders straightened and she stalked arrogantly towards the shelter, throwing a fierce glance at the watching faces. The girls drew up their veils and the eyes of the men slid away. Zara wished she had a great and fluent command of Urdu so that her tongue could have flayed them with insults. Perhaps it was as well she had not, for even children could be cruelly savage, and these men, though childlike in behaviour, were still men who must resent such words from a woman. They had been kind, according to their lights, she reflected, as she bent into the cave. Besides, the only word she knew that was in the least insulting was the one she had been told by Colonel Lacy that morning.

Shaitan meant devil and this Devil Sahib had been outside the Lacy bungalow last night. Why had he been there, actually inside the garrison, if he feared the soldiers? The hooded man who had joined him could not have been the Colonel. That was too ridiculous but there had to be a reason for Devil Sahib's presence in the garrison. She frowned, trying to recall a scrap of conversation between Ralph and the Colonel, the last time Ralph had come to dinner. Something about a missing consignment. Had it to do with rifles? Although the army did not use jezails like those of Raschid and Mahomet, British rifles might be preferred by some brigands. Had Devil Sahib been in the garrison for the purpose of stealing again from the arms store? A servant of Colonel Lacy's might conceivably be in the pay of Devil Sahib. If a key was necessary and the Colonel had it, how easy to steal into his room at that hour of the night. Zara wished that she had told Colonel Lacy of the meeting she had observed. It was too late now but she must certainly keep that knowledge from Devil Sahib. It would give him even more reason to silence her tongue, perhaps permanently.

Soonya brought a bowl of meat and rice to Zara. She said nothing and returned to the fire to squat beside Rahti. The small camp was very quiet and darkly shadowed. Everyone seemed to be waiting. The sound of booted feet came from the track that led to the pool and a moment later, the tall man strode into view. Mahomet and Raschid straightened from their lounging positions. Devil Sahib looked neither right nor left but strode past the girls towards the cliff track that had brought them on to this plateau. Raschid and Mahomet followed silently. Zara had watched the tall man closely as he had passed through the glow of firelight. The turban end still covered the lower half of his face but it was not on his face her eyes had lingered but on the rifle slung across his shoulders. It was not a jezail but a rifle of the type she had seen on the parade ground in the garrison.

Chapter Fourteen

Zara sat in the cave entrance until the last ember of the fire had fallen into ash. The girls had long since wrapped themselves in blankets and now lay merged with the shadows. The stars gave off a hard brilliance and the air was cold. The three men had not come back. Were they also sleeping, rolled into blankets under the cliff face? Why was she not asleep herself? Devil Sahib had said she would not be disturbed that night. But who could trust a brigand and a thief? She pulled

141

the blanket closer about her shoulders. And what if he did come back? She had little defence against such a large, strong man if he chose to force his will on her.

She shivered, feeling a wave of weariness engulf her. If they were to break camp at dawn, she must try to sleep and pray that her night would be undisturbed. She lay on the rough bed, her head on a folded goatskin, and fell instantly asleep.

When she woke it was to see daylight and her mind marvelled that she could have slept so soundly. She had expected to have passed a wretched night but this morning, in the misty gleam of sunshine, she felt refreshed and determined to plead again for her liberty. Last night Devil Sahib had been weary and angry, annoyed at this unwanted gift. She had seen him with the Rani, but what of it? He did not suspect her of seeing him in the garrison.

She moved into the open and smiled at the girls who were preparing breakfast.

'Will there be anyone by the pool?' she asked.

Soonya shook her head. She said nothing but her gaze held curiosity. 'We leave soon. They say you come with us.'

'I wish to talk to your leader again. I hope he will think it better to let me go.'

'Not here,' the girl said.

Zara stared. 'Not here? Where has he gone?'

Soonya gave her a pitying look. 'You think he tell me? I am only woman. We move, that is all.' She returned to stirring the pot.

Zara hurried down the track to the pool, conscious of the morning chill knifing through the thin cotton of her shirt. She performed her toilet quickly and the pool water in which she washed held an icy coldness. She longed for a hot bath, scented soap and clean clothes. Most of all, she needed a hairbrush. Even her fingers drenched in water could not bring order to the long dark hair. Another few days and it would resemble the coarse fibre matting of the veranda blinds.

When she returned to the fire, Soonya handed her the food bowl in silence. Zara bent to sit beside the girls but Soonya said, low-voiced, 'Better sit in shelter.' Her voice seemed to hold some warning.

142

Zara glanced, perplexed, at Rahti. The girl's gaze slid away and she pulled her veil higher but not before Zara had glimpsed the puffed cheek with its angry colour of a bruise in the making. Rahti's eyes had held a sullen resentment.

She jumped as Soonya hissed fiercely. 'Go now!'

Zara retreated with her bowl of hot thick oatmeal. Why had Rahti given her such a look? They had not even spoken to each other since Rahti knew no English. But yesterday she had smiled and been friendly.

Raschid and Mahomet swaggered into view, shouting loud commands to the girls then seating themselves at a distance from the fire. Both girls rose and carried food bowls at arms length before them. With bowed heads they presented them to the men. For a moment or two their presence was ignored, then the bowls were taken without a word or a look. Raschid and Mahomet ate and talked together as if no one else existed.

Zara realised then how Rahti had acquired her bruised face. A man shamed had to regain his authority by shaming another and since Rahti was Mahomet's woman, she was the logical choice. A cold chill seemed to settle in the pit of Zara's stomach. Had Soonya been beaten too? Did she carry bruised flesh under her clothing, though not as obviously as Rahti?

Devil Sahib had gone from the camp. Did that indicate he had accepted her, Zara Deane, as his woman and there was no more to be said on the subject? The chill in her stomach deepened until she felt her whole body tremble. If he should be angry or shamed, was she now to bear the brunt of it and be beaten like Rahti? But she was not a hillwoman, used to subservience, her mind cried. She was English and used to speaking her mind within reason. He could not expect a change of character, from independence to meekness, catering to his whims and accepting blows with the mute resignation of the hillwomen. That would be too shaming for her.

She put aside the bowl and tried to think. Perhaps if they came upon a village or town, she might escape, promising a rich reward to anyone who would get a message to Lahore. With food and water, a direction to Lahore, she might easily meet the search party. She remembered that she had not a

143

single coin on her. Buying food was impossible although some sympathetic farmer's wife might supply her.

She glanced towards Raschid and Mahomet. They were looking at her but the wide grins of yesterday were gone. There was nothing childlike in the stares today, but hard-eyed malevolence as if she were to blame for their shame at the hands of Devil Sahib. They averted their eyes and Mahomet spat on the ground. Zara tried to keep her expression stony but she shivered inside. Only Devil Sahib stood between her and the men who might beat her to death if the fancy took them. Since Rahti, and probably Soonya too, had been beaten, only their fear of Devil Sahib kept her from their fists.

Raschid rose and tossed his bowl at Soonya. He barked out an order, then turned away, followed by Mahomet. The two girls began to stack the cooking pots into a large wicker basket. They moved about the camp, gathering blankets and articles of clothing. Soonya came to Zara. She looked critically at Zara's dusty but well-fitting riding boots.

'Better no boots.'

'No boots?' Zara looked surprised. 'I know the ponies have no saddles or stirrups but I prefer to keep my boots on.'

Soonya smiled, that half-pitying smile again. 'Men take ponies. Women walk, carry baskets. Better no boots. Soon feet get hard.' She picked up the blanket and goatskins and walked away to add them to the second wicker basket.

Zara bit her lip angrily and stared at the stony uneven ground. Walk barefoot through that? Her feet would be torn to shreds before she had covered half a mile.

With hooves clattering, the two ponies surged on to the small plateau. Raschid and Mahomet looked down arrogantly from their lordly heights and snapped at the women, flicking Zara an indifferent glance. Raschid said something and Soonya shook her head. Raschid shrugged, wheeled the pony, overturning one of the baskets, and rode off without looking back.

Zara moved forward and helped repack the spilled basket. Rahti gave her a cold look and snatched the cooking pot out of Zara's hands.

Zara straightened. 'Will you tell Rahti,' she said to Soonya,

144

'that I am sorry she was beaten but I do not consider myself to blame for the actions of her man or yours. I had no wish to come here. They brought me and I could do nothing about it.'

'Rahti knows it is so but hurting just same.'

Zara softened. 'Yes. I am truly sorry. What can I do to help?'

Soonya shrugged. 'Maybe when hurting more, she let you carry basket.' She looked at Rahti's stiff face and rigid back as the girl placed the basket on her head. 'But now not good time.'

A shout from Raschid had Soonya bending down to pick up her own basket. The two girls walked out of the clearing in the wake of the ponies and Zara followed. There seemed nothing else she could do for the men glanced back continually as if they feared she might suddenly disappear. Where to, she wondered, looking about her. The whole area was just hill and rock with the occasional patch of grass and the glitter of water jetting from a cleft. She had thought to turn and see the wheatlands, the rivers, and human life spread out before her but they must have gone through a pass which cut off the view of the lower foothills. Behind and all about her were hills and rocks. The camp site had been well chosen and although the Himalayas lay ahead, only a mountain man could find the track that led down to civilisation.

Zara followed the swaying figure of Soonya. How gracefully she walked, her neck erect, balancing the basket upon her head. Only when they crossed a particularly rock-strewn patch did Soonya need to raise a hand to hold the basket steady. Otherwise its balance was perfect, leaving Soonya's arms free. Zara soon found that the girl's criticism of her boots was well-founded. The leather soles skidded, unable to grip as bare feet did. But Soonya's small feet were hardened, the soles thickened to withstand the rough ground. How could Zara with her soft English feet walk this track barefoot? She needed to be shod when she made her bid to escape. Rather blistered feet than raw, bleeding ones.

The sun was well into the sky now, the snow caps of the Himalayas soaring like crystal stalagmites into an upturned blue bowl of sky. Dark shapes of birds sailed overhead, their wide wings barely moving as the air currents took them in sweeping, wheeling flight. Hawks, kites, mountain eagles, all floating effortlessly, able to go where they wished. Zara's boots skidded again and she almost fell. This was no time for bird-watching, she decided, and remembered the beautiful kingfisher by the willow-shaded pool where she had halted with Farah before this nightmare began. How long ago that seemed. Her eyes stung with the memory of that double desertion. Farah's was instinctive and could be forgiven, but Ralph's had been deliberate. Perhaps self-preservation was instinctive too, but she could never forgive him.

The chill of the morning was gone now and the sun was fierce, beating down on Zara's shoulders under the cotton shirt. She still wore the split riding skirt over her breeches and was tempted to remove it to make walking easier; however some instinct warned her not to reveal the shape of her body in the close-fitting breeches. Raschid and Mahomet might see it as a sign of low breeding and lose whatever fragile respect they still held for her. Only a female of ill-repute exposed her body before the eyes of men. Respectable Indian women swathed themselves from top to toe in loose-fitting garments, faces veiled in modesty.

Almost without realising it, she found they had left the rock-strewn path and were moving over damp grass. The ground felt marshy and her aching legs and feet welcomed the change from hard rock to soft grass. The ground still held that early morning scent so familiar since she had arrived in India. She looked about seeing bushes and small clumps of trees. A small fertile valley, obviously well irrigated, flourished in the craggy hillside. Was this the new camp? She hoped so for she felt the rawness of her heels and knew she would find them blistered when she removed her boots.

The two men dismounted and disappeared into the bushes, leaving the ponies to crop the grass. Rahti unwrapped a cotton bundle, revealing some small flat cakes of bread. The men returned, took a handful each and retreated some distance away to sit on a fallen tree. Zara sat down beside Soonya.

'Is this the camp?'

146

Soonya smiled and shook her head. 'Many miles yet. Walk till dark.'

Zara's heart sank. Many miles yet and already her feet were throbbing painfully. She sighed and glanced at Rahti. The girl was looking at her. Soonya said something and Rahti hesitated, then held out the opened bundle.

Zara took a flat cake and smiled. 'Thank you, Rahti.' The spicy scent had come to her, making her aware of her hunger, but she took only one. She held Rahti's eyes, still smiling, and the girl shrugged, showing the faintest glimmer of a softening of her expression.

'I tell her,' Soonya said, 'that beating not fault of you. She knew that already and say for you to please Devil Sahib and he no more angry with Mahomet.'

The spicy bread seemed to lose all taste for Zara. She chewed and swallowed mechanically, every piece gathering into a heavy lump in the pit of her stomach. She coughed and Soonya handed her a mug of water from a goatskin container. When Zara had sufficient control of her voice, she asked, 'Will he come to the camp tonight?'

Soonya shrugged. 'Maybe yes, maybe no.' She glanced at Zara and a smile touched her lips. 'You like now carry basket for Rahti?'

Zara gave Soonya a searching look but the wide dark eyes stared back innocently if unconvincingly. Zara could not help laughing. 'Clever Soonya. I carry Rahti's basket to show that I agree and save her more beatings from Mahomet.'

Soonya giggled, putting a hand over her mouth. She showed pleasure at being called clever. 'Devil Sahib you will be liking. He have good face and always taking off clothes.'

Zara stared. 'What?' she asked faintly.

Soonya nodded vehemently. 'Not just spring when everybody go to river for washing but more time. Raschid see him go like fish all down river.'

'Fish? Whatever are you talking about?'

'Move like fish. Raschid he laughing at pushing water.' She thrust her arms forward then swept them sideways and Zara understood.

'You mean Devil Sahib can swim like – well, like a fish.'

'Like fish, yes.' She looked slyly at Zara. 'Maybe you like be fish too?'

Zara shook her head. 'No, I can't swim.'

As they rose to move on, Zara gave Devil Sahib one good point. A man who could swim and who did it frequently, must surely be a great deal cleaner than either Raschid or Mahomet who washed only in the spring. It was not much of a consolation but if she had to be his woman, he might let her have some facility for keeping herself clean.

A whirring sound above them brought Zara's head up sharply. A billowy pink cloud seemed to engulf the sun then passed as if propelled by a sudden air current. The cloud resolved itself into pink and white bodies, bright red bills and long legs like thin red sticks incongruously trailing behind.

'Flamingo,' she exclaimed. 'How beautiful and graceful in flight. Are we near a river or lake?'

'Many lake, not so much till rain come so they look. Soon many lake before snow.'

'Snow? Do we go so high?' Zara stared up at the mountains. So many places where nomads and hill people could hide. Brigands too, like Devil Sahib. She shivered. How could one girl be found in this immensity of mountain? How long would they go on searching before giving her up as lost?

Raschid's voice made her jump. She looked round to see the men already mounted. Soonya rose and picked up her basket. Rahti looked at Zara with the neutral expression of one who awaits to see if the terms laid out are accepted. Zara gritted her teeth against the scorching pain of her feet. She knew the blisters on her soles and heels had broken and the raw skin was chafing against the leather. Rahti was prepared to be friend or enemy, there was no in-between for a hillwoman. Zara picked up the basket.

They moved on. With the additional burden of the basket, Zara's progress was even more clumsy. Her arms ached from holding it aloft. Her carriage over rough ground was unlike Soonya's swaying motion but she was filled with a grim determination not to have Mahomet order Rahti to take the basket from her. She knew that both men watched her efforts,

148

with what emotion she had no idea, but her slitted eyes glittered defiance if their glances met. Everything about her ached, her feet were balls of fire, her vision blurred by sweat, but she went on, her only thought to keep the swaying back of Soonya in sight. She found herself blinking constantly for Soonya seemed to float and merge into the landscape, one moment ahead, then to one side, then nothing, then ahead again. Why couldn't the girl stay in sight.

They might have been walking for ever but suddenly the sky was dark and a gusty chill wind blew. Zara felt the sodden shirt cling coldly to her skin. It was not so hard now to open her eyes. Stars above, not the sun, and the change was bewildering. Rahti's face swam before her, arms reaching up for the basket. The girl was smiling as she prised Zara's stiff fingers from the wicker basket. Soonya was there too bringing Zara's arms down gently for they seemed to remain in that ridiculously upraised position even though the basket was gone.

'Very good, very good,' Soonya said soothingly and her palms rubbed Zara's flesh roughly, easing the aching joints. 'Rahti now friend. Raschid and Mahomet have much fear.'

'Fear?' echoed Zara dully. 'Fear of what?'

Soonya giggled behind her hand. Zara thought vaguely that it must be an Indian custom to cover an open mouth, even a laughing one.

'You, Missie Sahib. They say your eyes like tiger eyes, little yellow, much fierce.' She put her head on one side and regarded Zara thoughtfully. 'Sometime Devil Sahib have eyes little yellow when angry. Maybe he not angry tonight.'

If there was meaning in the words, Zara chose to ignore them. She looked about her. 'Is this the camp? Do we stay here tonight?'

Soonya nodded. 'We make fire. Raschid and Mahomet build shelter. When he come he bring fresh meat for pot. Rahti make chapatti.'

Zara did not need to ask who was bringing fresh meat. Instead she asked if there was a village near by.

'No, Missie Sahib.' Her face was questioning.

'If,' said Zara slowly, 'we are to walk a hundred miles a day,

149

I must have some sandals. Riding boots are for riding, not walking. I cannot go barefoot like you. I have never done so and my feet are soft.'

'I say boots no good,' Soonya said. 'Now knowing, yes? Shelter all done now. Missie Sahib take off boots?'

'Not until someone rides to a market and brings back a pair of sandals.'

Zara hobbled toward the leafy branch shelter the men had constructed. They moved away as she approached, avoiding her eyes. She looked after them with bitterness in her heart. If only she had tiger's claws as well as eyes, she would happily rend them apart for bringing her to this situation. She sat down, her back against a rock, and regarded her boots in miserable contemplation. They were probably half-full of mangled flesh. She had no ointment or bandages and even if she had, she could never fit her feet into the boots again. Her feet throbbed furiously but she dared not remove the boots.

It was a relief to let her body sag against the rock. She closed her eyes. Her lips felt dry and salty and the dried sweat on her body chafed like grit. Her only satisfaction was that she had kept up with the girls and given the two hillmen no cause to despise her. Had she been less than Charles Deane's daughter, she might have wept from sheer frustration and pain, but the Deanes had pride of family, if little else. Whatever befell them was hidden from the world while they schemed to make good without loss of face. Hadn't they both done just that, Charles with his marriage to Mrs Makin and she with her engagement to Captain Browne? But now her own plan had gone awry, even before she had been captured by the hillmen. Her head rolled on to her shoulder, her body sliding to the ground. Camp noises became muted and her mind stilled, sinking into darkness.

Perhaps she slept for only a short time. She came awake to a numbing cramp in the bent arm under her body. Cold and stiffness combined to make movement difficult. She rolled on to her back, holding down the gasps of pain as her limbs set up a protesting ache. They would have to leave her tomorrow. Unless one of the men gave up his pony, and that she knew was quite unthinkable, there would be no brave showing in the morning. This Deane was spent and she knew it. Looking up through the branches of the shelter she regarded the stars, cold, impersonal points of light, the same stars that had watched her hopeful journey by steamship and train, that had glowed brightly over garrison and Lacy garden and now shone down on a lone English girl lost in the mountains. Would she ever look at them again from another place? Her eyes pricked, but she fought back the tears of self-pity. Headstrong, Ralph had said, and he had been right. She should never have outpaced him, forcing him to follow her so far from the garrison. She deserved his anger, deserved to be left to her fate and fear had driven him to do just that. She could understand, perhaps forgive, but she could not forget the sword he had not attempted to draw in her defence.

She linked her hands behind her head and listened wearily to the stirring in the camp. The girls' high voices, the clatter of cooking pots, the thud of ponies' hooves. A new voice calling made her tense, a dull throbbing beginning in her breast. Had he come, the leader? She raised her head. There were three men now, standing to one side, and she saw the flash of a knife as the girls prepared whatever had been brought for the pot. Her shelter was just beyond the circle of light cast by the fire. She could watch, unseen, and be warned of the man's approach, not taken by surprise as in the cave. There was nothing she could do anyway and at the moment she was too tired to put up even a token resistance.

She saw him reflected in the firelight, tall and powerful-looking, his head inclined slightly towards Raschid and Mahomet who seemed to be explaining something, their words cutting in on each other. They glanced occasionally towards the shelter but the leader did not look in her direction. What were they telling him? Something about her? The way she had looked at them? Urging him to take stern measures against his woman who should not be allowed to show defiance to a lordly male?

The man spoke at last. It was a curt command and Raschid turned, removing a sack from the leader's pony. He handed it over and Devil Sahib slung it over his shoulder. Then he was walking towards her. Zara lay still and closed her eyes,

151

feigning sleep. She heard the soft thud of a bag being dropped beside her. She flinched involuntarily and heard a soft
laugh.

'You are not asleep and have no need to pretend. The men
said you did well today.'

'How kind of them,' Zara murmured, a caustic note in her
voice. 'It would have been kinder to offer me a ride.'

'Hillmen never let their women ride.'

Zara opened her eyes fully and saw the glint of teeth. A
swift anger rose, overpowering her caution.

'I am not a hillwoman and well you know it! If you think I
shall walk tomorrow, you are very mistaken.'

Squatting, he sank on to his heels, and regarded her
gravely. 'And why is that if I order it?' His voice was calm,
like that of a reasonable man awaiting enlightenment.

'Because my boots were made for riding, not walking.'

'Take off your boots then. Boots no good.' A large hand
closed round Zara's ankle and he gave the boot a tug.

'No!' Zara gasped, coming instantly upright. Red-hot wire
seemed to be piercing through her flesh and her face became
damp with perspiration.

The girls had tossed more wood on to the fire and the glow
now reached to the shelter. Zara saw the man frown.

'Such vanity,' he said with scorn. 'Why wear boots that are
too small for walking?'

Zara breathed deeply. How could she convince this man
that not all boots were the same?

'They are not too small when I ride, but my feet have grown
big with walking in the heat.' She paused. 'If I take off my
boots, my feet will not go into them again.' She eyed the tight
boots morosely and muttered in an undertone, 'Though I'm
sure they'll be all of a piece in rawness.'

'We will see,' the man said and drew a shining blade from
his waistband scabbard.

Zara's eyes flew from the blade to the man's face. 'No, you
cannot,' she gasped in alarm. 'They will be smaller tomorrow.'

The man paused, his brows upraised. 'Your boots? How
can this be?'

'No, no, I mean my feet! They are swollen tonight but –'

'But tomorrow worse. I will look tonight. You have no wish to become a cripple, I think, with untended sores?'

Zara shook her head mutely. If this man was determined to cut off her boots, she could not stop him, but her mind cringed from walking barefoot on the sharp, stony ground.

'Lie back,' he ordered.

She obeyed, covering her eyes with a forearm, expecting the pain of the knife blade slicing through her skin. She lay tense, feeling the run of the sharp edge as it moved from knee to ankle then across the top of her foot. The blade moved deftly, she knew the stitchings had parted, then she felt his hand on her bare skin just above the ankle. The touch was brief but now she felt the cold air on her foot and could hardly believe the boot was gone. The sheer relief of being able to move her toes freely brought her up on to her elbows. The ruins of her riding boots lay to one side and she found herself staring at a pair of red and white objects in fascinated horror. The skin on her toes and heels was fiery red and raw-looking. Deep indentations from the stitched leather panels were scored down and across the length of her feet. Blood still oozed through broken blisters.

'Thank you,' Zara said and shivered as a cool breeze fluttered the leaves. 'They feel so much better, almost – almost wonderful.' The pricking began behind her eyes as she stared at her ravaged, almost useless feet. She must not break down before this man and show him the depths of her misery, she resolved. Her feet would heal, of course they would, but not by tomorrow if he ordered another march. She steadied her breathing with an effort and looked up at him.

He was staring at her and in the fire's glow, his expression was of anger, his dark eyes almost hidden under thick dark brows drawn together in a scowl.

'Wonderful? You think these –' he stabbed a finger at her toes, 'are wonderful?'

Zara felt her control slipping. She had gone through fear and despair, the increasing hopelessness of her position, physical pain and the tension of not knowing what this man intended with her. All that was left was screaming hysteria and the man's outraged expression as he glanced at her toes seemed so farcical that Zara felt her mind waver in that direction. Her breathing became ragged, jerky, and she fought to hold back a hysterical giggle.

He must have heard the choking, gasping sounds for he gripped her shoulders and shook her until her head rolled wildly under the fierce digging fingers.

'Stop that or I shall hit you!' The voice came curt and icy cold, like the first blast of winter air when a door is flung open. Her body began to shake and he picked up a blanket and threw it across her.

'You will ride tomorrow,' he said, still in that curt voice. 'I shall order Mahomet to walk.'

'No, no, you must not do that!' Zara raised herself in alarm. 'Please, not that.'

He frowned. 'Is your brain addled too, woman? You complain of walking, now you have no wish to ride.'

'But not their horses, please. They will lose face and beat their women if one of them has to walk and allow me to ride. You said yourself that a hillman will not walk while his woman rides.'

'And you, Missie Sahib, reminded me that you were not a hillwoman.'

Zara pressed her hands over her aching eyes. 'I know, I know, but I will not take Mahomet's pony, nor that of Raschid.'

'Because of their women?'

'They have been kind to me. It would be a poor return if they were beaten for it. You are a hillman too. You must understand.'

'And how do you propose to travel if you will not ride?'

'I was hoping someone might get me some sandals from a bazaar. Very cheap ones, just to keep my feet from the sharp stones.' She stared at him pleadingly, her hazel eyes feverishly bright as they caught the reflected gold from the firelight.

He turned away from her to the small sack he had dropped when he entered. Out of this he drew a stone pot and a number of cotton cloths. Zara felt the blissfully cool ointment being smeared liberally over her entire feet, then the narrow

154

cotton cloths, like bandages, wrapped her feet closely from toe to ankle.

'That is – that is most kind,' she whispered, her mind still dizzy with amazement.

He did not look at her but thrust a hand into the sack again. A pair of wide-soled leather sandals with ankle strappings dangled from his fingers.

'Big size for big feet.' He seemed to find the remark amusing and pointed to her bandaged feet. 'Big now, but small later. Can move strings.' He gave her a brief grin and rose. 'Very good hillman, yes? Think of woman.'

He strode away towards the fire, leaving Zara with a weird feeling that she had been talking to two different people. These last words had been such as Soonya used, yet part of their previous conversation had been conducted very much in the King's English.

Chapter Fifteen

Zara drifted into wakefulness, blinking up at the stars. The camp was very still, only a few smouldering ashes glimmering in the circle of stones. Humped figures completely enveloped in blankets lay scattered and unmoving, like large boulders after a rockfall. The air was very cold and she realised it was that which had awakened her. The soft blanket had slipped from about her shoulders. She tucked it round her neck and turned on to her side. Her gaze fell on the large blanket roll beside her. She noted the intricate design of the weaving, the bright, almost garish, reds and yellows that seemed to offer more warmth than a plain grey blanket. Not only offered but gave warmth, she reasoned hazily, and curled herself close to the blanket roll. Warmth flooded through and about her and she began to drift into sleep again, only wondering in a vague way why her heartbeat should sound so extraordinarily loud.

When she woke again it was morning, one of those pearly dawns with only the rim of the world edged pale yellow. The stars, so bright in the darkness, were almost invisible as the sun took over the task of illumination. Zara stretched, pushing aside her blanket. She turned her head towards the blanket roll and reached out a hand to touch it. It wasn't warm any more, in fact it wasn't even a blanket roll, although the pattern was as she recalled it. It lay crumpled as if tossed aside by one of those recumbent figures. She frowned, then her heart gave a jerk as she realised the truth. Of course it was a rolled blanket but Devil Sahib had been inside it. The warmth had come from him and two hearts beat louder than one.

She peered out of the shelter, scanning the clearing. Three men stood together beyond the fire now being revived by Rahti. Dressed as usual in their stained tunics and baggy trousers, Raschid and Mahomet were smoking their small brown beedis. Devil Sahib was smoking too, but what appeared to be a slim, black cheroot. A plume of blue smoke drifted upwards on the still air. He turned to look at the girls and spoke a few words in Urdu. Soonya glanced up, nodding. She rose and wiped her hands down the sides of her tunic. She approached Devil Sahib and he handed something to her, then Soonya came towards the shelter.

'Devil Sahib say to take you in bushes. Little water coming from rock to wash face. He say to give you this.'

Zara looked at Soonya's grimy, open palm. On it lay a comb, a white bone, thick-toothed comb. Zara drew in her breath sharply. She glanced over at Devil Sahib but he had his back to her. She took the comb from Soonya and stared at it. When you have nothing, everything is a luxury, even a plain bone comb that might have been bought in any bazaar for a few annas. At this moment, it was more precious than the silver-backed dressing-table set her father had bought her when she was twenty-one.

'It's wonderful,' she said, then remembered the man's reaction to that word last night. Her breath caught on a giggle and that stupid pricking began behind her eyes.

Soonya was regarding her with a puzzled frown. 'You not wanting?'

'Indeed I do, very much.' Zara took the comb. 'You have one also?'

156

The girl shook her head. 'Too much hurting. Oil better and stick for scratching.' Her teeth showed in a grin. 'One day I see fat memsahib slap ayah. She screaming, ayah pulling out hair.' she looked expectantly at Zara. 'You pulling hair now?'

Zara grinned back. 'No, I am not, you sadistic creature! I shall wet my hair very thoroughly first. I have no intention of pulling out my own hair for your enjoyment. Where are my new sandals?'

'Sandals?' Soonya eyed them in surprise. 'Nobody been bazaar.'

Zara smiled. She rather thought she would keep Soonya in the dark. Her tongue would spread the word to the other three who might consider that Devil Sahib was being too soft with his woman. He had been kind in bringing ointment and cloth for her feet, the sandals and now the comb. She did not intend to show him in a poor light to his men. Any embarrassment to his dignity would rebound on herself. Since she was in his power, she meant to do nothing to earn his anger.

She tossed the blanket from her legs and stared at her feet. They hardly hurt at all, but she must reduce the bandaging or even these large sandals would not cover them. Unwinding the cloth slowly, she realised that Devil Sahib had wrapped round extra cloths for night-time comfort. The feet themselves were still bandaged neatly and protectively. The extra cloths she folded carefully and put into the pocket of her riding skirt. The sandals, stout-soled with very little upperwork, slipped on easily, to be held in place by the leather straps. She rose and took a tentative step. It was quite painless. How had he known which size to bring and, for that matter, how had he known that her riding boots would blister her feet? Since she was not a hillwoman it would be a logical conclusion to reach. He was not completely of the hills like Raschid and Mahomet. She doubted that they had ever been in the Rajah's palace or in the garrison town. Devil Sahib had been in both places so would know more about the English.

When they returned to the camp, Zara's hair lay wet and sleek to her shoulders. How different it felt from the thick rough tangle of the last couple of days. she tucked the comb securely into the pocket of her skirt, for it was something she would hate to lose. Her feet looked big and ungainly below the slim-fitting jodhpurs, rather like the elongated boots of a clown she remembered in London.

'Like some old General with gout,' she murmured.

A shadow fell across her and she looked up, smiling, expecting to see Soonya with a bowl of boiled oatmeal. Her smile faltered as she saw Devil Sahib. Behind him was Soonya who laid down the bowl and retreated without a word.

Devil Sahib stared down at her feet. His mouth seemed to twitch slightly. Zara drew up her knees and covered her feet with her skirt.

'Feet good?' he asked.

'Yes, thank you,' Zara said in a small voice and lowered her gaze. 'I can walk today.'

'Eat first,' he said. 'Not much journey. Just to high river. You take off clothes tonight.

Zara's head jerked up. She tried to read his expression but all she caught was the glint of teeth as he smiled and swung about. She watched the tall lean figure stride towards the pony lines. With his height, it was no problem to swing one booted foot over the rough flanks, then he was gone. Where did he go each day, she wondered, then sighed and picked up the food bowl. Tonight, he had said. Was that his way of telling her that personal freedom was at an end? That tonight she must become his woman?

She ate her porridge slowly and contemplated her position as calmly as she could, bringing all the platitudes to bear on the subject. What cannot be cured must be endured, and the favourite expression of her father, needs must when the devil drives. Very apt, she thought wryly, and since she was in no position to do anything about it, she must make the best of it. What was a well-brought up young lady to do in these circumstances? Consult a book of etiquette or write to the *Lady's Companion Magazine* for guidance? She imagined their reply:

My dear Miss Deane: while we have the greatest sympathy for you in your time of trouble, do remember that you are an English lady and must uphold the honour and dignity of the British Empire on all occasions. a lady must hide her true feelings and

158

meet adversity with a smile, keeping her mind on higher things.
Our thoughts will be with you, my dear Miss Deane.

Zara smiled in self-mockery and raised her eyes to the wide blue sky. Only God could release her from this situation and she was too much of a realist to believe that the British Army would come storming in with a last-minute rescue. They would not have the faintest idea where she was.

With her chin resting on her knees, she thought of Devil Sahib. Surely he had a real name in spite of what Soonya had said. His English was good, when he chose to use it. Had he received some education in an English-staffed school? There were many about. A well-educated brigand? A budmash, a thief? To bring her those sandals he must have gone to a village market or bazaar. Could there be one nearby? She doubted they would take the risk of passing through one. An Englishwoman in riding habit, escorted only by a group of hill people, must be unusual enough to cause comment. Of course, Devil Sahib would avoid habitation for his own reasons and since he had a pony, the sandals could have been purchased miles away.

Raschid's harsh voice cut through her thoughts and she looked up. They were striking camp, the men already mounted. Rahti and Soonya had the baskets packed. Zara rose, checked to assure herself of the safety of her comb, then caught sight of the small sack from which Devil Sahib had produced the sandals. The stone jar of ointment was still within its folds. The bag was of coarse hessian with a drawstring. The comb and cotton cloths were transferred and Zara looped the cord over her arm. It was her sack and contained her own belongings. She felt inordinately proud to possess something of her own, however pathetic. Perhaps she could add to it as time went on. Devil Sahib might bring her something else if she pleased him.

Dear God, she thought, appalled. I am beginning to think like a hillwoman, resigned to having a lord and master, a man who could use or abuse her at will. She thought of Rahti's poor bruised face. The girl had taken her beating without a sound, submissive and unprotesting. She, Zara Deane, did not intend to become that much of a hillwoman. She would not cower in silence, waiting for the man's anger to expend itself. Brave talk, she jeered to herself, what could she do against a man topping six feet in height with a body tough and strengthened by hard living? Not a great deal, but he would certainly be aware of her displeasure. Displeasure! How very genteel that sounded. She joined the girls, walking carefully on her bandaged feet. Rahti smiled and shook her head as Zara mimed her willingness to carry the basket, then touched her own cheek and pointed at Zara's All three girls looked down gravely at the two splayed white cotton lumps. Zara's mind went to the penguins in Regent's Park Zoo and she began to giggle as she remembered their ungainly way of walking.

When she glanced up, both girls were shaking with laughter, their palms clamped tightly over their mouths. They might have stood giggling helplessly all day but Raschid's impatient bellow had the two hillwomen reaching for their baskets with unsteady hands, their shoulders still shaking.

Soonya turned a laughing gaze on Zara. 'Rahti say she carry. Hurting feet come later than beating. Is good, all sharing, yes?'

Zara nodded. 'Very good.' It occurred to her that even in this short time she had grown quite fond of these two hillwomen. Perhaps because they were women, she supposed. At least they would understand her problems, having similar ones themselves. She would be lost without Soonya's grasp of the English language, too. The thought of travelling with only Raschid and Mahomet as company was frightening. With Devil Sahib away for the most part of the day, how much control did he exercise over the two men in his absence? Hopefully, enough, and they did have their own women.

They moved on, climbing higher, and the sun beat down, warming Zara's shoulders and drying her hair. The track twisted, curling round solid rocks, sometimes so narrow that the ponies had to be led. Here and there were surprisingly green valleys, a welcome relief for the eyes after the barren rock-strewn pathways.

Zara was glad of her pith helmet but her shoulders under

the thin shirt were prickling with heat and there was nothing she could do to protect them. Her legs in the tight jodhpurs, which she had only infrequently removed, felt prickly too, especially about the waist. Prickly heat, the curse of the fair-skinned Europeans in India, was already making itself felt. She thought of Delia Pringle who took so much care of her skin, the creams and lotions, the always present parasol. How would Delia fare in this position? She glanced at her hands and wrists. They were already honey-coloured. She supposed her face to be the same although she had not looked into a mirror for many days. Perhaps it was as well, she mused, for the elegant well-dressed Miss Deane would certainly not be found looking back at her.

A sound caught her attention. They were crossing a shallow stony valley beyond which were trees and glimpses of green. It sounded like water. Devil Sahib had mentioned a river. Not far, he had said. Was this where they were to camp? The mere thought of water made Zara lick her dry lips.

The ground rose a little as they reached the trees. Once within, those great-leaved branches must cut off the sun's rays. She tried to catch up the girls, hurrying on clumsy feet. Raschid and Mahomet had cantered ahead. The two hill-women continued their pace, the rhythmic sway of their bodies unvarying. Time was of no importance. Today, tomorrow, it was all the same. Life would go on, why be impatient to live it? It was a brief span, after all. The philosophy of the East, thought Zara, and slowed her own pace. What was she hurrying for? Fate had already mapped out her life.

Raschid and Mahomet were sitting on their ponies, gazing slightly downwards. Zara joined the girls on a slight ridge. Stretching out below was an almost perfect circle of thick green grass, bushes hanging heavy with fruit. Tamarisk and jacaranda stood high and willow trees, wide and dense, bowed to a narrow, glinting sapphire stream. Splashes of colour dotted the grass, wild flowers of every imaginable colour and thicker clumps had tucked and rooted themselves under the bushes. Zara stood entranced. A perfect valley, almost self-supporting with its watercourse and fruit, shade and

161

sunshine. A patch of lighter colour caught her eye and she recognised it as wheat.

As they moved over the grass, Zara saw that the small stream disappeared into the lift of the farther crest. It was from the other side she heard the splash of water. She questioned Soonya.

'This comes little sideways,' she nodded at the stream. 'Then go back join big river. Not so big now but when rain comes, very big. Cliff stop little getting too big so we stay now for little time. Plenty animal come.'

The ponies were let loose. Raschid and Mahomet drew their tulwars and began hacking at tree branches. The girls made for a circular stone fire pit under the lee of a jutting rock ledge. The tasks were performed routinely, the girls knowing exactly where the dry twigs were to be found to start a fire, the men with their piles of leafy branches, cutting and weaving the pliable stems into thatching.

Zara wandered towards the ridge. No one glanced at her as she passed. Rahti and Soonya were setting up a spit over the flames, the men had eyes only for the blades of their flashing knives. The ridge was not very high but afforded protection for the enclosed valley. Zara looked over the crest and caught her breath. The source of the river was up there in the mountains; it seemed to leap from them in a dazzling burst of spray to fall into a rocky gorge whose sides had eroded over the centuries. The water foamed and surged, a downward torrent until the lie of the land slowed its progress and it became milder, slower-moving and foam-free. She followed its winding course to a deeper indentation in the hillside almost directly below her. Here it formed a placid pool before winding between great boulders to become once again a river heading for the lowlands.

Beyond, the countryside was a pattern of green and brown, the wispy smoke of isolated habitations spiralling into the cloudless sky. Patches of cultivation merged with areas of rock and all part of the same foothills. She tried to see into the hazy distance. Lahore was down there. The garrison, Colonel and Mrs Lacy, Mrs Fraser, Delia Pringle – and, of course, the gallant Captain Browne! Had they given her up as lost? Was

Ralph putting a brave face on it, accepting sympathy as a broken-hearted lover on the verge of marriage? How sad to have his bride-to-be so cruelly torn from his arms within two weeks of their marriage! Poor young man, we must all be extra kind to him. How bravely he is taking it. What a comfort dear Delia must be, for she has suffered herself during that dreadful business with Major Deverill. Yes indeed, thought Zara savagely, what a wonderful opportunity for Delia to prove her worth by pointing out that Ralph must not blame himself, for though quite charming, of course, Miss Deane had a tendency to behave a little incautiously.

Zara looked down into the blue-green water of the pool. How tempting it looked. Not too deep, and a short grassy slope ran down to its rocky sides. In contrast to the fresh clean water, her body felt hot and sticky. She needed to bathe and change her clothes but both were impossible. Neither Soonya nor Rahti seemed to have any personal bundles. They were content to wear the same filthy garments for days on end. People on the move must, of necessity, travel light, but they were young women. Had they no feminine fancies for new tunics and trousers, even a fresh cap or veil? Perhaps there was a special time for new clothes. The end of a journey or a festival, perhaps with the settling into winter quarters.

Soonya's voice called to her and she went back to the camp. The shelters were in place. There were three of them, one a little larger and apart from the others. She remembered Devil Sahib's words. *You take off clothes tonight.* She avoided looking at the thickly thatched shelter where she must spend the night with the leader.

The girls were turning the chunks of meat on the spit. To one side a pot bubbled. Raschid and Mahomet were stretched out under the shade of a tree smoking their beedis. Did Devil Sahib bring them every night, Zara wondered? Neither man had left camp but fresh meat had come with the leader, along with the sandals he had brought for her. The cheroots he smoked, too, had to come from some larger village, one that had Europeans passing through, for they were superior to the small Indian beedis. If she could find such a place and have the luck to see a European, she might throw herself on his mercy and ask for protection. He must, at the least, promise that a message would be sent to Lahore informing them of her whereabouts and that she still lived.

Zara went to the small stream and knelt, cupping her hands in the water and splashing her face and neck. Without a towel, she had to wipe her forearm across her face, but the sun was warm. She had rolled up the sleeves of her shirt, no longer white but a patchy grey with stains of grass and perspiration. She regarded her bare arms. No longer white, either, but at least the honey colour was more pleasing than dirty white. How long before this cotton shirt fell into ruin? It was an alarming thought. Devil Sahib would have to buy her another or see his woman go naked! She smiled. No hillman would risk honour by allowing such a shameless thing. He might, of course, bundle her into one of those enveloping burkas, the purdah robe where a woman's view seemed as limited as if she were looking out of a Post Office pillar-box from the inside.

The sun was low in the sky when Devil Sahib returned to camp. He came through the trees, the pony's hooves thudding softly on the grass. Zara, sitting at the entrance to the shelter, watched him. He rode easily, relaxed, as if guiding the pony with knees and hands, untroubled by lack of saddle stirrups. Because he was tall and long-legged, the pony seemed too small. She pictured him riding a high-stepping stallion, like those she had seen on the parade ground, not a sturdy, rough-coated hill pony.

As he dismounted by the fire, Zara felt her nerves tighten. He was looking very grim. Firelight touched the hard planes of his face, etching shadows on cheeks and eye sockets. He dropped his rifle and pack, sinking on to his haunches by the fire. Mahomet led away the pony, saying no word, and the girls prepared a bowl of food. Rahti laid it before Devil Sahib and retreated into the darkness, casting Soonya a nervous glance.

Devil Sahib sat for a moment longer, frowning into the fire, then he picked up the bowl and ate with slow intent deliberation, the frown still on his face. Zara saw the men and girls moving quietly beyond the circle of firelight. Their brief sideways glances were cautious as if not wanting to be caught staring at the leader. Their faces were curious but wary. Zara supposed that experience had given them the key to the moods of the leader. A man in anger was best left alone. Zara studied the face under the turban. Was it anger? Some men in angry mood shouted and cursed like Raschid and Mahomet. This man's anger was contained, perhaps anger mixed with puzzlement. Was that why he was frowning? Had something gone wrong at the garrison? Had his accomplice not appeared with the Colonel's keys?

Colonel Lacy was not a fool. Losses from the armoury could not go unnoticed. A trap set, an ambush laid perhaps, from which Devil Sahib had barely escaped. The thought pleased and alarmed her at the same time. His capture would not free her. She might be glad that the army had caught a thief but he would not implicate himself in her abduction. No one knew of his existence, not even Ralph. What might Raschid and Mahomet do with her if Devil Sahib were arrested? They must dispose of her, that was certain. A shiver ran through her. What did they say? Better the devil you know. But she didn't know this man. A comb and a pair of sandals, a salve for the feet might be mere common sense. A pony with a damaged fetlock could not walk. Neither could a woman.

Her heart gave a jump as he rose in one lithe movement. He stared towards the shelter, then bent to pick up his rifle and pack. Zara held her back firmly against the rock wall and drew up her knees, watching his approach. Within feet of her he stopped, dropping the rifle and pack, then sat down on a tree stump. The firelight played on one side of his face and she saw his eyes were fixed on her. The glow of the fire seemed to turn the pupils gold. His eyes were of a lighter brown than Raschid's or Mahomet's. A different tribe, perhaps, or even a strain of European in his blood. When he spoke, she jumped.

'Who was your companion, the man who ran away in fear?'

Zara blinked. She had not expected this question. What good would it do him if she put a name to the coward? Where was this leading?

She shrugged. 'A man friend.' She tried to keep her voice casual. 'But not such a friend, after all.'

'I know it was a man friend,' he said in a hard deliberate voice. 'I knew that much from Raschid and Mahomet. I asked who he was.'

'Does it matter? Why do you want to know?' Even now she felt she must protect Ralph's reputation, though perhaps not Ralph's, so much as the army's. One cowardly soldier must not be allowed to tarnish the honour of the British Army.

'One more time I ask his name.'

Zara shook her head stubbornly.

'You wish to protect this coward, this toy soldier who flies like an antelope at the scent of danger?'

The hard flat voice, full of scorn, sent a shiver of apprehension through Zara. She stayed silent.

'You can love a man like that –' He shook his head in wonder. 'You disappoint me, Miss Zara Deane.'

She looked up quickly. 'How did you know my name?'

'How do I know the wind is blowing? Because it whispers its message through the trees and I am not deaf.'

'What – what else do you hear?' Zara asked uncertainly.

'I hear that a man has been invited to the British garrison to answer one or two delicate questions regarding your abduction. All very polite and discreet, naturally, but the invitation was quite irresistible, impossible to refuse.'

Zara frowned. 'I don't follow you. Why impossible?'

'Issued by a high-ranking body of British officers and reinforced by a troop of cavalry and an infantry regiment? How could the Prince of Batala refuse?'

Chapter Sixteen

Zara sat in stunned silence, her eyes wide with disbelief.

'The Yuvaraj? But that is ridiculous! Why should they suspect him?'

'Why indeed?' Devil Sahib's laugh was low and amused. 'Perhaps you, yourself gave them cause.'

Zara had the feeling that he was watching her closely. 'I? What do you mean?'

'The good ladies of the garrison remember – or are reminded – of a certain young lady's rather forward behaviour with the Prince.' His laugh seemed to mock her. 'It is not quite the thing to be so openly friendly – even with a Rajah's son.'

Zara stared at him suspiciously. 'You seem to be well-informed. May I ask how?'

'Of course.' His smile became bland. 'Did you think Raschid and Mahomet were my only followers?'

Zara thought of the man in the Lacy garden and shook her head. 'No, but what is to be done about the Yuvaraj?'

'Done? Why, nothing, Missie Sahib. The British may hold him in custody – protective custody, you might say, for feelings are a little high in the garrison – but eventually they will release him through lack of evidence. No one supposes that the Prince of Batala was personally involved, but he has many loyal followers. Meanwhile, there are those who have much to gain by clouding the waters and spreading ripples of suspicion in his direction.'

Zara said coldly, 'Including you.'

'Ah yes, that is true and since, like the Prince, I had no part in your abduction, I hold myself clear of blame.'

Zara gasped. 'How dare you say that, when I am here only by the stupidity of your men?' She was suddenly very angry. 'If you consider yourself so blameless, then for the sake of honour, return me to Lahore. I can then declare the Yuvaraj's innocence.'

'And my guilt?' His smile seemed almost gentle. 'You wish me to take the Prince's place? I regret that my honour does not extend so far. They are unlikely to hang a Prince, but a hillman –?'

'I could tell them it was a mistake and you have not harmed me.' It sounded weak, even to herself, and she bit her lip in frustration.

Devil Sahib laughed softly. She glanced up at him.

'You would plead for a hillman, Miss Deane? You might be forgiven a Prince but never a hillman.'

167

He took a cheroot from his tunic pocket and rose, walking to the fire. He touched a burning twig to the end of the cheroot. He stood for a moment watching the blue smoke curl upwards, then he returned to the shelter.

'Besides, Miss Deane,' he said, as if he had never left her side, 'you are forgetting the other interested parties.'

She frowned up at him. 'What others?'

He sat down on the tree stump. 'The Yuvaraj has enemies. Some will not be displeased to see him fall, whether by accident or design. This we know was by design.'

'We do?'

He slanted a sardonic sideways look at her. 'Think, Miss Deane. An accused must have an accuser. Who, in your acquaintance, might seek to divert embarrassing questions away from himself?'

Zara caught her breath. The pit of her stomach felt hollow and cold. Surely Ralph would not do that?'

'Well done, Miss Deane. I see by your face that a name has occurred to you. I was beginning to wonder if you were as bright as your reputation. It took you a little while, but yes, Captain Ralph Browne was the accusing party.'

'So you knew my companion's name all the time.'

'Yes.'

'But why should he accuse the Yuvaraj? He had no proof. He could have explained about the hillmen catching us in ambush and firing on us.'

'Perhaps he has some special reason for disliking the Yuvaraj. You, maybe?'

Zara shook her head. 'He would not go to such lengths because of me. He was a little jealous and lectured me on my behaviour, but surely it is ridiculous to suppose –' Her voice trailed away uncertainly. She was seeing again the meeting with the Yuvaraj and the money-lender on the hillside, the look of hatred on Ralph's face and the malicious amusement of the Yuvaraj. Ralph had grown very pale at the sight of Hassan. She frowned, trying to recall Ralph's explanation of his visit to the money-lender in the bazaar. A young officer in financial difficulties? Maybe, but knowing Ralph's coldness towards junior officers, she could not imagine any one of them confiding his secret to Captain Browne, a man who lived by regulations.

Devil Sahib was regarding Zara gravely. 'You know him better than I do. How would you read his character?'

Zara stared at the fire. 'Ambitious, very correct –' she stopped and frowned. Why was she talking of Ralph's character to this man? He was intelligent and spoke good English but he was still her captor, if not her actual abductor.

His grin was sardonic. 'Ah, Miss Deane, you have suddenly remembered that you are a well-born English lady and I am a wandering brigand, yes?'

'Confound you, yes!' Zara smiled reluctantly. 'Where did you go to school? Your English is excellent – when you choose to use it.'

He laughed. 'It is, isn't it? I having very good English man teaching poor boy.'

'It is a pity,' Zara said tartly, 'that he did not teach you a proper trade.'

'I have a trade, Missie Sahib.'

'Well, it's not making you very rich, is it? Why, Raschid and Mahomet haven't robbed a merchant in days!' She stared down at her dirty shirt and said, defiantly, 'Since I am your prisoner, the least you can do is provide me with another shirt. I have lived and slept in these clothes for days.'

He rose and tossed the cheroot butt away. He stretched out his hand. 'Come. You remind me that you are my prisoner. It is good to have things made clear.'

Zara swallowed, staring at the outstretched hand. 'Why couldn't she have held her tongue? How stupid to remind him that she was his prisoner. Could a man refuse the gift of a woman, however she had come to him? His command of the English language had lulled her into believing he also thought like an Englishman.

'Come,' he repeated and there was a note of hard impatience in his voice.

Zara rose slowly. She ignored his hand. 'Where?' It was almost a squeak and she had to clench her teeth to fight down the flutterings of panic.

His hand came out and gripped Zara's wrist. He pulled her

169

towards him. Her frightened eyes looked into his. She noted the strong bony planes of his face, the dark skin smooth over high cheek-bones, the long dark hair beneath his turban and the curly beard. His mouth was curved into a faint smile. Contempt, perhaps, at her show of timidity.

She drew in a deep, steadying breath and fixed her thoughts on her father. He would understand that when life gave you no choice, the only thing to do was accept gracefully and not whine about ill-luck.

Devil Sahib seemed to be waiting for some further comment. His mouth still smiled and one thick brow rose in question. Zara looked at him as coolly as she could.

'Well?' he asked.

Zara shrugged. 'I am yours to command, lord.' She tried to speak with weary tolerance and was gratified by the flash of anger in his eyes. It was a dangerous game to play and she knew it, but her pride was at stake. If this man took her as his woman he would find no response, no fight in her, only acceptance of her fate.

She relaxed in his grip. 'Shall we get it over then?' She found herself smiling sourly.

He frowned. 'Of what do you think?'

'My father.'

His brows shot up. 'Your father? He would grieve for you tonight?'

'He is not one for grief.' She almost smiled in amusement. 'He would say, needs must when the devil drives.'

Devil Sahib stared at her for a long moment. 'He is a bad father?'

She shook her head. 'No, he is a wonderful father and I adore him.'

'I don't understand. If I asked ransom, would he pay for your safety?'

'No. He has no money, which is why we both –' She stopped, annoyed with herself again. Why should she explain anything to this man?

'Tell me,' he insisted. 'Why you both – what?'

They were moving away from the shelter and crossing the clearing to the ridge. His hand still gripped her wrist. In the darkness it seemed easier to talk and what she said could make no difference anyway. She hunched her shoulders against the cool breeze.

'Since it has no significance now, I will admit that Father and I lived on credit. Our friends thought us rich and so we were but Father inherited the family weakness for gambling and lost all we had.'

'You did not despise him for making you poor?'

She shook her head. 'How can you despite someone you love when their faults are yours too?'

'You gamble also?'

'No. One gambler in the family is quite enough, but I confess to living above my income. It has always been the nature of the Deanes. Foolish, I know, but we are optimists to the end.'

'And what end was that?'

Zara lifted her face to the wind and smiled at the stars. 'The insanity of optimism may reap sane reality if one is diligent.'

'You speak in riddles, woman. Did your father become a brigand to gain wealth?'

'Nothing as difficult as that and not in the least dangerous. He married a rich widow.'

'I see.' He was silent for a moment, then glanced at her sideways. 'That is a good way. Your father's plan succeeded, but yours? You are not married.'

'No. I was to have been married in Lahore next week.' She sighed. 'There will be a delay.'

'A delay?' Devil Sahib laughed, the mockery plain in his voice. 'What was it you said – the insanity of optimism?'

'But you must release me sometime!' Zara said desperately. 'You didn't want me in the first place. I shall only be a nuisance to you and the soldiers will not give up. Do you want to be hunted for the rest of your life?'

'It would be ill-mannered to refuse a gift,' he said, musingly. 'And I don't have a woman to cook and wash my clothes, nor,' he said with slow deliberation, 'one who will warm my bed and attend to my needs with meekness and submission.'

The pale moonlight revealed his face as he turned towards

171

her. Zara said in a choking voice. 'For the love of God –'

'No. For the love of Allah. You must learn the ways of the hillmen and serve me well. I will not beat you unless you are rebellious. A woman's pride has no place in these hills. She is put on earth to serve man. That is Allah's law. You must obey.'

He pointed down the gentle slope to the pool Zara had seen earlier. 'We stay here overnight and you may wash in that water. It is quite safe until the rains come and then the river will rise and the pool be gone in a torrent of water.'

Devil Sahib dropped the small sack beside her and took the rifle from his shoulder. He sat down on a rock overlooking the pool and laid the rifle across his knees. He indicated the sack and glanced up into her pale face.

'It is time my woman was dressed in suitable garments. You will find them in that sack. It is not fitting to appear in English clothes. They will be buried later.' As Zara hesitated, he said harshly, 'The English do not come as friends in the mountains. The women might stone you to death.'

He drew a cheroot from his pocket and spoke the words so matter-of-factly, that it was a moment before Zara realised their impact.

'Stone me to death?' she asked in disbelief.

He shrugged. 'It happens. A woman needs a protector if she is not to come to harm. There are men, too, who may challenge the right of a protector. Think of these things, Missie Sahib, while you wash and decide which garments to choose.'

Zara looked at him with dislike. 'You intend to sit there while I undress and wash?'

'Naturally, but do not flatter yourself that I shall stare in amazement. All women are fashioned the same and I have known many women.' He turned away, bending his head to light the cheroot.

Zara picked up the sack and went down the grassy incline without another word. She reached the pool and glanced back. He was not looking at her but gazing over the hillside, the smoke from the cheroot idling upwards. She was angry, embarrassed, and fearful, all emotions mixed together, but she also had a great longing to peel off the tight jodhpurs and immerse her body in the clear water. The contents of the sack she emptied by the pool's edge and examined them curiously. Wide, baggy trousers in a dark shade of red, a black and red patterned tunic and a pair of soft leather silk-lined slippers with turned-up toes. At the bottom of the sack something clinked metallically. Her fingers encountered a round object and she drew it out. A silver bangle! Good heavens, she thought, with a spasm of amusement, a gift of jewellery to a woman who was herself a gift!

She glanced up furtively. He was still half-turned from her. Her hands fumbled to unbutton her riding skirt and then the jodhpurs. She sat down and stripped them off. The cotton shirt followed with her undergarments and she eased herself naked into the pool. Her feet found bottom and the water was cold, almost icy, but it was the most refreshing experience she had had in a long time. There was no soap, she had to rub her skin to rid it of accummulated dust.

Not until she climbed out, her drenched hair streaming coldly down her back, did she realise that she had no towel. She looked up towards Devil Sahib, then decided against pointing out this fact. He might misunderstand and consider her remark an invitation. She squeezed out the water from her hair and picked up her discarded shirt. The night air was suddenly cold and she shivered, rubbing her body vigorously. The trousers and tunic were made of a heavier cotton than her own shirt and surprisingly wind-proof. The bandages about her feet were soaking but now clean, and she removed them, rolling them carefully for possible future use. Her toes had healed but were still a little tender. The curly-toed slippers, juttees she thought they were called, proved comfortable. Her own clothes she gathered together. With the silver bangle resting on her palm, she approached the man.

He glanced up as she paused a few paces away.

'Clean now, Missie Sahib?'

Zara held out the bangle. 'This is quite unnecessary.'

He flicked a glance at it. 'Would you have me shamed as a man who cannot afford bracelets for his woman? Wear it, girl, it is the custom. A woman with many bracelets, even a jewelled ring through her nose is considered to have great

173

appeal for her man.' One brow rose quizzically. 'It is early days yet. Be content with one bangle. Maybe, in time, you will earn a nose ring!'

'A – a nose ring? Good God, are we cattle then, to be led by the nose? I beg you will restrict your generosity to bangles, if you insist on keeping face with your fellows.'

'The choice will not be yours, Miss Deane, and whatever I do, you will accept. I admire your spirit but keep it under control. In the hearing of others, you will act the submissive woman or face the consequences. A man is lord and master in these hills and a woman is little higher than a beast. Do you understand?'

Zara sank on to the grass, her knees giving way. She stared into the hard face.

'I understand you well, but you must understand that I am not a hillwoman. I am not submissive by nature, yet you threaten me with consequences when I know nothing of your customs. How can I know what is right or wrong and what are these consequences?'

'Quite simple. A disobedient woman is beaten. A bad woman is given away. If she is young and fair of face, she may be sold.'

'Sold?' Zara's voice was incredulous.

Devil Sahib shrugged. 'Merchants, camel traders. Life is hard for them and harder for their women. They are always needing replacement women.' He slanted a glinting look at her. 'Then there are the houses, of course, but I will respect your English upbringing on that score.'

There was silence between them and Zara stared almost unseeingly across the river. A chill wind of fear had her in its grip. Only this man stood between her and the fates he had described. She was completely in his power and if he demanded meekness and submission, how was she to refuse? To be sold to a camel trader or forced into a house of ill-repute was even worse than her present position. As he had said, she had no choice. Escape was impossible, the hope of rescue increasingly dim and her natural optimism had reached its lowest ebb. She looked down at the silver bangle on her lap and sighed.

'So be it,' she said and slipped it on to her wrist.

Devil Sahib turned to look at her. 'So. You have decided to become my woman.'

'Since the alternatives lack appeal, I see no other solution.'

'Good,' he said and drew her to her feet. 'You will not regret my protection. All men will treat you with the respect due to the woman of Devil Sahib. I will buy you bangles and ankle chains, maybe jewels for your hair. Is that not a pleasing prospect?'

He was smiling as they stood face to face. Zara realised vaguely that it was not a smile of triumph but rather one of relief. Because she had accepted her fate and would not fight him, thereby bringing disgrace to his manhood? Or was it that he was reluctant to beat her for fear of its preventing her carrying out her duties? Soonya had mentioned his reprimands to Raschid and Mahomet over their heavy hands.

The tears pricked her eyes as she looked into a future of living in these hills, her youth and looks fading into wrinkled old age, serving one man until he cast her aside for a younger, fresher woman. She blinked away the tears angrily and focused on the dark face. The sky was darkly purple behind his head and the breeze seemed to flatten his beard to his face. He glanced up at the stars and she saw his profile outlined by the glint of the river.

A feeling of having been here before touched her mind. A vague, fleeting thought, a memory of wind, movement, and water. She tried to hold on to that fragment of *déja vu*. That strong, hard profile, she scent of cheroot smoke, the timbre of his voice, could only be imagination. That memory belonged to a cultured, well-dressed Englishman, not a dark-skinned hillman, but a night-time stranger on the ship who turned out to be a cashiered officer.

She frowned, shaking her head. Similarity in build, how could it be anything else? That man by daylight, as he raised his panama hat mockingly to the ladies clustered by the rail, had been tanned of skin, but this man by daylight was very much darker. No European could ever look so dark. Red, perhaps, and sun-tanned in parts exposed to the hot Indian sun, but never the colour of mahogany as this man was. Of course she had never seen him unclothed . . . Her thoughts skittered to a halt and a shudder ran through her. She glanced up, her eyes wide with apprehension. That would come when he took her as his woman.

She began to turn away but his hands took her shoulders, forcing her to face him.

'The garments suit you but your hair must be plaited.' He looked into her eyes. 'You are well-favoured. I think you will please me.' His mocking smile came again. 'But the thought of being bedded by a hillman does not appeal, no?'

'It is not what I expected,' she muttered, low voiced.

'Do you pine for that cowardly English officer?'

Zara thought for a moment. 'Not exactly. I am my father's daughter.'

Devil Sahib's smile broadened. 'Splendid. You intend to emulate your father. Was this gallant Captain aware of your poverty?'

'Of course not. He thought me as I appeared, a rich woman.'

'And you thought him a rich man with a forgiving nature?' He laughed softly, with such amusement that Zara, her fears temporarily forgotten stared at him suspiciously.

'You seem to find that vastly amusing.'

'I do, Miss Deane.' His shoulders shook with suppressed laughter. 'Deceit is not confined to the fair sex as you seem to suppose.'

'What does that mean?'

'Just as your father required a rich woman, so does Captain Browne.'

'I don't believe you!' Zara said hotly. 'Captain Browne is rich by his great-aunt's inheritance. You are suggesting that he is marrying me for my money?'

'Indignation, Miss Deane? It hardly becomes you since your own aim was the same.'

She frowned. 'How do you know anything about the matter? You are implying that he, too, is poor. That is ridiculous for he bought me a valuable ring and paid for my passage, first class.'

'Ah no, Miss Deane. A certain unnamed gentleman did that.'

'Oh, my God, the money-lender,' whispered Zara and many puzzling facts fell into place. 'Hassan?' she asked.

Those dreadful mocking brows rose in astonishment. 'You know his name? Surely Captain Browne was not idiot enough to allow a meeting?'

Zara shook her head. 'No, the Yuvaraj did that. Why does he dislike Captain Browne? Why does he go out of his way to cause embarrassment to him only?'

Devil Sahib shrugged. 'Malice, perhaps? He is informed of every vice and delights in holding that knowledge over the heads of his victims.'

'But Ralph told me he was acting for some other officer. I saw him in the bazaar, you see.'

'What else could he say? You were not then secured in marriage.'

'Nor ever will be now!' Her body began to shake with laughter though tears streamed down her cheeks. 'Dear God,' she gasped, choking for breath. 'With deceit in common, we deserved each other.' Laughter shrilled her voice. 'What shock and disaster our wedding would have revealed.'

'Be quiet, woman.' Devil Sahib pulled her roughly towards him and she found her face buried in his chest. He held her so tightly that her struggles seemed feeble. She calmed herself with an effort and gradually her shaking stopped, the tears ceasing to flow.

When he released her, she looked up at him, trying to smile. 'I'm sorry. I just found it so ridiculously comical. I'm not usually given to the vapours.'

'No,' he said thoughtfully. 'I imagine not, nor to gossip either.'

'What do you mean?'

'The day of the durbar, when you saw me at the palace in company with the Rani, you told no one of it. Why was that?'

'The Yuvaraj once told me that the Rajah's judgements were according to the old ways. I don't know what the penalty is for – for taking a lover, but I would not wish to be the cause of any punishment to the Rani.'

'And what about me?'

'You? What of you? I had never seen you before. If you

risked anything, it was by your own choice, but the Rani is young and beautiful. She is married to an old man.'

'The Rani is well able to care for herself.'

Zara felt her mind quiver and that sensation of *déja vu* repeated itself. She shook her head to clear her wits. Tension and tiredness played strange tricks. She found Devil Sahib watching her intently. She felt bewildered, light-headed

'My dear Miss Deane, I thought better of your intelligence. How slow you are.'

Her mind turned in confusion. 'What are you talking about?'

He laughed softly. 'Your eyes are full of doubt and questions while your mind rejects the possibility and considers it preposterous. You are bemused by what you see and what you think, too diverse to contemplate seriously.'

'I don't know what you are talking about,' Zara repeated.

'I think you do but refuse to accept the possibility. Do you think I hold you prisoner simply because you saw me with the Rani? That is of little importance. I have been waiting for this other knowledge to touch your mind as it most surely would in time. It is not in my scheme of things to have that knowledge revealed.'

'I don't believe – you can't be –' Zara began, her mind in confusion.

'You must and I can.' He smiled with a wry twist to his lips. 'You learned my identity in Calcutta. A cashiered officer, one Major Richard Deverill, a disgrace to the proud name of the regiment, a vile creature who should have been hanged. Isn't that what they said?'

Chapter Seventeen

Zara stood very still, as if she teetered on the edge of a precipice and one false step would hurl her into oblivion. It wasn't true, how could it be; and yet he knew too much to be anyone else save a man acquainted with the garrison.

178

'But – but you can't be – not that man, I mean your skin and –' She waved a trembling hand to encompass his attire. 'How can you look so like –' She stopped, realising the foolishness of her babbling. Of course he was the cashiered officer. Her subconscious had recognised him without the acknowledgement of his words.

'How can I look like a hillman?' He was smiling. 'One can look like anything and anyone in this country. I could have shaved my head and worn saffron robes to appear a Bhuddist priest, but a shaven head did not appeal. Skin colour can be varied by the application of berry juice or even boot polish. As for beard and hair, that is only a matter of neglecting one's barber.'

'But why?' Zara asked. 'What is this impersonation for?'

'Now that, Miss Deane, is a question I am not prepared to answer.'

'Do they know that you are English?'

'Raschid and Mahomet? Yes, they know but the women do not. I trust you will keep it that way for your own good.'

'Why do they call you Devil Sahib?'

'I should have thought that was obvious. They are not educated to English names and find Deverill too complicated to pronounce. Come now, we have talked enough. It is time to sleep.' He took her arm in a strong grip and drew her down the crest towards the shelter.

Zara's heart quickened and she spoke in a strangled voice. 'It is foolish, I suppose, to believe that you might allow me privacy. You are – or were – an English gentleman.'

'Were, is the correct word.' The firelight touched the dark, glinting eyes as he regarded her sardonically. 'As a hillman, it is customary to have one's woman close by. You wish me to lose honour because of your fancy ways?'

'Damn your honour, Deverill! You lost that long ago but would it hurt to consider mine? Surely there is decency left in you to consider my position.'

'Your position, Missie Sahib,' he said coldly, 'is no higher now than Soonya's or Rahti's. You are the woman of Devil Sahib and will be accepted as such. Resign yourself to that for there is no way back to Lahore.'

179

Zara stumbled into the shelter, her face burning with shame and embarrassment. He picked up a blanket and thrust it into her hands.

'Wrap yourself in that and go to sleep,' he said curtly. 'My honour may have been lost but I have not yet become a rapist!' He turned his back on her, slung a blanket across his shoulders and lay down.

Zara did the same, falling at last into an uneasy sleep where bearded men with dark cruel eyes stared down, mocking and contemptuous, as she struggled to break free from an ever tightening circle. She woke gasping and shivering to a dark cold night, her blanket a tangle beside her. The steady breathing of a sleeping man was somehow comforting. With the blanket once more wrapped about her, she inched her way closer to the sleeping form, hoping he would not wake, but extend some of his warmth to her chilled body. Her last conscious thought was, strangely, of Delia Pringle. She imagined the incredulous horror on that haughty face, could she but see Zara Deane lying beside that despicable murderer and taking comfort from the warmth of his body in some God-forsaken niche in the Himalayas.

Devil Sahib was gone when she awoke. The cool, pearly light of dawn was tinted by a golden haze and she lay huddled in her blanket, thinking of last night's conversation. She knew she had offended him by damning his honour and decency, his curtness had made that obvious. Regret and bitterness over the events that resulted in his court martial must be constant companions. A future ruined by a drunken action that dismissed him from the service and deprived him of rank, must surely leave scars too sensitive to probe. She resolved to guard her tongue and temper for he was, she admitted wryly, her only protection. Murderer or brigand, she had no choice but to apply herself to the role of being Devil Sahib's woman. Deverill, she corrected herself, for now that she knew his name, it was less frightening than the name bestowed on him by the hill people. Would he still be curt when they met again? She really must apologise for her outburst in case he considered it preferable to rid himself of her in one of the ways he had outlined. Practicality, she decided, was her only protection. Better the devil one knows than the unknown quantity of a camel trader.

As she pushed aside the blanket, she realised with a stab of quite inexplicable gratitude, that he had laid his own blanket across her before leaving the shelter. A thoughtful gesture, so he could not still be angry with her, and her spirits rose. She looked down at herself with a slight feeling of shock, seeing in daylight the wide red trousers and tunic. The bangle on her wrist was of heavily chased silver and she knew that it must have cost many rupees. The soft slippers were embroidered in bright colours and looked too dainty for hard walking. But then, she had the strong leather ones for everyday use. She looked round quickly for her sack with its ointment and cloths and the precious comb.

Outside the shelter, she paused, feeling rather self-conscious in her strange clothes. Soonya and Rahti glanced up from the fire and their eyes widened. Standing by their ponies were Raschid and Mahomet. For a frozen moment, four pairs of eyes stared, then the men's faces split into wide grins and giggling, quickly stifled, came from the girls. Delight or derision, Zara could not tell which emotion was uppermost in their minds. She tossed her hair back and strode up and over the crest towards the little pool where she had bathed.

Thank God for bushes, she reflected, accepting that she had no alternative. Beside the pool lay her discarded clothing and the hessian sack in which Deverill had brought the new clothes. Would he let her keep them against the day when she returned to Lahore? Would there ever be such a day? She must continue to hope so and if he released her eventually, it would be too embarrassing to walk into the garrison wearing the baggy trousers and tunic of a hillwoman. She picked up Deverill's sack and was about to stuff in her skirt and jodhpurs when her fingers encountered something else. It was a small, pillbox-shaped hat of hard felt. Deverill had forgotten nothing. This was exactly the headgear that Rahti and Soonya wore. He had told her to plait her hair. In this outfit and with veiled cap in place, she would look exactly like the two girls, rather cleaner for the present but with only one

181

costume, there would soon be no identifiable difference. She was not even fair-haired and with her skin already tanning, her dark hair hanging in a tail, who would doubt she was just another hillwoman?

Carrying the little cap, she returned to camp, her old clothes stuffed into the sack. She must hope Deverill had forgotten his plan to bury her skirt and jodhpurs. The shirt he might allow her to keep if she protested at the lack of a towel, but her jodhpurs and riding skirt were too obviously English to risk retaining.

Back in the shelter she put the larger sack under the blankets and drew out her comb from the smaller sack. As she was combing her hair, Soonya appeared with a bowl of the usual oatmeal mixture. She smiled, her eyes bright.

'Missie Sahib look like us now. Devil Sahib buy much rupee clothes. Very good he liking you.'

Zara paused in her combing and saw what Soonya meant. The cloth of her own tunic and trousers was far superior to the cheap cotton of Soonya's garments. The girl caught sight of the silver bangle and gasped with delight.

'Such rich thing, Missie Sahib.' Her eyes came up slyly to Zara's. 'You pleasing him good last night?'

Zara bit her lip, trying not to smile at the frank childish curiosity. 'Mind your own damn business!' She felt her cheeks redden as Soonya giggled and clapped her hands, quite unoffended.

'That is good for soon Raschid say Devil Sahib have many lakhs of rupees. Maybe he give me little for fine tunic.'

Zara said very carefully and evenly. 'Many lakhs of rupees? How will he get that?'

Soonya shrugged. 'Not knowing where but Raschid say Devil Sahib have much bad feeling for soldiers. Maybe hurting them some good way for plenty rupee.'

She moved away and Zara sat still, the comb idle in her hand. It was just as she had suspected on first seeing that rifle on Deverill's shoulder. The thefts from the armoury in the garrison, with the aid of that hooded accomplice, were his work. Not just a few rifles but theft on a grand scale if Raschid was to be believed. How would one set about it? Ambush the

182

supply trains? One could not burst into the armoury and extract great quantities of rifles without the alarm being raised. But lakhs of rupees? A lakh was a hundred thousand rupees, many thousands of English pounds. One would need hundreds of rifles for that amount of money. And who was buying?

Richard Deverill might have come to hate the army but who was benefiting from his hatred? Who was he arming and why? Did a mysterious someone want to repeat the tragic events of the Mutiny and force the British out of India? The questions fluttered and clawed at her mind like a desperate bird caught in a net. Deverill might hate the army that had thrown him out but he was still an Englishman. Dear God, could he be a traitorous Englishman, a man so lost to honour that he betrayed his own people? Shaitan, a Judas, a traitor to his own kind!

Zara came to herself with a start. Soonya was kneeling before her.

'You dreaming good time, Missie Sahib. Now I put hair like Devil Sahib say.'

'What?' Zara spoke vaguely.

'We go soon. Must wear cap.'

Zara blinked. 'We move again? How many more times and where to, for heaven's sake?'

'Up there.' Soonya waved a hand. 'Sometime village. But for winter camp.'

'We are going to a village?'

'Very small. People passing many time, up and down mountain. Plenty traveller.'

As Zara sat with her back to Soonya while the girl plaited her hair, she thought of this village with its travellers. Afghans and Pathans making for their mountain homes before the rains came, or Punjabis and Kashmiris travelling south with their goats. This village sounded like a crossroads where stores were bought and travellers exchanged news and possibly more important things. Everyone knew of the swooping raids into the lowlands, the plundering of mule trains, the quick retreat into the mountain fastness. A wounded soldier, she had heard, would as soon be shot by his

183

comrades as taken prisoner by a fierce band of Pathans or any other tribesmen.

She pondered her method of escaping from Deverill. Alone it was impossible, but could she attach herself to a south-bound group of travellers? Once clear of the mountains, they must inevitably come across a British garrison, not Lahore, of course, that was too far south, but a small outpost, maybe.

Soonya had finished the plaiting and was arranging the veiled cap on her head.

'When coming on men, Missie Sahib must cover face, so.' She demonstrated and Zara nodded absently. 'Now giving me English legs like Devil Sahib saying.'

'What?'

'Now that you are hillwoman, he say to bury legs.'

'Damn,' muttered Zara in resignation. 'I might have known he wouldn't forget.'

She went into the shelter and reached for the larger bag. She pulled out the jodhpurs and skirt.

'The skirt is good. I could use it for – for a cloak in the cold.' She looked hopefully at Soonya.

The girl shook her head. 'Devil Sahib say bury English things. Too looking like memsahib thing. Memsahib's topee too. He say not seemly for hillwoman.'

Zara sighed. 'I suppose when I die of sunstroke, he will bury me too since I am too English thing!'

Soonya giggled, her dark eyes knowing and merry. 'He taking good care of woman who please him. Is it not so with English peoples? Woman has body to tempt man, yes?'

Zara thought of the devotion of the Lacys, the contentment of the Frasers. Who else? The wives she had met had not the earthy simplicity of this girl. Most of them accepted the necessity of receiving their husbands' attentions but viewed the act of love with dignified distaste, hinting, not subtly, that for the sake of the children, one was expected to suffer them. It was a duty, duly performed and not a subject to be discussed.

Would her marriage to Ralph have been like that? She rather thought so as his touch had not filled her with desire and, to be honest, she doubted that he had any stronger feeling for her. If she believed Deverill, Ralph was poor as herself. Deceit and poverty were not good foundations for marriage. Had they loved, it might have been different, deceit admitted then forgotten and a brave face to show the world in patent devotion. Some people were lucky in finding that special person, like Colonel and Mrs Lacy, her own mother and father, but how rare a thing it seemed to be.

'Thank you, Soonya,' she said and the girl, glancing into the sombre eyes of Missie Sahib, ceased her chatter and moved away, shaking her head at the change of mood. Why had Missie Sahib suddenly become silent? Had her own silly question brought a reminder of something unpleasant? But Devil Sahib was a fine man, strong and lusty. He would teach the Missie Sahib the importance of having a protector. What more could a girl want than enough food in her belly and a lusty man in her bed?

Zara packed the shirt and her new slippers into the sack. She took the precaution of bandaging her toes again before putting on the heavy, large sandals, and then left the shelter. The baskets were being packed and the men readying the ponies. Zara turned back, remembering the blankets. Since she was now officially one of this group, she could not expect to be waited on. As she folded the blankets, she wondered if she would be called upon to produce meals. That was something the servants did and her only experience had been toasting bread at the schoolroom fire. She might make tea and boil an egg but neither commodity had appeared so far. Soonya must teach her if it was required.

As they moved out of the camp, Zara glanced back at the ridge where only last night she had learned Devil Sahib's true identity. She was sorry to leave the small pool, and its privacy. Now they were going higher to this village where she must attempt her escape. Raschid and Mahomet, she had no doubt, would have been warned to watch her closely. Richard Deverill had no intention of letting her carry the news of his perfidy back to Lahore. If only she could find out something of importance, such as where the stolen rifles were going and for what purpose they were going to be used. How many more consignments had been lost since she had left Lahore? Rifles needed bullets, he would have to steal those too. Not cannon, they would be too difficult to spirit away but small arms and certainly bayonets. She suppressed a shudder as she thought of bayonets slicing through living flesh. Dear God, she must find out something.

Soonya's words came to mind. Woman has body to tempt man. No, that was unthinkable. Deverill was too clever to be fooled by a languorous body and seemingly innocent questions. A languorous body, indeed! She hadn't the faintest idea how one tempted a man into a passion of flaming desire where his tongue babbled freely. That, she reflected grimly, might be something else Soonya would have to teach her.

Progress up the mountain seemed easier today. It was no less rocky underfoot but the sandals with their roughened soles held balance better and the loose-fitting clothes allowed the air to circulate about her body. She was glad of the absence of boots and tight jodhpurs although she regretted their burial. The last vestige of Englishness had been taken from her by the orders of Deverill. Following in Soonya's wake, Zara found her body swaying in that same rhythm and felt surprise and a strange gratification. How much less tiring it was to walk in that relaxed fashion, hips swinging in a way that would have been considered fast and provocative by the garrison ladies. There would be less need of fans and smelling salts if English ladies discarded their tight corsets, multiple petticoats and boned bodices and wore the flowing garments of the Indians.

Zara recalled her own wardrobe of tight-waisted gowns, ruffled petticoats and stultifying corselets. She had been no different, but when she reached Lahore again, her whole wardrobe would be redesigned. She sighed. 'If' was a word more appropriate than 'when'. The higher they travelled, the more remote became her chances of seeing Lahore ever again.

From the narrow goat tracks they moved on to a wider, well-travelled road, the hard-packed earth witness to the passing of horses and cattle and the occasional imprint of iron-shod wheels. Zara felt her spirits rise. This must be the way to the village, the first evidence of civilisation. Surely there was a chance now to contact some south-bound traveller. She had no money, but Soonya's admiring gasp on seeing the silver bracelet from Deverill proved that it had a value which might be turned to advantage. The slippers too. They were of soft kind, elaborately embroidered, and might appeal to some better-off lady. With a few silver rupees in her possession to buy food, she could follow a party of merchants or even mingle with goat-herders making for the plains.

Soonya was at her elbow. 'Put up your veil, Missie Sahib. We coming village.'

Zara obeyed and looked forward eagerly. A few derelict thatched huts sagged by the roadside but further on she glimpsed buildings of more substance. Sheets of corrugated iron over stone walls, mostly three-sided with wooden stalls protruding, lined a wide, dusty street. Rather like an inferior bazaar, Zara thought, for the place had a desolate feeling. No Silver Raj and fancy carpets, no noisy throng of brightly coloured shoppers, but a dour assembly of men, casting critical eyes over tethered animals or merely staring about with hard, suspicious eyes.

Zara held her veil in place tightly and walked with lowered eyes past a line of resting camels. They looked quite mountainous with their long necks and haughty, raised heads, large teeth showing as they chewed with slow gravity. Their strong scent made her glad of the veil. The attendants smelled much the same, tall bearded men in goatskin waistcoats, their sashes bristling with knives and small axes. Every man had a rifle slung over his shoulder and a double bandolier of cartridges across his chest. No women were to be seen and Zara assumed them to be herded somewhere while men's business was being conducted. No man, she guessed, would do his own cooking and wood-gathering for fires.

She peered over the edge of the veil, searching for more friendly company. A line of ox-carts caught her eye. Small, wiry little men with yellow Mongol faces were loading sacks. She nudged Soonya.

'Who are they? I haven't seen men like that before.'

Soonya looked at the busy figures. 'Are Ghurka peoples from Nepal. They liking to be soldiers. Many Ghurka in your English army.'

Nepal? No, that was a country high in the east and very far from Lahore. They would not answer. Yet if they were friendly to the British? Even so, she could not communicate and they might well be heading home.

'Those men with camels,' she asked. 'Are they Afghans?'

Soonya nodded, her eyes bleak. 'Not trusting them. Taking things, then cutting throat. Very bad men. Not liking to be woman of Afghan. Much beating.'

Zara's hopes began to wither. Surely more travellers passed this way. There must be someone going south.

'How long do we stay here?'

Soonya shrugged. 'One night, maybe two. Devil Sahib tell when he come.'

'Where is he?'

'Not knowing. He having big talk with leader.' Her eyes slid nervously towards a villainous looking Afghan warrior. 'Not knowing. Forgetting quickly, Missie Sahib, Raschid say he cut out tongue.' Her eyes looked pleadingly into Zara's. 'Please forgetting I speak. Raschid come very angry I saying such thing.'

Zara gripped Soonya's arm. 'Hush, Soonya. I promise I will say nothing. You are my friend.' She smiled into the wide scared eyes, her voice soothing although her mind was stiff with shock. She forced herself to go on calmly. 'Where are we staying or must we make camp outside this village? I am hungry and thirsty. Where are the women of all these men? Are they resting somewhere?'

The questions came automatically, only half of her mind forming them. She had to think but first she must reassure Soonya that nothing of Raschid's boasting talk and Soonya's own indiscretion would go any further.

Soonya was relaxing visibly under this babble of questions. Like a child who has escaped punishment, she was eager to please and not by a breath refer again to a forbidden subject.

'There is tea room where women go. All sitting with babies. Much noise but I get Missie Sahib good tea. We go now with Rahti, yes?'

'Yes please, Soonya. Do you know, I have not tasted tea since I left Lahore. Is it good tea?'

'Very good, strong tea. Is made in samovar.'

They paused outside a long, low building, Soonya and Rahti lowering their baskets to the ground. Raschid and Mahomet rode on without looking back. It was obviously the custom followed by all men and needed no special ordering. The three girls entered the dark room. The windows were mere apertures without glass and heavy wooden shutters stood open to allow in a faint light. A haze of smoke made sight difficult until one had adjusted to the gloom. Some kind of wood-burning stove stood at one end of the room, an enormous samovar hissing above the flames. Strong and very stewed tea, Zara decided, but she would drink it, however revolting, for Soonya's sake.

'Sitting here, Missie Sahib, by door. Much smelling of camel not good.' Soonya smiled broadly, a simple child trusting in Zara's promise to say nothing. Of course Zara would hold her tongue. Who could she communicate with except Deverill, and he was the arch-villain of the piece.

She watched the two hillgirls elbow their way towards the wrinkled old woman dispensing tea from the tap of the samovar. It might have been brass in its early days but now it was so blackened by smoke it could have been any old iron cooking pot. The girls returned carrying metal bowls of dark brown liquid so steaming hot that their tunic skirts were used in the carrying. Soonya placed a bowl on the floor in front of Zara who peered doubtfully into its depths.

'What are those things floating about?' she asked.

'Little mint, Missie Sahib. Tasting good, you try.'

Zara tried and was pleasantly surprised by the tangy taste. One could grow accustomed to drinking tea without milk or sugar. As she sipped, she glanced outside. The ox-carts were lumbering away with their attendant Ghurkas. The camels of the Afghans still sat by the side of the track but the men had moved away and were squatting in a tight little group. A few paces away, two bearded Afghans stood, as if on guard, rifles cradled negligently across their chests. Although their postures appeared relaxed, there was nothing relaxed in their faces. Hard, dark eyes were alert and watchful, like senties guarding their chief's council of war.

By craning her neck a little and shifting her position casually, Zara studied the circle of intent faces. Her fingers tightened on the tea bowl and she no longer felt the hot metal. One face she recognised, and it took a reat effort of will to remain calm and lift the bowl to her lips without spilling the tea. Soonya's words should have prepared her but it was still a shock to see Deverill treating with the Afghans.

Soonya's voice recalled her. 'You finish tea now, Missie sahib. We go to rest house.'

'Rest house?'

Soonya nodded. 'Not much like bungalow where sahibs go but charpoys and place for fire. Coming soon very cold.'

Zara rose wearily. 'I'm ready to make good use of a charpoy and a hot meal. Lead me to it, my friend.'

They left the tea room, picking up their baskets, and walked on down the track. The group of Afghans had broken up and there was no sign of Deverill.

Zara glanced at Soonya. 'Are those camel men going over the mountains and back to Afghanistan?'

Soonya looked uneasy. 'Women not knowing men business. Bring trouble.'

Zara nodded and asked no more questions. The dirt track curved round the end of what looked like a large stone warehouse with high barred gates and before them lay a small thatched hut. Zara looked at the sagging roof and walls with dismay. The wooden door sagged on its hinges and the tiny windows appeared to be stuffed with goatskins.

'This is the rest house?' she asked incredulously.

Soonya nodded. 'Is very poor but only one and Devil Sahib make everybody else leave.'

'You mean he ordered out other travellers so that we could use it?'

Soonya grinned. 'For you, Missie Sahib.' Her eyes went sly. 'Raschid never do such thing for me. Devil Sahib liking his woman to have best place.'

'Best place?' Zara asked faintly as the musty odour of the place reached her. Dear God, it was as if a century of animal droppings had been stamped into the earth floor and a battalion of mice and spiders had occupied it in the absence of human habitation.

Something scuttled across the floor as she peered in at the doorway. She stepped back quickly, stifling a scream. The thing had been long and sleek, much larger than a mouse.

'What – what was that?'

'Mongoose, maybe.' Soonya shrugged.

'Mongoose? What on earth is that?'

'Very good things. Liking snakes. Catching good.'

'Snakes? Oh, no, don't tell me there are snakes here, too?'

'Snakes everywhere. Sahibs liking mongoose in gardens. Snake not liking mongoose.'

Zara moved hesitantly into the rest house, a misnomer if ever there was one. She could not imagine passing a restful night under the rustling thatch that crawled, no doubt, with cockroaches and spiders and heaven knew what else. The charpoys, their sagging webbing evidence of hundreds of weighty bodies, stood a mere foot in height from the floor, the frame supported on four wooden legs of indeterminate age. There were only two. She looked quickly at Soonya who smiled knowingly and waved a hand to the far side. A small archway, hung over by a large goat-hair blanket led into another room Zara had not noticed.

'I show you,' Soonya said and pushed aside the blanket. Some attempt had been made to sweep the room clean, the walls were less cobwebbed and the roof thatching showed fresher green in parts. The only object in the room was a charpoy, wider and more solid-looking than the two in the other room. Zara stared at it for a long moment. Was she expected to share this bed with Deverill? Of course she was, her commonsense told her. Deverill, in his role of hillman, was unlikely to roll himself in his blanket and sleep meekly on the floor while allowing her sole occupancy of that wide charpoy. The goat-hair dividing blanket was not so thick as to allow a fierce argument to go unheard and when did a hillman allow his woman to argue and go unpunished?

But Deverill was not a hillman and she was not his woman. They were both English. Would that weigh with him, persuading him to treat her as an Englishwoman? Why

191

should a disgraced officer, now dealing with enemies of the English, have any such reservations? She was already lost to the garrison and who would believe she had received honourable treatment anyway, if she were ever returned?

'Oh, devil take the man!' she muttered.

Soonya beamed at her. 'You liking then? Devil Sahib order all this.'

Zara smiled faintly. She must give the devil his due. There hadn't been much one could do to improve this room, but he had tried by having it cleaned to its limits. She really should thank him for that but the spectre of that wide charpoy was a dark question mark on her mind.

They returned to the other room. Rahti was preparing the fire. The cooking pots and blankets had been unloaded. Soonya looked at Zara.

'You wishing to wash again?' She spoke in a voice that implied the unwisdom of doing such a thing so often.

Zara laughed. 'Of course I do. Where do we find water?'

Soonya led her outside and back the way they had come from the tea room. Just before reaching it, she turned aside and pointed to a narrow stream that trickled its way from the direction of the hills. Since snow was always on the mountains, there had to be many such rivulets descending from the snowcaps.

'Thank you, Soonya. I will find my way back, unless you wish to wash too.'

Soonya shook her head. 'Water coming very cold. I not wanting fever. I go put blankets on charpoy. You coming soon, yes?'

'Very soon.'

Soonya nodded and went away. Zara toyed with the idea of not returning to the rest house but it would soon be dark and where would she go anyway? She had seen no other travellers. Perhaps tomorrow. With her toilet completed, she emerged from the turning and began to make her way back to the rest house. There was movement on the other side of the track. In the gloom she saw the weird unfolding of the camels, their strange protesting cries as their handlers tugged and prodded them upright.

192

They rose, heavier and more bulky-looking. She supposed they had been loaded while kneeling. Loaded with what? She peered intently. Long rolls of sacking had been strapped to their sides. The Afghan men were supporting the rolls as the camels rose to their full height. When the men took away their hands, the rolls sagged slightly as if heavy. Long sack-covered rolls? Somewhere in the region of four feet or so? Rifles?

She pressed her hands over her mouth but she could not stop the pounding of her heart.

This was the destination of those stolen rifles, but who was paying Richard Deverill lakhs of rupees to steal and deliver them to the Afghans? The Afghans themselves could not have that kind of money. They were taking delivery but for whom? Some disaffected minor rajah who planned to sweep down on the British outposts and carry the people with him? And Richard Deverill would be the engineer of the bloodshed that resulted. How despicable and hateful he was.

She turned blindly towards the rest house and froze. A large, dark form barred her path.

'Good evening, Miss Deane,' said Richard Deverill.

Chapter Eighteen

Richard Deverill's voice was as calm and polite as if they had chanced upon each other during a gentle stroll through the garrison gardens. Zara stared at him, unable to find words. His eyes looked down, amused, then rose to glance at the departing camel train.

'I'm glad,' he said mildly, 'that you did not decide to attach yourself to that train. It would have cost me money to get you back.'

Zara found her voice. 'You have been watching me,' she accused.

'Of course. I was interested to see what you would do.'

'Since I have no desire to go to Afghanistan, the point is academic.'

'Afghanistan?' He looked surprised. 'What makes you think they go there?'

'Wouldn't that be natural for Afghans? Soonya said –' she stopped. Even in the shadows beside the building, she sensed a tautening in his stance.

'Soonya said what?' His voice was still soft but held an undertone of something that chilled her. She remembered her promise to Soonya. What foolishness had made her mention the girl's name? This man had a clever and, quite natural in his position, a suspicious mind.

'It was probably the camels,' she said.

'They are not camels.'

'What?' Zara feld suddenly bewildered.

'A breed of them, yes, but shorter-legged, better equipped for mountainous regions. They were Bactrians. Didn't you notice the double hump?'

'Well, no. I didn't look as closely as that. I – I was thinking how villainous the men were looking.'

'And Soonya said – ?' The question was still there.

Zara kept her voice steady. 'You will, of course, be aware that my experience of India is limited to Lahore. Since I am forced into a position of unwilling traveller, I may as well benefit from the experience. I questioned Soonya on the people here. She pointed out the Ghurkas who were loading an ox-cart and when I asked about the camel men, she thought they were Afghans. I can only ask questions of other women, since we are far beneath the notice of such superior beings as men.'

She sensed a relaxation in his posture and sighed inwardly with relief.

'Just as it should be,' he said and gave her his mocking smile. 'Even so, Miss Deane, I believe you noticed the cargo and came to a conclusion.'

'Did I?'

'A woman who thinks she is unobserved does not hide her expression.'

'And you have great experience of women, I am sure.' Zara vented her scorn in sarcasm and was annoyed when he laughed.

'You recognised the size and shape of those rolls. Rifles, you said to yourself, and stolen from various armouries by that traitor, Deverill. Quite correct, Miss Deane.'

'But why? Why have you turned traitor?' Wide hazel eyes stared up in desperate appeal. 'Why? Is it revenge for being cashiered?'

'There's more to it than that. A small matter of finance.'

'Financial gain? You would sell your honour for money?'

He took out a cheroot and spent a few moments lighting it. His eyes were very hard when he looked at her again.

'Coming from you, Miss Deane, that remark is quite amusing.' His voice had a cutting edge. 'By your own admission, your father married for money and your own intention was to do the same. Why find it blameworthy in others?' His voice went on inexorably. 'Were you not prepared to dispense with honour and sell your body to a man for financial gain? There are many levels of betrayal and you are guilty of one.'

'But to arm the Afghans –'

'Did I say they were Afghans?'

Zara felt bewilderment again. 'Not Afghans?'

He blew out a plume of smoke. 'Not Afghans. They are hill tribesmen, mostly Pathans, but a fairly polyglot collection of hired villains. A couple of goats and they'll cut your enemy's throat for you. A racing camel and they'll wipe out an entire family, except for the nubile young girls.'

Zara felt her skin grow tight and knew she had paled. Deverill grinned, showing strong, white teeth.

'Perhaps I should have let you go with them, after all, if it's experience you want. They're heading south, too, but not quite as far as Lahore.' He tossed away the cheroot. 'And while I keep you here talking, they're well on their way. Isn't that a shame?'

Almost without being aware of it, Zara's arm swung out. She was filled with fury and wanted to pound the grin off Deverill's face. He caught her wrist without haste and jerked her forward into his arms. His face was very close to hers and he was still grinning. She could not pull free from his powerful arms. She glared defiantly.

'You think you can do as you like, don't you?' she hissed.

'I can and I will, make no mistake about that. You are my woman. Accept it.'

'Never –' she began but his lips were on hers and the kiss was like nothing she had ever experienced before. Her body seemed to melt in the heat of some fiery torch. She felt trapped, her brain a dancing feather seeking to escape the uprush of leaping flame.

When he drew back, Zara was breathless with shock and humiliation. That was all it had been, she thought angrily. He was humiliating her as a reminder that she was completely in his power.

'You – you –'

'Whatever you like, Miss Deane, but don't call me a cad or a rotter, please. Too Victorian for words. How about devil incarnate?' He laughed. 'Now that would be appropriate, don't you think? And you, Miss Deane, have the fire of the devil in you.' He held up a hand as Zara opened her mouth. 'Don't interrupt. My own experience of women – which I daresay has been less delicate than yours of men – convinces me that you would make the perfect devil's mate. Oh, yes, there is fire in you, Miss Deane. A veritable holocaust which no man has yet succeeded in igniting.'

Zara's cheeks were as hot as fire now. 'How dare you speak so coarsely! You are no gentleman, even if you did hold the rank of major. You probably bought that commission off some poor, deluded popinjay who ran into debt and –'

She gave a small breathless scream as his hands clamped about her waist. In one movement he lifted and flung her across his shoulder, one arm circling her thighs. Her fists beat at his back in helpless rage as he strode back towards the rest house, and in this undignified position, her head bobbing, he walked between the four occupants and straight into the back room. He bent slightly and tumbled her on to the charpoy. She lay gasping, staring up into the dark face with a heart full of hatred.

Deverill stared down at her sombrely and there was no amusement on his face. A thread of fear wove itself into Zara's anger.

'Within the hearing of these or any other people,' he said in a soft cold voice, 'you will hold your tongue and pattern your behaviour on Soonya and Rahti. It is a point of honour with a hillman to have his woman completely submissive. A defiant look alone may bring on a beating. Here, I am a hilllman and you are my woman. Do I make myself clear?'

Zara's throat was dry. She swallowed painfully, nodding. 'To hold to your masquerade, you would be prepared to beat me. Is that it?'

He nodded. 'I would be despised if I did not, and it suits my purpose to retain respect.'

'And what suits me is of no consequence?'

'None at all. The stakes I play for are too important. If you get in the way, you will suffer the consequences. Play the game my way and you might live to see Lahore again but understand me very well: I shall not risk my life to save yours.'

'Thank you,' Zara muttered.

A hint of a smile touched Deverill's lips. 'Think nothing of it. You are under my protection at the moment but don't abuse that privilege. It is all I can offer.'

Zara pushed herself into a sitting position on the charpoy and looked up into the dark face. 'You say I might live to see Lahore again. There will be an end to this business?'

'Eventually, yes. I don't plan to spend the rest of my life in the guise of a hillman.'

'What do you plan to do?'

The smile became a little cynical. 'A man may do much with money. You must agree with me there since your own inclinations run along those lines.'

Zara stood up and looked at him coldly. 'I sought only to sell my body, as you so delicately termed it, not my country nor my countrymen.'

'That's true and I give you credit for it. Soon I shall be a rich man. Wouldn't that be a tantalising prospect for a girl of mercenary nature?'

'How dare you suggest such a thing! I have nothing but contempt for you. To become rich in so base a way is despicable.'

'Such virtue and righteousness, Miss Deane,' he mocked. 'Does a millowner's wife consider the low wages paid to her husband's millhands when she is buying a Paris bonnet? Does a shipping magnate's wife grieve over the poverty of the seamen's families when a ship is lost with all hands on the eve of her daughter's coming-out ball? A blind eye and a little loss of memory are so much more comfortable than bothering one's mind on how the money was made. It is just there and must be enjoyed to the full.' He watched her through half-closed eyes, the smile still on his face. 'Does your conscience deny that philosophy? It happens just the same.'

'That's different,' Zara muttered.

'But not much,' he said equably. 'Some men succeed where others fail. There is no such thing as equality. That is an idealistic dream.'

'And you intend to become one of those who succeed and become rich?'

'Of course.' He reached out and lifted her chin so that she faced him. 'Are you so strong on conscience? Doesn't the idea hold any appeal for you? Attach yourself to me, Miss Deane, and you'll be wealthy beyond your dreams of avarice.'

'Attach myself to you? What an outrageous statement.'

He laughed softly, still cupping her chin. 'I am all you have at the moment. It would be in your own interests to please me in the way every clever woman knows by instinct, if not experience.'

Zara jerked her head away. 'How – how –'

Deverill sighed. 'If you say, how dare you, again, I shall run out of patience. I can take you whenever I wish and no one will interfere since you are known as my woman, but I prefer a willing partner.'

'Like the Rani?' Zara snapped. 'She looked very willing.'

Richard Deverill laughed. 'Do you know, that tone of voice hinted at jealousy.'

'Jealousy?' Zara was outraged. 'How ridiculous! Take your money to the Rani and smother her in jewels if you wish, and I hope the Rajah catches you and chops off your head!'

He grinned. 'What a devilishly waspish female you are, but I confess we make a pretty pair. Think about my offer, won't

198

you?' He started for the door curtain.

'I don't need to,' Zara hissed at him broodingly. 'Captain Browne and I may have deceived each other equally, but his proposal was an honourable one.'

Deverill paused at the entrance, his hand on the goatskin curtain. He turned, his dark eyes amused. 'Since you decry my honour, I can only make you a dishonourable proposal. What I have in mind does not require the blessing of the church.' His gaze moved over her with insolent slowness. 'Forget your prudery, Miss Deane, for I can see right through you to the sensuous woman you really are. Love should be enjoyed, not crushed into the straight-jacket of a genteel marriage – and that, I don't offer.'

The curtain dropped into place behind him and he was gone.

Zara sat on the charpoy staring at the gently swaying curtain. She hated to admit it, but there was much truth in his words. An experienced man could read the reponses of a woman's body with deadly accuracy, despite her attempts to hide them. Zara had glimpsed in others the hidden passions and thought never to know them herself. Ralph could never have fulfilled her foolish dream of romantic love – but was it really so foolish? While not accepting that Deverill was her idealised dream, she could not deny that he had a presence. Beneath that bushy beard, he was handsome. Beneath those loose-fitting hillman clothes, his body was strong and hard. Humour lurked behind his dark eyes, wicked, devilish, but certainly malicious.

He was a man who took what he wanted and to the devil with honour and convention. In no way could she imagine him reading his fiancée a lecture on her lack of conduct and unseemly behaviour. He would not frown and become tight-lipped like Ralph. He would probably roar with laughter and sweep his fiancée into his arms. Fiancée? Had Delia considered herself so? A smile touched Zara's lips. An ill-matched pair if ever there was one. Her smile died. What of the scandal? The drunken man lying beside the body of his murdered mistress? That was fact, the reason for his dismissal. Now, despite his physical attraction, and she could not in her heart refute it, he was a dangerous man without honour and compassion for his countrymen.

What happened to her was unimportant. What really mattered was that she must warn the army of its danger. Those Afghans or Pathans were heading south with enough rifles to wipe out any small garrison or outpost. This village was the collecting point. Now they were on their way to some hiddenn rendezvous to be placed at the disposal of a more powerful leader than Devil Sahib. What was he going to do, now that his task was over as events had seemed to indicate? Wait here for his payment or make doubly sure by heading south himself to join forces with the enemies of the government? This village had proved a disappointment to her plan of escape. A few shabby buildings and no sign that any European ever passed this way, which was why, she supposed, it had been chosen as the common meeting ground.

The door curtain whisked aside, startling her. Deverill looked in.

'Come out and eat,' he ordered. 'Don't skulk there like a sulky child expecting to be waited on.'

'I'm not sulking! Why should I?' she flared at him.

'Hold your tongue and come out,' he said curtly. 'It is time you began to take your turn with the cooking. Hill people don't have servants.' The curtain dropped into place again.

Zara swung her legs over the edge of the charpoy and stood up. She pulled the veiled cap from her head and flung it savagely across the room. Yes, she would hold her tongue in front of the others but he could not control her expression, nor the hatred in her eyes. She crossed the room, sweeping aside the goatskin curtain, and strode into the outer room. It was so small and filled to capacity with five squatting figures that her stride lost its effect for lack of space. Added to which, no one gave her a glance! Feeling slightly deflated, she squatted beside Soonya who filled and handed her a bowl without meeting her eyes.

They ate in silence but Zara was aware that Deverill was watching her. He leaned forward to refill his bowl from the cooking pot and she glanced at him covertly.

'You will veil your face at all times in the presence of men,' he said, very quietly but with an unmistakable note of warning in his voice.

Zara lowered her head submissively although she longed to scream and question his authority to give her orders, but there was something in his voice that hinted of the danger of disobedience. Why was he now insisting on this measure since all four hill people had seen her unveiled and wearing English clothing? Soonya and Rahti still wore their caps but the veils had been lowered to allow them to eat. Was it his intention to accustom her to veil her face automatically, thus making her indistinguishable from every other woman? This awe in which women looked upon men was ridiculous, yet men did have the power to make the lives of their women painful and uncomfortable.

The meal ended and the two girls began to gather the bowls. Zara glanced at Deverill. He was watching her through narrowed eyes. She gave a mental shrug and bent to help the girls. The hillmen produced their habitual beedis and Deverill drew a cheroot from his tunic pocket. Zara followed the girls outside. After the smoky, heat-filled room, the air struck coldly. She shivered and the grass beneath her sandals crunched with a slight beading of frost.

Soonya and Rahti seemed more relaxed away from the men. They wiped out the bowls with a handful of wet grass and Soonya smiled at Zara.

'Coming cold soon. Maybe getting sheepskin for coating.'

'I hope so,' Zara replied. 'Do they cost a lot of money?'

Soonya nodded. 'Devil Sahib, he buy, coming big village.'

'Big village? Where is that? Up there?' Zara jerked her head towards the mountains.

'Maybe, but thinking soon go down to nice camp where Missie Sahib lying first with Devil Sahib.'

Zara looked at her sharply but Soonya was smiling without guile or malice. She said something to Rahti and both girls began to giggle. Zara began to smile, reluctantly at first, but the giggling was so infectious that she laughed too. There was no way these hillwomen would believe that she and Deverill had spent the night together in celibacy. To them, when a man and woman lay together, the act of love was inevitable and entirely expected.

With the bowls and cooking pots, they moved back into the rest house. Soonya and Rahti picked up their blankets, retiring to the farthest corners where they lay down. Zara went through the curtained doorway and sought her own blankets. The wind had risen and strong gusts of freezing air sought out every chink and crack in the dilapidated building. Even the thatching, hastily and inexpertly repaired, could not repel the chill of a windy night. Zara wrapped herself in her blanket and lay down on the extreme edge of the charpoy. The webbing of the frame held no mattress and cold air rose from the earth floor. Even the poorest dak bungalow of Mrs Lacy's early travels could not have been as comfortless as this. Zara pulled the blanket over her head as she had seen the girls do, but her body still trembled with cold. The outer room must be far warmer since the hearthstone was there, but here she was cut off from any lingering heat by the heavy goatskin curtain.

The soft rumble of voices went on and the acrid smell of beedi smoke drifted in with every gust of wind. Sheepskins, Soonya had said. Sheepskin coats to keep out the cold. What a wonderful thought, but that was in the future, not now. The talking stopped and she heard the scrape of boots. Her body tensed. Now Deverill would come. She might pretend to be sleeping if she could control the shivering of her body. Her ears identified the sound of the curtain being moved, then soft footsteps approached the charpoy. She lay, her back to the room, her eyes tightly closed. A few vague sounds. Was he undressing? Surely not in this cold. At the thought, her body gave a convulsive shudder and she could no longer contain her trembling.

Then the charpoy sagged and because her arms were imprisoned inside the tightly rolled blanket, she could not prevent herself from rolling on to her back. Deverill looked down on her. He had discarded his turban and in the faint light of the moon rays creeping into the room, she saw his thick black hair, overlong and shaggy. He seemed to be smiling.

'Are you cold?'

'Of c-course I'm c-cold,' she stammered through a fit of shivering. 'How can anyone s-sleep in this c-cold?'

'I'll soon have you warm,' he said.

'D-don't bother.'

'It's no bother.' He reached out and pulled her towards him. 'Don't you know that proximity is the best protection in the cold?'

His own blanket he tucked about them both and gathered her into his arms, holding her close against the length of his body. Zara felt the immediate warmth enveloping her and she allowed her stiff resistance to ebb away. Pride had its place, but why should one freeze to death on a point of principle? Her head lay on his shoulder, her cheek pressed to his breast. His arms held her, his hands still, not seeking any further intimacy. Perhaps there was still something of the gentleman in him, at least for this night and in this cold. Her body relaxed and all thought drifted and wavered into nothingness.

It was dawn when Zara awakened. She assumed it was dawn for the room was in greyness, not the fresh pearly greyness of early morning on the lower slopes but the harsher light of a winter morning. Deverill was still beside her but his arms lay about her loosely. She raised her head cautiously. His breathing was steady. He was asleep. Zara examined his face under the wild disarray of black hair. His eyelashes, like his brows, were thick and black, the lashes as thick as any girl might envy. She tried to visualise him in a major's uniform, hair clipped short under an army cap. It was difficult to imagine, yet she could see him, tall, strong and handsome in military evening dress, dancing elegantly with the young ladies and flirting outrageously with the matrons. He would be like that, she was sure, for she recalled a certain gentleness in Mrs Lacy's tone when she had spoken of him. What had gone wrong and ruined a promising career? Drink and women were the usual things, and there was the evidence of both in the drunken stupor and the dead Indian girl.

In the lightening dawn, Zara searched his face, trying to find the marks of dissipation. His eyes were not pouched, his lips and chin were too firm to suggest gross indulgence. In

203

sleep, the planes of his face were hard boned, but unlined, yet there must have been a weakness somewhere. A self-controlled man does not get himself into a situation where the only solution is ignominious dismissal from the army. Such a waste, and now he was a thief and a traitor.

Dark eyes opened suddenly and Zara felt her scrutiny returned. She dropped her gaze, feeling a flush on her cheeks. How annoying to have him wake and find her observing him so intently. She waited for some mocking remark. Instead he ruffled her hair and spoke musingly.

'I dare say you could look quite pretty if you were clean and well-dressed.' Zara's head came up sharply, her sense of outrage reddening her cheeks still further.

'How –' she began hotly, then caught the mocking glint in his eye and went on with restrained hauteur. 'Whose fault it is, may I ask, that I am unclean and ill-dressed? This –' she cast a scathing look about the room, 'is not exactly what I have been used to. It bears no resemblance to Claridge's, you must admit, nor even the plainest country tavern in any part of England.'

'True,' he said. 'But you are coping with this life very well.' He regarded her through half-closed eyes. 'You will make a more fitting hillman's woman than a captain's wife.'

'Will I be given the choice?' Zara demanded.

He shrugged. 'I rather doubt it now.'

'What is that supposed to mean? That you will never release me?'

Deverill pushed himself upright and swung his legs over the charpoy. He looked at her for a moment and there was no amusement in his face.

'Think about it, Miss Deane. You have been missing from the garrison for several days now. You were abducted by wild tribesmen, according to all reports. What would your reception be if I returned you to Lahore unharmed and in good health?'

Zara frowned. 'What do you mean, my reception?'

'Would anyone believe your innocence unimpaired after your sojourn in the hills with men who take women as casually as a draught of water?'

204

Zara felt her stomach muscles tighten into a cold knot. She stared into Deverill's face and knew that he spoke the truth.

'You mean that they will never believe – they will see me only as a ruined woman, all reputation gone?' she asked unsteadily.

Deverill said nothing and Zara bent her face into her hands. She didn't need a reply to her question. Dear God, a ruined woman. They would call her that and perhaps worse names, not to her face but among themselves, not believing for a moment her claim to innocence.

Chapter Nineteen

Even after Deverill had gone, Zara sat on the charpoy staring into space. She knew he was right in his assessment of the garrison ladies. Any female who had been held captive by tribesmen as long as she had, must naturally have been raped. Mrs Lacy might believe, or pretend to believe her story, and give her a kindly reception, but the others? Not only the ladies, she reflected, but the officers with their sidelong covert glances, speculative, wondering just how low she had fallen. Bold glances, perhaps, calculating their own chances, for a woman spoiled was fair game.

The whole regiment would know the story, European and Indian alike. But she had to return to the garrison, if only to pack her clothes and arrange a passage back to England. Colonel Lacy would help her there. However distasteful the task, he would perform his duty conscientiously and send her to Calcutta. Packed off, back to England, just as that other poor girl had been, the one who was involved in a scandal with the Yuvaraj. Her thoughts went to the tall, elegant house in London. Father and Mrs Makin. Not Mrs Makin now but Mrs Deane. Father would understand but would his new wife welcome her return? Since she held the purse-strings, she would be within her rights to refuse a welcome for the black sheep. And what explanation would Zara give to Ralph's cousin, Eleanor Farnes, and all her friends? India had proved a disappointment? She had decided against marriage with Captain Browne? Very feeble, since Ralph might write to Eleanor himself with another explanation, a true, unvarnished report.

She rose wearily from the charpoy as Soonya put her head round the curtain.

'Come, Missie Sahib. Come quickly if wanting washing. We go soon. Men fetching ponies.'

Her head disappeared and Zara heard the clanking of metal pots being tumbled into the baskets. She strapped on the leather sandals, adjusted the protective bandaging and looked about her for the cap and veil. It lay in the corner where she had thrown it. The hessian sack lay under the charpoy and Zara checked that it held her comb, slippers and cotton cloths. Why bother to comb her hair, tumbled from the night's sleep? She might as well look as bedraggled as any other hillwoman. The cap and veil would do. With the folded blankets tucked under her arm, the drawstring of the hessian bag over her wrist, she passed into the outer room.

Even that room, so warm and smoky last night, held a damp chill now.

She glanced out of the doorway. It was raining.

'Rains come,' Soonya said unnecessarily.

Zara nodded and dropped the blanket, stepping outside. The icy coldness of the rain took her breath away and she walked as closely as she could in the lee of the wooden buildings. There were pools of water in plenty now but she headed doggedly, her face bent to avoid the sharp needles of rain, to the pool she had used last night for there were bushes about it. She hesitated on seeing a few other women with the same purpose in mind but she shrugged and chose a convenient bush for her toilet. At least they were all female, quite indistinguishable from each other with their rain-soaked tunics and dripping veils. The men, she supposed, went somewhere else. For these small mercies, we give thanks, she brooded miserably as rain lashed her face.

As she dipped her hands into the pool and splashed her

206

already wet face, she was conscious of curious glances from the other woman. Why wash, it is raining, they seemed to say and shrugging, went on their separate ways.

Zara rose, shaking her hands vigorously, more to regain circulation than rid them of water. She fought her way back to the rest house, marvelling that the damp track she had followed only minutes ago was now a muddy glutinous path, every identation filled with water. She staggered through the doorway, her sandals squelching, rain dripping off her chin. The first face she saw was Deverill's. She glared at him, but cautiously kept her voice low.

'What a lovely day for a stroll in the mountains! Where the hell are we off to now?'

She saw his lips tighten but the glint in his eyes showed him to be holding back a grin.

'Language, Miss Deane,' he rebuked, shaking his head. 'You follow where your lord leads, like it or not.'

'Most heartily – not! But where do we go? Up, down, or sideways?'

He rose from strapping a bundle. 'If it helps to know, we go up. Satisfied?'

'I see that Allah directs your steps, my lord,' Zara said with bitterness. 'I hope you carry pick and shovel in that bundle.'

'Why should I?' His tone was surprised.

'To bury my frozen body and rid yourself of an encumbrance. Or maybe you plan to leave me standing in some convenient rock cleft. That would eliminate the need of a pick and shovel.'

Deverill grinned. 'Are you cold?'

Zara stared at him. 'That's the damndest understatement of the century!'

He laughed and swung the bundle on to his shoulder. 'No wonder Captain Browne lectured you on propriety. You have a turn of phrase that must have distressed him and he such a correct fellow.' He moved to the doorway and paused, eyeing her sodden garments with open amusement. 'You'll survive, Miss Deane, if only to spite me and remain an encumbrance.' He looked into her face for a long moment then bent to drop a kiss on to her wet cheek. 'We're survivors, you and I.' Then he passed through the doorway and was gone into the slashing rain.

'Devil take the man,' muttered Zara, and looked at the two girls who had politely turned their backs on the conversation between the leader and his woman.

Soonya looked up shyly. 'Devil Sahib liking you. He not often laughing.'

Zara scowled. 'Like Janus, he is a man with two faces.'

Soonya's eyes opened wide. 'Two-face? Devil Sahib have only one face.'

'That's what you think. Devil Sahib is the most two-faced man I know.' She reflected on this statement for a moment. Weren't most people, come to think of it? Both she and Captain Browne had been two-faced in their dealings with each other. But never in such a traitorous and despicable manner as Richard Deverill. She sighed and picked up the rolled blankets, then the three girls left the relative comfort of the rest house and plunged into the driving rain.

Zara followed the now familiar back of Soonya, her own body adopting the swaying motion. Although the exercise of walking soon had her feeling warmer, she was conscious of the wide trousers flapping wetly against her skin and the mud oozing between her toes. Her resentment against Deverill grew with every step. He could have taken her on the back of his pony, but no, that would have lost him face with the hillmen. Such soft treatment of a woman would amaze and disgust them. She must act the hillwoman to keep his honour intact! If she had had the breath, she would have laughed aloud. Honour, for Richard Deverill? What did he know of honour?

The rain ceased, as abruptly as if a blind had been raised. Instead of a wet, grey curtain in front of her eyes, Zara saw a drenched landscape, glittering with rain-filled potholes. The sun blinked down, revealing diamond droplets on every leaf and blade of grass. As the sun's rays strengthened, the ground gave off its earthy smell in a low coating of mist. It was a smell Zara enjoyed, a reminder of those early morning rides in Lahore before the sun laid its burning hand over the landscape.

Ahead, Zara saw the three ponies cantering slowly, the men sitting at ease, their legs swinging as they talked and gestured. Zara's resentment grew. In spite of the sun's appearance, there was little warmth in it and water still dripped from her clothes. If only she had a towel.

'Soonya,' she called. 'Where are we going? Do we walk for ever?'

Soonya glanced over her shoulder and shrugged. 'Gujrat, maybe. Coming soon.'

Gujrat, thought Zara. Wasn't that where the dancers who had performed at the Rajah's durbar were from? What kind of a place was it? Her spirits rose a little higher. Perhaps, with people and bazaars, a place where Europeans might be and a place where she might plan an escape. This thought kept her mind occupied for the next hour and she almost forgot the discomfort of her sodden clothing.

They stopped once on the road to eat cold chapattis but Deverill seemed anxious to press on quickly. The sun had misted over and the clouds were dark with the threat of more rain. A wind had risen, a cold wind that seemed to freeze Zara's clothing until she felt encased in ice. She tried to catch Deverill's eye but his expression was stony and withdrawn. They moved on, the world hovering in half-darkness about them.

Lights pricked the distant hills and the pace increased, Raschid and Mahomet snarling over their shoulders at the panting women. Deverill did not turn and Zara glanced in futile anger at his erect back. They came at last upon dwelling-places, run down and ramshackle as outskirts often are, even in European towns. She looked ahead eagerly, seeing lights and hearing music, unmelodic to her ear but with a fascination of its own. Gujrat might be a town or village, she had no idea which, but there were people, playing and listening to music.

Her hopes faded a little as Deverill turned aside his pony, away from the sound, and led them through a narrow alleyway between stone-walled buildings close enough on either side for their occupants to hold conversations without raising their voices. Deverill halted at the last building.

Beyond this lay open country, bleak and dark. The men dismounted and Deverill rapped on the door with the hilt of his knife. He waited for a moment, then rapped again. Shuffling footsteps were heard and Zara surmised that a signal had been given and accepted. A chain rattled, a bolt was withdrawn and the door opened. A very old man, white-bearded and wrinkled with age, peered out. Deverill spoke a few words in a language Zara did not recognise as Urdu as the old man's face lit up. He grinned, revealing a few broken teeth in the pink cavity of his mouth.

To Zara's surprise, Deverill bowed, then embraced the old man. A wrinkled claw-like hand patted Deverill's shoulder and the door was opened wide. The men entered first, followed by the three bedraggled girls. The door was closed. Raschid and Mahomet were being introduced by Deverill and their greetings to the old man were deferential. He gestured to them to follow him and they disappeared through an archway into another room, none of the men sparing a glance behind. The girls laid down their baskets and stood in silence, dripping quietly on to the stone floor.

'And who was that?' asked Zara of Soonya.

'Devil Sahib father.'

'Father? But he was –' she stopped. The girls did not know Deverill was English. She went on. 'He was very old.'

Soonya shrugged. 'Maybe father of father but he call Devil Sahib "son".'

'I see.'

Zara looked about her. The building had more substance than was guessed at from the outside. The hall was clean and a flight of wooden steps to one side suggested an upper room or perhaps just a balcony where one sat during the coolness of evening during the hot weather. Soonya and Rahti seemed content to wait until ordered to move but Zara grew annoyed at this lack of courtesy since she could plainly hear the sound of conversation and the clink of metal bowls.

Mahomet appeared in the archway and beckoned. The girls moved forward. He allowed Soonya and Rahti through, then held up a hand as Zara drew level. He pointed to the flight of steps.

'Go now.'

'Where?' Zara stared hard at him. She could feel the warmth of the room beyond him and smell the fragrance of cooking food. Why was she not allowed in there?

He pointed to the steps again. 'Go now,' he repeated, avoiding her direct stare.

'Damn your eyes,' she muttered and turned. Short of shouldering him aside, she could not enter that room. She supposed Deverill to have issued the order and included him in her condemnation. A small, cold room upstairs, cut off from the heat of the lower floor and, no doubt, equipped as starkly as the rest house.

A door at the head of the stairs stood ajar. She moved into the room, prepared to be confronted by a sagging charpoy and, if she was lucky, a bucket and maybe a chatti pot of cold water. Her eyes widened as she looked about her. A young Indian girl raised a flushed face from the Victorian hip-bath she was filling with hot water. She smiled at Zara's astonishment and lifted a pot of cold water, pouring it into the steaming bath. Zara moved closer, staring into the water with undisguised amazement. She looked at the smiling girl who spoke in a soft, halting voice.

'He say, very special for you.' The girl took a handful of petals from a small bowl and tossed them into the water.

The scent of jasmine rose. The girl pointed to a towel and soapdish on a stool beside the bath.

'Good?' She looked anxiously into Zara's face.

'Very good and thank you, thank you very much.'

The girl smiled. 'Wet clothes I fetch later.' She pointed to a neat pile of garments set out on another stool beside a stove. 'You putting these.' She gave a little bow, her palms together. Zara returned the gesture and the girl left the room.

Zara sat in the hip-bath, breathing in the perfume of jasmine-scented water. She soaped and washed her hair, revelling in the sheer luxury and reluctant to end it. Beside the stove, she towelled her hair and body. Not in a long time had she felt so clean and warm. She withdrew her condemnation of Deverill, at least for the moment, since he had arranged this, but why had he not told her this morning when

211

she had complained of the cold? She could have spent the journey anticipating the pleasure. But that was not Deverill's way, she supposed. He had merely shrugged and told her that she would survive. His name should really have been Devil for he was devious and evil, a man who enjoyed inflicting misery, yet at the same time he could show kindness and thought for others.

She examined the clothing on the stool, excited yet despising herself for it. Another hillwoman outfit, of course, in green and bronze, identical save in colour to the damp garments on the floor. But a new pair of sandals, less heavy and she discarded the bandages. There was a cotton bodice and a pair of drawers too! She sank back on her heels and regarded them, trying not to laugh. Good God, had Richard Deverill gone boldly into a bazaar with a haughty request for English lady's undergarments? Could he have sent the young Indian girl? But would she have known what to buy and what size to choose? That thought sobered her. Maybe Deverill had watched her at the pool when she was naked. With his stated experience of women, he could judge garment size to a nicety. She smiled ruefully. Since he was her only audience, she could hardly play the role of outraged virtuous maiden. He would only laugh and most likely rob her of that too.

She rose and dressed in the new clothes. Automatically, she looked about for a mirror. The room was bare of one but a coat hanging on a wall hook caught her eye and she moved towards it. A sheepskin coat, heavy and protective. Was this for her, too? She tried it on quickly. It fitted well, the coat reaching just below hip level. The seams were hand sewn, the edges covered by strips of braiding. Large bone buttons and deep pockets made it a coat to defy all weather in the hills.

She had not heard the door open but Deverill's voice came lazily.

'You said you were cold. Does that satisfy you?'

Zara turned. He was leaning against the door jamb, arms folded, his eyes critical. He nodded as if in agreement with his assessment.

'The right size, I thought it would be.' His eyes changed

212

and Zara recognised the lurking humour. 'I trust everything else is – er – quite fitting, Miss Deane?'

Zara looked away, biting her lip in a fierce effort to restrain the impulse to laugh. She nodded, wordlessly, and there was a moment of silence. She risked an upward glance. He was laughing almost silently and her own lips began to twitch.

'Oh, confound you, Deverill!' She exploded into laughter. 'Everything fits and well you know it. I wish I could have been there when you asked the bazaar man for – for English bloomers!' Her voice choked on the words.

'He did eye me a little suspiciously, I will admit, but I knew he was a Hindu merchant who traded with Europeans. He probably robbed me blind, for I've no idea what price those things are. I've never bought them before.'

'Well, I dare say money is no consideration with you. The sheepskin coat must have cost a great deal and I thank you for it.'

The smile was still on his face but the humour was gone from his eyes. They were hard and cynical.

'Even though it was paid for by the sale of those rifles?' he said softly. 'What of your principles now, Miss Deane? Does your honour demand that you fling it into my face, along with your new clothes?' He waited, expectantly, his gaze now sardonic.

Zara thought of the cold, cutting wind, the slashing rain. She stared at Deverill. To retain one's honour and freeze to death with no one being aware of her sacrifice, seemed a pointless gesture. She had no wish to die, yet Deverill was making it clear that her acceptance or rejection of his gifts would place her in a different sphere. Accept and she would be as guilty of treason as he was. Reject and her bones might find a home in this wilderness.

She smiled. 'Like most people who have a mercenary streak in them, survival is what counts. I have no great wish for a glorious death in the name of honour, so I will suspend that virtue for the period of my captivity. You have my gratitude for this kindness.'

He nodded. 'You have made the decision I expected of you. Practical and lacking melodrama.' He paused and his eyes were less hard. 'You give me gratitude. In what practical form will I receive it?'

'I will learn to cook like Soonya.' Zara's reply was prompt. 'I will wash your shirts though I don't guarantee they will dry if the rain continues.'

Deverill laughed and pushed himself away from the door jamb. 'Very practical, Miss Deane, but not quite what I had in mind. However, we can discuss that matter later. Take off the coat and put on your veiled cap. The food is ready downstairs.'

He turned and opened the door. Zara hastened to obey and follow. They had eaten nothing for hours and the smell of food, growing stronger by the second as she trailed Deverill down the stairs, made her realise her hunger. The room they entered was large, with a rush-matted floor and a cooking stove set in an alcove. Raschid, Mahomet and the old man sat cross-legged on one side of the room, Soonya and Rahti on the other. Zara approached the girls, noting with relief that they too had had a change of clothing, but the bathing had been omitted. There were signs, however, that a half-hearted application of water on hands and face had been attempted. They both looked cheerful and smiled as Zara sat down.

The young Indian girl, probably the old man's grand-daughter, set empty bowls and beakers before them, then two large dishes of food. One contained a mound of boiled rice, the other a mixture of curried chicken and almonds, sliced eggs, chillies and some kind of vegetable. Fingers were used to heap individual bowls and they began to eat. The first mouthful made Zara gasp. It was the hottest-tasting curry she had ever known. Soonya grinned at her and obligingly filled the beaker from the metal jug by her elbow. Zara took a deep drink and gasped again. Looking into the beaker, she saw that it was not water as she had supposed, but a pale golden liquid.

'What is it?' she croaked, still gasping.

Soonya spoke to the young girl, then turned back to Zara. 'She say water with little rum to taste. Devil Sahib bringing.' She poured and tasted her own drink. 'Very good, yes? For warming, he say.'

Zara wiped her forehead with the sleeve of her tunic. It left

214

a wet stain on the fabric. She must fashion one of the old bandage cloths into a handkerchief if they were to eat like this with any regularity. Despite the heat of the curry she enjoyed the meal, taking cautious sips of the rum and water. Was rum a favourite drink of Deverill's? She associated it more with sailors. Had Deverill been drunk on rum when they found him beside the murdered girl? Rum did not seem somehow in character. Whisky, perhaps, or wine, she imagined him drinking, though she had smelt neither aroma on him during their meetings. Not even when he had kissed her.

Her body grew hotter at that thought. She knew in what way he expected her to show gratitude for the new clothes, but she would not submit willingly whatever he bought her. She sat staring into nothing, her mind in a heat haze of curry and rum. To submit would be another dishonour, like accepting the clothes bought with traitor's money. But no one would know of that either, an inner voice whispered in her ear. She was already considered a fallen woman, the voice persisted. Would a little more dishonour make her any less fallen? She blinked, trying to clear her mind. What was she thinking of? Well, Deverill, of course, her other self pointed out cynically. That tall, dark stranger with the handsome face and devilish sense of humour, the man who kept her guessing, infuriating her with his arrogance, then disarming her with an act of kindness.

She frowned into the depths of the beaker, wondering vaguely why she had not yet seen the bottom of it. She lifted it to her lips, then stared blankly at her empty fingers. Someone bent over her and then she was on her feet instead of being cross-legged on the floor.

'How strange,' she murmured and her head spun alarmingly.

'By Allah, you're drunk, woman!' a laughing voice said.

'Oh, no,' Zara said solemnly into the wavering face close to hers. 'I never drink. Why – why don't you keep still while I'm talking to you?' She tried to frown her disapproval but the world took a turn and she clutched at the figure for support. Then her face on his chest and strong arms lifted her. A low rumbling against her ear was the last thing she heard.

215

Chapter Twenty

Zara opened her eyes, then closed them quickly against the brightness of the day. She lay quite still, trying to think where she was, but the pounding in her head was not helping to capture coherent thought. She opened her eyes again, but narrowly this time. Instead of the intertwined palm leaves and fir branches she was gazing at a ceiling. She remembered then. They were in a house, an old man's house, where she had bathed and eaten an enormous meal that had ended with sweetly stuffed apricots. But she was lying on a charpoy, her head throbbing. Why? Of course, that rum and water from the never-empty beaker. Soonya had refilled it constantly without her noticing. Why should she do that? Had Deverill ordered it?

There was a movement on the charpoy beside her. Zara's head turned, too quickly for its own good, and the throb behind her eyes increased. She tried to focus her gaze.

'Who's that?' Her voice sounded querulous, she thought.

'A silly question, Miss Deane,' the familiar voice said. 'Did you expect someone else?'

Deverill leaned up on one elbow and looked down into the pale face on the pillow. His smile was malicious and she saw that his shoulders were bare, as was the chest with the dark curling hair upon it. She closed her eyes against the sight, then with a sudden jarring shock, realised her own body was naked.

'Oh, God!' she muttered and clutched tightly at the blanket. Without opening her eyes, she said, 'What happened?' She felt the charpoy quiver and knew he was laughing. 'I – I fear I drank a little too much.'

'A little too much?' The bed shook. 'You were as drunk as an owl, though why an owl I can't say, for I would have thought them teetotal, through and through.'

Zara lay for a moment in reflective silence. 'Drunk,' she

216

repeated. 'I have never been drunk in my life.'

'Then it was a new experience for you. How do you feel?'

'Terrible. On the verge of extinction. How can people enjoy getting drunk?'

'Some do, I assure you. It frees them from inhibitions.'

'Inhibitions? Like what?'

'Like being too prim and proper, worrying about principles and such things.' Zara, still with her eyes closed, frowned. 'I have no clothes on.'

'I know,' said Deverhill. 'I took them off.'

Zara heard him move, the sound of his breathing nearer. She sensed that he was waiting in anticipation her response.

'Why?'

'I was convinced you would wish it. After all, they were new and you would hardly want to crease them by wearing them in bed.'

He spoke in such a reasonable tone that Zara almost thanked him for his thoughtfulness, but she said nothing. There was more to come she was sure.

'Is there anything else you wish to know?' he asked softly, and without looking at him, she knew he was enjoying the moment. If she opened her eyes, she would find his own on a level with hers, watchful, teasing and so damn sure of himself!

'No,' she said briefly.

He sighed. 'Good. Though a little frayed at the seams, I can still retain my tattered guise of being an officer and a gentleman.'

Zara slitted her eyes and looked at him. 'A lady's honour is never discussed in the officers' mess?'

'Exactly.' He grinned cheerfully. 'My lips will stay sealed on last night's events.'

'Events?' Zara frowned. 'You said I was drunk.'

'Indeed you were – when I first put you to bed.'

Zara sat up quickly, forgetting her naked state, then gasped and made a grab for the blanket. She lay down again, pulling it about her neck. She glanced at Deverill and almost forgot her throbbing head.

'Are you trying to tell me something in your usual devious manner?'

217

'Not at all, Miss Deane. On the contrary, it was you who did most of the talking last night. I found you most charming and very entertaining.'

'I don't believe you. I was asleep.'

'As you wish, my dear.' His smile was so tolerant that she wanted to hit him.

'Damn you, Deverill, for a –' She stopped as someone banged on the door. 'Hell!' she muttered savagely and pulled the blanket over her head.

The charpoy creaked and Zara heard a murmur of voices, then the door closed. She peered over the edge of the blanket, hoping that Deverill had gone, but he was standing by the bedside, two steaming mugs in his hands.

'Good morning, Miss Deane. May I offer you a mug of freshly brewed tea?'

He might have just come in to wake her with morning tea as he placed one mug on the stool beside the bed, except that he wore only baggy trousers and his hair was in disarray.

Zara licked her dry lips and reached for the mug. 'Thank you,' she muttered without meeting his eyes. The tea was strong, no milk or sugar, but a few grains of something floated on the surface.

Deverill seemed to divine her questioning glance. 'I mixed in a headache powder. Thought you might need it before we leave.'

'Leave? Again? Isn't this place high enough for you?'

'Gujrat? It's not so high.' He sipped his tea. 'You'll be happy to know that we travel south this time. Not to Lahore, you understand, but we take a dog-leg route west after Gujranwala.'

'I've never heard of it.'

'Why should you? Most ladies go to Simla during the hot weather.'

'And after that?'

'After that, Miss Deane, is no business of yours.'

'Naturally not,' Zara said bitterly. 'You drag me up and down these mountains, scorch me with heat and half-drown me in the rain, threaten me with camel traders and getting stoned to death and then tell me it's none of my business.

218

You would have done better to have kidnapped a mountain goat!'

Deverill smiled. 'That's true. Mountain goats do not answer back, do not call me names, nor do they get drunk. With all these new-found qualities, my dear, I feel that Captain Browne is well out of a marriage with you. You would never have suited each other. You should be grateful for your abduction. Now you can marry some worthy in England who knows nothing of your reputation. You may trust in my guarantee of silence.'

Zara set down her empty mug with a bang. 'Would you kindly go to hell and leave me to dress in peace. When I need a homily from you, I'll ask for it!'

Deverill rose and picked up the two mugs. 'We move in an hour's time. Be ready.' He was still smiling as he left the room.

As Zara washed and dressed, she tried to recall the events of the previous night. She remembered falling into Deverill's arms and the deep-throated laughter rumbling through him as he carried her upstairs. After that, there was complete blankness. He had to have been the one who laid her on the charpoy and removed her clothes. No other hillman, however drunk, would have taken another man's woman. But Deverill had looked disgustingly healthy this morning. Only she had been drunk. Why suppose that everyone else had to be too?

She bent to strap on her sandals and the movement made her head spin. True, the throbbing in her head was less, but still there. She supposed she should thank Deverill for minimising it with his headache powder. The confounded man thought of everything, but only as it affected him. How could she march if she was laid low with a stunning hangover?

There was a tap on the door and the young Indian girl came in. She held out the dry, folded garments in which Zara had arrived. Zara took them, smiling.

'Thank you. It was very kind of you to take the trouble.'

The girl shook her head. 'For lady of Devil Sahib is honour. Food ready downstairs, memsahib.' She smiled shyly and went away.

Zara combed her hair and set the veiled cap in place. To the

219

Indian girl she was undoubtedly a European, yet she showed no curiosity at finding a memsahib dressed as a hillwoman and in company with four true hill people and Devil Sahib. It followed naturally that they were aware of Deverill's identity, as were Raschid and Mahomet. Where did this young girl and her grandfather fit into things? Did they know him for a traitor and approve of what he was doing?

Downstairs, she met Soonya and Rahti, both clear-eyed and cheerful. Soonya handed her a bowl of some thick mixture that held the tang of cinnamon.

'Missie Sahib looking tired. Not sleep much I thinking.' The sympathetic words were belied by the expression in her merry, knowing eyes. 'You tell me mind damn business, yes?'

'Exactly.' Zara scowled into her porridge, but Soonya giggled, unabashed.

In half an hour, they were on the road again. It was a crisp cold morning but the threat of rain hung heavily from the dark clouds. All three girls now had sheepskin coats and the men wore wool-lined waistcoats over their tunics. All, Zara assumed darkly, by courtesy of Deverill's ill-gotten wealth. She had to admit to the luxury of the coat and would have been a fool to refuse it. Her honour was gone anyway. Nothing would ever be the same again.

She brooded over Deverill's words that morning. He had said she talked during the night. She had no memory of it and he could have lied, yet how long did a person stay unconscious when drunk? Sleep it off, she had heard people say. A few hours, a whole night? And if she had talked, what on earth had she said, and, more important, done?

Her mind moved back to the meal itself, the consumption of watered rum from the never empty beaker, then the half-recalled conversation with herself. What had all that been about? She shivered suddenly and hunched her shoulders into the coat collar. Who else but Deverill? And her subconscious self, the part of her nature that should be rigidly suppressed, had won that argument in favour of Deverill's attraction, advising her to take the final step into dishonour. A well-brought-up young lady should never acknowledge such feelings, let alone have them! A proper lady did not cast her cap over the moon, or was it the windmill? She must, she decided, have windmills in her head to think she meant anything to Deverill. Go back to England and marry some worthy who has no knowledge of your reputation, he had said. Did that sound like a man who cared two straws what happened to her? She trudged on miserably. What had she said or done last night to make him so confoundly cheerful this morning? He had been amused, most definitely amused, but by what? She could remember nothing. Perhaps it was wiser not to try, but to ignore whatever happened, if anything did, and put it down to being under the influence of drink and not responsible for one's words or deeds.

She felt a little cheered by that solution and, as her headache had cleared in the fresh air, she looked about her. The land was more fertile here, still cold but with a freshening breeze and a break in the cloudy sky. The sun was trying to fight its way through and they were going south at last. That place he had mentioned, Gujranwala. She must wait until they reached it and then decide her next move. How far from Lahore? Someone would know. A dog-leg route west after Gujranwala. That information must give Colonel Lacy a rough idea from which direction to expect trouble. Was Deverill so sure of his captive that he let fall this useful information? He could be lying but that must not stop her from trying to escape.

It took them two days to reach Gujranwala. Deverill had been absent on the night they had camped in the dried-up bed of a nullah. Zara was glad of his absence and supposed, cynically, that he was following up his interests and making sure the camel train turned on to the right track. He was waiting for them in the town but once again he led them to a house on the outskirts. Here there were no occupants, no hot bath nor any pretty Indian girl to serve a delicious meal. However, Deverill had thought of everything in the way of food and water, firewood and more beedis for Raschid and Mahomet.

The building was single storey and lacking occupants; it lacked furniture too. No fireplace or stove, so the food had to be cooked outside in the small yard. In the absence of charpoys, they had to roll themselves into their blankets and sleep on the floor.

There had been little conversation. Deverill looked tired, Zara thought, and as soon as the meal was over, had retired into a corner with his blanket. Zara lay sleepless for a long time. She was not cold, the sheepskin coat prevented that, but the floor was uncomfortable. She dozed and wakened several times, her body aching with stiffness. At last she rose, unable to find a restful position. Five blanketed bundles lay still, save for the rise and fall of their breathing. The light was grey, they would soon have to wake anyway, so Zara picked up her hessian sack, now larger by a change of clothing, and crept outside into the yard.

A broken fence lay before her and beyond that, open country, dotted with bushes and rain pools. An ideal bathroom, she thought wryly, spacious and completely private. She took her time, waiting for the dawn light to strengthen. The girls would soon be roused to serve their men hot tea and food. Tea, she resolved, tea or coffee, maybe a little wine would be the only drinks to pass her lips in the future. Rum or any other strong drink, never! It gave one strange fancies and let loose inhibitions. Soonya and Rahti, like children, had no inhibitions. They were frank and literal-minded, accepting hardship and the pleasing of their men as the normal way of things. To lie with a man was the most natural thing in the world. Why should such a simple thing be hidden in a welter of white lace, tears and wedding-bells, pious words from a strange priest and the opening of matronly ranks to admit another sufferer?

Zara, bending over one of the rain pools, grinned at her reflection. It was completely absurd to make such a fuss about it, but that was the way of the conventional world. She supposed she would have gone through the same ritual in the garrison church with Ralph and thought it quite in order. Her smile died. That would never happen now, not with Ralph or any other man who knew her history. An outcast, a pariah, a girl to be avoided for fear of contamination, that would be her lot if she stayed in India. She rose, drying her face and hands on her old shirt.

The day was brightening, the birds beginning to wheel overhead. She glanced towards the house. Still no sign of anyone stirring. Rather than go back there, she would take a walk as far as that grassy ridge. A few goats were ambling on its summit and as she approached they became more numerous, turning into quite a flock. Did goats come in flocks, she wondered idly, or was it herds? Whichever was correct, there appeared to be hundreds of them, pouring over the crest, some with belled neck collars, the tinkling sounds adding to the bleatings.

A very small boy, scarcely more than three years old, she judged, bobbed up on the ridge, hooting in a high, shrill voice, urging the goats on with slaps from a short stick. The herd paid little heed and streamed down the sharp incline. The child ran and jumped, waving his stick, short chubby legs pounding along the crest. Buffeted by heavy bodies, he was swept along, over and down the incline. He would never keep his feet in that rush of bodies, Zara decided, then she saw the sharp, splintered rocks in the ditch below the incline.

The sure-footed goats were leaping them but the press of bodies hid them from the boy and even now, his body was outpacing his short legs. Zara began to run. The child would never stop in time to prevent himself from hurtling face down over the rocks.

She reached them a few seconds before he did and leapt to meet the boy in full uncontrolled flight. His eyes were wide with fear as she caught him and by twisting sideways, they fell together on the lowest part of the grassy slope.

'Aiyee!' screamed a voice from above and Zara, as breathless as the boy, looked up.

A tall woman in bright tunic and pleated trousers stared down, her face twisted in anguish, and a stream of words followed. Zara understood none of them. She climbed to her feet, lifting the child, and smiled up at the woman to show that the boy was unharmed. He was beginning to whimper and Zara walked up the incline with the child in her arms. She held him out and the woman's hands reached out.

'Good. Not hurt,' Zara said and smiled again. Although she

doubted the woman understood the words she must understand the smile.

There was a relaxing in the woman's expression. Her gaze went rapidly over the boy as if assuring herself of his undamaged condition, then she looked at Zara, and nodded. With the boy cradled on her hip, she beckoned with her free hand and pointed towards the black tent. Zara glanced past her to see more goats and several more black tents.

Something stirred in her mind. Goats, black tents, bold-looking women in bright clothes. Nomadic goat-herders? Up and down the mountains, always moving to fresh pastures. As if to confirm her conjecture, she noted the shawls, the heavy cotton shawls, a vital part of their dress. Before coming to India, she had read all she could about this vast continent, but with so many tribes and religions, such varied customs and cultures, complete knowledge would take a lifetime to acquire. These things she did remember, though, the importance of the shawl and its uses. A prayer mat, a pillow, protection from the wind and a sling in which to carry a baby. There was also a way, she had read, for a man creating for himself a rocking chair by a deft twining of the long shawl about his shoulders, crossing and tying the ends under his knees, so that he could rest easily on the ground.

At the tent of the child's mother, she was offered a mug of strong black tea. She accepted, smiling, and the little boy stared at her from his mother's arms, wide, solemn eyes over the grimy thumb in his mouth. The woman seemed to be questioning her, but Zara shrugged and spread her hands in puzzlement. Other women joined them, looking curiously at the newcomer, then smiled and nodded as the mother of the child spoke. A young girl was summoned, perhaps one with knowledge of a different dialect, Zara assumed, but still she did not understand.

She rose and bowed, handing back the mug. It was time she returned to the house. Glancing round, she saw the tents being dismantled, the packing up almost completed. They were leaving, moving on to fresh pastures for the herds. Where were they going?

'Go where?' she asked, pointing south, then turned to point north, her brows rising in question.

The woman stared, blank faced, then an old man paused in the act of tying the ends of his shawl behind his back. He looked at her and she saw his forehead corrugate into a frown as if trying to remember some long-forgotten words. His brow cleared and he gave a crow of triumph. The woman turned to stare at him.

'Sowt,' he declared. 'Go Shekhupura.'

Zara repeated the name in her mind. Shekhupura. There was something of memory there from the garrison. A good place for hunting, was that it?

'Lahore?' she queried hopefully.

'Soon by,' the old man said and nodded emphatically.

Zara felt a quick thrill run up her spine. Near to Lahore, did he mean that? Sowt or south, he had stated with confidence. She glanced behind her. There was no alarm from the house and these people were leaving and going south. She made up her mind.

Pointing at her own breast, then southwards, she looked a question at the old man. He shrugged and spoke to the woman. They nodded amiably and drifted away.

Zara bowed to the old man. 'I help carry.' She knew she sounded like Soonya but her disguise as a hillwoman was essential. If the old man had a few words of English, she must pretend the same until she had judged their attitude towards the British. Her race was not universally popular, she knew. They had brought roads and trains, schools and hospitals, imposed their judiciary system in an effort to create law and order, but not everyone welcomed these things, for it meant taxation and the abolishing of some ancient ceremonies. Now, a man could not plunder his neighbour's land with impunity, nor need a widow immolate herself in the burning ghat beside her dead husband. To be sure, the roads were safer for travellers since the British had stamped out thuggee, but Kali, the destroyer, was still a goddess although her followers had been eliminated. Perhaps she would rise again when the British left.

Zara came to herself with a start. Good heavens, she was

225

beginning to think like a superstitious hillwoman. The old man was holding out a wicker basket, full of cooking pots. She took it, settling it on her head. Then the whole milling camp was on the move. Zara remembered her cast-aside sack. She had to have that. The goats were passing within yards of where she had dropped it, and with a hurried crabwise movement had her catching it up before she merged herself into the centre of the striding women.

With luck, Soonya would tell Deverill that Missie Sahib had gone to wash. How long would he wait before becoming suspicious? Long enough, she hoped, for this nomadic group to be more than a dust cloud on the horizon. After all, she was similarly attired except, she thought uneasily, for the sheep-skin coat. At the first possible moment, she must slip it off. But then, what to do with it? Too bulky for her sack and if she dropped it, the goat women would wonder why she had thrown away a costly coat.

The nomads moved on, the long striding women covering the ground quickly. Zara glanced back once, but the sweep of the countryside was empty and her spirits began to rise. As the sun rose too, she solved the problem of the coat. Choosing a belled goat, she draped her sheepskin coat, wool side uppermost, over its back. The two shaggy skins blended well together and her free hand held on to the goat's collar. She was not quite ready to lose sight of the coat completely in case something unforeseen happened.

Zara strode along beside the goat, her face lifted to the sky. The breeze was fresh and invigorating, she could hardly believe that she was free for they must have marched for at least three hours. An urgent shout from behind made her swing round. The group had stopped, only she had marched ahead, the goat ambling passively beside her. She frowned, trying to think of a reason for this sudden stop. The shawls were being unknotted from shoulders and waists, men and women alike. Were they going to eat and rest on their folded shawls? There was no sign of food being unpacked. She approached them slowly, still holding to the goat's collar. There was no grazing here, the ground had become stony with only the occasional tuft of grass protruding from a rocky hillock.

She stopped a few paces away and looked at the goat people, a puzzled frown on her face. All eyes were on her and as she gazed around seeking reason, she realised with a jolting heart that their stares held hostility. What had she done? Her eyes searched for the old man. He was watching her too, a gentle sadness in his gaze. Of them all, he was the only one who stood. He raised a hand to quell the muttering that had begun and came slowly towards Zara. She stared into the old face, still not understanding the gravity of whatever she had done.

His words when they came were faltering and reminded Zara of some long unused machinery being forced into action again. Between each word there was a pause.

'You are of us?'

'I am hillwoman,' Zara said slowly, trying to read his meaning.

He made an impatient move of his hand. 'Us,' he said.

'I don't understand.'

'For Mahomet?'

Zara's eyes widened. 'Mahomet? What did he mean? Mahomet and Raschid? She scanned the way they had come. There was no one in sight. She shook her head, frowning in puzzlement.

The old man spread the fingers of his hand, palm down and lowered his arm groundwards. He wants me to kneel, Zara hazarded, and obediently sank to her knees. She looked up at him and he sighed, his eyes clouding over. He raised both hands, then dropped them in a gesture of resignation, turned and walked away. Zara looked past him to the goat people, all of whom were on their knees facing her.

As the realisation hit her that he was referring to the prophet Mahomet, not the hillman, Mahomet, the first stone took her on the forehead.

Chapter Twenty-one

It was quite a small stone but the shock of the sudden attack took Zara completely by surprise. It had been thrown by a young boy, taking his cue from a group of muttering women. They were Muslims, she realised now, intensely devout, fanatically so, with the time for prayer governed by strict routine. Five times a day, wherever they were and in any condition, the prayer mats went down. Every good Muslim should know this and those who did not were outcast.

The woman whose child Zara had saved from injury was arguing with the sullen group of females, some already rising to their feet, the rest watching, hate-filled eyes on Zara. The mother seemed to be arguing in her favour, as if aware of her obligation, but her protests were drowned in the rising murmur. She threw Zara a look of apology, then turned her back, gathering the child to her.

It seemed to signal the end of restraint and the stones began to fly. Zara came to her feet and made a wild grab at the curly wool of her sheepskin coat as the goat plunged away with an indignant bleat as a stone ricocheted off its head. With the coat affording some protection, slung round her shoulders, she turned to run. A sharp, heavier rock struck the back of her knee and she went down, rolling desperately to avoid the shower of earth clods and stones.

The women were yelling and screaming, the animal sounds far more frightening than the attack itself. It was like the baying of hounds with the fox in view, the most terrifying sound in the world to the hunted animal. Zara regained her feet, breath sobbing in her throat. She glanced back. Some were pursuing, their faces snarling masks, eyes black and bright with mad excitement. A sharp-edged stone scored her forehead and the blood ran down into her eyes. She swayed, shaking her head to clear her vision. Against these long-legged, hard-muscled women she would be no match, she

228

knew. Their lives had been spent walking the plains or climbing the hills. The hardness of life could only be compensated by a similar harshness of religious belief. There was no softness in them, except perhaps for their babies. She could only run for her life.

A harsh crack split the air, so sharp that Zara's head rang with the sound. Then there was such utter silence she thought she had become deaf. The scene was the same, the crowd of women, arms upraised, fingers clutching stones but time had stopped. The picture had frozen like models in a tableau.

Time moved on. The upraised arms were lowered and the shrill screams died into muted murmurings. Zara, still dazed and half-blinded by the trickling blood, watched the boldest women scuttle back to the companionship of their kind. No more stones came, which was odd, considering that a moment before, the women were racing in for the kill.

Zara wiped the blood from her eyes with the sleeve of her tunic and looked again. Their concerted gaze was upwards to the craggy rock with the tufted grass growing from it. Zara followed the direction of their eyes. A man stood on the rock. Towering high above the goat people, he looked like a giant, feet planted apart, the breeze rippling his tunic and trousers. The rifle tucked into his shoulder was unwavering, the barrel pointing steadily into the midst of the group.

Zara's heart jerked and she gave a half-strangled choke as her breath caught. She should have known he would not let her go so easily, but dear God, how glad she was to see him at this moment! She jumped as his voice cut through the murmurings.

'Come here, Zara Deane.' His eyes were still on the goat people.

Zara hurried, stumbling up the side of the crag until she was behind him.

'Mount the pony,' he ordered and she obeyed.

Deverill moved the rifle barrel slowly and deliberately over the massed bodies beneath. He spoke in a slow even voice but the menace was there. The words, Zara could not understand, but it was obvious the goat people could. Then he turned and slung his rifle over his shoulder. He did not look at her as he swung himself up behind her. The pony started forward, increasing its pace, and Zara clung to its mane. She half-turned towards Deverill.

'Shut up,' he said curtly. 'One word and I'll throw you into the nearest pit.'

Zara stared forward, tears and blood washing her cheeks. That brief glance had shown her a harder face than ever she had seen, the eyes like flint. Not exactly a welcome-home look but what did she expect? How was she to know the goat people would treat her like that? She guessed that he had declared her a runaway from her master. It was an explanation they would accept. A runaway woman had to be disciplined, beaten into submission. That was the hillman's way. Soonya and Rhati knew that only too well.

But Deverill would not beat her, would he? Neither of them was a hill person. In spite of the daytime warmth she shivered, holding the coat tightly about her shoulders. To keep up appearances he might. Why should he consider her feelings when he needed his disguise as a hillman so desperately? Would he shame her in front of Soonya and Rhati, Raschid and Mahomet? She had disobeyed and been caught. To them it was simple. A woman deserved her punishment.

She stared ahead, not recognising the countryside. This was the way back to that mean little dwelling. She did not dare question Deverill. Those flint-hard eyes had been murderous. With clenched teeth, she held on to the mane, trying to keep her balance. He had not touched her, not put an arm about her waist to hold her steady. If she fell off, he would probably just ride on! She tried to whip up anger against him but was miserably aware that she was more frightened than angry. If only he would say something!

He brought the pony to a swerving halt, so abruptly that Zara almost went over its head. He dismounted.

'Get off,' he said and looked at her with cold eyes. 'Go and wash yourself. You look disgusting.' He moved away and sat on a rock with his back to her, reaching into his tunic pocket for a cheroot.

Zara slid from the pony's back on to unsteady legs. Wash,

she thought dazedly, then heard the trickle of water. She stumbled towards the sound. Another of those rivulets that spurted from the rock-face. Something bumped against her knee and she realised that her drawstring bag had remained on her wrist during the whole episode with the goat people. Relief made her eyes water. She still had her precious comb and change of clothing. Nothing that Deverill had given her had been lost. She dropped the bag and coat beside the tiny waterfall and took off her veiled cap.

The icy water stung the cuts and grazes on her face and hands. With the aid of one of the cotton cloths, originally the outer bindings for her feet, she washed the drying blood from her eyes. Her forehead was sore where the heavy stone had struck it but the cut was not bleeding any more. Had Deverill not arrived in time – she shivered, remembering the snarling faces.

A shadow fell across her and she looked up, startled. Deverill towered over her, looking down without expression. She reached for her cap, sensing that he was still angry. He moved closer and Zara shrank away, unable to control the shaking of her body. His hands curled into fists, then unclenched.

'I should beat you to death, you damned, foolhardy idiot of a woman!' he said explosively. 'God knows you deserve it for going off with the goat-herders. What the devil possessed you?'

'They – they were going to Shekhupura,' she muttered.

'You seemed in a poor way of reaching the place when I arrived,' he said drily. 'What happened?'

'It was going well until they stopped. I didn't know why. I couldn't understand what they shouted at me.'

'Naturally not, since you are not a Mahommedan and don't speak that particular dialect. Go on.'

'The old man was kind at first then he said something about Mahomet.'

'And I suppose you told him that Mahomet was in Gujranwala as far as you knew. What next?'

Zara's voice quivered with humiliation at his tone and she stared at the grass. 'He gestured for me to kneel.'

231

'And you did, of course. Towards the group?'

'Yes.'

There was total silence for a moment, then a muffled grunt from above. Zara kept her eyes down.

'And that is why they became angry?'

'Yes.'

'You're a fool.'

'I know.'

'Not only do you choose the most fanatical tribe of goat people, you query the prophet and kneel with your back to Mecca!'

'I didn't realise until it was too late.'

'You could have been stoned to death.'

'I know.'

'You're the most idiot girl I ever met.'

'I know.'

'Good God! Is that all you can say?'

Zara rose slowly and faced him. 'Am I allowed to thank you for saving me?'

'I'll allow that if you promise never to repeat the performance – and I don't mean only with goat people. No merchants, camel traders or travelling circuses.'

Zara's hesitation was so fractional that anyone else might not have caught it, but Deverill grasped her roughly by the shoulders again and shook her. His voice was angry again, savage and biting.

'Is it a death-wish you have, woman? Don't you understand that I am your only protection? God knows if you're worth my trouble when you go on this way. You're a fool and a pest!'

Zara's head hurt and she felt bruised all over. The grip on her shoulder was painful.

'I didn't ask –' she began, then her head was jolted to one side as he struck her on her cheek with the flat of his hand.

'Neither did I!' he snarled and flung her away from him.

Zara stumbled back and fell to her knees by the trickling waterfall. She bent over, her head ringing from the blow, her vision blurred. Sickness welled up in her and she retched, her face almost touching the water. She had not eaten since the

232

scratchy meal last night and though she had now lost what remained, the cramping pains went on, doubling her over. Her face ran with perspiration and her body shivered without control, her entire being hot and cold at the same time. Never had she felt such misery and degradation. If only she could die or pass into unconsciousness. Either would relieve her from this agony, and at the moment, she didn't care which one came first.

As she gasped and retched, a wet cloth was pressed to her forehead. An arm lay about her shoulders, holding her firmly. Deverill eased her back gently and wiped her face with the cloth dipped into the water.

Though her eyes still smarted and her head ached, Zara sensed a softening of Deverill's mood. She winced as the stomach cramp came again.

'Did – did you have to hit me?' she asked, touching her sore cheek.

'Yes,' he said shortly. 'You'd drive a saint to distraction and I haven't the time to waste on tracking you down. And –' he went on ominously, 'you haven't given me that promise yet.'

'All right,' Zara sighed wearily. 'You have it.' The iron band round her head was easing a little, the nausea less violent. She knew Deverill's shrewd eyes were on her.

'Did you share food with the nomads?' he asked in a quieter voice.

'No, only tea.'

He grunted. 'God knows what they put in their tea. Ground leaves of cannabis, I suspect. The crop is grown in plots all over the place. Hold on to this cloth.'

He left her but was back in a moment, unscrewing the cap of a small flask. The cap made a small cup and he poured in a measure from the flask, adding a little water from the fall.

'Drink this,' he ordered, then a smile touched his lips. 'Not rum, I assure you.'

'What is it?'

'Brandy.'

'But I don't –' she protested weakly but he clamped her fingers round the cup.

233

'Do as you're told and don't argue for once in your life. Don't you want to feel better?'

Zara raised the silver cup to her lips and drained it. Diluted by water, the brandy sent a soft glow surging through her body. It was comforting and she stopped shaking. Even her stomach seemed to accept the soothing liquid, releasing its cramping grip. She began to feel human again.

'Better?' asked Deverill.

Zara nodded. 'You remind me of Mrs Fraser.'

He frowned, pausing in the act of screwing the cap on to the flask. 'Mrs Fraser?'

'Her reticule, rather. It carries a remedy for all occasions, from headache powders to safety pins.'

'Ah, I see. No safety pins, I'm afraid, but brandy is a useful remedy on occasion, like this one.'

'And rum on others.' As soon as she had said the words, Zara wished them unspoken. How foolish to remind him of that night.

'Brandy and rum,' Deverill said musingly. 'What next, I wonder, Miss Deane, will you add to your credit? Will you try a little arrack, the local fire-water?'

'No, I will not, and I only drank that rum and water,' she said defiantly, 'because it was cold and Soonya said it was warming.'

'Exactly. And continued drinking it to keep out all future chills.'

'You drank it too,' muttered Zara.

Deverill laughed. 'Did I? How would you know when you were drunk and incapable? I assure you I was far from incapable.'

Zara turned her face away. 'I know,' she said in a muffled voice. 'You removed my clothes.'

'In the dark, Miss Deane, and only to preserve your new outfit. I took no other liberties. I prefer my bedfellow to be in full possession of her senses.'

Zara's gaze came round slowly. 'You said I talked. What did I say?'

'Not very much and most drunks mumble a lot.'

234

Zara winced. 'A drunk! What a thing to call me! Was nothing intelligible?'

He grinned. 'I gathered a gem or two, such as you wouldn't take Captain Browne now if he offered you the Crown Jewels.'

'I imagine it will be the other way about, if I ever go back.'

'So do I. Don't look so woebegone. You didn't love the fellow, never did, so now you are free to really love someone else.'

Zara looked about her, then back up at Deverill. 'Someone else?' she echoed. 'Such a wide choice you offer, I am overcome.'

'Well, there's always me.' His eyes took on their mocking glint. 'I'm quite willing to be loved. You've only to say the word.'

'And you'll make me number one in your zenana, or is it harem?' Zara answered, her tone equally mocking.

'There are worse fates – like marriage to a man you don't love.' He regarded her silently for a moment, still smiling. 'You're not averse to me, I know.'

Zara stared at him. 'What? How did you come by that ridiculous idea?'

He laughed aloud. 'You told me so, but lay it at the door of the rum you drank. I won't hold it against you. Now, pray, mount that pony. We'll go and eat at some inferior establishment which allows women inside.'

Zara veiled her face in stricken silence, intent on avoiding Deverill's gaze. He wasn't looking at her, however, he was tossing her sheepskin coat over the pony's back. He must have been lying to tease her, she decided, then wondered uneasily if her rum-laden sleep had been quite as blank as she supposed. She could easily have railed against Ralph, but could she really have given Deverill the impression that she found him attractive? It was possible, for she remembered vaguely her own self-questioning on the subject of honour, that seductively honeyed voice making clear Deverill's attraction. But that was the rum, she defended herself, it made people silly and say things they didn't mean.

'Come along,' called Deverill peremptorily and Zara

235

started. She picked up her bag and went towards the pony. Deverill was waiting. He took her by the waist and lifted her to sit sideways to the pony's neck, then swung up behind her. He put an arm around her shoulders.

'Lean against me. You'll be more comfortable, and what's in that bag you're clutching to your breast as if they were the Crown Jewels?'

'To me they are. These things are all I have in the world.'

He didn't say anything but settled her against his shoulder. Zara relaxed her tired body and closed her eyes, comparing this ride with the rough, angry gallop away from the goat people. She didn't know where they were going and didn't really care as long as Deverill was with her. It had been a foolish move to go off with the goat people. Deverill was, as he had said, her only protector, not in the way that Soonya meant, but as one who spoke her language and was himself English. Merchants, camel traders, travelling circuses and goat people, she would obey his ruling on not attaching herself to any of those, but a party of English people? That was a different matter. They would not cower while a hillman retrieved an Englishwoman from their midst.

The pony came to a halt and Zara opened her eyes, blinking. For a moment she was loath to leave the haven of Deverill's arms but he was already setting her upright before swinging down.

'Hang on to the Crown Jewels,' he said and lifted her from the pony's back. Zara looked at the long, low building, white-walled and with a thatched roof.

'Keep up your veil and walk three steps behind me,' he ordered.

'Yes, lord.'

He gave her a quick look, half-frown, half-smile, then pulled open the door. Zara followed into a noisy, smoky room but she was only aware of the wonderful odour of food. Before she had time to examine the long counter of hissing, bubbling and frying pots, Deverill had pushed her into a small cubicle, a bench seat on each side of a plain wooden table.

'Keep your face to the wall,' he hissed as a man approached, a tin tray under his arm.

He and Deverill became involved in what appeared to be heated argument, then the man withdrew.

Zara peered up cautiously. 'Was he objecting to my presence?'

'No. We were discussing the bill of fare.'

'Really? It sounded like a preliminary to pistols at dawn.'

Deverill smiled. 'Not at all. It's customary to discuss price and freshness of meat, which market supplied the vegetables and who ground the spices.'

'Why?'

'If you find sand in your brown sugar as makeweight, you'll know who's responsible.'

Before Zara could ask what he had ordered, the food came. Dishes, mountainous with mutton and rice cooked in a spicy sauce, bowls of grated coconut, chutneys, fruit and yoghurt.

Another argument seemed to ensue, then the man returned, carrying a small brass samovar and two thick glass beakers.

'Freshly brewed tea with nothing added,' Deverill explained. 'I refused to accept two measures from the large samovar you see on the counter. It's topped up daily and God knows what its murky depths conceal.'

After they had eaten and drunk the fresh tea, Zara ventured a question. 'Where are we going now?'

'Back to the small valley. The others have gone ahead to set up camp.'

'Where the pool was? Will I be able to bathe again?'

'Of course, although the water will be higher in the river, the pool will be safe. Can you swim?'

'No.'

Deverill paid the bill and they left the tea room and mounted the pony. The sun was on the horizon as they reached the camp. Zara expected some awkwardness between herself and the hillgirls but they greeted her cheerfully. Whatever their private thoughts, they seemed to accept it as quite natural that Deverill should find and bring her back. The facial cut and bruise on her cheekbone, she supposed, would be attributed to Deverill's beating when he caught her. Another few weeks and they would forget entirely that she had ever been anything other than a hillwoman.

Deverill left the camp after supper. Zara watched him ride away. Was she glad or sorry to see him go? Her feelings were a little confused on that point. When he was with her she felt safe as if his presence held the world at bay. A certain bereftness was hers when he was not there, like the feelings she had experienced when she faced the hostile goat people. Lonely and very frightened, then Deverill had come. Despite his moods, she preferred his hostility to that of the goat women. It was natural, of course, both being English, she told herself, as she turned into the shelter and prepared for bed.

For a long time she lay, trying to quell that inner voice, the wickedly insidious voice that had whispered in her ear through a haze of rum. Because you are both English? What has that to do with anything? He is a man and you are a woman. But he is a man of dishonour, her mind protested. And what are you, may I ask, the voice went on, save a woman of dishonour? And isn't it a fact that a man of rakish habits and dubious reputation takes the eye of the most proper young lady in preference to the sober, earnest young man? Look at your own father. A handsome, expensive rake, if ever there was one! Yet he could have had his pick of a dozen women since your mother died.

But he was kind and charming, a man of style and humour, she protested. Well, the voice demanded? Can you deny those things to Deverill? Father was not perfect but he was not a villain! Of course not. He just avoided paying his bills, gambled his fortune away and married a rich woman to save himself from prison. What makes you so high-minded about improper doings? Being here at all is improper and Deverill is most attractive.

Zara turned her face into the pillow, trying to ignore the cynical voice. All right, Deverill is attractive, but he's bad and wicked, too. Now shut up and let me go to sleep. To sleep and dream of lying in Deverill's arms? The voice was fading into the background as she drifted but it left behind a fragmented memory of painted pictures unrolling frieze-like across the wall of a small room in the palace of Batala.

The sun was rimming the horizon when she woke. A band of gold shading to lemon, then fading into the violet of early dawn, met her eyes. Then her blood stirred and pounded so loudly she could almost hear it. Deverill was back! He sat at the entrance to the shelter, fully dressed and smoking a cheroot.

Zara lay still and watched him. If only he and not Ralph Browne had been Eleanor Farnes's cousin, had proposed marriage to her in London and met her ship in Calcutta, she knew he would not have been as patient as Ralph. Nor would she have delayed putting off the marriage date. She imagined a Deverill in love, sweeping aside all protestations, carrying along his fiancée in a wave of excitement. Had she been that fiancée, she knew she would have allowed herself to be swept along and gloried in becoming his wife. But Deverill was not Ralph Browne. Deverill had not proposed marriage. He was willing to be loved, he had said, but if she wanted marriage, some worthy gentleman in England must suffice.

Zara stirred restlessly under her blanket, cursing the fate that had brought her into contact with a man she could love but must not. There was no future in becoming Deverill's woman, however enticing the prospect. One day he would be gone with his lakhs of rupees, no longer the need to pose as a hillman, but to appear somewhere else in the role of wealthy English gentleman.

Deverill turned his head. 'You are awake. Come here a moment.'

Zara threw aside the blanket and joined him at the entrance. 'You were gone all night.'

'Yes. I went to Lahore.'

She felt her heart jump. 'Lahore? Wasn't that dangerous?'

'I needed to gather news.'

'And did you?'

'Yes. Some good, some bad.' He turned to look into her face. 'They've called off the search for you. Since it's now well over a week, you're presumed dead. The Yuvaraj has been released and is back in the palace.'

'So everything is back to normal,' Zara said in a small voice. 'Life goes on.'

'Not quite. The Yuvaraj is up to something and that worries me.'

'Why?'

'Because I fear he will involve the Rani and that worries me more than anything else. I must go to her.'

Chapter Twenty-two

Zara stared out over the clearing, her eyes not seeing the activity of the camp. She felt very cold, her heart a heaviness in her breast. The Rani? He was worried about the Rani. Why not, she thought dully. He was the Rani's lover. Why shouldn't he be concerned for the woman he loved? It was well known that she and the Yuvaraj were hostile towards each other. Did he know she had a lover and intended acquainting the Rajah of that fact?

Zara felt Deverill's eyes on her. She had to say something. 'What do you think the Yuvaraj is planning to do?'

'I shall have to go to the palace to find out. The Yuvaraj must be dissuaded from any rash action against the Rani.'

'What sort of action?'

'He believes she is partly to blame for his arrest since she verified that he was not in the palace at the time you disappeared. Captain Browne –' his tone became cynical – 'was most happy to receive that verification. The Rani may only have answered a simple question put to her, but the Yuvaraj, who dislikes her intensely, will assume she involved him deliberately. He is a man who never forgives an injury or an imagined injury.'

'Does – does he know about you?'

'Yes.' Deverill's expression was brooding. 'That's another card I must prevent him from playing.

For the rest of the day, Zara moved in a dream, speaking when spoken to but hardly aware of her surroundings. Deverill left camp in the middle of the afternoon and Zara went to the pool with her precious sack. The river was more swollen than it had been before but the pool was still contained between its rocky rims. The water was colder but she was so sunk into gloom that she barely noticed until she climbed shivering to the bank.

Dried and dressed again, she huddled into the sheepskin coat and sat with her arms about her knees. Her thoughts of last night had flowed away as swiftly as the river. Even her inner voice was hushed. Deverill, worried about the Rani, had gone to shield her from any malicious act of the Yuvaraj. In the Rajah's palace he could be in great danger. The Rajah, primed by the Yuvaraj, might well be waiting for him, expecting his visit to the Rani. She, herself, could be locked away, full of terror for her lover's life. A man did not ride into danger for a woman he did not love. Zara dropped her forehead on to her knees. It followed, then, that Deverill loved the Rani. There was no other explanation. The offer he had made to her was no higher than one he might have made to any girl who could be bought for a night's entertainment. And she, Zara Deane, had almost given in to the temptation! How degraded she would have felt had she done so and been told this morning that he was desperately worried for the Rani's safety. She should have remembered that dark head bent over the Rani's in the palace and realised what it meant.

She rose to her feet swiftly. Confound Deverill and confound the Rani too. Let them be discovered by the Rajah or betrayed by the Yuvaraj. What did she care if the old man chopped off both their heads! Had she no more spirit than to sit here in heart-sore misery like some moon-struck Victorian maiden? She strode back into camp, her hair flying, her eyes glittering with anger. She would not be made a fool of by that two-faced Deverill. Batala could not be far away, so neither could Lahore. All right, he had a pony, but the walking she had done over these accursed mountains had given her legs a new strength. She could walk to Lahore. No need to attach herself to any traveller. All she wanted was an idea of the direction. She could question Soonya, pretend concern for Deverill, perhaps, and ask which way he would come in from Batala.

Surveying the recumbent, blanket-rolled bodies, she knew she must leave the questioning until tomorrow. However simple Soonya might be, she would not appreciate being dragged from sleep to answer what must only be a casually phrased query. Zara entered her own shelter and rolled the blanket about her.

Deverill did not return the next morning. When Zara awoke, she half-expected to see him sitting by the shelter entrance, smoking his cheroot, but the space was empty. A sense of loss touched her, then she was angry with herself. A long, loving night with the Rani, no doubt, she reflected cynically. Much too tiring to make haste back to this camp before the dawn had fully broken. She went down to the pool to wash. When she returned, the girls were starting the fire. Raschid and Mahomet were squatting by a tree, smoking and conversing in low tones.

The porridge was cooked and served, the sun burst over the horizon in a flurry of red and gold and Deverill still did not come. The bowls were scoured, the men fed their ponies, the light steadied under its blue dome and time passed. No sign of Deverill.

Raschid and Mahomet polished the wire-bound jezails, glancing about occasionally, muttering the odd comment to each other. Soonya and Rhati were silent and Zara sat quietly beside them, studying their faces, glancing over now and then at the two men. Something was in the air, a sense of waiting, and, as time passed, a feeling of unease pervaded the camp site. Zara felt it strongly as she watched Raschid and Mahomet move restlessly, their expressions sombre. The girls were quiet too, possibly taking their cue from the men, but was it for Deverill they were uneasy? Surely he was in no danger. He had said quite calmly that he was going to the palace of Batala to see the Yuvaraj and the Rani. He knew his way about and must surely have an escape route planned as he must have had on previous occasions.

She felt her own feelings of unease rise. Had he been caught? Why wasn't he back? The palace would be awake and crawling with servants by now. She remembered her own vicious hope that the Rajah would catch him. Perhaps he had and now Deverill lay dead or imprisoned in one of those dungeons the Yuvaraj had joked about. No, please God, not that! He was reckless and uncaring but she hadn't meant that. Not really, though she hated him for loving the Rani, she knew she wanted him for herself. It was scandalous and improper and she would never admit it to him, but please, dear God, don't let him be hurt.

As the day wore on, Zara found her own restlessness increasing. Something must have happened to Deverill. Perhaps he would never come back. She pushed aside the thought but it returned again and again like a persistent mosquito. She squatted beside Soonya.

'Shouldn't he be back?' she asked in a low whisper. The low tone seemed appropriate, for Raschid and Mahomet spoke only in whispers.

Soonya nodded, slanting a quick look at the men.

'He said he was going to the palace at Batala,' Zara went on. 'Did you know that?'

Soonya nodded again but said nothing.

'Where is it? I mean from which direction will he come? Will Raschid and Mahomet go and search for him?'

Soonya shrugged but her eyes flickered towards the crest over which lay Zara's pool. 'No need look before. Always come back when say.'

'But not today. What will Raschid and Mahomet do if he doesn't come back before dark?' An unpleasant thought filtered into Zara's mind, but it was one she dared not put into words.

If Deverill never came back, what would the men do with her? If his death was proved, she would become an embarrassment, to put it mildly, an encumbrance to be disposed of as quickly as possible. Without Deverill's protection she was nothing to them. What need had four travelling hill people with an English girl, one who might bring them trouble? Turn her loose to inform on them? In their eyes that would be folly. Far better a silent tongue in a quiet grave and who would know or care? The search had already been called off. She was already dead to the garrison. She shivered, trying to shake off the morbid feeling, for it was morbid. Good heavens, Deverill was only a few hours overdue. Anything could have delayed him, a lame pony, a detour because a river

243

crossing was impassable, even a sudden decision to visit the people he was supplying with rifles.

She jumped as Raschid's voice, low and intense, called to the girls. They rose and moved over to the men. All four squatted in a tight circle, heads bent. Why were the girls being drawn into the whispered discussion, Zara wondered uneasily. They were rarely consulted about anything. She kept a close watch on the group. Occasionally Raschid or Mahomet glanced her way, convincing her that she was the topic of the talk. Soonya shook her head at one point. Was she defending the Missie Sahib? But Raschid frowned and Soonya's head went down. Surely they were not already discussing her future in the same way as she had herself a moment ago? But why not? There was nothing illogical about it. A woman needed a protector, Soonya had said long ago. Without one she is nothing, the prey of any man to use as he wished and discard in the same manner.

The girls rose and came slowly back to the ringed fire stones. They sat down, neither looking at Zara. She wanted to ask but was afraid of the answer. Her skin felt cold but her hands were damp with perspiration. Her mind kept repeating the words like an incantation. Come back, Deverill, come back. Go to the Rani if you must but come back to me because I love you. Think of the Rani but hold me in your arms. Show one of your faces to me and I won't ask for more. Damn you, Deverill, you must come back!

Her head came up as she heard the sound of ponies' hooves. Raschid and Mahomet were mounted. For a second her hopes flared, then they died. There was no third rider. The two men wheeled their ponies and galloped away. Zara caught Soonya's glance and grasped her wrist firmly.

'They are going to look for him?'

Soonya nodded but her eyes showed no brightness. They were calm, accepting, her expression as fatalistic as if this search was a mere gesture to be gone through.

'They will find him,' Zara said firmly, refusing to accept the lack of hope.

Soonya shrugged. 'Maybe. Too long time gone.'

'Nonsense!' Zara said hotly. 'He could have had an

accident. It is far too soon to give up hope.'

'Devil Sahib come always when say. Maybe She-Devil catching.'

'What?' Zara stared at her. 'Who is She-Devil?'

Soonya's lips curled in a cynical smile. 'Rajah woman. Make plenty web for catching.'

'The Rani? But he – I mean they –'

'Rajah woman liking men. Very bad woman. Devil Sahib very clever, maybe Rajah woman more clever.'

'But how – why?'

'Rajah woman not liking Rajah. Old man not good lover. Rajah woman much better liking dead. Devil Sahib knowing this.'

'You can't mean he is helping her to kill the Rajah? I don't believe it!'

'Maybe yes, maybe no.' Soonya shrugged. 'Rajah get sick this day, that day.'

'Poison?' suggested Zara in a horrified voice. 'You can't think –'

'He not back. Maybe Rajah catching.'

Zara stared across the quiet camp site, her mind full of conflicting emotions. This was just talk, hillwoman's gossip. Deverill wanted to be a rich man. Surely he would want to enjoy those riches without involving himself in anything so mad as to help the Rani dispose of her husband? He might love her but that risk was too great even for Deverill. What would he gain? The throne of Batala would fall to the Yuvaraj, the Rani retire into widowhood, perhaps a very secluded widowhood, if the Yuvaraj had anything to do with it. There could be no benefit for Deverill in any way. He was not a man to risk all for love of a woman, especially one he could not show off to the world. It was too preposterous. As a wealthy English gentleman in London, the matrons of that town would be only too delighted to present their daughters to a handsome dashing man-about-town. That was Deverill's plan. Murdering Indian Rajahs for love of their wives was quite out of character. And since the Rajah was of the old school of thought, he might very well leave orders for his wife to join him on the funeral pyre. Zara felt a cold touch on her

245

spine. The idea of enforcing that order might appeal most strongly to the Yuvaraj, in a private place and away from English eyes!

Zara narrowed her eyes on Soonya. 'How do you know so much about the Rani?' she demanded. 'We have been travelling for more than a week, barely seeing anyone.'

'We seeing many people but Missie Sahib not understanding talk. Everybody know of Batala. Rajah is great lord like –' she wrinkled her brows in an effort to find a comparison, 'like palace of pukka Sahib, ayah and chokra boy know all things and telling servants of other sahibs.'

Zara had to admit to the truth of that. Backstairs gossip was like the grapevine in the jungle. News and speculation passed quickly from kitchen to kitchen. The same method applied whether here or below stairs in a London house. Servants were aware of things almost before their employers.

She rose and began to move restlessly about the camp. The feathery-headed tamarisk and willow threw long shadows over the brilliant red and purple flowers of the oleander beside the stream. Zara looked up at the sky. Night was coming, the second night of Deverill's absence. If Raschid and Mahomet did not find him before darkness, what would they do? How long had she, herself, left before they struck camp and faded into those immense hills.

Rahti lifted her head, Soonya too. Zara heard the hooves then. The men were coming back. Zara's spirits rose. A glimpse through the trees had shown her three ponies, the dense leaves masking all but their legs. They had found him, perhaps hurt but alive. The three girls waited, their eyes on the clearing between a thin stand of trees. Three ponies swept into view. Three ponies but only two riders. Zara gasped, her hands flying to cover her mouth. The third pony dripped blood from a cut on its flanks, its eyes were wild and froth coated its muzzle.

Rahti and Soonya moved forward slowly. The men dismounted but Zara stayed where she was, frozen in horror. Raschid spoke soothingly to the pony and gradually it stopped trembling and became calmer. Mahomet began to examine the pony's injuries. A discussion on how to treat the animal seemed to be in progress. Zara forced herself to move and ran towards the men. Mahomet glanced at her then pointed to the deep slash mark on the flanks. He looked grave.

'Damn the pony,' Zara almost screamed. 'Where is Devil Sahib?'

Mahomet raised his brows and looked at Soonya. She spoke quickly, he answered in what seemed a casually worded reply. Soonya nodded and turned to Zara.

'They not find Devil Sahib, only pony.'

'I can see that, but what do they think happened?'

'Pony very frightened, running far each time they come close. Somebody cutting him like with tulwar, Mahomet say. Devil Sahib not anywhere.'

'They must go and look again. He is lying hurt somewhere. He must be found.'

Soonya looked towards the dying sun. 'Coming dark soon. No good, Maybe tomorrow.'

Zara turned away to hide the fear on her face. Tomorrow might be too late. How could an injured man survive a cold night in these hills? An injured man? Perhaps he was already dead, the pony escaping while Deverill was hacked to pieces. She felt very cold and sick as she retreated to her shelter.

Soonya and Rahti made preparations for the evening meal as if all things were normal. They had to be, she supposed, dully. People still ate and slept, women did their duty and life went on. She couldn't believe Deverill was dead, despite the evidence of the injured pony. Yet who would attack a pony if it was riderless? The blows had to be aimed at its rider, wild blows from many tulwars, the pony accidentally receiving one.

Soonya stood before her, offering food and tea. Zara took the tea, shaking her head at the food bowl. Soonya shrugged and returned to the fire, now casting light over the scene. The twilight was so short in India, the stars were already appearing in the deep blue sky. Zara felt warmer for the hot strong tea but she knew she could not sleep as the hillmen and girls were preparing to do. It was going to be a very long night. Was she to fill it with images of horror, pictures of Deverill's body disintegrating blow by savage blow as the tulwars cut deep, until nothing remained of that reckless renegade?

Setting down the tea mug, Zara scanned the already blanketed figures. She could not stay brooding in this shelter. It was too confining, too full of Deverill's presence. She had to walk, by the pool or the river, anywhere, just to move and stop her mind filling with morbid images. If he was dead, it was his own fault. No one made him go to the palace. He knew the risk he took. Was it the Rajah's doing or had it come about through the Yuvaraj's hatred of his stepmother? Perhaps the Yuvaraj himself had played the card Deverill had sought to prevent.

She snatched up her bag and coat, moving soft-footed to the ridge. Did it matter who was responsible if he was dead? She stared at the hard brilliance of the stars. Who cared that one man had perished bloodily? They had seen it all before.

Beside the pool, she dropped her coat and bag. The surface of the water was dark and very still. There was no wind tonight. If Batala lay somewhere out there in the darkness, Lahore could not be far beyond. Could she walk there? Would Raschid and Mahomet give her the chance? They were sleeping now, decisions put off until tomorrow. If she crossed the river now and kept on walking –

The thought of slinking into Lahore was suddenly a bleak prospect. To return with her tail between her legs like some beaten alley cat was not to be thought of for a Deane. She stared down into the pool. It was a tempting thought. Go out in defiance, make her own choice. But not in this pool, the water wasn't deep enough. A soaking was all she would achieve.

She turned from the pool and began to follow the river. If Deverill was truly dead, there was little point in living. Like her father, she could only know one passion. But unlike her father, she had never experienced it. How ironic that now Deverill was denied her, she wanted him with an intensity that was frightening. Like Soonya's Raschid, Deverill had been her protector, but he had not benefited from his protection as Raschid had done.

As she followed the river, the moon bathed gullies and

248

rocks in a flat grey light, touching the water with silvery sheen. It certainly looked deeper here but she continued to move on, avoiding the reedbeds and trailing vines. Deverill might still be alive. She could not imagine him blotted out for ever. Only the sight of his dead body would convince her of that. She halted and stared moodily at the water. Suicide was a coward's way out and a defect of the spirit.

A slithering sound in the bushes made her jump. A snake, some nocturnal hunter? The night fell into quietness again and she listened intently, conscious of her bare, sandalled feet. A plop from the river made her jump again. A fish or that snake sliding into the water? She stood quite still, her head turning slowly. Of course there were night creatures in every country, owls, bats, frogs, but in England they were harmless. This was India, full of wild hogs, tigers, mountain bears, all kinds of dangerous things.

The night sounds began to intrude upon her senses. They must have been there before but only now had she become aware of the rustlings and strange tiny cries. Were eyes watching from those bushes? She glanced back the way she had come. The river wound placidly away and the pool was out of sight. What madness to be so far from camp. The instinct to run almost overwhelmed her but she knew that a fast-moving creature was irresistible to a carnivore. Don't run from a tiger, someone had said. Stand quite still and he will go away, unless he is hungry! What a comfort to know that, the unfrozen cynical part of her mind jeered. Did one ask? Did they hunt by night? A twig cracked and her whole mind froze. Only her eyes moved, searching the bushes and darkness of crevices.

Across the river something moved, a darker shadow against shadows. Zara strained her eyes. A bush, surely, the leaves moved by some rooting creature. The wind, but there was no wind. She blinked, concentrating on it, aware that her frozen body was damp with sweat. The bush moved again and changed shape. Dear God, it wasn't a bush at all, but some large ambling creature. Moving slowly but somehow disjointedly, it grew larger. It was coming towards the river! Well, they drank there, didn't they? Her flickering glance upriver caught the line of stones, stretching from one bank to the other, the moonlight reflecting the glint of water droplets on their flat surfaces. Stepping-stones, used by man and animal alike before the river floods submerged them. And this creature was heading straight for them. Hardly straight, really, for there was something unsteady in its gait. A mountain bear walking upright? Whatever it was, she should run now but her legs trembled and refused to obey.

Then it was on the stepping-stones, sliding and splashing through the water. She listened to the angry grunts as it stumbled and skidded. Skidded? Did bears skid on pads that were as hard as leather? Did they curse like sailors in bar-room brawls?

Zara's throat gave a dry, choked scream, then she was running towards the stepping-stones, her body and mind as unfrozen as if she had been struck by lightning.

'Deverill!' she screamed as the figure stepped off the last stone. 'Deverill!' Zara's voice rose higher as she reached him and flung herself into his arms.

They teetered on the edge of the river and Zara's arms were around his neck, her face pressed against his. He smelt of ashes, horses and sweat but it was the most delightful perfume she had ever encountered.

'Deverill, oh Deverill,' she kept repeating, her voice cracking with relief and joy.

His arms closed about her, pulling her deeper into his embrace.

'A right royal welcome indeed.' His voice came soft and caressing. 'But restrain your joy, my sweet Zara. Do you want to wake the neighbours?'

Chapter Twenty-three

'Neighbours? What neighbours?' Zara's voice quivered tween tears and laughter.

'Who knows? Voices carry a long way at night and I'm not out of the wood yet.'

Zara sobered. 'I'm sorry. It's just that you are alive when we all thought that you were dead.' She looked at him closely. 'Are you hurt? Forgive me, I should have asked first.'

His face was streaked with dust and his eyes looked tired. He regarded her thoughtfully. 'Weren't you the one who hoped the Rajah would chop off my head?'

'I didn't mean it, of course I didn't. I was angry.'

'And now?'

'I'm not angry, just relieved that you are alive.'

'Is that all? Just relieved?' A faint smile touched his lips. 'Which would you have me accept, your words or your welcome?'

Zara put her arms about his neck again and held him tightly. 'You are welcome in my heart, lord,' she murmured against his lips. 'Two nights without you were as two years in my sight.'

Deverill's lips were hard on hers. They had the tang of salt. He drew back, looked down at her and smiled ruefully.

'You smell as fresh as the dawn while I disgust even myself. Let's go to the pool where I may wash away this filth.'

'Are you hurt? You didn't say?' Zara looked at him anxiously. 'You were limping as you came to the stones.'

'Oh, that –' he paused. 'Well, perhaps you'd better give me your arm before this mood of tenderness passes.'

'It won't,' Zara said firmly. 'I have made up my mind to it.'

He glanced at her quizzically. 'Without benefit of clergy? I never promised you that.'

'I know and I don't care. They'll all believe it anyway.'

His eyes became sardonic. 'So that's the reason, is it? You want your defiance to have some basis in fact?'

Zara shook her head. 'That isn't the reason.' Her mind noted subconsciously that for a man with an injured leg, he was moving over the ground at a sharp pace. The pool was coming into sight rapidly. 'My reason, should you need to be told, is that I love you.'

Deverill said nothing for a moment and Zara's bold front began to crumble a little. He would laugh. He loved the Rani. It was an absurd statement for her to make but if he gave back a mocking laugh, she would die of misery.

251

He stopped walking and swung her abruptly towards him. 'Say that again!' he demanded.

'I love you,' Zara whispered in a choking voice. 'Dammit, Deverill, don't you know anything?' Only by the supreme effort of forcing anger into her voice could she withstand the hurt when it came.

'You love me? A cashiered officer, a traitor to his country, a thief who arms rebels with stolen rifles and a lover of the Rani? How can you?'

'I don't know,' Zara shook her head helplessly. 'I can't explain it to myself so how can I to you? Whatever you are, I love you.' She tried to smile and to make her voice light with self-mockery. 'Such a declaration, most unseemly, quite shocking when directed at someone else's lover.'

She tried to turn away but Deverill did not release her. He looked at her intently. His voice was not mocking as he spoke.

'If I take you at your word, the responsibility is yours, remember that. I don't deny that you attract me physically but there's an end to it. I offer you nothing else. What they say of me is true.' He paused. 'I wish to heaven you had stayed in the garrison where you belong.'

'I never want to return to the garrison.'

'You think to spend your life in this fashion?'

'We could be together.'

He shook his head. 'No. When my business is done, Devil Sahib will disappear. There is no place in my life for a Devil Memsahib.'

Zara felt her heart contract at the thought, but if those were his terms, she had no choice but to grasp the fleeting happiness.

Deverill began to slip off his grimed clothes by the pool. He glanced over his shoulder and smiled.

'Like drinking, swimming is best done in company. Join me?'

The moon on the water, the strong muscular body of Deverill and the gentleness of the night air, all combined to fill Zara with a sense of heady exhilaration. He had not rejected her but admitted her attractiveness for him. Forget his way of life, forget even the Rani. What mattered was his love here and now and her own longing to receive it. She pulled her tunic over her head and discarded the voluminous trousers. Deverill gave a throaty chuckle and she glanced at him.

'My God, those bloomers. They must have been designed by an architect in the dark.'

'Well,' Zara began, then realised she was staring at Deverill's nakedness.

'My God,' she gasped. 'You're –'

'I always swim like this,' he said mildly. 'It saves getting one's clothes wet, don't you think?'

Zara opened and closed her mouth again, feeling the blood pound in her ears. He was magnificently nude, just like the marble statues in the museums.

'I'll spare your blushes, my love,' he said, laughing. 'I'll go in first, but don't let those bloomers follow me. Three is definitely a crowd if those things join us.'

He slid into the water, still laughing, and Zara looked down at the frilly bloomers and began to giggle uncontrollably. Edwardian bloomers in a hillside pool on the slopes of the Himalayas! She took them off together with the cotton chemise.

Deverill glanced up as she hesitated at the water's edge. She saw his eyes scan her body with an appreciative gleam in them, then he held up his arms. Zara leapt and was caught. Deverill let himself fall backwards, pulling Zara with him and they both went under.

As they surfaced, Zara gasped, shaking back her hair. Deverill grinned. 'Sorry, I should have told you to take a deep breath. One always does before submerging.'

'You might have warned me that we were about to do that. How could I know? I don't swim.'

'Your education has been sadly neglected, my love, but I'm not of a mind to teach you swimming tonight. Put your arms round me and hold me close.' His own arms were about her hips, pressing her to him.

Deverill began to kiss her mouth, lingering expertly until Zara's own lips softened and parted. The sensation of standing on the sandy bottom of the pool, being embraced

253

from breast to knee, was as startling to Zara as the movement of Deverill's body. His fingers stroked and caressed her, filling her with such excitement that she could have sworn the pool contained heated water. Her limbs felt heavy and languorous, her flesh aflame with heat and the stars swung dizzily in the sky. She had no resistance to the pressure of his hands on her thighs, no thought of retreat as the male hardness sought and found her. A stab of pain, then the slide into a world of blissful sensation where even the stars paled into insignificance.

And later, on the grassy bank, rubbed dry and glowing, Deverill made love to her again. Zara could not remember climbing out of the pool, only the gentle caressing hands that must have lifted and laid her on the grass.

Deverill was looking down at her and Zara blinked the stars out of her eyes. He smiled and kissed her lightly.

'Better climb back into that maidenly edifice, my love. In case you hadn't noticed, the night has turned cold. Let's see if we can creep back into shelter without disturbing the camp.'

Zara nodded, realising for the first time that the night had chilled. She pulled on her clothes as Deverill did the same and they walked hand in hand towards the camp.

'You're not limping,' Zara said in a puzzled voice. 'I thought your leg was hurt.'

'Not a scratch on me,' Deverill said cheerfully and swung up the boots he was carrying. 'See? They only managed to slash the heel completely off one of them. I didn't fancy walking from Batala in bare feet over the rocks, so I wore them although they were dashed uneven.'

'But you asked me to help you.'

He grinned, unabashed. 'I know. I thought you would be kinder if you believed I was hurt. What made you think I was dead, by the way?'

'Raschid and Mahomet went out to look for you. They brought in your pony. It had a long slash on its side.'

'Ah yes, poor beast. I smelt ambush as I left the palace. Quite literally, too.' He laughed quietly. 'Bushes don't smoke beedis. They must have got tired of waiting and lit cigarettes. Fools to think I wouldn't catch the scent.'

'What did you do?'

'Headed the pony into them and rolled off at the last minute.'

'But who were they? Why did they plan to ambush you?'

He put an arm about her shoulder and kissed her cheek. 'You're a beautiful, loving creature, my dear Zara Deane, but the less you know, the better.'

'You don't trust me?'

'I don't trust anybody in this business. Be content with the role you have chosen and don't ask questions. You know what happens to inquisitive hillwomen.'

Zara looked at him doubtfully. 'You wouldn't –'

'But I would.' His eyes were on her but she found no comfort in their hardness. 'Not even you will be allowed to endanger what I am doing. Don't look for a knight on a white horse, my dear. It's a profitless occupation these days.'

When Zara woke the next morning, she was alone. She could hardly believe what had happened last night for the dawn was exactly as it had been every morning before. Only the ache in her lower body convinced her that she had not dreamt the whole thing. Trying to recall their conversation, her thoughts were constantly thrown into confusion by the memory of Deverill's naked body, the feel of his hands and lips on her own and the whirling vortex of consummation. So full of relief and love had she been to find him alive, the truth had burst from her, but he, she recalled, with a slight chill, had not made the same declaration. He didn't love her but found her physically attractive. She grinned to herself. What man would refuse a girl who flung herself at him, babbling of love? To be fair he had said there was no place in his future for her. The responsibility was hers alone.

She unrolled herself from the blanket and looked out of the shelter. The fire was burning and Rahti was stirring the inevitable oatmeal mixture. Raschid and Mahomet were by the ponies. Deverill was there too, examining the cut flanks of his own pony. Obviously it would not be rideable for a few days since the deep cut was exactly where a rider might be expected to sit. Zara swallowed hard as she realised the significance of that position. Had the tulwar or sword found its intended mark, Deverill might have been missing a leg or part of his stomach.

She picked up her sack and made her way to the pool. There were too many 'might haves' in her life. She might herself have missed Ralph at Eleanor's house. She might never have come to India. She might have ridden somewhere else on that fateful morning. She might never have met Deverill. As she looked into the pool, the water lay placid, looking back at her with an innocent blue face as if the turmoil of last night had never occurred to ripple its quietness.

On her return to camp, she joined the girls by the fire. They smiled.

'Devil Sahib back,' Soonya said. 'But Missie Sahib knowing that.' She looked at Rahti and the two girls gave stifled giggles. 'Much better,' Soonya continued. 'When man go away, one, two nights. Much strong when coming back.' She repeated her words to Rahti and they both giggled again.

Zara smiled. Neither girl would ever believe that she had not been Devil Sahib's woman from the beginning. Well, it was true now and she differed in no way from Soonya and Rahti save by race and origins of birth.

Soonya spooned the porridge into the metal bowls. 'You take Devil Sahib, yes?'

Zara, who had been about to retreat into the shelter with her own bowl, paused. Of course he would expect to be served by his woman, just as Raschid and Mahomet did.

She walked with the girls towards the men, copying the girls' actions as they presented the bowls at arm's length, heads bowed.

'Breakfast is served, lord.' Zara murmured in her most servile tone.

Deverill took the bowl from her, without even looking or interrupting is conversation with Raschid. Zara felt her colour and temper rise and she withdrew, tight-lipped. After last night, he might have looked at her, even smiled, but her reception had been no whit different from Soonya's or Rahti's. She took her own bowl to the shelter and ate her porridge in smouldering silence. Bedding a woman was no

256

new experience to him, but he might have spared a tender glance for the girl he had so recently deflowered.

What a ridiculously melodramatic word, her inner voice, roused from smug content, opined scathingly. If ever a girl enjoyed being deflowered, you did! So don't expect a man like Deverill to moon about, looking soulful. He's an opportunist, not a poet and no one ever changed a man's nature yet.

Zara put down her empty bowl with a shrug of acceptance. It was the voice of commonsense. Enjoy the here and now and let the future take care of itself. When Deverill came to the shelter entrance, she was able to smile on him without a feeling of aggrievement.

'Thank you for breakfast,' he said, smiling. 'It's the custom to ignore the serving wench. Anything else is bad form.'

'Thank you for telling me. I shall resist the urge to pour it over your head in future.'

'Do that. Otherwise I shall be forced to beat you in public.'

'You're forgetting –' she began stiffly.

'No, my dear, you're forgetting and that could be dangerous.' He was still smiling but his eyes were cool. 'You're my woman now but don't try for advantage. I am not to be swayed a hair's breadth from my course.'

What did I tell you, Zara's inner voice asked? Out loud Zara said, 'Yes, I can see that nothing will be allowed to stand in your way. You really are quite ruthlessly determined, aren't you? May I ask a question?'

Deverill's eyes became wary. 'You may but I don't guarantee any answer. What is it?

'Last night when I met you, you smelled of ashes, among other things. Why was that?'

Deverill stared at her for a long moment, then began to laugh. 'Ashes? I should think so. I dived into what I thought was a natural ditch but it happened to be an ashpit behind the palace. I thought I should choke to death before the hunt had passed me by.'

Zara then asked the question she really wanted answered. 'What would Raschid and Mahomet have done if you hadn't come back at all?'

'Merged back into the hills and lost themselves.'

257

'With me? Or would I have been lost on the way?'

'They have their orders.'

'That's comforting,' Zara said drily. 'The tulwar or the jezail?'

'Neither.' He rose, looking down from his great height. His brown eyes were more amused than mocking. 'Let doubt create wisdom in tongue and action, uncertainty shape your behaviour.'

Zara gave him a look of pure disgust. 'You've been listening to Mahomet again.'

'Which one?' He smiled down at her. 'You mean the one in Mecca, I suppose. At least I think you do, even if you're not quite sure where Mecca is.' He turned away. 'I'll be home by sundown, my dove. Be ready to receive me.'

He strode away and mounted Raschid's pony. They exchanged a few words then he put the pony into a trot and left the clearing to disappear into the trees.

Zara sighed. He was a most aggravating man, could never answer a straight question unless it was a trivial one, and she still didn't know what he planned to do with her when his business was finished. Lose her somewhere in the hills? He hadn't given a direct reply to that question. What orders to Raschid and Mahomet? They wouldn't tell her and Soonya didn't know. *Be ready to receive me tonight*? How confident he sounded. And with good reason, she acknowledged wryly. In the matter of last night's seduction, he could quite fairly claim that hers had been the moving spirit. Oh, confound the man, she would go over to Soonya and ask to be taught how to make chapattis!

Soonya nodded gravely as Zara expressed her wish to learn the art of hill people cooking.

'Very good,' she said. 'Man always expecting much food when there is little, and not care how it is coming. See?' She pointed towards the small patch of wheat. 'It is ready for bringing before much rain come. You help?'

'Of course. Show me what to do and I will help.' Anything, Zara thought, to keep her mind off Deverill. Had he gone to the palace again? In spite of the danger, was the Rani so irresistible that he had to make sure of her safety? She felt a hot, jealous anger surge through her, then it was followed by the cold certainty of her own rejection when Devil Sahib disappeared as he had said he would.

She followed Soonya and Rahti across to the wheatfield, carrying a large round basket.

Soonya had given her a short-bladed knife and for the next few hours she cut and hacked at the tough stems, loading her basket to capacity. She had thought it a small plot but the bending and gathering was as wearying as if it had been a ten-acre field. A scythe would have cleared it more quickly, but Soonya looked blank when Zara commented on the fact. Zara thought of the horse-drawn reaping machines of England and sighed for a pair of heavy shire horses.

'It would be quicker if Raschid and Mahomet helped,' she gasped, easing her tired back. The men were sitting in the shade near the camp, smoking and talking. Zara caught Soonya's shocked eye and smiled. 'All right, I know. Women work in the fields while men discuss important issues, like when is the next meal going to appear and haven't the women cleared the field yet.'

The task went on with the loaded baskets being carried back to the hard ground, emptied, and the corn spread to dry thoroughly. The sun was well past the meridian when the last stalk had been cut. The walk back through the sharp stubble made Zara wish for her old riding boots but Soonya and Rahti showed no discomfort. There was still no respite for Mahomet pointed to the sky and Zara, looking up, saw the dark clouds hovering. Rahti hurried to the fire, rousing its embers and setting a pot to boil, while Soonya produced two open-work wicker baskets and began to strip the ears of corn from their stalks. Zara joined her, trying to work as swiftly and neatly as Soonya but her fingers soon became sore from the rough stems. In spite of the threatening rain, the air was hot and Zara wondered why Soonya had not sought the shade for this task.

'Corn dry quick here,' Soonya explained. 'Raschid angry if not all finished today.' She looked skywards. 'Wind maybe come soon for toss basket.' She glanced at Zara's red and scratched fingers. 'Missie Sahib not doing this before?'

'Never!' Zara said with heart-felt vehemence. 'And I hope I am not here for next year's harvesting.'

'Who know that?' Soonya shrugged expressively and Zara paused to stare at her.

'Don't say things like that. I shall be in England next year, please God.'

Soonya grinned. 'I forgetting you not hillwoman but Devil Sahib be saying what you do. Man always say and he your man, yes?'

Until he disappears, Zara thought gloomily, and then what? She bent over her basket again.

The women took a short break to eat and rest, then work began again. As Soonya had predicted, a late afternoon breeze blew up and was sufficient to whirl away the chaff from the tossed baskets. Raschid and Mahomet roused themselves enough to build a small shelter to house the corn. Tomorrow, Soonya promised, she would show Zara how to grind the corn into flour. Zara nodded and retreated tiredly to her shelter.

The sun was lowering itself in the sky, a flamboyant picture of reds and golds. Almost sundown. Be ready to receive me, Deverill had said cheerfully that morning. After a day's labour in the wheatfield, Zara thought sourly. She was no Rani, lying on a silken couch, eating sweetmeats and being massaged with scented oils! Yet, she could not deny the rise of a tingling excitement as she awaited his coming. But not like this, she decided, all dusty and sweat-stained. If she could not receive him in perfumed splendour, a little honest fresh water would have to do. She took her sack and went to the pool.

The water was deeper but she was still able to stand. She must ask Deverill to buy her soap and a towel, or perhaps bring them from the palace. The Rani, she was sure, would have an abundant supply. Didn't men ever consider that a woman needed more than a comb and a change of clothes? The tunic and trousers she had worn that day, she rinsed through and laid on the bank to dry. Hesitating for a moment, she washed the undergarments and laid them out too. Tunic and trousers must suffice for this night unless Deverill decided otherwise.

Returning to the camp, she unfolded the blankets and

made them into a bed. She lay down, suddenly weary from the muscle-stretching day. In a few moments she would go to the fire and help the girls cook the supper. Her eyelids drooped and she fell into a light doze. A few moments only, she thought hazily, then I'll get up. As the smell of cooking meat reached her, she sat up. It was quite dark and the fire blazed brightly. Blinking, she looked at the figures around it. Five people she counted. Five? They were all eating and Deverill was one of them! Why had no one roused her?

She came out of the shelter unsteadily, still a little dazed by sleep. Deverill glanced over his shoulder as she approached. His gaze was sardonic.

'So, you're hungry enough to join us, are you?'

'I must have fallen asleep. Why didn't someone call me?'

'No one will call you in future, by my order. Neither will you be waited on like some lady of quality. Your place is to serve your lord and he happens to be me. Now sit down and don't answer back. My temper is not at its best tonight.'

Zara obeyed, catching the brittle note in his voice. She filled her bowl from the communal cooking pot and ate in smouldering silence. She would like to have jeered, asking if his mistress had been unkind that day and teased him into a bad temper, but she remembered the heaviness of his hand on her cheek, and wisely decided on discretion.

The meal over, the three men retired to smoke their cigarettes, or in Deverill's case, his cheroot. Zara helped to clean the bowls and fill the chatti pots with fresh water from the little curving stream. Even that was deeper than before, filling from the melting snow of the mountains. With the tasks finished, the girls separated to enter their own shelters.

Zara glanced over to where Deverill sat. His words at supper had given her an uneasy feeling, as if he intended her to become so much the hillwoman that he could leave her in their company without a qualm when he disappeared. They have their orders, he had said. Would either of them be foolish enough to risk approaching the garrison? It was something else he had in mind for her, she was convinced.

He came at last and Zara watched him in silence as he stretched himself out on the bed she had prepared.

'Take off my boots,' he said and Zara knelt at his feet. One day, she threatened the boots silently, I shall see that you pay for this. In spite of her sore fingers she managed to remove the boots.

'I think you had better start taking lessons in Urdu,' he said.

Zara sat back on her heels and regarded the face etched by the firelight.

'Why?' she asked. 'Why should I speak Urdu?'

'Because I do and it might come in useful for your future.'

Zara thought about it for a moment. 'Since our futures diverge when your business is accomplished, you had better explain why I should find it useful. And while you do, you might oblige me by giving me a reason for those remarks at supper.'

'It is in your own interests to speak and act like a hillwoman. I shall not always be here to protect you. Had you been able to communicate with those nomads, you would not have risked being stoned.'

'Oh, I see. Your concern is in my own interests, not yours.' She could not hide the slightly derisive note in her voice. 'When you disappear, you will go with the noble feeling that you have done your best for me.'

Deverill leaned on one elbow. 'Are you deliberately misunderstanding me?'

'How would I know that, when I don't understand you at all?'

'When we first met,' he said patiently, 'you took me for a wild hillman. Had we not chanced to meet on board ship, that impression would have remained and I should have let it be so. Appearance and knowledge of the language give rise to no suspicion. Don't you understand that to merge into the lifestyle of a hillwoman is your best protection? To have Soonya wait on you and converse in English would attract immediate attention.'

'From whom?'

'Good God, woman, this valley is not private property! When the rains come, so will the travellers. They'll water their ponies at the stream and graze their sheep and goats all

262

about this area. A fair-skinned woman is an asset in some establishments. Do you want to be spirited away one dark night by appearing superior?'

Zara shook her head, appalled by the thought. To be abducted again and forced into a life of shame, from which there was no escape, made her present position seem luxurious in the extreme. Was he telling her the truth?

As if in answer to her thought, Deverill said. 'Believe me, Zara, I don't lie to you on that score. Talk to Soonya tomorrow.'

He reached to grasp the hands that lay in her lap. 'Now, to more pleasant pursuits.'

Zara's exclamation as his hard fingers gripped hers, made him pause, frowning. He lifted her hands, palms uppermost, and examined them. 'How the devil did you get your fingers into this state?'

'By doing already what you are asking me to do.' She smiled, ridiculously pleased by the concern on his face. 'Being a man, you wouldn't have noticed that the corn has been cut, the ears removed and de-chaffed, or whatever it is called. We did it all today, the three of us, the girls, that is, not the lordly men. Tomorrow, we grind it!' she finished triumphantly.

'Well, I'll be damned!' Deverill said and laughed, wrapping his arms about her shoulders and pulling her on to the bed. 'I hope you're not too tired for me tonight.'

'Would it matter if I were?'

'No,' he said and kissed her, his hands moving over her body. They paused and he gave a low chuckle. 'Where are the unmentionables? Removed for my benefit?'

'Not at all,' Zara said primly. 'They needed washing, that's all.'

'Well, there's a convenient thing,' Deverill murmured, pulling the tunic over her head and easing off the baggy trousers.

Zara shivered as his hands touched her breasts and his sensitive fingers brought her body to a hot flaming desire. Her arms closed round him and she met his passion with equal fierceness.

Chapter Twenty-four

It rained the next morning and the corn grinding had to be done in the shelter. Since Deverill had taken his usual departure before Zara awoke, she put her mind to the task of pounding the corn in the concave vessel with a pestle-like stone as the crushing instrument.

Soonya grinned at her. 'Very good we fetch yesterday. Much rain coming.'

Zara nodded, wiping her forehead with her sleeve. 'Hot work. How do you say that in your language?'

Soonya told her and Zara repeated the words, to the great amusement of Rhati. Throughout the morning, Zara endeavoured to memorise the simpler words of Urdu, refusing to be put off by the giggling of both girls.

'Why you wanting, Missie?' asked Soonya.

'Maybe useful sometime,' Zara answered with a shrug. She hoped fervently that her almost nonexistent command of Urdu would never be put to the test. If any traveller came this way, she must not only fade into the background but claim dumb idiocy if caught unaware.

It began to rain more heavily and Zara remembered the washing she had laid out to dry. There was little point in retrieving it now and the sun would shine later and be warm enough to dry it. By the time they had finished the corn grinding, the rain had stopped. The ground gave off its pungent earthy scent and the oleanders by the stream seem to shake themselves and glow more vividly.

Zara watched carefully as Rahti slapped the chapattis into shape and laid them to cook on hot stones. Mahomet had brought in a stem of plantain holding a quantity of small, banana-like fruit and he tossed down a handful of pomegranates and papaya fruit. After the meal was finished, Zara judged it time to collect her washing, and proceeded towards the pool.

264

The sound of bleating caused her to glance upriver. A large flock of sheep moved like a dirty white blanket over the freshly washed rock and grass. The river itself was fuller and wider than it had been, the stepping-stones almost gone from view. She glanced into the pool. That, too, was fuller, the water lapping the rock barrier that separated it from the river. As the waters flowed down from the glaciers, swelling the river, her own private pool must lie submerged while the rains lasted.

Collecting her dry clothes, she glanced upriver again. The sheep were nearer and dark heads bobbed among them. They might pass the hidden valley without being aware of it, unless they knew of its existence, but a scarlet tunic and feringhee undergarments laid out to dry must attact anyone's notice. She bundled the clothes together and returned to camp.

Throughout the day, the sound of animal and human voices drifted over them but no one, it appeared, decided on a river crossing. Later, Zara supposed, the travellers would appear from other directions, coming from the western approaches. All sound died away as the afternoon advanced. Across the vastness of the foothills, other camp fires on which other evening meals steamed, would be rivalling the twinkling stars.

Deverill came and Zara showed no emotion, serving him, her lord, in exactly the same way as the two girls with their own men. Only when the pots had been scoured and the men had smoked their cigarettes did she follow his beckoning hand to the shelter. No word had passed between them over supper and she felt that she had behaved in superb hillwoman fashion. She hoped Deverill might comment on this but he appeared to take it for granted. As she looked at him fully for the first time, she noted his withdrawn expression.

If Deverill wanted conversation, he should start it, she decided. Since he had not spoken at supper, she could not guess his mood and instinct warned her to remain quiet. He sat for so long in brooding silence that Zara jumped when he spoke.

'They've sent for the English doctor from the garrison but I doubt he'll find anything suspicious.'

'Suspicious?' Zara echoed, her mind flying to Soonya's comments on the Rajah's fluctuating health. 'You mean like poison?'

Deverill nodded. 'What they don't know about deadly herbs is not worth knowing. On the other hand it could be natural causes. Far more likely.'

'And much more convenient,' Zara observed cynically. 'Though traditional beating of breasts must be observed.'

Deverill turned his head to look at her. He was frowning. 'What are you trying to say?'

'Surely an old man can be supposed to have died of natural causes. It happens every day without causing suspicion.'

To her surprise, Deverill laughed. He reached out and tugged her hair gently.

'My sweet Zara. What a sour tongue you have when it suits you. I detect a note of jealousy in your voice and that pleases me. Are you supposing the Rajah is being poisoned by his wife?'

'Why not? He is an old man and the Rani has taken a younger lover.' She lifted her chin to stare at him defiantly. 'Who better to know that than you?'

'You are out on one point, my sweet. It is the Yuvaraj who has fallen sick, not the Rajah.'

'The Yuvaraj?' Zara's eyes widened in astonishment.

Deverill chuckled. 'Exactly. I dare say it's over-indulgence and the doctor will prove it, but the Prince is creating a fuss about poison. Since we know how he hates the Rani, you may guess where he points the finger of suspicion.'

'But you don't – or won't – believe him?'

Deverill paused. 'I don't know. I wouldn't put it past her to give him a fright. She can be a vengeful woman, I don't deny it, to those she hates.'

'Why does she hate the Yuvaraj?'

'She is a Rajput, a strong-minded woman who despises the submissive role. She has a certain influence over the Rajah, something not to the taste of the Yuvaraj. He goes out of his way to disparage her. Since she is not his mother, he treats her as a mere woman of the zenana.'

'I can understand her feelings on that score,' Zara said

drily. 'If she really has poisoned the Yuvaraj, she might make a better job of it next time. Of course, the Yuvaraj might retaliate in the same fashion.'

Deverill nodded. 'It's an interesting thought, isn't it? A minor power struggle. What will happen when the Prince succeeds to the throne is anybody's guess.'

'If he lives to succeed,' Zara said. 'Heirs-apparent are not immortal.' She had meant it as an idle remark but Deverill looked at her sharply, almost angrily.

'Do you know what you are saying?' he demanded.

Zara's jealousy of the Rani spilled over in an angry stream. 'Yes, I do,' she snapped. 'You describe the Rani as a woman who likes power. If she rids herself of the Yuvaraj for good and all, she has only to wait for the Rajah to die to become all-powerful. Why, she might even help him along a little if she is so clever with her deadly herbs.' She paused for breath. 'It is not so fantastic, remember the Borgias and the Pharaohs –'

'Be quiet!' Deverill snapped and Zara felt herself quail under his icy stare.

'This is madness, the talk of a jealous woman. I thought better of you than to concoct such a ridiculous story. Do you think the Rani would risk her position at this point?'

Zara looked down at her hands, her flare of anger withered. 'I'm sorry. You are right. I am jealous. The doctor is bound to find nothing suspicious. The Yuvaraj will recover –'

'Damn the Yuvaraj!' Deverill said violently. 'I'm not concerned with him. My entire future rests on the Rani. She must come to no harm through any unwise action of her own or the Prince's. There must be no suspicion.' He rose. 'Dear God, I can't take that risk –'

He was out of the shelter, his words trailing into the darkness. Zara sat in frozen silence, stunned by the anguish in his voice. A pony whickered, then hooves pounded out of the clearing. After that, there was nothing but the sounds of the night.

Zara wrapped the blanket about her and lay down on the bed, feeling drained and hollow. The anguish in his voice still rang in her ears, like the slow tolling of a funeral bell. That anguish had been for the Rani. Any hope that she, Zara Deane, had entertained of replacing the Rani in his affections, had gone like the morning mist under the sun. No man could speak of a woman in such agony of tone without being possessed, body and soul. She tried to think clearly. The Rani was strong-minded, perhaps a woman of fierce temper. If the Yuvaraj goaded her into retaliation, she might well have dosed his food with poison, not to kill, just to frighten. Was she capable of killing? Deverill must have thought so, or why would he go off so violently to protect her?

Hadn't it occurred to him before her own outburst, that what he called a minor power struggle between the Rani and the Yuvaraj might develop into a major battle? She would want to retain her influence with the Rajah, while the Prince would be happy to have her banished in disgrace, and it would not suit Deverill to have his mistress banished to heaven knew where. She fell into exhausted sleep.

Morning brought no alleviation to her spirits. The day was grey and wet. Deverill was not in the camp nor had she really expected him to be. When he came back, if he ever did, nothing would be the same again. By her own outburst of last night she had severed any link between them. He might use her, but coldly and possibly brutally, since she had disparaged his mistress.

The hillmen and girls huddled miserably in the rain, Raschid and Mahomet in bad temper as the rain made fire-lighting impossible out of doors. Under one of the shelters, the girls did their best, but the wet sticks smouldered reluctantly, giving off choking smoke and little heat. The porridge was only half-cooked when the men demanded food and the fault was naturally attributed to the stupidity of Rahti and Soonya.

Soonya turned a smoke-streaked face to Zara. 'Where Devil Sahib go in big rush?'

'To the palace, where else?' Zara said moodily. 'Gone to protect the Rani.'

Soonya grunted, dropping the corners of her mouth. 'Who protect him from Rani?'

It seemed a rhetorical question and Zara made no answer but shrugged.

Towards midday, the rain stopped and at last the sun came out. The atmosphere of the camp brightened and the girls carried out damp blankets and clothes to spread on the ground. Zara examined the contents of her own shelter but found everything dry. Mahomet and Raschid must have made a better job of roofing for Devil Sahib, she supposed.

The heavy downpour must have added inches to the river. Had the little pool disappeared? As she walked towards the edge, Zara played a childish game with herself. If the rim of the pool was visible, Deverill might come back in better mood and she would try to heal the breach between them. If there was no sign of the pool where they had first made love, if the rushing river had submerged it completely, it would be as if nothing had ever happened there. Just another incident in his life, without significance, but to Zara it had the awakening moment of physical love, something a girl does not forget.

She stood on the crest looking down. There was nothing but the fast-moving river. It had been ridiculous to suppose anything else. A concoctor of dreams, that was all she was. To dream of sharing a life with Deverill when he had clearly stated that his future lay with the Rani.

Upriver, the stepping-stones had gone too, and only the beaten earth tracks on either side of the river remained, indicating their position. Zara stared over the river towards Batala. It wasn't visible, but Deverill had come from that direction, limping on his broken-heeled boot. The hills sloped unevenly downards, dotted with sheep and goats. The sun was brighter and the view quite extensive. The tents of the nomadic goat and sheep herders were being dismantled with practised ease, billowing canvases furled and strapped along the backs of mules and ponies. From where she stood, she could hear the shouting of women, the yells of scampering children beating the flocks into movement. An untidy, milling flurry of animal and human. Someone must have given the signal, for the assembly moved as one, dust and earth clods rising in their passage.

Zara moved her gaze from the descending array and

glanced higher up the hills. Two lines of white tents caught her eye. Two very straight lines, so unlike the irregular siting of the goat people's tents that she frowned, trying to focus upon them more intently. Horses she saw, but no other animals. Figures moved and there was precision and orderliness about the movements.

Zara's heart gave a jerk. She had become so accustomed to the camp sites of the hill people that her brain was not reacting as it should. Dear God, she was looking at a British army camp site! As if to stamp all doubt from her mind, the blast of a bugle soared and held upon the still air.

What message was in that trumpet call? Muster for breakfast, grooms to the horse lines, strike camp? Oh no, please God, not that. She had to reach them before they decamped and rode away. Let it not be an exercise in brisk efficiency, the officers counting the seconds to test their men. It was her only chance to break from this life, forget Deverill and his desperate concern for the Rani, get back to Lahore and start a new life in England.

But first she had to cross the river. Why did it have to rain so much and hide the stepping stones? There was no other way across. A strong swimmer might have fought the current but she could not even swim. She began to run upriver towards the beaten earth of the crossing tracks. Would the stones be visible? She peered into the water. They had to be there and there was no other way.

On the edge of the river, she paused, staring down. Only the waves breaking and creaming showed some underwater obstruction. By keeping level with the track on the opposite bank, could she keep her balance and ignore the splashing wavelets? How deep? Perhaps knee-deep, for the stones were not to be seen. As she hesitated, the bugle shrilled again. It had to be now or lose the chance, perhaps for ever. She spread her arms and took the first step. The iciness of the water made her gasp. She stood for a moment, swaying. It was only ankle-deep, nothing at all difficult about it. A second step and she discovered the slipperiness of wet stones. Neither were they of equal height. The water rose to her knees in places, folding the wide trouser legs about each other, so that she had to bend and pull them apart while maintaining her balance. She wanted to search out the British camp, to see if they were still there, but she dared not take her eyes from the opposite bank.

Progress was slow and painful. Twice she skidded and fell to her knees, grabbing at the stones to stop herself from being swept away. In that position the spray rose over her, soaking her tunic and hair. Since the rain had weakened the banks, the river had drawn into its grasp earth and twigs. The water was muddy and Zara felt its grittiness slapping at her arms and neck. She stayed on her knees, crawling over the last few stones, then climbed out, dropping into a gasping heap. Soaked and muddied, her hair a wild, wet tangle, who on earth would recognise her as Miss Zara Deane, English lady of reasonable quality?

They didn't have to recognise her, she told herself. All she had to do was ask for the senior officer, reveal her identity and ask that a message be sent to Colonel Lacy in Lahore. She rose to her feet and looked anxiously towards the camp. Relief made her feel dizzy. They were still there. Ten, fifteen minutes of swift walking and she would be there. She began to walk, holding out the wide trouser legs in an effort to dry them. After the icy river, the sun was good and she shook back her hair. Her step faltered only once when she thought of the officers there. Not Captain Browne, please God. Major Fraser, even Colonel Lacy himself, she could bear, but not Ralph, please.

As she approached the camp, she noted the armed sentries on its perimeter. They stood relaxed now, since they alone possessed the hillside. Last night, the guards would have been on the alert, discouraging any approach by the goat people begging food or coin. About twenty yards from the nearest sentry, Zara stopped. The sun had almost dried her clothes and she brushed her hands down her tunic to rid it of dried mud. Then she ran her fingers through her hair and wiped her face on the tunic sleeves. It was the best she could do.

Glancing up, she found the sentry watching her curiously. She began to walk towards him. He was young, a private soldier by his uniform, and she smiled as she drew nearer. He

271

frowned and took a firmer grip on his rifle.

'Halt,' he called hoarsely, and brought round the rifle.

Within five yards of him, Zara stopped. 'Good morning,' she said and smiled again.

'Be on your way,' the boy said and made his voice low and threatening. He glanced round nervously and she saw the relief on his face as a large, burly man rounded a tent and stopped dead.

'Sergeant,' the boy called. 'This 'ere woman won't go away. Begging likely.'

The sergeant, thick and red-faced, walked forward. He stared Zara up and down.

'Your folks have gone and there's nothing to hang about for. Get off with you.'

'I wish to see your commanding officer,' Zara said flatly, eyeing the sergeant through narrow eyes.

'Do you indeed.' The sergeant grinned insolently and Zara felt her anger begin.

'At once,' she snapped.

'What for?'

'None of your business.'

The sergeant's face turned redder and he glared at her. Zara realised her folly. She should not have spoken that way in front of one of his men. She jumped as his voice came in a bellow.

'Get your filthy self away from here. Go and peddle your wares back in Lahore. Officers don't have no truck with scruffy wenches like you. I wouldn't touch you myself, let alone this lad here. Ain't that right, Barker?'

The boy's grinning reply was drowned in the thud of hooves on the grass. Zara looked in that direction and saw the horse lines breaking up as officers came out of their tents. She craned to see a face she knew but the big sergeant blocked her view. Then, in a moment, the calm camp site burst into a flurry of activity. Officers swung themselves on to their horses, shouting orders that were repeated down the ranks by sergeants to corporals, to private soldiers. Tents collapsed to be furled with rapidity, boots clattered, urgent voices called, commanding, ordering, chivvying infantrymen into line. The bugle blasted again and Zara panicked. They were moving, she hadn't got through to any officer and this grim-faced sergeant was advancing on her with threatening gestures.

'Out of it,' he roared.

'An officer, for the love of God!' Zara shouted, panic flooding through her. 'You can't go yet. I am Zara Deane. You must tell him.'

'What, disturb my officer to tell him there's an Indian wench called Zaradeen as would like a word with him? Do you think I'm mad?'

'I'm not an Indian wench,' Zara screamed above the noise. 'I'm English, can't you see that?'

'Ho, yes, I can see you're an English milady,' he said with heavy sarcasm. 'They're always wandering about, dressed scruffy like you and with mud in their hair. Ain't that right, Barker?' he called over his shoulder to the young soldier.

The boy nodded sheepishly. 'All the time, Sergeant,' he agreed.

Zara looked desperately at the lines of soldiers preparing to march. 'Take a message, please, it's vitally urgent.' She tried to move past the sergeant but he blocked her way, still grinning, his rifle held horizontally.

'Be off, there's a good lass or you'll be in real trouble.'

Zara's temper snapped. 'I'm Zara Deane, damn you, as English as you are and I won't go away. Fetch an officer, man, and don't be a fool.'

The sergeant's smile died and his expression turned ugly. 'Fool, is it? No common trollop calls me fool. I've been patient, God knows, but that's going too far.' He reversed his rifle and held it by the barrel. 'I'll give you a second to clear out, then you'll get a whack with my rifle butt.'

Zara drew in a deep breath. The man was immovable and completely intractable. She had no alternative but to scream as loudly as she could. Surely an officer would come to investigate. She noted a movement in the sergeant's eyes, his gaze rose and he was no longer glaring into her face. Without looking down, he reversed his rifle quickly and brought it up to his shoulder in the firing position. Zara turned her head and saw where his gaze lay.

Covering the ground with immense strides came a large black horse, heading directly towards them. The speed of its passage billowed the robes of the rider and his turban tail streamed behind him like a regimental pennant. The rifle slung over his shoulder, a tulwar in his sashband, made the sergeant's action understandable. The barrel of his rifle held steady on the newcomer who slowed his horse to a canter. A broad grin lit his face as he looked from the sergeant to Zara.

'May Allah bless you, General Sahib,' he called, then in a flashing moment he was out of the saddle with one hand buried deep in Zara's hair. He jerked savagely and Zara screamed in pain. The black horse had fooled her for a few moments but the face and voice were Deverill's. His hand was so deeply entwined in her hair, the pull so severe, that her neck was strained backwards. Tears of anger and pain flooded her eyes.

'Don't –' she gasped but her plea was ignored. Deverill was talking to the sergeant.

'A bad bargain I made, General Sahib, when I buy this woman from rascally camel-trader. Good and obedient, he promise, but what do I get? Woman who answer back, never make food worth eating and run away all the time. She have great wish to be English camp follower, you understand, General Sahib?'

The sergeant had lowered his rifle and was chuckling now. 'I do indeed. She was wanting to talk to my officer and calling me a fool, would you believe, when I refused to fetch him.'

Deverill clicked his tongue. 'She much big trouble. Very wise man you are, General Sahib, to say no.'

'She said she was English.'

'Always she saying that and making up name. What name this time?'

The sergeant pondered a moment. 'Didn't sound very English to me. Something like Zaradeen – yes, that was it. What are you going to do with her?'

Deverill sighed. 'Beat her, of course, but maybe not too hard for she is one of the Blessed of Allah.'

'Eh? What's that mean?' the sergeant asked.

From the corner of her eye, Zara saw Deverill describe a

circle in the air close to the side of his forehead. The sergeant nodded and grinned. Zara, still with her hair held viciously in the strong fingers, felt a boiling fury. She relaxed her knees and sagged as if in a faint. The pressure eased from her scalp. Deverill loosened his hold and looked down on her.

Zara met his eyes with a blazing hatred. 'He lies!' she screamed suddenly. 'He is a –' The breath caught in her throat as Deverill's hand clamped over her mouth. She kicked and struggled to free herself, but Deverill pulled her forward and held her face hard against his chest. It was almost impossible to breathe, let alone scream.

'I will take her away now, General Sahib. A little opium maybe to calm her.'

'Poor mad thing,' the sergeant said and there was a hint of real sympathy in his voice. 'Don't be too hard on her. She can't help herself.'

'You have kind heart, General Sahib,' Deverill said piously. 'I keep her, for my own heart is kind and maybe when I meet Allah, he will know this good thing I do and give me very special houri, yes?'

Zara felt herself lifted on to the horse's back but Deverill followed too quickly to allow her to take more than one gasping breath. Her face was clamped to his breast again.

'Just one thing, friend,' called the sergeant as the horse began to move. 'I'm not a general, just a sergeant.'

'But a very good sergeant, Sahib. One day maybe you make great general.' He raised a hand in salute. 'May Allah guide your steps, Sergeant Sahib.'

The sergeant's chuckle faded as Deverill put his horse to the gallop. Zara's hope of rescue faded with the sound and she lay limp and defeated in Deverill's arms.

Chapter Twenty-five

It seemed only seconds before they were at the river bank. Deverill slid Zara to the ground and dismounted.

Hang on to the left stirrup,' he ordered. 'This horse is well able to swim across and you will be protected from the current on that side.'

He positioned himself on the horse's offside, took a short grip on its bridle and led it into the river. The horse went willingly, as if well used to river crossings, and struck out strongly for the opposite bank. Zara hung on to the stirrup, her body and legs submerged. There was no bottom that she could reach and her limbs floated aimlessly, dragged along by the horse's movements.

Her mind was still numbed by her failure to escape and the shock of Deverill's appearance. How had he come to be there at precisely the wrong time? Did it make any difference? She hadn't exactly made a great success of her encounter with the sergeant. A more servile approach would have been more appropriate, but eagerness and impatience had made her speak sharply. Too sharply for the dignity of a stolid British sergeant who took her at face value, a scruffy, mudstained camp follower with an impertinent tongue.

She stared at the closing opposite bank. What a complete shambles she had made of the whole thing. Now she was back in Deverill's power. Her head ached from the tugging of her hair and her mind burned with the shame of his description. One of the Blessed of Allah. A madwoman, bought from a camel trader! He would pay for this treatment, she vowed, but the future looked obstinately depressing.

The horse climbed out of the river, dragging a sodden Zara clinging to the stirrup. She let go and sank to the grass, streaming muddy water. She lay still, uncaring, as the horse showered her with still more water as it shook itself. A squelching of boots on the grass, then Deverill was looking down at her. She stared through him, hating him for what he had done.

'Get up,' he said.

Zara lay unmoving, as if she had not heard.

Richard Deverill's gaze rested on the white, drawn face. Those hazel up staring up almost sightlessly, had a dull, quenched look. They were very speaking eyes, he knew, sometimes sparking with anger, sometimes tender with love, but always alive. Now they were blank, as if the spirit had gone, leaving an empty shell. He shook away the fancy. This girl was not lifeless and could never be spiritless while breath remained in her body. She was wet and exhausted, stunned by her recapture, but the old Zara Deane would return, he was convinced. Meanwhile, she must make the best of it until he decided otherwise. Yet he was disturbed by her apathy. He bent and took her arms, pulling her to her feet. She stood, swaying, staring at nothing. Holding the bridle of the horse with one hand, he used his other to grip her shoulder and propel her to the ridge. Over the crest he paused and called. Raschid came running, a wide grin on his face as he saw the tall, black horse. Deverill left him to take the animal, removed a saddlebag, and guided Zara quickly into their shelter.

Raschid had not glanced at Zara, having eyes only for the horse. He led it away towards Mahomet and both men began to rub down and groom the animal. Deverill put his hands on Zara's skin. It was very cold. Opening his saddlebag, he brought out a large, rough towel. Before Zara could make any protest, Deverill had stripped off her tunic and chemise and was rubbing her skin with hard, vigorous strokes. He pulled down the soaking trousers.

'Step out of them,' he said quietly. 'I'll rub you down, or, if you prefer it, dry yourself.'

'I can do it myself,' Zara said dully and began to shiver.

'Hurry then,' he said in a curt voice. 'I'm damned if I want a sneezing, snivelling wench in my bed.'

His words, as he had intended, brought a little colour back to Zara's face but her eyes stayed dull and there was no anger in them. She was still shivering as Deverill caught up a blanket and draped it about her.

277

'Lie down and rest. You've had a busy time.' He hadn't meant it as a jibe but Zara's lips tightened and she turned away her head, folding the blanket tightly about her. She lay down with her back to Deverill and the shelter entrance. He saw that she was still shivering and frowned. Shock and reaction to what had happened, he supposed. Hot food and drink was the answer.

Thank God he had been in time to intercept her at the British camp. It had been pure coincidence that he had been returning at that moment. Since Raschid's pony had gone lame, he had borrowed the black stallion from the palace stables, one of the Yuvaraj's mounts but the Prince was unaware yet of its absence. It was good to be mounted on a well-trained horse again, a nostalgic reminder of his army days, more than six months behind him now.

He strode from the shelter towards the camp fire. 'Make strong, hot tea for Missie Sahib,' he told Soonya and handed her the packet he had taken from his saddlebag.

Soonya nodded but said nothing. One did not question Devil Sahib, even without that black look on his face, but she wondered at the unusual request. It was not time to make food, the sun was not yet sinking. Was Missie Sahib ill? Raschid would not have noticed if she, herself, had fallen dead at his feet but there was something of worry on Devil Sahib's face. She pondered on it as she boiled the water and tossed a handful of tea leaves into it. Maybe, he like the Missie Sahib very much. Soonya had caught a quick glimpse of Missie Sahib's face as she was pushed into the shelter. She nodded sagely to herself. Very white face. Memsahibs go like that when sickness come. She had seen it for herself in Lahore. The hand stirring the pot paused. But in Lahore, English doctor sahib giving medicine. No doctor sahib here. She began to stir the brew vigorously.

Zara lay huddled in the blankets, her mind foggy with misery and shame. Why had Deverill brought her back again? Why couldn't he have left her at the British camp? She knew the answer, of course. He could not risk her telling them all she knew about his activities. But he had taken a risk in galloping right up to the sentries, without knowing how much

278

she might already have revealed. If it hadn't been for that obstructive sergeant, her tale could have been told and Deverill arrested as he rode up. Now she was back in the shelter again with nothing achieved. She gave a low moan of despair and frustration.

'Missie Sahib,' a voice whispered. 'Here very hot tea like Devil Sahib say.'

Zara ignored the whisper. How could she face Soonya and pretend nothing had happened? She lay still, her eyes closed.

'I am leaving here,' Soonya's voice said after a pause.

There was a long silence after that and Zara drifted into a half-doze which dulled the headache and kept her safe from reality. She didn't want to think or move, just lie here and die. The garrison thought her dead and after today, Deverill might decide it best for his own sake that she should be so. The doze deepened into sleep and her mind emptied.

Deverill had been watching the entrance to the shelter as he had talked and given his orders to Raschid and Mahomet. They had ridden out an hour ago, Raschid proudly astride the black horse, and it was now dark but no movement had come from the shelter. He had seen Soonya go in with the mug of tea and now she and Rahti were cooking the evening meal. He debated on whether to enter the shelter and decided against it. She would come out when she was hungry. He was rather looking forward to seeing her stride out, spitting fire from her eyes in a venomous glare. Shock at her recapture would be replaced by anger, if he knew his Zara. His Zara? Yes, dammit, his Zara! She loved him. A girl could not pretend to the extent of responding so passionately to his love-making. He had offered her nothing but that had not deterred her. He thought of the respectable young ladies of the garrison, those he had known in his days as Major Deverill. Some of the prettiest had flirted with him but like a bargaining counter, they were concerned to receive value in rank and position. An officer with a private income was high on the priority list of fresh maidens. But a disgraced officer was something else. No more limpid glances of encouragement, no fluttering fingers in his hand during a waltz and really, that Major Deverill has misread entirely their natural courtesy. He grinned to himself as he recalled the vehement denials of flirtatious behaviour. He glanced again towards the shelter. Still no sign of Zara.

Although she was not here by her own choice, she had taken a disgraced officer into her heart and given him everything a woman could give. And what return had he given? Not even the assurance of a safe return to Lahore. Why hadn't he reassured her on that score, for he intended it all along, not yet, but when his business had finished. It was cruel to let her believe he would abandon her in the hills. He frowned. Why had he done that? To keep her submissive and eager to please him? Perhaps that had been true at first, for nothing must endanger this operation, but now he knew with certainty that a meek and self-effacing Zara Deane was not what he wanted.

His admiration was all for the raging tigress, the waspish-tongued virago, the girl who walked the hills with cynical resignation and shared the discomforts of Soonya and Rhati without putting herself above them. In short, he wanted her exactly as she was. He glowered at the shelter entrance. Why didn't she come out and play hell with him? That quenched look still disturbed him. Come out, damn you, Zara Deane! Don't expect any apologies from me!

Raschid and Mahomet trotted their ponies back into the clearing, swung down and came to squat beside Deverill. Talking and listening to their reports took his mind off that dark, silent shelter. The business was progressing well. Soon, it would all be over and this company of hill people disbanded, Devil Sahib laid to rest. The smell of cooked meat came to him. He glanced at Soonya who was filling the food bowls.

'Time to eat,' Deverill said and the three men rose.

Soonya's hand hovered uncertainly over an empty bowl. She glanced at Deverill.

'Leave it. She will come,' he answered and began to eat.

Since he had made it plain to Zara that she would not be waited on or called when food was ready, he could not now change that ruling without loss of face. She would come, late

280

perhaps in a gesture of defiance, but come she would, he was convinced.

The meal eaten, Deverill made conversation with Raschid and Mahomet. The girls were silent but aware of Devil Sahib's brooding anger. They had no idea why he should become increasingly angry. If Messie Sahib was sick, that should not make him angry. Soonya would have liked to take Missie Sahib's bowl to her but the look on Devil Sahib's face kept her quiet. She saw him glance covertly once or twice towards the shelter. Was he going to beat Missie Sahib? Not if she was sick, surely, but there her thinking was at the beginning again. Devil Sahib was angry.

The three men withdrew to smoke. Soonya and Rahti cleaned bowls and prepared for the night. Zara had not appeared and Deverill's short answers to the comments of Raschid and Mahomet caused the men to fall into uneasy silence. They drifted away to join their womenfolk but Deverill sat on. For half an hour he sat, his eyes dark with anger, staring at the shelter. Damn the girl's defiance! Let her go hungry. He would not allow food to be taken in. Fuelling his anger with such thoughts was becoming difficult. Unease and concern were creeping into his mind. He remembered the dazed, white faces of young recruits returning after their first wild skirmishes in the mountain passes. Wide, shocked eyes, unbelieving expressions, a tendency to stare vacantly as reaction set in. Yes, that was it. Just reaction. It would wear off.

He rose, tossing the cheroot butt into the fire, and strode towards the shelter. At the entrance he stopped. The mug of tea he had ordered especially for her was standing untouched on the earth floor. Somehow he could not feel angry at her ignoring it. He crossed towards the blanketed figure and peered down. She was so still, she might have been dead. A stab of fear clutched his heart and he knelt, listening intently. A faint sound reached him. She was breathing, thank God. Of course she was breathing. Young, healthy girls did not die of shock or disappointment. But the breathing was shallow and the face, so white before, had a red spot on each cheek. He laid a cool hand on her forehead and was shocked to find it hot.

281

Her skin was damp with an unnatural clamminess. He sank back on his heels and regarded her thoughtfully. Was this just the aftermath of shock or was it a fever? How could she contract a fever without anyone else being affected? But she was not a hillwoman and did not share their immunity to the ailments that affected newcomers to this land.

He dropped his turban and tunic to the floor and removed his boots. Tomorrow he would see how she was but tonight there was nothing to be done. He took his own blanket and wrapped it about them both, holding her tightly in his embrace. Sweat out a fever, the old India hands used to say. That might be the cure and tomorrow the old Zara, full of fire and fury, would be back. That was the way he loved her. Sleep claimed him on that comforting thought.

Zara woke and wished she hadn't. Her body felt leaden and the pain in her head was still there. She tried to lick her dry lips but her tongue seemed too heavy to move. What was the matter with her? She closed her eyes and tried to think but her mind would not concentrate. Like fragments of dreams, pictures came and went. A big man with a rifle stared pityingly, then a bigger man dragged her by the hair. She remembered the pain of that and, through watering eyes, the cruel face of Devil Sahib. Everywhere she turned he was there, blocking and checking her. Although her body ran with perspiration, she began to shake with cold. That drenching in the river, muddy water swamping and choking her as the horse plunged through. The taste of churned-up mud was still in her throat. She coughed and gasped at the rasp of pain in her chest. Lie still, try for unconsciousness again, she thought, better that way.

But somebody was there, lifting her head. Go away, you'll bring back the pain, she tried to say, but her tongue wouldn't form the words. Tears of frustration ran down her face and she moaned. Something pressed hard against her lips and liquid slopped over as she tried to push it away. Some drops fell into her mouth and the taste made her feel sick. Not water, nor tea, nor anything she had ever tasted before. A vile mixture like muddy water again. She fought to avoid the insistent thrusting of the beaker to her mouth but the hands that forced her were too strong.

'Drink,' a voice kept saying and she was suddenly too tired to resist.

She drank and her stomach protested. There was a bowl beside her and she jerked herself over it and was violently sick.

'Good,' the voice said, and she thought how stupid it must be. Then a damp cloth was wiping her face and that was not stupid but comforting, like the warm blanket and the lowering of her body. Then there was nothing again.

When next Zara woke, she lay quite still, not wanting the pain of that other awakening. Her mind seemed clearer, her body lighter and the throb in her head less violent. She lay for a long time with her eyes closed, not quite believing in the absence of pain, and half-afraid that if she opened her eyes, someone would make her drink that foul mixture again. There was no sound, it might be safe to open her eyes. She slitted them and looked out. Her breath came out in a low moan. Someone was there, after all, sitting very still and very close to her. It was Deverill and he had a beaker in his hand.

'No, no!' she gasped and put both hands over her mouth, shaking her head fiercely.

'A cup of hot tea?' he asked. 'Soonya thought you would like that.'

'It's not tea,' Zara mumbled through her fingers. 'I hate it, take it away!'

'But it really is tea, on my word.'

'Your word!' There was no disguising the bitter note in Zara's muffled voice but Deverill showed no reaction.

'Take Soonya's word then.' He glanced towards the entrance. 'The poor girl has had the water pot on the fire these two days, waiting to brew tea.' He spoke in Urdu to a crouching figure and Soonya rose and approached the bed. Deverill handed her the beaker. Soonya knelt and Deverill left the shelter. As the sunlight caught his face, Zara felt a sense of shock. He looked unkempt and drawn, lines of weariness etched round his eyes and mouth.

'Is true tea, Missie Sahib,' Soonya said. 'You smelling first.'

Zara obeyed, sniffing warily. It smelt like tea and she sipped a drop.

'Yes.' She nodded. 'It is tea. Thank you.' She drank thirstily and Soonya beamed.

'Very good Missie Sahib better. Devil Sahib much unhappy.'

Zara frowned. What had Deverill said? These two days?

Soonya was going on. 'When you come here with Devil Sahib and big horse, I thinking you not looking good but Devil Sahib saying nothing.'

'Last night do you mean?'

'Not last night, Missie Sahib. That being three nights back. You very sick all time since. I making medicine, getting herb and thing.'

Zara remembered the dreadful-tasting liquid that had been forced on her more than once. She shuddered.

'Medicine? It tasted like muddy water.'

Soonya giggled. 'Yes, very bad tasting, but doing much good. I get secret from wise guru in my village. It make you better, yes?'

Zara smiled wanly. 'I'll take your word for it, but it did make me sick.'

Soonya nodded. 'That is best way, then no bad thing left. Now you hungry, yes?'

'Very,' Zara said, surprised that she should find the thought of food suddenly irresisible.

Soonya went away and returned after a few minutes with a bowl containing a thick, meaty broth. With it came a wooden spoon. Zara glanced at Soonya who shrugged and eyed the spoon with respect.

'Devil Sahib making. All time sitting here, not going to palace.'

Zara frowned, recalling the low voice and gentle hands that had eased and tended her.

'You mean he looked after me himself?'

Soonya nodded. 'We fetching water, making medicine.'

'But why was I sick? I don't understand. I was all right when –' She stopped, wondering how much Deverill had told them.

284

'You very hot after corn grinding and go to river. Devil Sahib say you drinking bad water.' She gave Zara a reproachful but apologetic glance. 'Peoples and goats using river. Is better to wait until water come clean.'

Zara thought about that. The goat-herders had moved off before she attempted her crawl over the stones. Perhaps there were other herders higher up and the thrashing of the black horse dragging her by its stirrup had stirred up some unclean water. She remembered her own gasping breaths. Yes, she could have swallowed some river water.

She ate some of the broth but her stomach was still rather reluctant to accept it all. The effort exhausted her and she lay back, still feeling weak, and half-afraid that she might be sick again.

'Where is Devil Sahib now?' Zara asked.

'He go to palace but he say giving you this.' On Soonya's extended palm lay a cake of bright pink soap. 'Night you fell sick, he bringing towel too.'

Zara looked from the pink soap to the gaudy green towel. If only he had thought to bring them much sooner, she might have presented a better appearance at the British camp. In spite of the bitterness of that thought, she was touched that he had brought them at all. And he had cared for her himself, according to Soonya. That must mean he felt a responsibility towards her. She closed her eyes. Responsibility. It was something positive, she supposed, and showed that he did not want her death on his conscience. But what did that prove? That he would release her when it was time for him to disappear. But where, and more important, to whom? Sell her to another camel trader? He had told the sergeant he had bought her from one. To cover his own tracks, that must surely be wiser than sending her to Lahore where she would be free to tell her story to the authorities. Her mind drifted into sleep again.

Just before dawn, Deverill returned to camp. He entered the shelter and stood looking down on the sleeping girl. Still very pale with cheeks hollowed by the swift bout of fever, only allayed by that witch's brew of Soonya's, she appeared crushed and defenceless. He had brought her to this, he

285

thought with a nagging feeling of guilt. It was that guilt which had made him stay by her side during the last two days. She might have died on him and he didn't want that, yet the risk was still too great to allow him to send her to Lahore. He had been tempted to ride for the garrison doctor but explanations would have been difficult and dangerous.

He knelt beside her and laid a finger on her skin. Quite cool. She was recovering. In a few days her strength would return and with it her spirit. He looked forward to that, yet things could hardly be the same again. After the fiasco of her second attempt to escape, for which she must blame him bitterly, he could hardly expect the return of a loving, giving Zara Deane. That would be too much to expect and his mind lingered with real regret on those moments of rapture. He sighed and rose, moving to the entrance.

A sound made him glance over his shoulder. Zara's eyes were open but clouded by sleep. In hazy half-recollection, she was back in her bedroom at the Lacy bungalow, staring into darkness at the man stepping out from the shelter of the trees.

The dark face touched by lamplight, the smile and outstretched hand were the same but the eyes were not fixed on that approaching figure but on her. He had seen her. He was staring straight at her. Her breath came in a strangled gasp. Unbidden, the word forced itself from her stiff lips.

'Shaitan!' She covered her face with her hands as she saw the smile freeze on the dark face.

Chapter Twenty-six

Deverill stood motionless for a moment, then moved back to kneel beside the bed. He took Zara's hands and pulled them away from her face. Her eyes were wide, aware now but uncertain.

'Where did you hear that?' he asked.

Zara shook her head. 'I don't remember.'

'I think you do. Tell me.' The voice was soft but demanding an answer.

'In the garden.'

'Which garden?'

He didn't seem angry and Zara took a little heart. 'In the Lacy garden.'

Deverill frowned. 'Perhaps you'd better explain. I don't understand.'

'I – I was to be a house guest of the Lacys until my marriage.'

'I see. And the garden? You were in it?'

'No, in my bedroom which faced on to the garden. It was hot, I couldn't sleep so I opened the shutters.'

'And stood in the dark taking the air, I suppose.'

'Yes.'

'You saw me waiting?' At Zara's nod, he went on. 'And you also saw the person for whom I was waiting? Yes, you must have done to have heard that word. What did you do about it?'

'Nothing.'

'Nothing?' Deverill frowned. 'Why not?'

'Because I thought – perhaps the other man was Colonel Lacy, at first that is – and if he was deceiving his wife, it was none of my business.'

'At first, you said. Couldn't you see him?'

'No, he wore a sort of hooded robe.'

'Ah, yes. And what was your second thought?'

'That he was some house servant sneaking out to go to Lahore.'

Deverill laughed softly. 'To sample the delights of a certain quarter, I suppose you are implying?'

'Even then I was wrong.'

'Tell me your third thought,' Deverill said encouragingly. 'I am eager to learn.'

Zara stared at him stonily. 'He was your informant and most likely stole the keys of the armoury from Colonel Lacy while he slept. I know now that you took those rifles. Do you deny it?'

'Of course not. You are absolutely right. Why didn't you tell Colonel Lacy of your suspicions?'

'I didn't have any then, although I did ask him at breakfast what the word "Shaitan" meant. He seemed a little surprised but said it meant devil.'

'And you pursued it no further? You told no one else?'

'That, in case you've forgotten, was the day I ran into Raschid and Mahomet!' Despite its weakness, Deverill detected a dryness in her tone. He smiled.

'I begin to think it was a lucky chance encounter.'

'For whom?'

'For me, primarily. Although I did not appreciate it at the time, you were, in fact, the only witness to my meeting with my contact in the Lacy garden. In addition, you just happened to be the one who saw me with the Rani at the palace. I could not have chosen a better captive if I had tried.'

'How very convenient.'

'Yes, isn't it? You understand why I can't allow you to escape?'

Zara closed her eyes. 'Very well indeed. Why didn't you leave me to be stoned to death by the goat paople? And for that matter, why force medicine on me when you could have let the fever take me? You would have been rid of your witness either way.'

'My dear Zara,' Deverill said in a shocked voice. 'I have no wish for your death. That will be of no benefit to me at all. I have other plans for you.'

'Yes, of course, I should have realised that. I am worth nothing dead.' She opened her eyes and gave him a weary look. 'I am very tired. Would you mind leaving me now. I am sure the Rani can provide you with better amusement than I can.'

To her surprise, Deverill leaned over and dropped a kiss on her forehead. 'Get well soon, my dear. I have missed you in various ways.' He smiled and went away.

Zara regained her strength in body but her mind remained troubled by Deverill's words. Did he plan to sell her? That, or ransom her back to the garrison were the only ways whereby he would benefit. And who, in the garrison, would consider her worthy of ransom? Not Ralph, that was certain, but maybe the army would consider it a duty to secure the release of an Englishwoman, even a fallen one, and ship her quietly back to England.

It was some days before Zara resumed her camp duties. She learned to make chapattis and corn bread and use the correct mixture of herbs and spices for the cooking pot. But all these things she did with a listless air and was ever watchful when strangers came near the camp. Soonya and Rahti were a little puzzled by her lack of animation but put it down to the after-effects of the fever.

Deverill found himself sharing their puzzlement. Although Zara appeared to have recovered well from the fever, she was pale and withdrawn, her eyes watchful. Whenever he returned to camp he would catch the flashing glance, then she would turn away, a slight relaxing of her rigid stance. Almost, he thought, as if she expected him to be accompanied. Something was very wrong, he decided, and determined to discover what it was. Since she had revealed, two nights ago, that she had seen him in the Lacy garden, she had been strangely silent. Where was the old Zara, the one who speared him with her tongue? This girl was a pale shadow and he missed the original. He must bring her back.

Instead of staying with Raschid and Mahomet to smoke his cheroot, Deverill followed Zara to the shelter. She sensed him behind her and jumped nervously.

'I want to talk to you,' he said.

Zara heard the flatness of his tone and a shudder ran through her. So, it was coming, all that she feared. She wrapped herself in a blanket and waited, staring out across the camp.

Deverill sat at the entrance and put a light to his cheroot. He sat for a while as if savouring the suspense and Zara gritted her teeth. Her nerves were tightly drawn. Still he said nothing and Zara's nerve broke.

'Well, tell me, damn you, Deverill! Whose offer have you decided to accept?'

He looked at her in surprise. 'What are you talking about?'

'You said you wanted to talk to me. We have only one subject in common. Is it a camel trader or a rich, fat merchant?'

A slow smile began to grow on Deverill's face. This was the old Zara and without a word from him.

'Which would you prefer?' he asked and cocked an eyebrow at her. 'I'm in a generous mood.'

To his utter dismay, Zara's face seemed to crumple, her eyes became large opaque pools of horror, her skin turned ashen. Without a sound, her body fell limply into a huddle of blanket.

He tossed away the cheroot and gathered her into his arms, holding her to his chest like a father with a child. Brandy. Where the devil was his flask? He fumbled in his sash pocket and found it. Good God, he thought, stunned, had she really believed he would sell her to the highest bidder? Of course she had and he had only himself to blame for that belief.

He unscrewed the cap with one hand and held the flask to her lips. Carefully, a drop or two only, an unconscious person cannot swallow. He managed to trickle a drop between her slack lips. As he waited in dread suspense for her to recover, he cursed himself fluently in several dialects. She had shown such spirit and defiance during the weeks of her captivity that he had come to expect a continuance. How abysmally wrong he had been and how insensitive she must think him. The fever had done more than weaken her body, it had stripped her mentally, making her as vulnerable as a child to the casual remark of an adult.

She stirred in his arms, her delicate, blue-veined eyelids fluttering above the dark lashes. Her cheeks were still deathly pale but consciousness was returning. He trickled a few more drops of brandy between her lips and noted, with relief, the convulsive swallowing.

'Zara, forgive me,' he muttered, half under his breath. 'Drink just a little more.'

Her lashes fluttered and her eyes opened, half-focused, seeing only the intent face so close to hers. He thought she was going to faint again for her eyes looked blank and he spoke quietly.

'I didn't mean it, Zara, believe me. I would not sell you for a mountain of gold. I was joking, though a poor sort of joke it turned out to be. I expected – God knows what I expected –

but it wasn't this reaction. Forgive me, please.'

Zara listened to his voice and her mind tried to make sense of his words.

'You said –' she began weakly, then closed her eyes again. She was so tired that nothing made sense. Her body felt hollow, even her mind seemed empty, unable to catch any coherent thought.

Deverill's murmur came insistently and she tried to listen and create some meaning.

'Too soon,' he was saying. 'I didn't allow for your lowness of spirit.'

Zara found herself sinking back into that blessed state of unconsciousness. His voice was fading but her mind accepted the sincerity of his promise not to sell her.

Deverill looked down uncertainly. She wasn't listening, he knew, but her colour was better. If the brandy had sent her into sleep, that was good. Perhaps some of his reassurances had got through. He wrapped the blanket about her and laid her on the bed of fern and pine leaves, then discarded his own clothes. Pulling the other blanket forward, he took her in his arms and draped the blanket abaout them both. His heart still pounded from the shock of her collapse. Careful treatment, not sardonic humour, was what she needed until her recovery was complete. He lay awake for a long time, planning his course of action.

When Zara awoke the next morning, she remembered little of the night before, save a few sparse fragments of the conversation. She frowned, trying to gather the pieces together. Had he really said he would not sell her? Could she trust him? A joke, he had said, yes, she remembered that, but the humour of it evaded her.

She started as Deverill walked briskly into the shelter, a mug of steaming tea in his hand. He stood, looking down at her, and Zara returned the look without expression.

'Thank God you're awake,' he said. 'I thought you had died on me last night. Quite a shock you gave me. I had to resort to the brandy flask again.' He knelt, offering her the mug. 'Really, Miss Zara Deane, if you continue this taste for brandy, I can see you proving an expensive wife.'

291

Zara accepted the mug gratefully and eyed him over the rim. 'I see you're in humorous mood this morning.' Her tone was caustic and her eyes glinted angrily.

Deverill was delighted and relieved by the return of her sharp tongue. 'I apologise for that stupid remark last night. It was in very poor taste.'

'But your promise not to sell me. Do you still hold to that?'

'I hold to it.'

'Then what, precisely, do you intend?'

'You may take it that I intend you no harm, no more, that is, than you have suffered already. In due course, I shall return you to Lahore.'

'When your business is finished?'

'Yes.'

'When will that be?'

'A few days, perhaps. All the arms have been delivered to the secret location. There only remains the arrival of the leader and the signal to begin operations.'

'Are you the leader?'

Deverill shook his head. 'No, just a mercenary recruited by the one who hopes to wield power and drive the English from the land. A very ambitious project but already doomed to failure.' He laughed softly and Zara stared at him, frowning.

'But if it fails, how will you become rich? Isn't that your ambition?'

He smiled, good-humouredly. 'You know little about mercenaries, my dear. An efficient one demands payment in advance.'

'So, if it ends in disaster, you have nothing to lose.'

'But a great deal to gain.'

'I'm not sure that I follow you there.' She paused, thinking, and he watched her, still smiling.

'What, in your opinion, would a good mercenary do in the aftermath of a battle where one or the other party has fled?' he asked.

'Repossess the arms he had already sold once?' Zara hazarded a guess and Deverill's smile widened.

'What a good idea. And sell them back to the army?' He

292

laughed aloud. 'I believe you must have had a buccaneer in your family to think of that. What a splendid scheme.'

'But one which would have its dangers, especially for you. The army might be less forgiving for a second offence and hang you.'

'Yes, you do have a point there. On the other hand my – er – principal might seek revenge for failure and want to chop off my head.' His chuckle brought the glimmer of a smile to Zara's lips.

'You seem remarkably unconcerned by either eventuality, so I take it you will be far away by the time the outcome is resolved.'

'It would be the wisest course to pursue, I do agree on that.'

Zara watched him broodingly. A few days only, then their paths would divide, he to his rich reward and she to the anonymity of England. She turned her gaze away and stared out of the shelter to look at the grazing horse and ponies.

'A splendid fellow, isn't he?' Deverill had followed the direction of her gaze. 'A real pleasure to ride.'

Zara sighed. 'It seems so long since I rode my mare, Farah. Even she will have forgotten I ever existed.'

'Come riding now,' Deverill said, touched by the note in her voice.

Zara's eyes opened wide. 'Riding? What would Raschid and Mahomet say? After all, hillwomen don't ride.'

'But you're not a hillwoman and they know it and, in any case, be damned to what they think or say. I'll take you riding if I choose, providing you promise not to try and escape. You'll only be on a pony, mind, and I'll be on the black horse so there'll be no contest if you do decide to make a run for it. But please promise you won't.'

'All right, I promise.' Zara's eyes sparkled. 'It would be wonderful to ride again. Where shall we go.'

'To Batala.'

Zara caught her breath. 'Not to the palace!'

He took her hand in a strong clasp. 'Well, I do have to return the Yuvaraj's horse and collect Raschid's pony.' He grinned. 'No more questions. Come on. Put on your cap.'

Zara crammed the cap over her tousled hair, pulling the

veil across her face. She hadn't felt so animated since before her bout of fever. To be out in the open, away from the camp, a sturdy pony between her knees and the wind on her face.

There was no saddle for the pony but Zara did not mind that. Sitting astride and wearing trousers gave her much more freedom and control than mounted primly on a leather sidesaddle, keeping her skirt in place and trying to look ladylike in front of the garrison people. Here, there were no rules of etiquette to be observed and she rode as if charging into battle. The black horse maintained equal speed and Deverill, glancing into the flushed face and glowing eyes, grinned at the return of the old Zara. She answered his grin with one of pure happiness and he recognised the bleakness of a future without her.

Those nights of passion before the fever struck had to be forgotten. She must be given the chance of a return to civilised society, to mix with her own kind, here or in England, and become once again the young lady of fashion he had seen on the ship. The only thing he could give her was freedom of choice to decide her own future. Those loving words and actions when she thought him dead were only the natural reaction of a girl deprived of her protector and the only man of her own race with whom she had come into contact.

On the tree-lined hill that swept down into Batala where the palace stood square and brooding, Deverill drew rein. They stared down in silence, only their own and the horses' breathing breaking the quiet. The occasional foreshortened figure hurried from door to door and across the courtyard. No one glanced up the hill and probably would not have seen them anyway as Deverill had reined in under the shadows of the trees.

Zara glanced at the tall figure on the black horse. His gaze was moving slowly over the balconies and windows. Looking for the Rani, she supposed, with a stab of jealousy.

She said, 'How do you propose to return the horse and get Raschid's pony?'

'The stables are behind the palace, so we shall circle that way and I shall ride down.' He looked at her. 'And you will come part way with me. Where I can keep an eye on you.'

'Don't you trust me? I gave you my promise.'

'I know, but I don't want you falling into other hands while I am down there.'

Zara glanced about her. 'It seems fairly deserted at the moment. I shall try not to get abducted again.'

Deverill did not return her smile. He was studying the palace again.

'I wasn't thinking of tribesmen.' He leaned over and took the reins from her hand. 'Come, we'll move to those trees beyond the palace corner. Wait for me there.'

When they reached the trees on a small plateau, Deverill handed back the reins. 'Don't answer any signal but mine. If I wave you off, get back to camp as quickly as possible and tell Raschid.'

'Are you expecting to be ambushed again?'

'No, but please do as I ask. All right?'

Zara nodded. 'Very well.'

Deverill rode down the slope and Zara followed him with her eyes until he rounded the corner and disappeared from sight. She felt slightly nervous on her own. He must have enemies in the palace to be so cautious. Whoever had tried to kill him before must still be there. The Yuvaraj, who knew him for the Rani's lover and who hated her, or the Rajah, suspecting his wife but playing a waiting game?

The pony wandered a little distance from where Deverill had left her, deciding the grass was greener further on. Zara did not check it for the trees extended along the plateau. She had a better view now beyond the corner where Deverill had disappeared. Each movement of the pony widened the view and she glimpsed stone buildings with wooden doors set about a paved square. Were these the stables? She slid from the pony's back and tied the reins to a tree.

A few yards ahead were bushes and she ran, crouching, to their shelter. Here was a much better viewpoint. If Deverill ran into trouble she would know it sooner and be able to ride swiftly back to camp to tell Raschid. She peered through the bushes her eyes on the empty yard, but casting an occasional glance over the palace doors and windows. Deverill was a long time. What had happened? Had someone seen him on the hillside and taken swift action to ambush him?

She blinked against the sun and stared down. There was no sign of the black horse nor any hill pony. Perhaps there was another stable area.

Then she saw the black horse being led towards a loose-box by a groom in palace livery. From an archway, beyond her vision, there must be another yard, but where was Deverill? The syce opened the stable door and ushered in the black horse, closing the bottom half of the door. He turned towards another loose-box and in a moment was leading out a pony. He tied its reins to a ring on a central post, then disappeared back, presumably to the passage from where he had come.

Deverill walked into the yard then and Zara breathed a sigh of relief. There was nothing hurried about him; she could see the glint of his teeth as he smiled. He was talking to someone standing in the shadow of the palace wall. His hand reached out and he nodded before turning towards the pony. Zara narrowed her eyes on the still figure by the wall. Quite tall, wearing Indian dress, a man, she guessed, then he moved forward slightly and the sun struck something that glinted in the folds of a silk turban.

Zara remembered that flashing jewel. She had seen it before, on the day she and Ralph had encountered the money-lender in high company. It was the Yuvaraj and she saw the two men exchange friendly salutes as Deverill urged the pony forward.

Zara scrambled out of the bushes and ran back to her own pony. She untied the reins and led him quickly back to the spot where Deverill had left her. Tumbling herself on to the pony's back, she waited. Deverill and the Yuvuraj? They seemed on the friendliest of terms yet she would have supposed him only too willing to use his stepmother's lover as a weapon against her? Deverill had said that the Yuvaraj knew of their relationship. Surely that was enough to disgrace the Rani in the eyes of the Rajah? Why hadn't he used that lever? She felt a sense of bewilderment. It could not, then, have been the Yuvaraj who had set the ambush for Deverill when he had barely escaped with his life. The Rajah, then? It had to be the Rajah.

She felt her nerves tauten. Neither the Rani nor the Yuvaraj could save Deverill from that absolute ruler if he should choose to strike. What incredible foolishness possessed Deverill that he should venture into the palace in broad daylight, putting himself within reach of that old, hard-eyed man whose word was law?

Chapter Twenty-seven

As Zara watched Deverill come round the corner and canter the pony towards the hillside, she wanted to scream out for him to hurry. There was still time for a body of armed and mounted men to sweep out from cover and surround him before he reached the shelter of the trees. But he didn't hurry, didn't even look back. She was the one damp with nervous perspiration, not Deverill. But nothing happened, no outcry, no pursuit.

Since Zara had been told to remain exactly where she was, there was nothing she could say to Deverill without revealing that she had disobeyed him and crept to a better vantage-point. He wouldn't know she had seen the Prince so the face she showed must be calm. He came up the hill and joined her.

'The prince will be happy to find his favourite horse back in its stall,' he said.

'And Raschid glad to have his own pony back, I expect.' She glanced into the dark face and could not help saying. 'Weren't you afraid of being ambushed again? And you were out of my sight for a time so how could you have waved me off?'

He raised a dark eyebrow. 'But you, my dear Zara, were not out of my sight for a moment. Those particular bushes do not grow scarlet flowers.'

Zara felt her own cheeks turn scarlet. 'Oh, confound you, Deverill, do you miss nothing?'

He laughed. 'Very little, my dear, and a soldier, or an ex-soldier, learns to sense ambush, but I was in no danger today.'

'Well, there may be other attempts at other times.'

He shook his head. 'Not from the same source, I received assurance of that. I believe you witnessed that too.'

Zara stared at him. 'Are you saying that it was the Yuvaraj who set that ambush?'

'Yes, but he had no idea it was for me he set it.'

Zara spoke drily. 'Do you mean the identity of his stepmother's lover makes all the difference?'

'Oh, yes.' Deverill's smile was teasing. 'The Prince and I are old friends.'

'So you're given the freedom of the palace and the Rani for old time's sake? You'll be telling me next that you're both old boys from the same public school in England.'

Her tone was so tart that Deverill laughed. 'Not quite, but the Prince is most understanding.'

'Well, I am glad that he understands because I understand nothing.'

'Don't try,' he advised. 'It will be safer if you know nothing, believe me. The less you are involved, the better.'

'Does the Prince know about me?'

'No. It is best that no one knows anything. You can return to England without a stain on your reputation.'

'Hah!' Zara kneed the pony into a gallop. 'You are all consideration, sir. I am most obliged to you.'

Deverill grinned at the straight, retreating back as Zara put the pony into full flight. She was a fighter. He liked that. If things went wrong with him and Devil Sahib disappeared, not as he had told her he would, but by the thrust of a tulwar, she would accept and be strong enough to remake her life. He didn't hurry his pony but caught her up as she approached the river.

Zara peered into its depths. The water level was very high. She looked doubtfully at Deverill.

'Can these ponies swim over?'

He nodded. 'They're small but strong and quite used to rough crossings. Let them go on their own. I'll take you across.'

'The current looks fierce.'

'So am I.' He grinned at her. 'Will you trust yourself to me?'

'I don't have much choice, do I?''

'That's true. I should teach you to swim but it's the wrong season and too late, anyway.'

Too late, thought Zara. Yes, it was too late for everything. A few more days, then all this would be over, this life, this uncertainty, but most of all the passion this man had awakened in her. Would it ever lie dormant again? Could any other man rouse her to those heights?

'Yes, too late,' she murmured, half to herself, and allowed Deverill to guide her into the water.

'Put your arms round my neck and your legs about my waist,' he said. 'Rest easily on my back and for both our sakes, don't choke me.'

Before Zara could answer, he plunged into the river. The water seemed colder than ever but that was perhaps after she had been so hot before, Zara's brain said logically. She clung to Deverill with an illogical fear of being swept away. The current was strong and even though he was a good swimmer, they reached the opposite bank some fifty yards downstream. They came out pouring water and Deverill fell on his face, gasping. Zara unclasped herself and lay panting beside him.

Deverill turned his head towards her, rivulets of water running from his hair and beard.

'All right?' he asked.

Zara nodded. 'Have you always had a beard?' she asked irrelevantly.

He smiled. 'No, not always and I can't say I like the damned thing or the length of my hair for that matter. Why do you ask?'

'I don't know. It just came to me that you would be more presentable without it. I don't like them myself.'

'Really? Did you have one then?'

Zara gave a stifled giggle. 'Don't be a fool.'

299

'I once saw a lady in a freak show with a magnificent beard, though to tell the truth, I wouldn't have fancied to kiss her.'

'Perhaps she was really a man.'

'I never thought of that; but why are we lying here, soaked to the skin, and discoursing on beards? I can think of better ways to pass the time.'

'In the middle of the day?' Zara rolled over on to her stomach and Deverill grinned. 'Did I say what they were?'

'No, but neither did I, so take that smug look off your face.'

Deverill came to his knees, still smiling. 'You were thinking of food, of course.'

'Of course, weren't you?'

'Later, I think. We both have to change so let's make a start.'

They crossed the ridge and went towards the shelter. The two ponies had made their own way and were being rubbed down by Raschid and Mahomet. Deverill called something to Soonya who smiled and nodded. Rahti's hand went to cover her mouth.

'What did you tell them?' asked Zara.

'I told them we would be ready to eat in half an hour.'

'Half –' began Sara, but Deverill was already stripping the tunic from her.

The sun still streamed into the shelter almost an hour later. What was time, thought Zara lazily, running her fingers down the strong, bronzed back. Time was so fleeting, especially in her case, for Deverill had said there was little of it left. She must make the most of it and enjoy this passion at whatever hour of day or night. Deverill's lips were on her breast, his fingers on her thighs. When he raised his head she cupped his face between her hands. They stared at each other and Zara knew this was a face that would stay in her mind for ever, blotting out all others. His love-making was so intense that she wondered, without any sense of alarm, if the result might be a pregnancy.

She kept the thought to herself and it gave her a warm feeling. He would never be lost to her if she had a child, perhaps a son who would grow up exactly like him. A daughter, maybe, dark-eyed and wilful, a combination of

300

their joint personalities. Time would tell. In England, she could pose as a widowed mother, but the problems attached to survival in that condition seemed far away and unimportant. She blinked as a ray of sun across the entrance showed the passage of time.

Deverill moved. 'We should dress.' He kissed her.

'And eat. I'm hungry,' Zara answered. She stretched, arching her back.

'Don't do that,' Deverill admonished, grinning, 'or we shall be here another hour and I've work to do.'

'What work?'

His face took on its guarded look and he rose and began to dress.

Zara caught at his hand. 'Please, Deverill, won't you tell me the truth?'

He paused and looked at her with a gentle half-smile on his lips. 'Haven't you believed anything you've seen or heard? It's all true, you know.'

'I just can't think of you as a common mercenary.'

'An uncommon one then, my dear, but I have to see this thing through to the end. My fine future depends upon it.'

'Yours and the Rani's, I suppose,' Zara said on a bitter note.

'Mine and the Rani's,' he agreed. 'Yes, you could say that our fates are intertwined.'

'And will you kill for her?'

He was silent so long that she felt he would not answer, but at length he said, 'I hope it will not come to that.' He gave her a long searching look. 'You know, of course, that I was court martialled on such a charge?' He drew his hand away and Zara stared down at her spread fingers.

'I heard but I don't believe it. You are capable of many things but I would put you above murder. It takes a mean, vindictive man to kill with deliberation and whatever you are, you are not like that.'

He bent and lifted one of her hands to his lips. 'Why, ma'am, I thank you. My heart is touched by your words.' The mockery was back in his smile.

'But not sufficiently to give up this madness,' Zara persisted.

301

He shook his head. 'I'm afraid not. Had we met in earlier times, who knows?' He shrugged and continued dressing. 'Think of me kindly sometimes, my dear, as I shall certainly think of you and your loving embraces.'

Zara realised, with humiliation, that her words had made no impression whatever on his determination to go on with this madness.

Deverill left camp after the midday meal but returned as darkness fell. When he made love to her that night, he showed such tenderness that Zara knew in her heart that it was over. This was his silent farewell, so gentle and loving that she wanted to cry out with the pain of it. But pride held her silent. He had never said he loved her, the Rani occupied his thoughts while she, Zara Deane, was near at hand and more than willing to be loved. What man would refuse bodily pleasure, even though his heart was not engaged?

As she watched the three men the next morning, Zara knew that her instincts had been right. The cleaning of rifles and the sharpening of tulwars, the examining of pony hooves, all proved that here was the moment of parting. Soonya and Rahti were preparing bundles of food for the journey, Zara supposed, to the secret rendezvous where the mercenary army waited. She sat beside the shelter entrance, hoping for a last word with Deverill, but to her dismay, the three men mounted their ponies and rode out without a backward glance. Zara could not decide which emotion was uppermost in her, dismay or anger at the callous abandonment.

Anger and hurt pride won. The sight of Soonya and Rahti beginning to dismantle the camp convinced her that the men would not be back. The girls had had their instructions but Deverill had given her none. What was she supposed to do? In due course, he had said, I shall return you to Lahore. In due course? What did that mean? If he intended disappearing before the outcome of the operation, why should he come back at all and risk his own freedom to return her to Lahore? She had believed him. How foolish that had been. A man on the run with a fortune to protect was unlikely to give her another thought.

She rose and crossed to the girls. 'Why are you striking camp?'

Soonya looked up from folding blankets. 'Devil Sahib not telling you?' She grinned slyly. 'Maybe you not hearing words when Devil Sahib loving you?'

Zara ignored the remark. 'Where is the new camp to be?'

Soonya waved a hand towards the mountains. 'Safe place up there. We go now. Men come tomorrow. Too easy find this place.'

Zara looked at the mountains thoughtfully. Once up there, she would never find her way back to Lahore. Was that what Deverill intended, despite his fine talk? And if only Raschid and Mahomet returned, what then? The more she thought about it, the more convinced she became that Deverill would not return but leave her to whatever fate the two hillmen decided. No, indeed, she would not go into those hills again. It would be sheer foolishness, like signing her own death warrant.

She nodded to Soonya. 'I will pack my things.'

In the shelter, she gathered up her towel, soap and comb and changed into the cleaner of the two costumes. If she carried too large a bundle to the river, Soonya might wonder at it. Going to wash before the oatmeal was cooked was quite legitimate in Soonya's eyes, so she packed the smaller sack and included the embroidered slippers. The sheepskin jacket she wore for the air was still cool. The girls glanced incuriously as she passed. They were accustomed to Missie Sahib's peculiarity of washing every day.

When Zara reached the river, she wondered how she should cross it. Since that ride to Batala, she was pretty sure she could find her way there on foot. The Rajah was trusted by the British and would not refuse his protection to an Englishwoman. Deverill was not working for the Rajah. She could not imagine such an old man planning intrigue against the British. He would know their strength and not suppose a motley band of mercenaries would have the power to drive them away. Yes, she must appeal to the Rajah, even warn him that something was being planned. Deverill had said he would be far away when the action started. She despised herself for considering his safety. He deserved to be punished for what he and the Rani were planning, but somehow she shrank from placing him in danger. He was merely the Rani's tool, the experienced military man she had seduced to her cause. What of the Yuvaraj? He was not a stupid man. Did he just accept that his old friend Deverill was his stepmother's lover and think no more about it?

While she thought, Zara had been moving briskly upstream. The stepping-stones were quite submerged but she went on up the hillside, hoping for a narrower crossing, more stepping-stones, a ferry boat, anything. She just had to cross the river. She thought again of the Prince of Batala. With all his cunning, his followers and informers, surely some knowledge had filtered through to him of the secret place, the accumulation of weaponry, and the growing number of tribesmen heading in that direction. What would he make of it?

She remembered the handshake in the stable courtyard. Was Deverill's principal the Rani or the Yuvaraj? The only thing those two had in common was, possibly, the removal of the Rajah. If this was accomplished, what then? To safeguard his position, the Yuvaraj must dispose of the Rani and she, if power was her objective, must remove the Yuvaraj.

Dear God, thought Zara in dizzy discussion with herself, was Deverill playing both sides against the middle, lining his own pockets, and secretly working for two principals? Two sides, and the middle man was the Rajah. If there was to be a victim, it could be none other than the old Rajah of Batala. All right for Deverill's pious hope that killing could be averted but now she felt distrustful of him. He had not denied the killing that had led to his court martial. Perhaps he really was mean and vindictive and she was too blinded by love to see it.

Her steps quickened. Love made fools of everyone, giving the loved one qualities they didn't possess. While the senses ruled the body, there was little sense in the head. How Deverill must have laughed secretly at her frank admission of love. Of course he would remember her loving embraces, if only to recount them humorously to his next mistress, whether Rani or someone else. Oh, damn you to hell,

Deverill, Zara thought crossly. I'll take no pleasure in seeing you hang but, please God, don't ever let me see your lying face again. Go to the devil in your own way but keep out of mine.

She stopped suddenly. A tree, uprooted by one of the swift storms, lay half-submerged in the water. Its roots still clung to the bank but the wide-spread branches reached almost to the other side of the river.

Here was where she must cross, even if the spread branches sagged under her weight. Not so much of a weight, she reflected ruefully, since her bout of fever. She felt herself to be all sharp bones and angles, hollow-cheeked and quite unlike the Zara Deane who had ridden out from the garrison long ago with Captain Ralph Browne. Naturally she was different, for the hard life of a hillwoman had fined her down to positive leanness. Those well-fed matrons of the garrison would eye her with astonishment, and consider her gawky, no longer a rival to their own charges. So let them, she thought, as she tested the roots of the tree. They would not see too much of her for she would take passage for England at the first opportunity.

The tree roots seemed firmly anchored to the ground although the split trunk had toppled. It must serve as a crossing-place. There was no point in trudging higher up the hill in the hope of finding a better crossing. That would take time and she must reach Batala before sunset. She hung the drawstring of the hessian sack round her neck and slid her arms into the sheepskin jacket. The sleeves might get wet but the coat itself would protect her from the night's cold if she should lose direction and have to spend the night on the hills. No, that was unthinkable, her message must reach the Rajah before anything happened.

At first she crawled quickly along the trunk of the tree, then as it thinned into a mass of branches, she had to choose the branch she thought strongest and proceed more cautiously. Inevitably, her hands and the jacket sleeves sank under the water but she was pleased with her progress. A few more yards and she could grasp the thick reedy tufts standing out from the opposite bank. More caution as the leafy branches gave, almost toppling her into the river. Her trousers became soaked. At last she was able to take a firm grip on the strong tussocky grass opposite. A violent heave which thrust the branches well under the water, then she was scrabbling for a more secure hold, wriggling her stomach on to dry land. Like a gaffed fish, struggling for breath, she lay for a while, feeling the exultation of achievement. She had crossed the river, that deep, frightening river, without anyone's aid.

When Soonya and Rahti missed her, they might come looking to the river bank, but she doubted they would search very long for their orders were to head into the hills for another camp site. At last she was free and this time there was no possibility of encountering Deverill. Climbing to her feet, she tried to squeeze the water from her trousers and jacket sleeves. The veiled cap was still in the shelter but she felt she had no need of that, and anyway her plan was to avoid all contact with other travellers. She thought of combing her hair as she removed the sack from about her neck but no, her tangled hair could hang in its present state of disarray, half-masking her face.

A careful study of the landscape, trying to recall the special features, occupied her for a few moments. The camel-thorn bushes, yes, they had passed close by yesterday. That was the first objective. Beyond the bushes she recognised a peculiar diagonal crack in the rock from which dripped water into a clump of bright orchids. She walked on, her sandals squelching, until the sun began to dry the leather. They were hard and uncomfortable but the scree and thistle were harder and she forced her mind to discount the rubbing leather.

Heartened by her recall of particular features, she trudged on as the sun rose higher. Her trousers were dry now and she carried the coat with the sleeves reversed to aid drying. Several times she paused, eyeing the countryside. That grove of plantain trees, had they passed it yesterday? Looking at the small bananas, she realised her hunger. A pocketful of bananas to eat on the journey was better than nothing. In the shade of the grove she rested and removed her sandals. What luck that she still had the ointment and bandages in her sack. Now her feet reminded her of that other time when Deverill had cut away her riding boots. No matter, and really she should stop associating everything with Deverill. That was an episode in her life, the sooner forgotten, the better. He was no good, as the army had found out. Now it was her turn and she must accept it.

What time was it? Mid-afternoon? She began to hurry, her feet easier in the bandages. If she didn't sight the palace before the brief Indian twilight faded into blackness, she would be hopelessly lost. A touch of panic flared and she pushed herself on. They had looked down on the palace from a stand of trees. Was she too low or even too high? She stared round the empty landscape, no longer seeing anything familiar, and her spirits began to droop but she must go on. Higher then, up to the top of the next slope where she could obtain a longer view. Of course the hills rose and rose into the mountains but the garrison carriages going to the palace durbar had not laboured up hills, merely followed a gentle slope.

A cool breeze had arisen as Zara laboured up to the ridge. Distances on horseback seemed short, but on foot it was interminable. The sun was losing its brilliance as she reached the crest, to stand panting against a tree. The sky was darkening, red, not golden any more and the blueness was turning grey. Twilight already and where was she? In a grove of trees, for sure, but did it help? A pinprick of light caught her eye, another and then another. She began to laugh, half-hysterically. Without those lights she would not have known that she had been staring down on the palace for a full minute. It had, in the dusk, seemed yet a further part of the mountain but now that some understanding servant had begun to light lamps, it was coming to life and revealing itself.

Her knees felt weak and she sank to the grass. A few minutes to decide on her next move while she tidied herself. She must comb her hair, rub her face and hands with the towel, creating some semblance of respectability, or she would be driven off as a beggar. There was little she could do, failing water in which to wash. She studied the palace. Not the front entrance she had entered in the company of Colonel Lacy and his officers. Too many hallways and doors flanked by guards. Through the stable yard, the way Deverill had gone, seemed a better way. Would there be guards there or just palace servants? How could she know until she made the attempt and that was surely the only reason for her being here at all? Heavens, she thought, can one walk in unannounced and demand to see the Rajah? As with a doctor or lawyer, there must be appointments or special times to present petitions. How far would she get?

She rose in sudden decision. Her business could not wait. Even now, the rebels might be on their way. She slid into the jacket, slung her sack over her wrist and hurried down the hillside, heading for the stable yard behind the palace. She blessed the darkness now. With luck she could slip into one of the palace doorways, avoiding servants and guards alike. The latter might take her for a serving girl but how was she to know where the Rajah had his quarters?

Under the shadow of the palace wall, she moved cautiously, listening. The horses must be stabled by this time, the syces retired to their own living quarters. The smell of cooking grew stronger in her nostrils as she edged round the corner. The stable yard was deserted and a quick survey of the doorways revealed that most were open to the night, letting in the cool air in return for the dissipation of cooking smells. Two open doors were dimly lit and no sound came from them. Hugging the wall, Zara approached the first. The aroma of food was less strong here but a hurrying figure passed a few yards down the passageway, making her draw back as she peered in.

The second door then. Staring down the length of stone-flagged corridor, she saw no sign of life, no servant or guard, which was not to say she wouldn't run into one, lurking somewhere about, but that chance had to be taken. The Rajah was rich and well-served. No one could approach his royal person unobserved. She remembered Colonel Lacy talking to him. In English or in Urdu? The Colonel could well be fluent in the Rajah's own language but could the same be said for the Rajah's English? Well, surely he had an interpreter? The Yuvaraj would understand and so, she suspected, would the Rani, but neither of them could be entrusted with her message. It had to be the Rajah.

Once in the corridor, Zara moved as silently as she could. Faint murmurings came to her from hidden rooms but in this warren of a palace, how was she to find the one she sought? Look for luxurious surroundings, she advised herself, but luxury was better suited to the Yuvaraj than the austere Rajah. She jumped as a door banged and stood for a heart-thudding moment, expecting a rush of feet, but nothing happened. On again down the corridor, eyeing each closed door fearfully. The corridor turned and voices became louder. There was even music and her spirits rose. Who would play music except to the royal household?

The end of the corridor opened on to a large hall. The scent now was of flowers, but stronger, aromatic, like burning joss-sticks or sweetly perfumed herbs tossed into a glowing stove. Carvings, statues, potted plants stood about. Yes, it had to be the central place. How lucky she had chosen that particular doorway. A glint of steel flickered and she froze against the wall. The central place indeed, but had she forgotten those enormous, hard-eyed guardians of the Rajah's person, those fierce tribesmen whose fingers had never left the hilts of their tulwars while the foreigners had remained at the durbar?

Edging closer to the arched doorway, she tried to think what to do. If she burst straight in, those tulwars would flash and cut her down before she could utter a syllable. Hover by the entrance and smile ingratiatingly at the guards? That would be worse, for an unveiled, smiling woman who looked into a stranger's eyes was of the lowest class and obviously without shame or morals. And such a woman to insinuate herself into the heart of the palace would be an effontery punishable by heaven knows what.

A small potted palm cut off her view. The guards were here but was the Rajah? She looked over her shoulder. Could she find a servant girl and try to get over the urgency of her plea to see the Rajah? A girl familiar to the guards and one who might understand a little English? She began to retreat slowly. Perhaps the kitchens would have been a better place to start. She half-turned to hurry back along the passage. A door opened, sending out a stream of dazzling light and in that unseeing moment, Zara stumbled into the shoulder of a man leaving the room. He swung about quickly, a hand at her throat, pressing her hard against the wall. Then she was jerked savagely off her feet and dragged into the room where the lamplight revealed her fully.

She choked for breath under the hard fingers and tried to pull them away.

'No, no,' she managed to gasp and the pressure eased slightly, but a dagger glinted in the light.

The harsh questioning voice in Urdu had Zara attempting to shake her head.

'English, English,' she gasped.

'English?' the voice asked and she heard the astonishment in it and sought to take advantage.

'Yes, yes, and I must see the Rajah. It is very important –' She stopped in mid-sentence for she had glimpsed, as so often before, that large brilliant jewel in the snowy folds of the turban.

The dark, frowning face of the Prince of Batala was regarding her with undisguised suspicion.

Chapter Twenty-eight

'Speak!' the Yuvaraj snarled and the cold blade of his dagger lay across Zara's throat. 'The truth or I will spit you like a goat.'

'Highness, please,' Zara drew in a shuddering breath. 'I am Zara Deane.'

'You are an evil-smelling beggar woman out to steal. How did you get through the guards? I shall have them flogged for their carelessness –'

'No, Highness, please listen, I beg of you. I cannot help my dress or evil aroma but truly I am Zara Deane. Surely you remember me from the garrison.'

The Yuvaraj frowned. 'The English girl who was taken by

hill brigands? She is dead. How can you claim to be her?'

'But I am, I am!' Zara pleaded in desperation. 'They dragged me from camp to camp, all over the mountains. I expected to be killed but they were not at all brutal.'

'They let you go? That is hard to believe.'

'I escaped after the men had left camp. Only the women remained. Please help me by sending a message to Colonel Lacy in Lahore. They all think I am dead.'

Was it a mistake to say that, she wondered, with a jump of the heart, for the Yuvaraj was eyeing her strangely. Dead is dead, after all, and the timing irrelevant. Dear God, had she made her final mistake?

But the Yuvaraj removed his dagger from her throat and stepped back, unable quite to hide the fastidious wrinkling of his nose.

'Yes, I believe you really are whom you claim to be though Allah himself would not recognise you.'

Zara gave a shaky laugh. 'I doubt it in any case, Highness, since I am not of your religion.'

'Very true.' The Prince gave her a slight smile. 'You are hungry and thirsty, I expect. How far have you travelled and from which place and direction?'

The question seemed casual, much too casual and Zara heard a faint alarm bell in her mind, but she smiled and spread her hands.

'I cannot give you any names since we never camped near habitation. Several times we moved but always in the hills and never in company with others. How far I have walked, I have no idea, save that I escaped early today.'

'I see.' The Prince's face was impassive. 'I will order food for you.' He opened the door and called an order, then walked over to the small latticed window and stood silent, staring into the darkness.

Zara longed to slump on to the divan, her body was trembling with fatigue, but until the Prince sat down or gave her permission to do so, she dared not move for fear of offending him. When there was a tap on the door, he swung round and as if seeing her tiredness for the first time and accepting her English status, he waved a hand towards the divan.

311

'Thank you, Highness,' Zara murmured and sank with relief into its comfort. The servant placed a tray on the table beside her and if he was shocked that his lord was feeding a beggar woman, he gave no sign but withdrew discreetly. The heaped dish of chicken and almond curry steamed so deliciously that Zara's mouth watered. She glanced at the Yuvaraj for permission to eat in his company.

He nodded, acknowledging the courtesy with a faint smile. 'How well experienced you have become with our customs, Miss Deane. Unlike you English, we do not sit at food with our women. Ah, but the servant has brought you no refreshment.' He half-turned towards the door, then paused. 'No, I will serve you myself. I keep many fruit juices by me.' He opened a small wall cupboard, revealing several flasks of coloured liquids. His hand hovered for a moment, then he lifted out a flask and beaker. 'Orange juice, Miss Deane?'

'Thank you, Highness,' Zara said.

Why did she feel that the hovering fingers and bland smile hid something that rather pleased him? He was being the perfect host. Why did she have this prickly feeling that he was playing a game? Against his father?

As if he had read her thoughts he asked, 'Did you have any specific wish to see the Rajah?'

'I – I thought that if I was allowed to see him, I could ask for his protection and – and tell him about these people who abducted me. May I be permitted to approach him?'

'Is there more to tell him than you have confided in me?'

'Well, no, not really – '

'Then, Miss Deane, I will appoint myself your protector. There is much ceremony in an approach to the throne, many courtesies to be gone through and, if you will forgive me, your appearance would not commend you.' His smile was charming but the dark eyes were watchful. 'Have no fear, Miss Deane, the Rajah will be informed by me of your arrival.'

'Thank you, Highness.' Zara continued eating. She could not force a meeting with the Rajah and on the face of it, the Yuvaraj was being most obliging.

'You have not tasted your orange juice yet,' he said

surprisingly. 'I was hoping for your opinion as it is a new variety of orange from China.'

Zara lifted the beaker the Yuvaraj had filled. 'I am sure it will be excellent.' She noticed that the Prince had no beaker. 'Won't you join me?'

'Of course.' He went again to the cupboard and drew out another flask. 'I prefer the taste of papaya juice myself so you may empty the flask by your side.'

He filled his own beaker and drank, watching her over its rim as she drank the orange juice. It had the accustomed taste but something else had been added and she could find no name for it. Cinnamon, lemon? There was a residue of bitterness but she must praise it.

'It is very good, Highness,' she said, smiling and setting down the beaker.

'But you have drunk so little,' he chided.

'Forgive me, I am far too hungry but I shall drink it presently.'

He nodded and drained his own glass. 'Please excuse me now, Miss Deane, I have many duties to attend, but you will not be disturbed here and your message will reach the Rajah.'

Zara blinked, feeling a sudden lethargy overcome her. Those brilliant black eyes blurred for a second, then the Prince was gone from the room. Zara leaned her head against the wall, her appetite gone and a fuzziness clouding her mind. She could not be so tired so abruptly. Her lips felt dry and she reached for the orange juice. She stared into its depths. A glass was all she had taken and until that moment, her mind had been clear. The taste had been slightly bitter. What had been added? And why the mild reproach from the Yuvaraj who should not care one way or the other if his guest drank or not? Unless he had some purpose. The Prince always had purpose and always to his own advantage.

Poison? No, surely not, but she felt he was not above adding some drug to the fruit juice. And he had not joined her but had taken his drink from another flask. She closed her eyes then forced them open again. If he had drugged her, it was to keep her from warning the Rajah and that meant he was in Deverill's plot too. Overthrow the Rajah? Was that it?

It was an effort to make her limbs answer but she struggled off the divan, resisting the lure of its soft cushions. Staggering to the wall cupboard, she grasped the flask the Yuvaraj had drunk from and tilted it up to her mouth. Dilute whatever small amount had entered her system and walk about. Walk, damn you, she told her legs as they wobbled under her. She concentrated fiercely. If she had drunk that whole flaskful she would have been incapable for hours, even days.

Across, back, across the room again, breathing deeply as she passed the lattice window. She finished the papaya juice without noticing and after a while, she began to feel better although drenched with perspiration. At the door, she paused. Slip down the corridor and out into the open, that is what she would do. Her hand went to the door handle and turned it. Locked. Of course it was locked. Why hadn't she considered that? The Prince had quietly locked the door on her, expecting when he came back to find her curled up on the divan, as deeply asleep as anyone could be. She looked at the flask of orange juice. If one long swallow of the stuff affected her in this way, what would have happened if she had drained the flask? Eternal sleep?

Her body shuddered convulsively and fresh perspiration soaked her. A terrible sickness rose from her stomach and she looked about wildly for some receptacle. There was no doubt, the curry spices, and whatever drug had been used, sent spasms of protest through her. Just in time she reached a tall, no doubt priceless, painted jar. Gripping its gold-trimmed rim, she bent over violently sick. She gasped for air. Better, much better, almost back to normal, if anything could be called normal in this devious double-dealing place.

Wiping her face and hands on her own towel, she looked about. The door was locked but there might be a chance of escape through the small lattice window. On examination, she had a moment of despair. It was not an opening window but a solid glazed pane, criss-crossed by wooden slats. It would have to be broken or dug out of its frame. Perhaps the latter idea, to prevent noise, might be better, she thought, peering at the plasterwork. It looked old. With a little persuasion it might well crumble and flake away.

314

A tour of the room and fittings brought her to a low cupboard which seemed a repository for discarded knives, all jewel-hilted but blunt-edged. Did the Prince buy himself a new dagger each time his current weapon needed sharpening? She picked out the least blunt and returned to the window. The plaster must have been as old as the palace for the knife sank in, dislodging chunks of the stuff. She worked at a furious pace, fearing the Yuvaraj might come back any moment to check her condition. Poking and prodding, blinking away sudden spurts of powdery plaster, she cleared the bottom sill. Leaning her forearm against the glass, she began on one side. There was a slight tilt to the pane and Zara stopped hacking and placed the flat of her hand on the lattice work. It moved again as she put pressure on it. Renewing her efforts, she pushed and hacked at the same time. Like the roots of a tree coming slowly out of the ground, the window groaned, creaked in protest, then quite suddenly it was not there any more.

Zara's mind seemed to go blank for a moment, then she saw the stars clearly without the barrier of lattice window. It had gone, fallen into the darkness of the wall outside. After that first, unbelieving moment she moved softly, throwing her coat and bag into the night. Yes, the dagger too, she decided, as she dragged the divan under the opening. It couldn't be a long drop, thank heavens, the Prince had not taken her to an upstairs room. She climbed over the sill and hung for a second by her fingertips before letting go. The ground came up with a thump that jarred her bones, then she scrambled up, feeling about for her possessions. It was lighter than she had supposed but the air was cool and she shivered, dragging on her coat. She found her bag easily but had to feel about for the blunted dagger. With that in her hand, she felt safer. If any wild mercenary sought to detain her, she had a weapon with which to strike.

Since self-preservation was the only thing left to her, no chance of seeking out the Rajah again, she felt the stirring of something primitive within her, a force that ancient man would recognise as a fight to the death in self-defence. Zara was not truly conscious of this interpretation but only knew that a determination was in her to kill if necessary, without qualm or civilised thought.

The ridge, where she had spied on Deverill, where was it? The other side of the palace? She ran, half-crouching under the stone walls. A corner. She peered cautiously. Not the stable yard, perhaps she was on the other side. Steal a horse and ride to Lahore? Which direction? Oh, God, she didn't know and might be riding directly into the path of the mercenaries. Hide until it was all over seemed the wisest plan for there was nothing she could do to help or hinder anyone. Run, get away from the palace walls and find a high spot from where to get her bearings. She began to run, directly away from the palace. The ground rose slowly but headlong running was dangerous, there were ditches and unexpected rocky obstructions. She slowed and began to pick her way more carefully but still the landscape was unfamiliar.

A rock tripped her and she stumbled to her knees, half-falling into a stiff bush whose sharp twigs raked her cheek. She stayed on her knees, feeling the threads of blood trickling down her face. Confound this blundering about in the darkness, she might just as well huddle under this bush until morning. She turned to look at the palace. Even if the Prince had found her gone, he would have no idea where to search in the dark. In any case he had more important things on his mind. Even if she succeeded in reaching the Rajah, would he have taken her word over his son's? Of course not, and for that matter, what could she have told Colonel Lacy, even if she had reached Lahore? A plot against the Rajah? Was she sure? How did she know? By whom and for what reason? All she knew was what Deverill had chosen to tell her. Lies or the truth? Her head drooped forward. What a vague story to tell a logical man like the Colonel who could only come to Batala at the request of the Rajah.

Zara stretched out on the grass, feeling her fighting spirits evaporate. What was there to fight? The only sounds were rustling leaves, the chirrup of cicadas and the faraway moan of cattle. Hours seemed to pass, the night growing colder and she huddled in her coat, the ridiculous knife in her hand. There wasn't a soul about she could stick it into and nothing more dangerous than a whining mosquito to attack her. Well, she was free, that was something, and at first light she could find the Lahore road from Batala. Walk right into the garrison and astonish everyone? She remembered the big sergeant and the young soldier. Looking as she did, she would not get past the first sentry at the garrison gate. Better wait until dark, then slip into the compound and make for the Lacy bungalow. That stately butler, the khitmagar? He would take her for a beggar too and order her away and be well within his rights. She must find a place to skulk until she caught sight of Mrs Lacy. What a horrible shock dear Mrs Lacy would get. Well, that was tomorrow. Tonight, there was nothing to do but sleep, although she wished she were not so dreadfully hungry.

Another sound slowly seeped into her consciousness, a distant humming that grew louder by the second. No, not quite a humming, more of a drumming as if a goat herd was on the run. Not at night, surely, she reasoned, and laid her ear to the ground. It came louder then, vibrating through the earth. She raised her head, listening. Horses, yes that was it, for there was no chorus of bleating. The rebel attack, it was beginning, it had to be that. She came to her feet and looked down on the palace. It stood glowing with lamplight, silhouetted against the dark night like some theatre tableau. No mercenary army could miss it. A frontal attack, perhaps, with encircling arms taking in the courtyards and stables? She began to run towards the pillared frontage.

A phrase of Deverill's passed through her mind. Doomed to failure. Why? Had he warned the Rajah while pretending to work for the Rani or the Yuvaraj? She kept running until she was on the hillside overlooking the wide courtyard where the garrison carriages had halted. There, she dropped to her knees, listening to the thunder of hooves. Surely the sound penetrated into the palace. Where were the guards, the outpouring of armed tribesmen loyal to the Rajah? She couldn't yet see the attacking force but from the palace there was no sign of alarm.

Moving cautiously now, she ran, half-crouched, towards a stand of trees surrounded by bushes. A clicking sound halted her steps and she dropped to the ground. The bushes rustled, more than was possible even in the breeze. Someone was there, lurking and hiding like herself. Then she heard the whispering. More than one person, but who were they? Friends of which side? But no friends of hers, she was convinced.

The echo of a rifle shot flung itself harshly round the hillside. The sound was repeated, then another and another. The steady drumming of hooves seemed to break step as if the riders had split apart to attack separately or take evasive action. The rattle and crack of rifles and small arms shattered the night and now Zara could see the advancing horsemen. They were scattering in all directions, firing wildly and at no visible target that she could see. But resistance was there for horsemen threw up their arms and toppled from saddles.

A bugle blared, and the sharp commanding blast made Zara jump. Out of the ground men rose, aiming, firing, reloading and advancing with well-practised ease. Such military efficiency could only have been taught by the British army. The army? They were here and it didn't need the sight of a red-coated figure to convince Zara that the Rajah had been prepared for this attack and had enlisted the aid of the Lahore garrison. A drumming of hooves from a different direction jerked her head round. A body of red-coated mounted men swept down the hillside, cutting off the retreat of the disorganised mercenaries. Swords flashed in the moonlight and the clash of steel, the cries of men and horses alike, filled the air with fierce sound. The mercenaries gave ground, were driven into a tightening, narrowing circle, then all sound died away. It was over. Tulwars and rifles fell to the ground. Red coats advanced in a thickening circle and the net closed.

Torchlight flared in the palace courtyard as servants spread in a wide arc. The scene was as macabre as any imaginings of hell. Men and horses lay still, robed figures knelt clutching injuries, heads lowered in sullen acceptance of the will of Allah. The flames from the torches flickered this way and that, touching first a blood-stained turban, then reflecting on the unwavering fixed bayonets of the red-coated infantrymen who would stay unmoving until the next command.

Zara rose to her full height. Now the battle was over, this was her chance to find Colonel Lacy. As officer commanding the garrison, he would be here, no doubt of it. Shouted orders rose to her and the infantrymen broke the circle to form into two straight lines, reaching from the encircled mercenaries to the palace entrance. Between these two lines the rebels moved, followed closely by the mounted men. The torches were held high by the palace servants, illuminating the bearded faces of the defeated. Zara scanned them fearfully and breathed a sigh of relief. Deverill had said he would not be there but he had lied so often that she could no longer trust him. However, thankfully, his face was not among them. Far away with his bags full of rupees, she thought cynically, his promises as substantial as the sand of the desert.

Zara remembered the whispering bushes and glanced about. The rifle shot had wiped them from her mind but was anyone still there? No sound came from them. Since she had been lying flat on her stomach in the shadows watching the battle, anyone could have passed her unnoticed, but now she must hurry down the hillside and try to intercept Colonel Lacy. Caution was unnecessary now although the wavering torches showed ridges and hollows she would do well to avoid.

Her sandalled toe caught a rock, sending her stumbling sideways, dislodging a shower of rattling pebbles. There was a sharp exclamation and a black shape loomed in front of her. Before she had time to regain her balance, her shoulder cannoned into a hard, yet yielding figure. Her own forward movement took the man off balance and he fell back with a choking cry, Zara's elbow in his stomach. The shock took away Zara's own breath but she recovered first and was on her feet quickly. Her relief as she saw the red jacket was enormous and she drew in a gasping breath.

The solder rolled and came to his feet, reaching for his fallen rifle. He gripped it in both hands, the bayonet flashing in her direction. The young white face staring into hers was oddly familiar, then she remembered.

'Barker, isn't it?'

The youth blinked. 'I don't know you. What do you want?'

Zara saw the wariness in his eyes and smiled. 'It's all right. I'm English, too. I want to find Colonel Lacy.'

The boy peered, then his eyes went wide. 'Gawd, you're the madwoman we met on manoeuvres.'

'No, I'm not,' Zara said tartly.

'But your man said –'

'He wasn't my man. He was my kidnapper. Now, for heaven's sake, listen and stop pointing that thing at me.'

The boy backed a few paces. 'Keep away from me.' His gaze flickered sideways. 'Sergeant!' he called hoarsely, his gaze searching the darkness.

'What is it, lad?'

Zara remembered the voice of the large red-faced sergeant. Dear God, not him again! A giant figure loomed up and Zara knew he would take her request no more seriously than he had before. She had to do something quickly before those great hands reached out for her.

The young soldier was beginning to gabble. 'That madwoman, Sergeant, she's here again and demanding to see the Colonel.'

As he spoke, his grip on the rifle lessened. Authority was here and would put everything right, his stare seemed to be saying. Zara sprang, wrenching the rifle from the relaxed fingers. She leapt two steps up the hillside, then swung on the boy, the bayonet point only inches from his neck. He made a choking sound and his face turned ashen. The sergeant stared up, his jaw slack.

'Now you give that back, do you hear?'

'I hear,' Zara said coolly. 'Now you hear me, Sergeant. Fetch Colonel Lacy this instant or you'll be short of one young soldier. Do you understand?'

'You're mad. You can't go round –'

'I don't go round decapitating soldiers,' Zara interrupted. 'But there's always a first time if you persist in argument.' She regretted the remark as she saw the boy begin to shake but went on in her coldest tone. 'Fetch Colonel Lacy, if you please.'

'And who shall I say wants him?'

'Tell him the name is Deane. He will know me.'

The sergeant looked at her steadily. He had recovered from

320

the shock of her action and now his voice was placating.

'Ah, yes, I remember you now. Zaradeen was your name, wasn't it? Always running away from your man. Now that is naughty, isn't it? You'll be in trouble when he catches you again. We won't say anything, will we Barker, if you give the lad back his rifle.' His smile was ingratiating but his eyes held cunning.

'What is your name?' snapped Zara.

'Wilson,' the man replied, caught offguard. 'Sergeant Wilson, that is.'

'All right, Sergeant Wilson. Pray convey my respects to Colonel Lacy and say that Miss Deane wishes to have a word with him. Is that too much to ask?'

'Of course not, Miss.' He grinned and made a mock bow. 'You speak right pretty. Where did you learn such fine talk? Tell you what, Miss. Give the lad his rifle and I'll take you myself to see the Colonel. How about that, eh?'

'Sergeant Wilson,' Zara said in a gritty voice. 'I'm neither stupid nor a fool. You will do as I say unless you want Barker's blood on your hands. I am not a mad native girl but an Englishwoman. Surely you are aware that a girl was kidnapped by tribesmen a month ago?'

'Eh, Miss, you're not that one? She's dead, she is.'

'For the love of God,' Zara exploded. 'She's talking to you now! Why the devil can't you get it into your thick skull and fetch the Colonel? The boy is quite safe unless you try any tricks. I warn you, Sergeant, my patience is not inexhaustible. Get the Colonel before he goes into the palace.'

'All right, Miss, I'll try. Don't hurt the lad, will you?'

'That depends entirely on you. Sergeant. Hadn't you better get moving?'

Not until Zara had seen the sergeant stride hurriedly over to the group of officers standing by their horses did she move her position.

'All right, Barker, you can sit down now,' she said, sinking on to a rock herself and laying the rifle across her knees.

The boy slumped to the ground like a puppet doll whose strings had been cut. He turned a white face cautiously towards her.

Zara smiled, feeling sorry for him. He could not be above eighteen, she judged.

'Don't worry, Barker. I never had any intention of hurting you. It was all I could think of to get your sergeant moving.' She suddenly felt rather sick and very weary. 'Have you any food on you, Barker? I haven't eaten since yesterday morning.'

'Sorry, Miss. We were only issued rations for the night.'

It took a moment for Zara to comprehend the boy's words. 'When did you leave the garrison?'

'Mid-afternoon, Miss. Orders were to circle the palace half a mile away, then move up and get dug in under cover of darkness.'

Zara stared at him. 'You mean you were already here and waiting for the attack?'

'Yes, Miss.'

'But how did you know there was going to be one?'

The boy shrugged. 'Don't know, Miss. Officer's orders, that's all I know, seeing I'm only a private and do what the sergeant tells me.'

'Somebody from the palace must have sent warning of trouble and asked for the army's help.' She frowned. 'And in very good time too, since you were dug in overnight.'

'Looks that way, Miss, and I did overhear –' he stopped, biting his lip and looking down at the two approaching figures, the Colonel and the Sergeant.

'Go on,' urged Zara. 'Tell me quickly. I won't give you away. You overheard what?'

'Sergeant Wilson, Miss, talking to another sergeant. I shouldn't have listened but I was on sentry-go and heard tell there was a message from the Prince.'

'The Yuvaraj?' Zara's mind spun. Why had he locked her in that room with drugged fruit juice if not to keep her from warning the Rajah? Whose interests was he protecting, if not his own?

The figures were coming rapidly and Zara had no time to work things out, if indeed, her brain was capable of it, and that she doubted very much with all these devious pieces on the chessboard.

'Here, Barker.' She stood quickly and offered him his rifle. 'Cut along into those trees. I know it's a military offence to lose your rifle and I don't want you to be put on a charge, so I'll swear the sergeant mistook the matter.'

'Thank you, Miss,' the boy said and smiled for the first time before fading into the shadow of the trees.

Zara drew out her own, or rather the Prince's, blunted dagger and moved to where the sergeant had last seen her. The dagger she held in full view before her, turning it so that the jewelled hilt caught the light from the torches. The blade was far shorter than the bayonet but it would serve if the sergeant was quick-witted enough to recognise her motive and had not already told the true story to the Colonel.

'There she is, sir,' said the sergeant and the two men paused, looking up as she stood slightly above them.

Zara made a showy pass or two with the dagger, willing the sergeant to understand, then she smiled at the tall, lean-faced officer.

'Good evening, Colonel Lacy, or is it good morning? I confess to having lost track of time these past few weeks.' Her voice wavered a little but she fought for control. 'And how is my dear friend, Mrs Lacy?'

'All right, Sergeant. Carry on,' the tall man said quietly.

Sergeant Wilson saluted smartly, cast a bewildered glance about for the missing soldier, then seeming to accept that discretion was the most effective move at this point, turned and hurried down the hillside.

'Zara, my dear, dear child,' the colonel said. 'What a time you have had. I am more sorry than words can say.'

Zara had prepared herself for curtness, distaste or outright rejection, but never had she expected such gently voiced words. The night turned hazy as if through rain but it was her own tears running hot and scalding down her cheeks.

Colonel Lacy's arms encircled her and she tried to pull away.

'I am too dirty and smell dreadfully,' she protested between gasping sobs.

She heard his low chuckle. 'No matter. I have you safe, my dear, and we shall soon be back in Lahore.'

323

Chapter Twenty-nine

Colonel Lacy glanced over his shoulder. The last of the prisoners were passing beneath the portico of the palace entrance.

'I must go, my dear. The Rajah will be expecting me in the audience chamber.'

'I will wait for you here, Colonel.'

He looked down into Zara's face. 'No, I think it better that you come into the palace, too.' He smiled. 'Less risk of losing you again.'

'I wouldn't be too sure of that,' Zara said with feeling. 'I would rather not enter the palace again.'

'Again? Do you mean that you have been in there already this night?'

'Yes. When I escaped from – from the hillmen, I sought to warn the Rajah of this attack but I was unable to reach him.'

'What prevented you?'

'The Yuvaraj.'

Colonel Lacy frowned but his gaze was curious. 'In what way?'

'He caught me creeping down a corridor and naturally took me for someone disreputable. I thought he was going to cut my throat, but after I had convinced him of my identity, he could not have been kinder. He ordered food and served me himself with orange juice.'

'That sounds reasonable. What was your objection to his treatment?'

'The orange juice was drugged and he locked the door on me,' Zara said flatly.

'Yet you are unfettered on this hillside. How did you manage that?'

Zara showed him the Prince's dagger. 'I dug the old plaster out of the window and escaped that way.'

Colonel Lacy eyed the blunt dagger then Zara with smiling

approval. 'Zara Deane, I salute your ingenuity. My wife did say that you were out of the ordinary and I have good reason now to endorse her opinion a hundredfold. The Prince, to his cost, has not dealt with your kind before. Come, we must hurry now. One does not keep a Rajah waiting.' He took her arm and they began to descend the hill.

Zara protested. 'Colonel, I cannot enter the palace in company with your officers. I look like a beggar woman and I should die of shame if any of them recognise me.'

'Surely you are curious to see the end of this drama?' His smile was irresistible. 'After all you have been so much part of it.'

'Have I? The whole thing has been most bewildering, but yes, I do admit to intense curiosity.'

'Well, then?'

'I still will not enter with you but go the way I did before. I was within sight of the hall when the Yuvaraj caught me.'

'He won't catch you again, my dear. You have my word on it.'

Zara nodded. 'As long as you have him safe.'

'He's very safe, don't worry about it.'

They parted and Zara hurried round the palace wall, passing the broken window through which she had escaped and finally finding her way to the courtyard with its kitchen doors.

She selected the same dark hallway, still deserted, and went down it quickly, but as cautiously as before. The army might not have caught all the mercenaries, one or two could be hiding in these innumerable rooms, but all was silent as she approached the hall. The same perfume came to her, she glimpsed the potted plants and the guards with their tulwars sheathed. The only thing different was the hum of noise, the clink of steel and the sound of booted feet.

The audience chamber – it had to be that for the guards were here – blossomed with light as if every lamp in the palace had been brought. Zara blinked in the brightness and hovered in the shadows to decide where best she might conceal herself. Those potted palms were not quite flush with the walls and she inched her way behind the guards and into the cover of

325

long, broad leaves. Between two tubs almost touching each other, she lowered herself until she crouched, her back against the wall. These were young trees, short-trunked as yet but well-leafed. An ideal spot, she decided, and began to survey the scene before her.

The hall was very large and in the immediate centre, row upon row of robed and dusty figures sat cross-legged, eyes downcast. Beside every door stood armed men in the uniform of the Rajah's bodyguard. By craning her neck a little, Zara could see the Rajah, gaunt craggy face impassive, while to one side of his raised throne stood the grouped British officers, Colonel Lacy among them. Zara felt easier for knowing he was there. Then she stiffened and almost gasped aloud as a tall elegant figure crossed her line of vision. The jewelled turban, the immaculately cut jodhpurs, the shining boots were the Prince's.

He made a deep obeisance to the silent figure on the throne then turned towards the British officers. His hand went out and was taken by Colonel Lacy. The two men shook hands and exchanged smiles, then the Prince moved to stand beside his father. The smile died on his face as he stared at the sitting figures.

The curtains beside the throne were drawn back by armed guards and the Rani swept in. Her attire was as rich and elegant as the Prince's.

A beautiful, olive-skinned woman, Zara thought, with good facial bones and the strong nose of her Rajput ancestry. A gleaming curtain of black hair flowed over her slim shoulders, reaching almost to her waist. Although Zara's view of the Rani was in profile, she remembered from the durbar those brilliant kohl-ringed eyes, black and magnetic. No wonder Deverill had found this woman irresistible. Oh, damn Deverill! Why must he persist on slipping unannounced into her conscious mind so often? She concentrated on the Rani.

All eyes rested on her as she made obeisance to the Rajah. Both he and the Prince looked down on her impassively but neither she nor they spoke. The Rani rose and disappeared behind the silk curtains. Zara frowned, more puzzled than ever. The end of a drama, the Colonel had said. Certainly it was the end of the uprising, the game of power or whatever it was, but who had won or lost? The mercenary army had been vanquished but who, apart from Deverill, had set it up in the first place?

The Rajah made a gesture with his hand. A staff of office, held by someone unseen to Zara, rapped twice on the floor and all sound died away. Judgement was beginning. Since it was conducted in Urdu, Zara could not follow it, but one by one the seated men rose and made explanation or plea to the Rajah before being led away. The hall emptied and Zara was no wiser than she had been when it was full.

The Rajah raised himself from his throne and descended the two steps. He did not shake hands with Colonel Lacy but gave him the traditional namaste, palms pressed together, fingers touching his forehead. The officers responded with military salutes then the Rajah passed between the silk curtains. There was a relaxing of tension and the Yuvaraj joined the officers. Servants hurried in carrying trays of refreshments. The Colonel and the Prince began a leisurely stroll across the hall, talking low-voiced. Colonel Lacy's eyes glanced about, lingering on doorways. Was he looking for her, Zara wondered? The whole business seemed to be over and it was time to return to Lahore.

She gave one of the palm leaves a tweak. As it flipped back into position, she saw that Colonel Lacy had caught the movement. His mouth twitched and he took the Prince's arm, directing him towards the palm. The Yuvaraj raised questioning brows and Zara heard the Colonel's voice.

'Highness, I should like you to meet someone you thought safely tucked away. One should never underestimate the ingenuity of women, don't you agree"

'Indeed, but what –'

He stopped as Zara pushed aside the palm leaves and stood upright before them.

'Good evening, Highness, or by now, good morning.' She spoke in a cold voice, her gaze steady on his. 'Forgive me if I don't thank you for your hospitality.' She paused. 'However, you have my apology for making use of a valuable vase in my – er – distress.'

327

The Prince was looking at her with amazement. 'By Allah, you're right, Colonel. I thought to find you sleeping yet, Miss Deane, as I have just been telling the Colonel. How did you get away?'

Zara handed him the dagger. 'Yours, I believe, Highness, and incidentally, you now lack a window to that room.'

The Prince smiled wryly and looked at Colonel Lacy. Both men began to laugh. Zara felt anger grow in her.

'I see nothing humorous in the situation. I am very hungry and tired. I want to go home.' She grew even angrier as her voice wavered.

The Prince stopped laughing and grew concerned. 'I will order food for you and something to drink. Tea perhaps? I promise you will suffer no ill effects. Please come to my private quarters. You too, Colonel, for I see Miss Deane is highly suspicious of me.'

'Perhaps you'd better explain, Highness,' Colonel Lacy said, taking Zara's arm and leading her after the Prince.

'Of course. The fact is, Miss Deane, your arrival was well meant, I have no doubt, but inconvenient. We could not risk an interruption in events. Luckily, I was the one to come upon you in the corridor. I could only do as I did. I expected you to sleep through it all and stay out of any possible danger.'

They were in the same room as before. Colonel Lacy pushed aside the divan to examine the empty window frame.

'A neat job, that, my dear,' Colonel Lacy said. 'Don't you agree, Highness?'

The Yuvaraj joined him, running his fingers over the rough plaster. He turned back and looked at Zara. His voice held amusement and respect.

'I certainly underestimated your determination, Miss Deane, but really it was quite unnecessary to go to so much trouble. You were quite safe.'

'Perhaps you should have explained the situation to me, Highness, instead of resorting to drugged fruit juice.'

The Prince spread his hands. 'Forgive me, but there was no time and how could I be sure you would believe me?' He moved to the door. 'The food I promised you will be here directly.' His dark eyes flickered over Zara. 'Perhaps hot

328

water and a change of costume?' He was gone before Zara could do more than nod.

She looked at Colonel Lacy, standing with hands clasped behind him. 'I daresay,' said the Colonel, 'he will make a good ruler when his time comes, with the right advice, naturally.'

'From the army?'

'Of course, and I have the very man in mind, on whose friendship and advice he already respects.' He smiled down at Zara. 'It has been a long, complicated business but now it is over.'

'Well, I'm still in the dark,' Zara complained. 'I thought the Prince planned to overthrow the Rajah, now it appears that he is completely loyal. Is that right?'

'Perfectly right. He – and others – kept us well-informed on every move.'

'But the gathering of that secret army? It was not a secret from you since you were in position when they attacked. I – I know who organised it, but who was the leader?'

The Colonel's brows rose. 'My dear child, I thought you would have guessed after the scene in the hall.'

Zara shook her head tiredly and sank on to the divan. 'I don't understand Urdu and everyone I suspected was present.'

'Didn't you notice that the Rani was unveiled and with her hair loose?'

'Yes, now that you mention it. I was too confused to understand anything.'

'It was rather like the unfrocking of a priest, the taking away of position. She was among the leaders and we concentrated on her capture and whisked her into the presence of the Rajah. She will be returned to her family in disgrace, rejected by the Rajah. Since she plotted through intermediaries and the Rajah was reluctant to believe her willing to harm him, she had to be handled cleverly to bring her into the open. The Prince suspected her but had no proof.'

'Didn't she try to poison him?'

'No. The Prince was mistaken. His accusation was rash and could have ruined everything it had taken so long to achieve.

We had to take him into our confidence to avoid any outburst and convince him that the matter was being well-handled.'

Sounds drifted in through the window space, the shouting of orders and the shuffling of many booted feet. The Colonel glanced up.

'I gave orders for the men to be marched back to the garrison. I shall escort you myself, providing the Prince will oblige us with a horse.'

'But of course, Colonel.' The Yuvaraj had entered at that moment, followed by a servant carrying a tray of food, another with samovar and a third empty-handed.

The Prince raised an enquiring eyebrow at Zara. 'The – er – vase you mentioned, Miss Deane. Allow me to have it removed.'

'Why, yes,' Zara said faintly. 'The one with the peacock design.'

The Prince spoke rapidly and the servant who had entered empty-handed clasped the tall jar to his chest and left the room. Zara kept her eyes down as he passed, watching the servant pouring tea instead. The strength and aroma of it reminded her so much of the tea she had drunk in the hills, sugarless and without milk, that her thoughts went inevitably to Deverill. She must not mention him to the Colonel. It would be folly to bring up old history and might result in a hunt for accomplices of the Rani.

She remembered, too painfully, the anguish in Deverill's voice when she had suggested the Prince's accusation of poison by the Rani might have some truth in it. What had he said before rushing off to the palace? Something about his whole future hinging on the Rani? Well, where was he, now that the Rani was unmasked? Very conspicuously absent from those mercenaries in the hall, so what price his love for the Rani?

As she ate and drank, the Colonel and the Prince had been standing in conversation by the window space. A tap on the door brought their attention round. A woman, eyes lowered, entered and spoke. The Prince nodded. He looked at Zara.

'This is one of the bath women, Miss Deane. Will you permit her to escort you to the women's quarters to bathe and change?'

330

'Yes, indeed, Highness.' Zara rose. 'I thank you for your courtesy.' She hesitated. 'Please excuse my lack of it earlier.' She followed the woman out of the room.

Half an hour later, a very different Zara Deane stared back at her from the full-length wall mirror in the zenana. It was the first time an Englishwoman had ever been permitted in the women's quarters of the palace of Batala. Scrubbed clean of dust and perspiration, her hair washed and brushed until it gleamed, she was dressed in trousers and tunic of thick, honey-coloured silk. The garments, she suspected, might well have belonged to the Rani, but she was too thankful to be rid of her own stained clothes to be bothered by that thought.

With the outfit she wore the embroidered slippers Deverill had given her and, after a moment of thought, she slipped on again the wide silver bangle. The leather sandals that had carried her over hill and rock, she discarded. Staring at her reflection was like staring into the face of a stranger, a thinner, hollow-cheeked stranger whose eyes looked larger above the more prominent cheekbones. With her tanned skin and the filmy honey-coloured veiling draped about her face, she could well have passed for a member of the zenana.

Returning to the room she had left half an hour before, she found Colonel Lacy alone. He rose from the divan as she entered.

'How splendid you look, my dear,' he said, smiling. 'But I am sure you will not be reluctant to wear your own clothes once again. The Prince asked me to make his farewells. He was summoned to attend his father. I think there will be better understanding between them after this.' His face softened as he looked at Zara. 'You have been very brave, my dear. I am sorry you had to go through it all but secrecy was essential.'

Zara stared at him. 'Are you saying that my abduction could have been prevented?'

'No. That was pure accident but once done, could not be undone. On Captain Browne's evidence, we suspected the Prince of having a hand in it, but that proved false. We had word of you and knew you were alive and in Deverill's care. He sent word that no harm would come to you.'

'Deverill?' Zara was startled. 'And because of that, you called off the search? You believed him?'

'He gave me his word, Zara.' the Colonel said quietly. 'And whatever you may believe of Richard Deverill, he never breaks his word. In view of what happened tonight, we had no men to spare for a mountain search. Since you moved from place to place, it would have been pointless to try, for it might have placed you in more danger. There was too, his own personal danger and we thought it wiser to hold back and accept his promise to keep you safe.'

'So, he could have released me any time and sent you my direction but instead he chose not to do so. I find that incomprehensible and unforgivable.' Zara felt fatigue begin to shake her body and knew that tears of weakness were not far away.

'The operation had to come first, my dear, without regard to anyone's comfort. Surely you knew Deverill was working for us?'

Chapter Thirty

Zara made no reply but stared at the Colonel from wide, shocked eyes.

'Damn and blast the man!' Colonel Lacy said explosively. 'Why the devil didn't he confide in you? He should have known he could trust you.'

Zara smiled thinly. 'He trusted no one. He told me that himself.'

Colonel Lacy picked up Zara's sheepskin coat. He had regained his temper and he held it out to her to slip her arms into its sleeves.

'It is late and you are tired. Let explanations wait until we have you back in Lahore. My wife will be overjoyed to see you again.'

'Will she?' Zara murmured as they left the room. 'I doubt if anyone else will.'

She pulled the veil over her face, partly from habit and partly from fear of being recognised by the Colonel's escort. Not that it made much difference now, she supposed, for word of her return would soon be the talk of the garrison. Talk and sly glances, speculative stares and false solicitude in the hope of gleaning some morsel of repeatable scandal.

Colonel Lacy cupped his hands for her to mount the borrowed horse. Without thought she settled herself astride the mount, catching only one raised eyebrow from an English officer. Riding astride was not quite the thing for a lady but she glared at him, her eyes glinting golden in the torchlight, and he averted his gaze quickly. That brief encounter strengthened her somehow and she resolved never again to ride side-saddle. Let them all talk and stare, she was Zara Deane, returning with head held high and the light of battle in her eye, not some self-abasing sheep eager to be taken back into the fold.

They reached the garrison as the dark of night gave way to a grey dawn. The sun was the merest hint on the horizon as they halted before the Lacy bungalow. The escort had left them and Zara and the Colonel were alone. But only for a moment as a dressing gown-clad woman with hair flying rushed onto the veranda.

'Oh, James darling, you are back. I have not slept a wink for worrying about you all night. Did everything –' The voice trailed away as she became aware of the silent figure on the horse behind her husband's. Her hands went to her mouth, the blue eyes widening.

Zara dropped the veil from her face and looked down unsmiling on Mrs Lacy. 'Good morning, ma'am,' she said, steeling herself for the inevitable reaction.

Mrs Lacy gasped and dropped her hands from her mouth. 'Zara! Is it really you? Oh, my poor dear, come down this instant and don't look at me as if you were a housemaid who has sent my entire Crown Derby dinnerware crashing to the ground.' Her arms came up and the blue eyes shone with tears. Zara dismounted, feeling absurdly weak and tearful herself. Mrs Lacy's arm went about her and Zara felt the pent-up stiffness of her body relax in that comforting embrace.

'Take care of her, my dear,' said Colonel Lacy gently, dismounting and taking the reins of both horses. 'Tea and bed are what I recommend and the sooner the better.'

Mrs Lacy glanced fondly at her husband. 'Don't lecture me, James Lacy. I know exactly what Zara needs and as to tea, I can take a hint that you would not be averse to a cup of tea yourself. In fact, we shall all have tea.'

She guided Zara down the passage to her bedroom. It was exactly as she had left it, even to her spare pair of riding boots standing by the chair. Fresh towels hung from the washstand and the bed was turned down. Zara smiled at Mrs Lacy.

'It looks as if you were expecting me – or someone.'

'This is your room, my dear, and yes, I was expecting you, if not today, tomorrow.'

'But how could you? Even Colonel Lady didn't know I was at the palace.'

'The palace?' Mrs Lacy looked startled for a moment then recovered herself. 'I didn't expect you from that direction, but never mind. You are here now and I will not pester you with questions or James will be cross with me. Get into bed, my dear, and I will bring you a cup of tea. Are you hungry?'

'No, thank you. The Yuvaraj gave me supper.'

Mrs Lacy's brows rose again in surprise. 'The Yuvaraj? Well, I am really at sea now, but do take off that lovely outfit and slip into bed.' She held the filmy veiling in her hand. 'Quite beautiful.'

'Yes, isn't it? The Rani has good taste.' Zara removed the borrowed clothes and slipped her own nightdress over her head. She emerged to find Mrs Lacy standing in bemused silence. Zara climbed into bed and drew up the sheets. 'Dear Mrs Lacy,' she said, half-laughing. 'You are a study in confusion but your husband will enlighten you, I'm sure.'

'Well, yes, but I was sure it would be Richard –' she stopped as she saw the laughter die on Zara's face to be replaced by a closed-in look. She laid down the veiling. 'I will bring you that cup of tea, then you may sleep for as long as you wish.'

Zara slept for twelve hours and woke in some bewilderment until her mind caught up with events. The whitewashed

334

ceiling at which she stared had looked down on her for as long as the reed thatching, yet the shelter roof seemed more vivid in her mind. Why? Because she had slept under it with Deverill, the man who had taken her love but not trusted her, the man who had forced her to live the life of a hillwoman when he could have freed her.

She pushed back the sheets and slipped out of bed, crossing to the window. There were still things she had to know and only the Colonel could tell her. What time was it? The sun was lowering itself redly towards the horizon and dusk was creeping over the garden. Cheerful sounds reached her from the kitchen quarters, the clang of cooking pots, high singing of a young girl. Colonel Lacy would be home for dinner and be able to answer her questions.

A gentle tap on the door brought her head round. The anxious face of Mrs Lacy looked in. Seeing Zara awake and standing by the window, she smiled.

'My dear, you were fast asleep when I returned with your tea this morning. I looked in several times to no effect but now I wonder if you are rested enough to join us for dinner.'

'I am quite rested, thank you, and shall be pleased to join you.'

'Splendid.' She hesitated. 'There have been several kind enquiries about you –'

'Kind?' Zara's voice was edged with cynicism. 'Curious, you mean! Except, perhaps for Mrs Fraser. I imagine the ladies are agog to see for themselves what a girl who has been held captive by hillmen looks like? Will they expect me to show signs of torture or rape? How disappointing if I look just the same.'

'Oh, my dear, you must not be bitter. These things will soon be forgotten, given time.'

'I don't intend to wait for that moment. I shall leave for England at the first opportunity.'

'But Captain Browne, what of him? He has enquired almost daily since you disappeared, hoping for news of you.'

'News of my rescue or confirmation of my death? Don't look so shocked, Mrs Lacy. Can you imagine such a conventional man prepared to accept without question a bride whose reputation has been sullied, even by rumour? My being alive will put him in a quandary. Take my word for it, Mrs Lacy, and see if our gallant captain does not find some reason to withdraw from our engagement.'

Mrs Lacy regarded her for a moment in silence, then, 'You have become harder, my dear.'

'It is a habit one acquires, living the life of a hillwoman,' Zara returned flippantly with a shrug. 'It is the only way to survive.'

After Mrs Lacy had gone, Zara washed and dressed in clean undergarments. She examined her wardrobe of clothes carefully, selecting a scarlet silk gown. An appropriate colour, she mused, smiling at her reflection as she fixed the diamond earrings in place. Scarlet for a scarlet woman, a woman ruined, fallen, disgraced or whatever the ladies chose to call her. If any of them, by complete chance, of course, strolled by the Lacy bungalow that night, she would be Zara Deane, elegant, unruffled and quite without shame. She would allow no one to look down on her, she vowed, touching her cheeks and lips with rouge.

When she joined Colonel Lacy on the veranda, he smiled, unspoken approval in his eyes.

'Shall we take sherry out here, my dear Zara?'

'But of course, Colonel, just as we have always done. I have one or two questions I hope you will be good enough to answer.'

He handed her a glass of sherry. 'Yes. You deserve to know the truth.' He sat down and waited.

'Do you remember,' Zara began, 'the morning I asked you what the word "shaitan" meant? It was the day I was captured by the hillmen.' The Colonel nodded and Zara went on. 'I asked you because I saw a man in the garden, obviously waiting for someone. That someone wore a hooded robe and addressed the man I now know to be Deverill, as "shaitan".'

The Colonel's lips quirked. 'My old dressing gown, my dear. Since secrecy was the game, I addressed him that way as he was commonly known by the native troopers as Devil Sahib.'

'And I thought he was a servant handing over keys to the armoury, stolen from your bedside. Captain Browne spoke of rifle thefts and I assumed the worst, especially after meeting Deverill. Were they really stolen?'

'Yes, they had to be to make the whole thing plausible.'

'What made you suspect the Rani?'

'We didn't at first. We had only vague rumours to go on, some hint of trouble coming to Batala but from whom and where, we had no idea.' Colonel Lacy filled up their sherry glasses and leaned back in his chair. 'We needed more definite information and infiltration seemed the best way.'

'What?'

'A spy in the enemy camp,' he said, smiling. 'But there quite openly, not skulking about in dark corners. Since Major Deverill had represented the army at the wedding of the Rajah and Rani, I decided he was just the man for a spot of intelligence work. Since he was also one of our best marksmen with a rifle, I offered his services to the Rajah as tutor for his personal bodyguard. That gave Richard the excuse to be in and out of the palace. He soon learned of the emnity between the Prince and the Rani. He used his – er – charm on both to gain their confidence.'

'And naturally he succeeded,' Zara said, remembering Deverill's anguish over the Rani.

If the Colonel heard the caustic note in Zara's voice, he made no comment on it.

'Quite,' he said. 'The Rani was unhappy and told him that the Prince sought ways of disgracing her. She needed to send a message to her people in Rajputana but knew that the Yuvaraj would intercept any courier. Richard was sympathetic but said there was nothing he could do as a representative of the army unless requested by the Rajah. The Rani quite understood that the army could not be involved but she asked if he would come to the palace in a personal capacity, if she felt her life threatened by the Prince. It was agreed that she should send her trusted Rajput maidservant with a message if danger was imminent.'

'Why didn't she complain to the Rajah?'

Colonel Lacy smiled. 'The Yuvaraj is a very persuasive young man and a mere woman's word against his would not convince the Rajah.' His face sobered. 'Clever as Richard is, the Rani outwitted him and he fell into the trap she had set. The result was the court martial.'

Zara gasped. 'You mean that was real, not part of your plot?'

'It was real enough.'

Zara felt a cold chill run through her. 'So it was all true, everything people said, the murdered girl and Deverill lying drunk on the floor?'

The Colonel nodded. 'Yes, there was no denying the facts. The girl was heard to scream and one of our patrols went to Richard's bungalow to investigate. The scene was exactly as stated in the military court. Mine and Major Fraser's voices were the only dissenting ones on the panel of judges. Because of his good record, the court was divided on the question of hanging.'

Zara flinched and clasped her suddenly cold hands together. 'Thank God for that,' she whispered.

'The sentence was ignominious dismissal from the army and a recommendation that he be shipped back to England.'

'To England? But why is he still in India?'

The Colonel smiled blandly. 'There was some sort of confusion at the prison where he was being held and he managed to escape.'

Zara gave Colonel Lacy a suspicious glance. 'That remark sounds too innocent to be innocent. You helped him to escape. Why?'

'Because a man I was talking with only fifteen minutes before has not the time to drink himself into insensibility.'

'That's all?'

'No. I visited Richard in his prison cell and the lump on the back of his head was more consistent with a heavy blow than a mere fall to the floor in a drunken state, as the doctor declared.'

'And the dead girl? The one they said was his mistress, at least Delia said it.'

'Was nothing of the sort. She was the Rani's maidservant bringing, Richard supposed, a message from her mistress, and in obvious terror of something. To calm her and make sense of her words, Richard brought out the brandy bottle. That was all he remembered.'

Zara sipped her sherry and felt her hands shaking. She set down the glass. 'You are saying that he didn't kill the girl?' Her relief made her feel light-headed.

'I told you that he fell into the Rani's trap. She planned it very carefully and the girl was taken to Richard's bungalow by two of the Rani's men. The poor child knew what was to happen and showed her terror by screaming as the men took Richard from behind. They had only time to empty the brandy bottle over him and stab the girl before the patrol arrived. Since Richard stank of brandy it was assumed he was drunk.'

'And all this made you suspect the Rani?'

'On the contrary, we couldn't imagine the Rani sacrificing one of her Rajput girls. It seemed inconceivable as Richard was her friend. After his – er – escape, he went to the palace in disguise. The Rani greeted him warmly and swore that the Prince was bent on eliminating her true Rajput servants and eventually herself. She declared that he secretly hated the British and he had promised her that any Englishman she befriended would suffer. It was at that point, Richard doubted her story.'

'Why was that? Wasn't it plausible?'

'Not in Richard's view because he and the Yuvaraj were friends of many years' standing.'

'Ah, yes,' Zara said. 'I remember him saying that. And the Rani didn't know of it?'

'No. She hadn't been at the palace long enough.' The Colonel's mouth twisted into a wry smile of amusement as he went on. 'So, Richard became her devoted follower. As a disgraced British officer on the run, he fell in with all her plans, while keeping me secretly informed by dead of night visits to the garden. It all came to a head last night, as you know.'

Zara thought back to her very first meeting with Richard Deverill. 'The ship, Colonel, the one that brought me to Calcutta. He was on board. I met him a few times during the last week of the voyage.'

'Did you now? He didn't tell me that.' The Colonel's voice was amused.

Zara flushed, biting her lips, then squared her shoulders and looked steadily at the Colonel.

'The truth is, the weather was hot, the cabin stuffy for Delia Pringle would not have the porthole open, so I went on deck for air.'

'There's no crime in that, my dear, and Richard is a gentleman.'

'But why was he on board? He didn't embark in England. He told me that much.'

'He went down country overland to visit a retired officer, a man who had been adviser to the Rani's father in Rajputana. He needed to know the Rani's background, to understand if she was capable of sacrificing a loyal servant in her own interests. She was.' Colonel Lacy said grimly. 'The officer recalled many instances of the Rani's cruelty. Richard needed to return quickly so we arranged for your ship to reduce speed while Richard took a fast boat out to her and boarded.'

Zara nodded. 'Thank you for telling me, Colonel. What happens now? Will the sentence of the court be lifted?'

A hint of worry crossed Colonel Lacy's brow. 'I'm afraid not. It will stand unless fresh evidence can be found to prove Richard's innocence. That is going to be very hard.'

'But surely the Rani can be brought and accused of planning everything?'

'The Rani's judgement is in the hands of the Rajah. Her disloyalty was to him, not the army. We are in no position to interfere.'

'So Deverill's career is still ruined and he remains an outcast?'

'I fear so. You have seen the Rani. Does she look the kind of woman who will confess to more than she considers necessary? The Rajah will banish her but as an ally of the British, he might decide on a more severe punishment if she confesses to bringing about the disgrace of a British officer.'

'But if Deverill tells the Rajah –'

'She will deny it. Wouldn't any sane woman in her position?'

Zara sighed. 'Yes, you're right. There is no way back for him.' She leaned back in her chair remembering Deverill's anguished words. 'My whole future depends upon the Rani.' He hadn't loved her as Zara had supposed, only hoped to be reinstated in the army if the Rani was unmasked. But that was done now, and Deverill no nearer to clearing his name. ' Shall we go into dinner, Zara?' Colonel Lacy asked gently. 'My wife has held herself discreetly apart while we talked, but I don't think we should keep her waiting any longer. Come, my dear.'

Chapter Thirty-one

Zara woke to a new day where the air was fresh and birds swooped from tree to tree, crying their freedom in the dawn light. Free, thought Zara moodily, as free as she was herself. But Deverill? Was he ever to be free again? Only in the mountains, perhaps, with Raschid and Mahomet.

She rose and washed, dressing herself in riding clothes, buttoning her white silk blouse as she contemplated the orthodox riding skirt that should hide her jodhpured legs. English legs, Soonya had called them. Zara surveyed herself in the mirror and tied back her hair. A month ago she would have wrapped the skirt about her and reached for her topee as a matter of course. But that was a month ago and she was no longer the same girl, so why adhere to the same conventions? If the ladies of the garrison wanted something shocking to gossip about, she was quite prepared to give it to them. Her figure was good, her legs long and slender in the well-cut jodhpurs, so she would discard skirt and topee and ride Farah, astride.

On the veranda she found Colonel Lacy having an early breakfast. His brows arched as he saw her stride towards him but he made no comment until he had poured a cup of tea for her.

'Dressed for battle, my dear?' he asked, amused. 'Splendid girl.'

Zara shrugged. 'I might as well be hung for a sheep and I

never was a lamb. They'll believe the worst anyway, so I'll give them good measure. Besides, I rather prefer riding astride. Will there be a suitable saddle for Farah, if you allow me to ride her?'

'You may and there is.' He rose, touching his lips with the table napkin. He looked down at her, the humour lurking in his gaze. 'There will be callers today, but you will scatter them to the winds, I have no doubt.' He glanced across the maidan. 'Here comes your first, but please be gentle with this lady. She has true affection for you.' He moved to the veranda steps as Mrs Fraser hurried up, panting.

'Is it true? Is she all right?' She caught sight of Zara who had risen. 'Oh my dear, how wonderful to see you back and looking so splendid.'

'My words exactly,' murmured Colonel Lacy, giving Zara a twinkling grin as the syce arrived with his horse.

'Good morning, Mrs Fraser,' Zara said evenly. 'As you see, I am well.'

Mrs Fraser embraced her warmly and Zara relaxed a little.

'All that matters is that you are safe and well and the subject is now closed. If that teapot is not quite empty, my dear, I would appreciate a cup of tea. I left mine half-finished when ayah gave me the news. Isn't it strange how servants know everything before anyone else?'

She stayed only time enough to drink a cup of tea, then she looked Zara over and gave an emphatic nod.

'So hot and unnecessary those riding skirts. Aren't men supposed to know we have legs? A queer sort of fellow who's never seen a woman's leg! If I had your figure, my dear –' She sighed. 'Ah, well, I haven't and to be truthful, I never had. I must run now.' She moved towards the steps.

'Mrs Fraser,' called Zara as the lady paused, glancing back. 'Thank you,' finished Zara.

As Mrs Fraser hurried away, Zara called to the syce and ordered Farah to be saddled. As she waited, she glanced idly over the maidan, then stiffened.

An open carriage was following the path round the green expanse and heading directly towards the Lacy bungalow. There were two occupants, a man and a woman. A few yards

342

short of the bungalow, the carriage halted. Captain Ralph Browne descended. He spoke briefly to his companion, Delia Pringle, who handed him a walking cane.

Zara sat very still, watching Ralph limp forward. Delia did not glance towards the bungalow. Zara waited, schooling her expression to blankness as Ralph reached and negotiated the veranda steps. Despite the effort, he looked pale rather than flushed. Zara waited. After a moment's uncomfortable silence, Ralph spoke.

'Good morning, Miss Deane. I am happy to see you looking so well.'

Miss Deane? Such formality between a still engaged couple. Aloud she said, 'Thank you.'

Ralph paced a few steps then turned to face her. 'I'd like to explain what happened –'

'I know what happened,' Zara said coldly. 'I was there.'

'If that confounded horse hadn't bolted –'

'You refer, of course, to my horse?'

'Well, yes, but mine too and the brute threw me later which was why I arrived back here in such a state.'

'I wondered where you would lay the blame. First the horse and then the Yuvaraj. Why him?'

'It was a natural assumption,' Ralph said stiffly. 'Since you and he seemed to get on so well together. I warned you about becoming too familiar with him.'

Dear God, thought Zara, such pomposity was past belief and she knew that Ralph had really come to believe his own fiction.

'Nothing to do with the Prince being aware of your debts, of course, and for that you hated him.'

Her tone was so sharp that Ralph jumped as if he had been stung. Zara softened her tone and smiled at him. 'Well, never mind all that. I shall pay your debts when we are married.'

Ralph swallowed audibly. 'Married?'

'We are still engaged, Ralph,' Zara said with sickening sweetness.

His pale blue eyes flickered and Zara derived intense enjoyment from his appalled expression. She watched him calmly, guessing that his mind was darting here and there in a frantic chase to find reason for breaking the engagement. She had no intention of marrying him but it gave her a savage pleasure to see him squirm. Dear God, what a virago she had become! His face cleared suddenly.

'But it was you, Miss Deane, who doubted that we should marry at all. I distinctly remember you saying that we were totally unsuited to each other. I confess I took that as a hint that you wished to terminate our engagement.'

Zara rose to her feet. 'Oh, bravo, Ralph. Is that why I now see you in company with Delia Pringle? Have you been toying with the poor girl's affections? What happened to your leg?' she asked in an abrupt change of subject.

'I – I fell off – I mean, over, something a couple of days ago.'

'Just before the attack on the palace?'

'Well, yes. It put me out of action for that.'

'How convenient. Perhaps you will be able to fall off – or over – something every time courage is required.' She put as much scorn into her voice as she was able.

Ralph's colour deepend and there was open hostility in his eyes. 'I find that remark highly offensive. I demand an apology.'

'Demand away, you won't get one. Just bear in mind that there are two other witnesses to your actions that day and I know where to find them both if I wish. Now, wait here until I return.'

When Zara came back from her bedroom, Ralph stood white-faced and apprehensive. Zara held out her engagement ring. Ralph took it dumbly. Zara glanced at the waiting carriage.

'I do hope that you and Delia will be happy. You really deserve each other. Good day, Captain Browne.' She made a dismissive gesture with her hand and Ralph turned without a word and began to limp down the veranda steps.

The syce was leading Farah forward. Zara went down the steps at a run and swung herself astride the mare. She cantered past Ralph towards the carriage, then reined in. Delia looked up, startled.

'Congratulations. You've landed your fish at last, Delia –

even though it's one I threw back myself. I'm sure he's more to your taste than mine. Good day.' She laughed at the shocked expression on Delia's face as she took in Zara's attire.

Outside the garrison gates, Zara gave Farah her head. The mare was fresh and Zara's feeling of freedom communicated itself. Both horse and rider went headlong for the first two miles, then Zara checked their progress for the going underfoot was changing. The grass was still lush and the occasional paddy field a brilliant green, but the rising ground showed stony.

Although the mood of freedom was on her, freedom at least from her engagement to Ralph, the cloud that was Deverill stayed on her mind. Could one hate and love at the same time? Logically, he could not have afforded to trust her, yet illogically, she resented that lack of trust. He was still in disgrace, nothing could change that, however much he had hoped that by unmasking the Rani his honour could be regained.

Zara glanced up at the sun, feeling its warmth on her shoulders. Time to go back to the garrison and begin her packing. She would miss this country, even those impassive snow-clad mountains hiding secret valleys, winding rock-strewn tracks and bleak huddles of villages. Already there were workers in the fields on the lower slopes and she stared about, trying to imprint every scene upon her mind. There, surely, was the little pool where she had dismounted to wait for Ralph, the willow and the feathery tamarisk dipping to the water. Hadn't she loosened Farah's girth strap there? Well, that was an action not to be repeated, for it had been the start of everything.

She threw a last glance at the pool, then her fingers froze tightly on the reins. Farah halted, obedient to the unconsciously given signal. She tossed her head and blew gustily, bridle clinking. Zara stared at the robed figure kneeling by the pool, half-shadowed by the bushes. The man's head came up sharply, water running from hair and beard. Sun glinted off the steel in his hand and Zara choked down a cry and stared about wildly. Oh, no, not again! How foolish to come even this far! But there were no horsemen in sight, no Raschid and

345

Mahomet. She thrust down her panic and looked again at the man. He hadn't moved and she was mounted on a fleet-footed mare, safe enough if he made any move.

He was grinning at her, she realised with a start of alarm, then that familiar mocking voice came.

'Have you come to pick my bones clean, like the vultures up yonder?'

Zara stared, feeling her body tremble with sudden weakness.

'Deverill!' she gasped and almost fell as she scrambled out of the saddle. Then she was running towards him and he moved round the pool, opening his arms to her. She fell into them, feeling the wetness of his beard on her cheek.

'Deverill, I never thought to see you again. Why are you here? Isn't it dangerous?'

'Why so?' he asked.

'The Colonel has told me everything. I'm so sorry. What can I do to help?'

He held her away from him and studied her face. 'You want to help me? After all I made you suffer?'

'I still resent your not trusting me but I understand that you couldn't take the risk. That's all over now and I'm truly sorry it didn't work out the way you hoped.' She paused, eyeing him. 'Was there any money? Soonya talked about lakhs of rupees.'

'Gross exaggeration, I'm afraid. A few hundred rupees was all I could get out of the Rani before the operation. Very distrustful woman, that.' He grinned. 'The lakhs were to be the reward of success, but personally, I think a dagger in the heart would have been my reward. That lady has a way with witnesses.'

'You sound very cheerful, not like a man without a future. Still, a few hundred rupees is something, I suppose.'

'Those went to pay off Raschid and Mahomet. I recruited them as messengers. They knew nothing, just did as I told them. Easy money at the end of it! As for you, my dear, you'd best forget me and marry your Ralph.'

'Too late. He was a poor fish and I threw him back.' She grinned at Deverill. 'Guess who caught him?'

Deverill laughed. 'Who else but Delia? She's been angling long enough. They'll suit each other.'

Zara frowned. 'Oh, damn. I gave him his ring back too, That should have brought in a few hundred rupees. There's my own jewellery, too. It will be a start.'

'What are you suggesting? That I take money from you?'

Zara looked at him quickly. 'Please don't be offended. I'm only trying to help.' She was relieved to see the smile on Deverill's face.

'I'm not offended. I am very touched by your suggestions, but no, I can't do it. I must make my own future. Will you join me?'

Zara felt her heart jump but she kept her voice steady. 'Give me one good reason.'

'I love you.'

Zara nodded. 'That's good enough.'

Then they were both laughing and Deverill pulled her to the ground and began kissing her under the shade of the willow. He paused long enough to say, 'We'll get married in the garrison church. Colonel Lacy will give away the bride.'

'What?' Zara pulled free of him and sat up. 'Are you mad? They'll arrest you on sight.'

Deverill smiled lazily. 'I don't think so, my love. After all, I do have the Rani's full confession in my tunic.'

'Confession? Why on earth should she confess to more than is necessary? That's what Colonel Lacy said.'

'And very true. The condition of her agreeing to sign a confession was that we would hold it back until she had reached her own people.'

'We?'

'The Yuvaraj and I. It was his idea that we should visit the Rani and send the guards away on some pretext.' Deverill stretched out an arm and picked up the scissors Zara had mistaken for a dagger. 'We gave her the choice of confessing on paper the events leading up to my court martial or returning to her family without a hair on her head. The Yuvaraj swore he'd shave her head himself. He was truly disappointed, I believe, when she caved in.'

Zara remembered the beautiful waist-long hair of the Rani.

What woman wouldn't flinch from having such lustrous hair cut off?

'You didn't give her much choice, did you?'

Deverill's eyes hardened. 'More than she gave me, so don't waste your sympathy. I can't say I liked it, but it was the only way.' His eyes lost their hard look. 'That's the last act of Devil Sahib, I promise you. Now, kiss me, woman, and my name is Richard, in case you've forgotten.'

'Yes, Richard,' Zara said meekly and lay back, linking her arms about his neck. 'Incidentally, what were you doing when I rode up?'

'Trying to give myself a haircut and beard-trim with the pool as mirror.' He grinned. 'Not good, eh?'

Zara chuckled. 'Terrible! You look even more villainous. Let me try.'

'Presently, my love. I haven't finished kissing you yet.'

'Don't you know the sun is high and the workers are in the fields?'

Deverill stared into the laughing hazel eyes. 'What the devil has that to do with anything?'

'Ralph said that once when we were out riding and I asked him if he wouldn't like to walk by the pool and make love to me.'

Deverill grinned. 'What a stupid fellow he was, to be sure.' Then his strong brown fingers began to unfasten the pearl buttons of her silk blouse.